STARWATER
STRAINS

✦

STARWATER STRAINS

◆

GENE WOLFE

TOR®

A Tom Doherty Associates Book
New York

STARWATER STRAINS

Copyright © 2005 by Gene Wolfe

This book is printed on acid-free paper.

Edited by David G. Hartwell

A Tor Book
Published by Tom Doherty Associates, LLC
175 Fifth Avenue
New York, NY 10010

www.tor.com

Tor® is a registered trademark of Tom Doherty Associates, LLC.

Library of Congress Cataloging-in-Publication Data

Wolfe, Gene.
   Starwater strains / Gene Wolfe—1st ed.
      p. cm.
   "A Tom Doherty Associates book."
   ISBN-13: 978-0-765-31202-0
   ISBN-10: 0-765-31202-6
   1. Science fiction, American   I. Title.

PS3573.O52S73 2005
813'.54—dc22

                                              2004060115

First Edition: August 2005
Printed in the United States of America
   0 9 8 7 6 5 4 3 2 1

Copyright Acknowledgments

✦

The title of this book is taken from
"Lady Rosemary,"
a poem by C. S. Cooney;
and this book is dedicated to them.

✦

Contents

✦

Introduction

✦

Pieces like this ought to be about the stories, or so it has always seemed to me. Unless you've read one of my earlier books, there's no reason for you to be interested in me. And if you have, there's still not much: you can't buy me or take me home from the library. These stories are what you're getting, the things you must now give your time to possess. If I could write this the way I want to, I would spend its words telling you how others have reacted to the stories behind it. I can't, because in most cases I don't know. Someone warned me once that writing stories was like sailing rose petals into the Grand Canyon.

"Viewpoint" was written for Al Sarrantonio, who had paid lots of money for a story called "The Tree Is My Hat." Have you watched reality shows on TV? Every time I do, I'm struck by the unreality of them. The contestants have to pretend that they can't see the cameras or the director and his crew when we know perfectly well they can. But they're in it for the money, and that's what they have to do if they are to have any hope of getting it. Al wanted sf for his new book, and I tried to think of a way to do a reality show for real, with real guns and a real government clawing at the money.

"Rattler" is a collaboration with Brian Hopkins. Brian wrote *El Dio de los Muertos* and edited *13 Horrors*, and has written and edited a lot of other things. He is from Oklahoma, though. I like him, and I don't mind that Oklahoma people are smarter than Texas people like me; but they don't have to keep talking and talking about it the way they do. That was why I started listening hard when he said he was going to get himself a new truck with a manual transmission, because he couldn't abide a pickup that was smarter than he was. We got to talking about trainability, guide trucks for the visually impaired, and so forth. It went on from there.

Damon Knight used to say he got most of his stories by fixing other people's. Things in those stories would bug him—Damon was easily bugged—so he'd change everything that bugged him; and by the time he did, he had a different story. I don't do it much, but a while ago I read a story in which visiting aliens were taken for gods by Earthlings like you and me. It bugged me enough that I wrote "In Glory like Their Star."

When I sent "Calamity Warps" to Kathe Koja, she said it seemed very autobiographical. Which in a way it was. Calamity Jane was really Rosemary's dog, and I never liked her as much as I should have. She was a better dog than I deserved; let's leave it like that. And fast! Why, when she was young— well, you wouldn't believe me. For the first three or four years she was determined to learn Human and used to practice her language lessons when she and I were alone in the house and I wasn't looking. Calamity could give you the creeps.

"Graylord Man's Last Words" is a simple little twenty-ninth-century story about a poor kid sent to live with a servant in the house of a rich man. Dickens would have made a novel of him, and it would have been wonderful.

"Shields of Mars" was written for Peter Crowther, and when I started I called it "Swords of Mars." Then it hit me that the atmosphere factory those two guys worked in was in fact shielding Mars.

"From the Cradle" is one of my favorites. Greg Ketter owns Dreamhaven, a wonderful bookstore in Minneapolis. He wanted to do a book of stories laid in bookstores, one of the best anthology ideas ever. I was eager to get into his book, and did.

As you've seen, a lot of my stories come into being because somebody wants a story touching a particular topic. If I like the topic, I try to write the story. "Black Shoes" was a little different. I met Brian Hopkins at a World Horror Convention at which we were guests, and when it had been over for a while he told me he'd been asked to edit an anthology of stories by past WHC guests. I said sure—then couldn't think up an idea. Dean Swift wrote his meditation on a broomstick to prove that a writer could write about any subject, and I reminded myself of that one evening as I was getting dressed to go out to dinner. When I looked down at the objects I was holding, I knew what I was going to write about, but I still didn't know whether I could make my idea work. A wonderful audience at Windycon loved it, and I've liked it ever since.

"Has Anybody Seen Junie Moon?" is and isn't a Lafferty story. It isn't a story Ray Lafferty might have written—or at least I don't think it is. (With Lafferty, you could never be sure.) But he's behind it, laughing at my story and me. Which is better than okay. Like "Shields of Mars," "Junie Moon" was written for Peter Crowther, who put it in *Moon Shots,* which is better than okay, too.

"Pulp Cover" is about the covers I love on *Startling Stories, Thrilling Wonder Stories,* and *Planet Stories.* Not to mention *Amazing Stories,* that truly amazing magazine. If you're at all familiar with those old pulps, you'll be way ahead of me when you read "Pulp Cover."

"Of Soil and Climate" first appeared in *Realms of Fantasy,* as did "Calamity Warps" and "Rattler." If you enjoy these three stories, you may join me in thanking the editor, Shawna McCarthy.

Sometimes you open the back door and find a story there, wagging its tail and hoping to be fed. I think it's a good idea to take these stories in, feed them, and buy them flea collars. "The Dog of the Drops" came like that.

"Mute" is a story I wrote for the program book of the World Horror Convention at which Judi Rohrig introduced me to Brain Hopkins. If you don't like it, blame Rich Lukes and Tina Jens; they co-chaired the con. Save some blame for John Everson, who took it. It was nominated for the Stoker Award but didn't win.

"Petting Zoo" is a favorite story of David Hartwell's, the master editor who edited this book and most of my others. Do you like dinosaurs? I loved them when I was a kid, and I've noticed that Hobbes's buddy Calvin loves them at least as much. Perhaps David feels the same way.

"Castaway" is about birds and spaceships. It's a story not many people like, although those who like it seem to like it a lot.

When Lee Martindale asked me for a story for *Such a Pretty Face,* she asked me not to submit "a fat-gene story." I warned her that "The Fat Magician" was a fat Gene story, but she took it anyhow. I've written four or five stories about Sam Cooper, Ph.D.; perhaps there'll be enough for a collection someday.

Gordon Van Gelder, an editor to whom we short-story writers owe much, bought "Hunter Lake" from me, and many other stories. C. S. Lewis subscribed to *Fantasy & Science Fiction,* as do I. Why don't you join us?

"The Boy Who Hooked the Sun" was written for the late Jan O'Nale, who used it in a greeting card. It's a brown book story, like those in "From the Cradle." May the earth lie lightly on you, Jan.

"Try and Kill It" is a rarity among my stories—one Gardner Dozois liked well enough to run in *Isaac Asimov's Science Fiction Magazine*. Gardner no longer edits it, but he remains one of the friendliest guys I know.

"Game in the Pope's Head" impressed Ellen Datlow; I've loved it ever since. The Pope's Head was a London pub back when Sherlock Holmes walked among men, and this is a Jack the Ripper story. I hope you like it.

"Empires of Foliage and Flower" was a chapbook from Cheap Street, Jan and George O'Nale's little publishing company. Jan once said that when Saint Peter asked her what she had done that might get her into heaven, she'd tell him she'd published this. I hope it worked.

Nick Gevers pointed out that "The Arimaspian Legacy" should have been in *Innocents Aboard*. He's right. It, too, was a Cheap Street greeting card.

"The Seraph from Its Sepulcher" is about a lonely missionary on an alien planet. They will be there, just as we will.

"Lord of the Land" is a Lovecraft story as well as a Sam Cooper story. If you've sat in a rocker on the front porch of a farmhouse, cooling your face with a fan from a funeral parlor, you'll be kind to this story. If you have not, well, it wasn't written for you.

"Golden City Far" closes this book you're holding, as it does Al Sarrantonio's *Flights*. It's about dreams, high school, and finding love, which is as good a recipe for a story as I've ever found. This is my seventh collection from Tor, and it's high time I thanked you for reading. I owe you far more than I can ever repay.

—GENE WOLFE

STARWATER STRAINS

✦

Viewpoint

✦

I have one question and one only," Jay declared. "How do I know that I will be paid? Answer it to my satisfaction and give your orders."

The youngish man behind the desk opened a drawer and pulled out a packet of crisp bills. It was followed by another and another, and they by seven more. The youngish man had brown-blond hair and clear blue eyes that said he could be trusted absolutely with anything. Looking at them, Jay decided that each had cost more than he had ever had in his entire life to date.

"Here's the money," the youngish man told Jay softly. "These are hundreds, all of them. Each band holds one hundred, so each bundle is ten thousand. Ten bundles make a hundred thousand. It's really not all that much."

"Less than you make in a year."

"Less than I make in three months. I know it's a lot to you." The youngish man hesitated as though groping for a new topic. "You've got a dramatic face, you know. Those scars. That was your edge. Did you really fight a bobcat?"

Jay shrugged. "The bullet broke its back, and I thought it was dead. I got too close."

"I see." The youngish man pushed the packets of bills toward him. "Well, you don't have to worry about getting paid. That's the full sum, and you're getting it up front and in cash." He paused. "Maybe I shouldn't tell you this."

Jay was looking at the money. "If it's confidential, say so and I'll keep it that way."

"Will you?"

Jay nodded. "For a hundred thousand? Yes. For quite a bit less than that."

The youngish man sighed. "You probably know anyway, so why not? You can't just go out and stick it in a bank. You understand that?"

"They'll say it's drug money."

For a moment the youngish man looked as if he were about to sigh again, although he did not. "They'll say it's drug money, of course. They always do. But they really don't care. You have a lot of money, and if it gets into a bank Big Daddy will have it in a nanosecond. It'll take you years to get it back, and cost a lot more than a hundred thousand."

Though skeptical, Jay nodded. "Sure."

"Okay, I didn't want to give you this and have them grab it before five. They'll take a big cut of anything you spend it on anyway, but we've all got to live with that."

Jay did not, but he said nothing.

"Count it. Count it twice and look carefully. I don't want you thinking we cheated you for a lousy hundred thou."

Jay did, finding it impossible to think of what so much money could buy. He had needed money so badly that he could no longer calculate its value in terms of a new rifle or a canoe. It was money itself he hungered for now, and this was more than he had dared dream of.

"You want a bag? I can give you one, but that jacket's got plenty of pockets. It's for camping, right?"

"Hunting."

The youngish man smiled the smile of one who knows a secret. "Why don't you put it in there? Should be safer than a bag."

Jay had begun to fill them already—thirty thousand in the upper right inside pocket, twenty more in the upper left, behind his wallet. Twenty in the left pocket outside.

"You're BC, right?"

"Sure." Jay tapped the empty screen above his eyes.

"Okay." The youngish man opened another drawer. "As a bonus you get a double upgrade. Couple of dots. Sit still."

Jay did.

When the youngish man was back behind his desk, he said, "I bet you'd like to look at yourself. I ought to have a mirror, but I didn't think of it. You want to go to the men's? There's a lot of mirrors in there. Just come back whenever you've seen enough. I've got calls to make."

"Thanks," Jay said.

In the windowless office beyond the youngish man's, his secretary was chatting with a big security bot. Jay asked where the restrooms were, and the bot offered to show him, gliding noiselessly down the faux-marble corridor.

"Tell me something," Jay said when the bot had come to a stop before the door. "Suppose that when I got through in there I went down to the lobby. Would there be anything to stop me from going out to the street?"

"No, sir."

"You're going to be standing out here waiting for me when I come out, right? I'd never make it to the elevators."

"Will you need a guide at that point, sir?"

The blank metal face had told Jay nothing, and the pleasant baritone had suggested polite inquiry, and nothing else. Jay said, "I can find my way back all right."

"In that case, I have other duties, sir."

"Like talking to that girl?"

"Say woman, sir. To that young woman. They prefer it, and Valerie is an excellent source of intelligence. One cultivates one's sources, sir, in police work."

Jay nodded, conceding the point. "Can you answer a couple more questions for me? If it's not too much trouble?"

"If I can, sir. Certainly."

"How many dots have I got?"

"Are you referring to IA stars, sir?"

Jay nodded.

"Two, sir. Are you testing my vision, sir?"

"Sure. One more, and I'll let you alone. What's the name of the man I've been talking to? There's no nameplate on his desk, and I never did catch it."

"Mr. Smith, sir."

"You're kidding me."

"No, sir."

"John Smith? I'll bet that's it."

"No, sir. Mr. James R. Smith, sir."

"Well, I'll be damned."

Scratching his chin, Jay went into the men's room. There were at least a dozen mirrors there, as the youngish man had said. The little augmentation screen set into his forehead, blank and black since he had received it between the fourth and the fifth grades, showed two glimmering stars now: five- or six-pointed, and scarlet or blue depending on the angle from which he viewed them.

For ten minutes or more he marveled at them. Then he relieved himself, washed his hands, and counted the money again. One hundred thousand in crisp, almost-new hundreds. Logically, it could be counterfeit. Logically, he should have shown one to the security bot and asked its opinion.

Had the bot noticed his bulging pockets? Security bots would undoubtedly be programmed to take note of such things, and might well be more observant than a human officer.

He took out a fresh bill and examined it, riffling it between his fingers and holding it up to the light, reading its serial number under his breath. Good.

If the bot had called it bad, it would have been because the bot had been instructed to do so, and that was all.

Furthermore, someone had been afraid he would assault the youngish man the bot called James R. Smith, presumably because metal detectors had picked up his hunting knife; but Smith had not asked him to remove it, or so much as mentioned it. Why?

Jay spent another fifteen or twenty seconds studying the stars in his IA screen and three full minutes concentrating before he left the restroom. There was no bot in the hall. A middle-aged man who looked important passed him without a glance and went in.

Jay walked to the elevators, waved a hand for the motion detector, and rode a somewhat crowded car to the lobby. So far as he could see, no one was paying the least attention to him. There was another security bot in the lobby (as there had been when he had come in), but it appeared to pay no particular attention to him either.

Revolving doors admitted him to Sixth Avenue. He elbowed his way for half a block along a sidewalk much too crowded, and returned to the Globnet Building.

The security bot was chatting with the young woman in her windowless room again. When she saw Jay she nodded and smiled, and the doors to Smith's office swung open.

Smith, who had said that he would be making calls, was standing at one of his floor-to-ceiling windows staring out at the gloomy December sky.

"I'm back," Jay said. "Sorry I took so long. I was trying to access the new chips you gave me."

"You can't." Smith turned around.

"That's what I found out."

Smith's chair rolled backward, and he seated himself at his desk. "Aren't you going to ask me what they're for?"

Jay shook his head.

"Okay, that will save me a lot of talking. You've still got the hundred thousand?"

Jay nodded.

"All right. In about forty-seven minutes we're going to announce on all our channels that you've got it. We'll give your name, and show you leaving this building, but that's all. It will be repeated on every newscast tonight, name, more pictures, a hundred thou in cash. Every banger and grifter in the city will be after you, and if you hide it, there's a good chance they'll stick your feet in a fire."

Smith waited, but Jay said nothing.

"You've never asked me what we're paying you to do, but I'll tell you now. We're paying you to stay alive and get some good out of your money. That's all. If you want to stay here and tough it out, that's fine. If you want to run, that's fine too. As far as we're concerned, you're free to do whatever you feel you have to do."

Smith paused, studying Jay's scarred face, then the empty, immaculate surface of his own desk. "You can't take those chips out. Did you know that?"

Jay shook his head.

"It's easy to put them in to upgrade, but damned near impossible to take them out without destroying the whole unit and killing its owner. They do that to make it hard to rob people of their upgrades. I can't stop you from trying, but it won't work and you might hurt yourself."

"I've got it." Jay counted the stars on Smith's screen. Four.

"The announcement will go out in forty-five minutes, and you have to leave the building before then so we can show you doing it."

The doors behind Jay swung open, and the security bot rolled in.

"Kaydee Nineteen will escort you." Smith sounded embarrassed. "It's just so we can get the pictures."

Jay rose.

"Is there anything you want to ask me before you go? We'll have to keep it brief, but I'll tell you all I can."

"No." Jay's shoulders twitched. "Keep the money and stay alive. I've got it."

As they went out, Smith called, "Kaydee Nineteen won't rob you. You don't have to worry about that."

Kaydee Nineteen chuckled when Smith's doors had closed behind them. "I bet you never even thought of that, sir."

"You're right," Jay told him.

"Are you going to ask where the holocameras are, sir?"

"In the lobby and out in the street. They have to be."

"That's right, sir. Don't go looking around for them, though. It looks bad, and they'll have to edit it out."

"I'd like to see the announcement they're going to run," Jay said as they halted before an elevator. "Can you tell me where I might be able to do that?"

"Certainly, sir. A block north and turn right. They call it the Studio." The elevator doors slid back, moving less smoothly than Smith's; Kaydee Nineteen paused, perhaps to make certain the car was empty, then said, "Only you be careful, sir. Just one drink. That's plenty."

Jay stepped into the elevator.

"They've got a good holo setup, I'm told, sir. Our people go there all the time to watch the shows they've worked on."

When the elevator doors had closed, Jay said, "I don't suppose you could tell me where I could buy a gun?"

Kaydee Nineteen shook his head. "I ought to arrest you, sir, just for asking. Don't you know the police will take care of you? As long as we've police, everybody's safe."

The elevator started down.

"I just hoped you might know," Jay said apologetically.

"Maybe I do, sir. It doesn't mean I tell."

Slipping his hand into his side pocket, Jay broke the paper band on a sheaf of hundreds, separated two without taking the sheaf from his pocket, and held them up. "For the information. It can't be a crime to tell me."

"Wait a minute, sir." Kaydee Nineteen inserted the fourth finger of his left hand into the Stop button, turned it, and pushed. The elevator's smooth descent ended with shocking abruptness.

"Here, take it." Jay held out the bills.

Kaydee Nineteen motioned him to silence. A strip of paper was emerging from his mouth; he caught it before it fell. "Best dealer in the city, sir. I'm not saying she won't rip you off. She will. Only she won't rip you off as badly as the rest, and she sells quality. If she sells you home-workshop, she tells you home-workshop."

He handed the slip to Jay, accepted the hundreds, and dropped them into his utility pouch. "You call her up first, sir. There's an address on that paper too, but don't go there until you call. You say Kincaid said to. If she asks his apartment number or anything like that, you have to say number nineteen. Do you understand me, sir?"

Jay nodded.

"It's all written out for you, and some good advice in case you forget. Only you chew that paper up and swallow it once you got your piece, sir. Are you going to do that?"

"Yes," Jay said. "You have my word."

"It better be good, sir, because if you get arrested you're going to need friends. If they find that paper on you, you won't have any."

Jay walked through the lobby alone, careful not to look for the holo camera. Those outside would be in trucks or vanettes, presumably, but might conceivably be in the upper windows of buildings on the other side of Sixth. He turned north, as directed. Glancing to his right at the end of the next block, he saw the Studio's sign, over which virtual stagehands moved virtual lights and props eternally; but he continued to walk north for two more blocks, then turned toward Fifth and followed the side street until he found a store in which he bought a slouch hat and an inexpensive black raincoat large enough to wear over his hunting coat.

Returning to the Studio, he approached it from both west and east, never coming closer than half a block, without spotting anyone watching the entrance. It was possible—just possible, he decided reluctantly—that Kaydee Nineteen had been as helpful as he seemed. Not likely, but possible.

In a changing booth in another clothing store, he read the slip of paper:

Try Jane MacKann, Bldg. 18 Unit 8 in Greentree Gardens. 1028 7773-0320. Call her first and say Kincaid. Say mine if she asks about any number.

She will not talk to anybody nobody sent, so you must say mine. She likes money, so say you want good quality and will pay for it. When you get there, offer half what she asks for and go from there. You should get ten, twenty percent off her price. Do not pay her asking price. Do not take a cab. Walk or ride the bus. Do not fail to phone first. Be careful.

It took him the better part of an hour to find a pay phone that looked secure. He fed bills—the change from the purchase of his raincoat—into it and keyed the number on Kaydee Nineteen's paper slip.

Three rings, and the image of a heavyset frowning woman in a black plastic shirt and a dark skirt appeared above the phone; she had frizzy red hair and freckles, and looked as though she should be smiling. "Hello. I'm not here right now, but if you'll leave a message at the tone I'll call you back as soon as I can."

The tone sounded.

"My name's Skeeter." Jay spoke rapidly to hide his nervousness. "I'm a friend of Kincaid's. He said to call you when I got into the city, but I'm calling from a booth, so you can't call me. I'll call again when I get settled."

None of the clerks looked intelligent. He circled the store slowly, pretending to look at cheap electric razors and souvenir shirts until he found a door at the back labeled DO NOT ENTER. He knocked and stepped inside.

The manager flicked off his PC, though not before Jay had seen naked women embracing reflected in the dark window behind him. "Yes, sir. What's the problem?"

"You don't have one," Jay told him, "but I do, and I'll pay a hundred," he held up a bill, "to you to help me with it. I want to rent this office for one half hour so that I can use your phone. I won't touch your papers, and I won't steal anything. You go out in your store and take care of business. Or go out and get a drink or a sandwich, whatever you want. After half an hour you come back and I leave."

"If it's long-distance . . ."

Jay shook his head. "Local calls, all of them."

"You promise that?" The manager looked dubious.

"Absolutely."

"All right. Give me the money."

Jay handed the bill over.

"Wait a minute." The manager switched on his computer, studied the screen, moved his mouse and clicked, studied the result, and clicked again. Jay was looking at the phone. As he had expected, its number was written on its base.

"All right," the manager repeated. "I've blocked this phone so it won't make long-distance calls. To unblock it, you'd have to have my password."

"I didn't know you could do that," Jay said.

"Sure. You want out of the deal?"

Jay shook his head.

"Okay, you've got the place for half an hour. Longer if you need it, only not past three thirty. Okay?"

"Okay."

The manager paused at the door. "There's a booth out here. You know about that?"

Jay nodded. "It won't accept incoming calls."

"You let them take calls and the dealers hang around and won't let anybody use it. You a dealer?"

Jay shook his head.

"I didn't think so." The manager shut the door.

One oh two eight. Seven seven seven three. Oh three two oh. Three rings as before, and the image of the heavyset redhead appeared. "Hello. I'm not here right now, but if you'll leave a message at the tone I'll call you back as soon as I can."

The tone sounded.

"This is Skeeter again," Jay said. "I've got money, and Kincaid said you and I could do some business." He recited the number from the base of the manager's phone. "If you can give me what I want, this is going to be a nice profitable deal for you." Hoping that she would not, he added, "Ask Kincaid," and hung up.

He had slept in a bod mod at the Greyhound station, had left his scant luggage in a storage locker; that luggage was worth nothing, and seemed unlikely to furnish clues to his whereabouts when a criminal gang came looking for him and his hundred thousand.

The forty-five minutes Smith had mentioned had come and gone. His image had appeared in the Studio and millions of houses and apartments.

They might be looking for him already—at the bus station, at the Studio, at any other place they could think of. At the MacKann woman's.

The phone rang and he picked it up. "Skeeter."

"This's Jane, Skeeter." The loose shirt was the same; but the dark skirt had given way to Jeens, and her hair was pulled back by a clip. "Kincaid said to call me?"

"That's right," Jay told her. "He said we might be able to do business, and he gave me your number."

"He must be getting to be a big boy now, that Kincaid."

"He's bigger than I am," Jay said truthfully.

"How old is Kincaid these days anyway?"

"Nineteen."

"He gave you my address? Or was it just this number?"

"He gave me an address," Jay said carefully. "I can't say whether it's right or not. Have you moved recently?"

"What is it?"

Jay hesitated. "All right to read it over the phone?"

"I don't see why not."

The door opened, and the manager looked in. Jay waved him away.

"What address did he give you?"

Kaydee Nineteen's paper lay on the desk. Jay held it up so the small woman seated above the telephone could read it.

"The print's too small," she told him. "You'll have to say it."

"It doesn't bother you?"

"Why should it?"

Jay sighed. "I don't know. When I was in college, I used to play chess. Now I feel like I'm playing chess again and I've forgotten how." He reversed the slip of paper. "Building Eighteen, Unit Eight in the Greentree Gardens?"

"That's it. When will you be here?"

The black raincoat had slits above its pockets that let Jay reach the pockets of the camouflage hunting coat under it. Extracting a bill, he held it up. "Can you read this?"

"Sure."

"I'll give it to you if you'll pick me up. You've seen me and how I'm dressed. I'll be in that little park at the corner of Sixth and Fortieth."

"No," she said.

"I'll be there, and I'll buy. I'll pay you this just for the ride." He hung up, rose, and left the store, waving to the manager.

There was a hotel down the street; he went in and stood at the front desk, a vast affair of bronze and marble. After five minutes a black woman in a transparent plastic blouse asked, "You checkin' in?"

"I'd like to." Jay laid two hundreds on the counter.

"We can't take those." She eyed them as though they were snakes. "Got a credit card?"

Jay shook his head.

"You got no bags either."

Jay did not deny it.

"You can't check in here."

He indicated the hundreds. "I'll pay in advance."

The black woman lowered her voice. "They don't let us take anybody like you, even if you got two dots."

In a department store a block away, Jay cornered a clerk. "I want a light-weight bag, about this long."

The clerk yawned. "Three feet, sir?"

"More than that." Jay separated his hands a bit.

The clerk (who probably called himself an associate) shook his head and turned away.

"Three and a half, anyway. Forty-two inches."

"Soft-sided?" The clerk clearly hoped Jay would say no.

"Sure," Jay said, and smiled.

"Wait right here." Briefly, the clerk's fingers drummed the top of a four-suiter. "I'll be gone awhile, you know?"

Jay removed his slouch hat and wiped his forehead with his fingers. The hat had been a comfort in the chill air of the street, but the store was warm.

None of the milling shoppers nearby were giving him any attention, as far as he could judge; but of course they would not. If he was being watched, it would be by someone some distance away, or by an electronic device of some kind. Looking around for the device, he found three cameras, none obtrusive but none even cursorily concealed. City cops, store security, and somebody else—for a minute or two Jay tried to think who the third watchers might be, but no speculation seemed plausible.

Men's Wear was next to Luggage. He wandered over.

"What do you want?" The clerk was young and scrawny and looked angry.

With your build you'd better be careful, Jay thought; but he kept the re-flection to himself. Aloud he said, "I had to buy this raincoat in a hurry. I thought I might get a better one here."

"Black?"

Jay shook his head. "Another color. What've you got?"

"Blue and green, okay?"

"Green," Jay decided, "if it's not too light."

The clerk stamped over to a rack and held up a coat. "Lincoln green. Okay?"

"Okay," Jay said.

"Only if you turn it inside out, it's navy. See?"

Jay took the coat from him and examined it. "There are slits over the pockets. I like that."

"Same pockets for both colors," the clerk sounded as if he hoped that would kill the sale.

"I'll take it."

The clerk glanced at a tag. "Large-tall. Okay?"

"Okay," Jay said again.

"You want a bag?"

Jay nodded. A stout plastic bag might prove useful.

The clerk was getting one when the clerk from Luggage returned. He frowned until Jay hurried over.

"This's what we call a wheeled duffel," the luggage clerk explained. "You got a handle there. You can carry it, or you got this handle here that pops out, and wheels on the other end. Forty-four inches, the biggest we've got. You got a store card?"

"Cash," Jay told him.

"You want a card? Ten percent off if you take it."

Jay shook his head.

"Up to you. Hear about that guy with all the cash?"

Jay shook his head again. "What guy?"

"On holo. They gave him a wad so somebody'll rip him off. Only they see what he sees, so I don't think it's going to work. They'd have a description."

"They see what he sees?"

"Sure," the clerk said. "It's his augment, you know? Anytime he sees you they see you."

"Can they spy on people like that?"

"They don't give a rat's ass," the clerk said.

The angry Men's Wear clerk had vanished. Jay's new reversible raincoat lay on a counter in a plastic bag. He unzipped his new wheeled duffel and put the raincoat inside.

Outside it was growing dark; beggars wielding plastic broom handles and pieces of conduit were working the shopping crowd, shouting threats at anyone who appeared vulnerable.

The little park was an oasis of peace by comparison. Jay sat down on a bench, the wheeled duffel between his knees, and waited. Traffic crawled past, largely invisible behind the hurrying, steam-breathing pedestrians. Some of the drivers looked as angry as the Men's Wear clerk; but most were empty-faced, resigned to driving their cubical vanettes and hulking CUVs at four miles per hour or less.

"Ain't you cold?" An old man with a runny nose had taken the other end of Jay's bench.

Jay shook his head.

"I am. I'm damned cold."

Jay said nothing.

"They got shelters down there," the old man pointed, "ta keep us off the streets. Only you get ripped off soon's you go to sleep. Right. An' they don't give you nothin' ta eat, either. So if you was ta give me somethin', I could get me somethin' an' go down there an' sleep without bein' hungry. Right."

"You could get a bottle of wine, too," Jay said.

"They won't sell it 'less you got the card." The old man was silent for a moment, sucking almost toothless gums. "Only you're c'rect, I'd like to."

"Sure," Jay said.

"I used ta get Social Security, only it don't come no more. There's some kind a problem with it."

"You could get yourself a sweater, too," Jay suggested. "Winter's just getting started."

"If there was enough I could," the old man agreed. "I could sleep in one a them boxes, too, 'stead a the shelter."

"A bod mod."

"Yeah, right."

"I slept in one last night." Jay considered. "I didn't like it, but they're probably better than the shelter."

"Right."

"You said you were cold. Would you like my coat?"

The old man appeared to hesitate. "You said you wasn't. You will be if you give it."

Jay stood up, pressing rubberoid buttons through plastic buttonholes.

On Fortieth someone leaned down on the horn, a muted keening that suggested a dying whale.

"You're givin' it?"

"I am," Jay said. He held it out by the shoulders. "Put it on."

The old man pushed an arm into one of the capacious sleeves. "Lady over there wants you, is what I think."

"Those cars aren't moving anyhow." Jay waited until the old man's other arm was in the other sleeve, then fished a hundred out of his hunting coat. "If I give you this, are you going to tell those beggars with the sticks?"

"Hell, no," the old man said. "They'd take it."

"Right." Jay put the hundred in his hand and sprinted out of the park, thrust shoppers aside with the duffel, and strode out into the motionless traffic.

A red-haired woman in a dark gray vanette was waving urgently. He opened the right front door and tossed in the duffel, got in, and sat down, smelling dusty upholstery and stale perfume.

"Don't look at me," she said. "Look straight ahead."

Jay did.

"Anytime you're with me, you don't look at me. You got that? Never. No matter what I say, no matter what I do, don't look."

Assuming that she was looking at him, Jay nodded.

"That's the first thing. They've already seen me on the phone, but the less they see of me the better."

"Thank you for coming to get me," Jay said.

"I wasn't going to," the woman told him bitterly, "but you knew I would. You knew I'd have to."

Jay shook his head again, still without looking in her direction. "I hoped you would, that's all. You said you wouldn't, but after I'd hung up I decided that if I were you I'd have said the same thing, so they wouldn't be waiting for us if they were listening in."

"They were listening. They're listening now. They can hear everything you hear and see everything you see."

Mostly to himself, Jay nodded. "I should have known it would be something like that."

"They put our call on the news. That dump in Greentree? There's a mob there. I went there thinking I'd wait for you, and there must have been five hundred people, and more coming all the time."

"I'm sorry," Jay said, and meant it.

"I'll have to get a new dump, that's all." The woman fell silent; he sensed that her jaw was clenched. "Anyway, I came. I probably shouldn't have, but I did. Did you see my license plate?"

He searched his memory. "No."

"That's good. Don't look at it when you get out, okay?"

"Okay."

"Did you think Jane MacKann was my real name?"

"It isn't?" The thought had not occurred to him.

"Hell, no. This isn't even my car, but the guy I borrowed it from is kind of a friend, and he'd have to steal new plates. So all they know is a green car, and there are lots of them."

"My color vision's a little off," Jay told her.

"Yeah, sure. A lot of guys have that." The woman paused to blow the vanette's horn, futilely, at the semibus ahead of her. "Anyway, I came and got you. So you owe me."

Jay fished a hundred from a pocket and gave it to her.

"This isn't for your heat. This's just for the ride. You tell me where, and I'll take you there and drop you, okay? That's what you're paying me for now."

"If I tell you, I'll be telling them as well?"

"I guess so. I didn't watch it, but that's what the people I talked to said."

"Suppose I were to write it on a piece of paper without looking at the paper. Then I could pass it to you without looking at you, and you could look at it."

The woman considered. "That ought to work. I've got a pen in my purse, if you've got paper."

"I do." Jay hesitated. "You said heat. I want a gun."

"Sure. That's heat."

"Slang."

"No, it's just what everybody says. Or it's tons if you got more than one. Like, I got fifteen tons stashed around now. So immediate delivery on them. What kind you want?"

Jay stroked his jaw, trying to reduce a hundred dreams to the pinpoint of a single gun small enough to fit into his wheeled duffel.

"Lemme explain my pricing structure to you while you're thinking it over," the woman said, sounding very professional indeed. "Top of the line,

I got submachine guns and machine pistols. That's mostly nine-millimeter, but there's some other stuff too. Like right now, on hand, I've got this very cool little machine pistol that's seven sixty-five."

She had paused to see whether he was interested; he sensed her scrutiny.

"It's what we used to call a thirty-two, only this one's got seven point sixty-five on the slide."

He shook his head and said, "I understand."

"Okay, under that is your high-cap autos. Only they're not really full auto, they're semi. One I got's a nine that holds seventeen rounds. Honest to God. Twenty-five hundred for any of those."

Jay did not speak.

"Where you draw the line is eleven, okay? If it holds eleven or under, it's low-cap. Twelve or better is high."

"These are handguns you're talking about."

"Yeah. Sure. Low-cap is two thousand. Or eighteen hundred if it only holds eight. There's a lot of these single-stack forty-fives around, and eight is all they'll take. So eighteen hundred for one in good shape. Then if you want a real buy, you get a revolver. I've seen some that hold eight, but it's mostly six, and nine times out of ten six will do it if you're careful. Twelve, thirteen hundred and you can get two, so that gives you twelve rounds and you got two guns in case one breaks. It's a really good deal, because most people are too dumb to see that it is."

"I need a rifle," Jay told her. "Don't you have any rifles?"

"The Feds melted them down, or most of them," the woman said dubiously.

"I know. But I hunt my food, for the most part." Jay cleared his throat. "I'm not from around here at all. I'm from Pennsylvania."

"So you don't really want to shoot anybody?"

"Deer," he told her. "Deer, and black bear. Rabbits and so forth now and then. Birds. A shotgun would be better for those, but I can't carry both back with me, and if I had a rifle I could shoot birds sitting sometimes." Doubting her comprehension, he added, "Ducks on the water. That sort of thing."

"I don't have one in my stock. I don't have a shotgun, either, and the shells are really hard to get these days."

He nodded sadly. "I suspected that they would be."

"Listen, we're just sitting here in this traffic. Would it bother you too much if I banged on my laptop some? Maybe I can find something for you."

"No. Go ahead."

"Okay, turn around the other way. Not toward me, away from me. Push slow against the harness."

He did, and the vanette announced, "I am required by law to caution you that your chance of survival in a high-speed crash has been reduced by sixty-two percent."

The woman said, "We're not even crawling, you idiot."

"The vehicle which strikes me may be traveling at a high rate of speed, however," the vanette replied primly.

Jay had contrived to turn a hundred and eighty degrees, so that he was kneeling in his seat and peering into the immensely cluttered rear of the vanette.

"Chinese red," the woman said.

He picked up the only red object he saw and held it up, careful not to look at her. "Is this it?"

"Sure."

Turning away from her again, he resumed a normal posture. "Would you like me to open it for you?"

"You can't. There's a thumbprint lock." She took it, and from the corner of his eye he saw her prop it against the wheel and plug a wire into the instrument panel. "You watch traffic, okay? If the car in front moves, tell me."

"All right," he said; and added, "Where are we going?"

"Nowhere." She sounded abstracted, and he heard the quick, hard tapping of her fingers on the keys. "We're going nowhere, Skeeter." More taps, and a little sound of disgust.

"They know that name already, huh? From when you phoned." The woman appeared to hesitate. "Yeah, I guess they have to. You can call me Mack."

"All right. Can't you find me a rifle, Mack?"

"Not so far. I got one more place I can try, though." She tapped keys again.

He said, "The car in front's moving."

"About time."

"Can I ask a question?"

"Sure. You can ask me a thousand, only I might not answer any."

"Who is 'they'?"

He felt her incomprehension.

"You said they probably know my name. Did you mean the holovid people who gave me the upgrade?"

"Globnet."

"Yes, Globnet. Was that who you meant, Mack?"

"No. The Feds. Big Daddy."

"So they can collect taxes on my money? I haven't refused to pay them. I haven't even been asked to pay."

Traffic had stopped again. Jay heard the rattle of its hard plastic case as the woman shifted her laptop back to the steering wheel. "They know you won't pay. Say, would you like a carbine? He's got a carbine."

Jay felt his heart sink. "Not as much as a rifle. Hasn't anybody got a rifle?"

"Not now. They might have something later, but maybe not. You never know."

Unwilling to surrender the new rifle he needed, Jay changed the subject. "How could the government possibly know I won't pay the tax?"

"How much did they give you? The holovid people?"

"That's my affair."

"Okay. Whatever it was? Have you still got it all?"

"No," Jay said. "I gave you a hundred."

"So you don't. So you wouldn't pay the whole tax because you couldn't."

He felt her hand on his arm.

"They want it all. The works. You'll find out. Not all you've got now, the most you ever had. Traffic like this—how many choppers do you think we ought to hear?"

He shook his head.

"About one every hour, maybe a little more. Three in a hour, tops. They been goin' over every three or four minutes lately. I just timed the last two on the dash clock. About three minutes."

From the corner of his eye he saw her hand reach out to rap the instrument panel. "Hey, you! Wake up there. I want you to open the sunroof."

The sunroof slid smoothly back, and the interior of the vanette was abruptly frigid. "Watch them awhile," the woman told Jay, "it'll keep you from looking at me."

He did, craning his neck to see the bleak winter sky where the towering office buildings had failed to obscure it. "Won't our open roof attract their attention?"

"I don't think so. There must be a couple of thousand people stuck in this mess who're wondering why they're flying over all the time."

"Black helicopters." Jay spoke half to himself. "Out where I live, way out in the country, people make jokes about black helicopters. Somebody in town did once, that's what I'm trying to say, one time when I came into town. He said the black helicopters would get me, and laughed, and I've remembered it for some reason."

"Sure."

"It's supposed to be like flying saucers, something crazy people see. But here in the city it's real. I caught sight of one a moment ago."

"Sure," the woman repeated. "They're looking for drugs out there is what we hear. Flying over the farmers' fields to see if they're growing pot in the middle of the cornfield. They're not really black, I guess. People who've seen them up close say they're UPS green, really. But they sure look black, up there."

"They must have binoculars—no, something better than binoculars. Isn't there a chance they'll see me down here and recognize me?"

"Mmm," the woman said.

"If the Government is really after me at all, I mean. The holovid people said it would be criminals." Jay paused, recalling his conversations with Smith. "Mostly criminals, unless I put the money in a bank."

"Okay, close it," the woman told the vanette, and the sunroof slid shut as smoothly as it had opened. "You're right about the binoculars," she told Jay. "They'll have something better, something they won't let us own. But I'm right about the Feds being after you. Ten minutes after the broadcast, they'll have had a dozen people on it, and by this time there could be a couple of hundred. They'll be another news tonight at eleven, and we'd better watch it."

Jay nodded. "If we can."

"We can. The big question's how good a look they've had at you. Been looking in any mirrors lately?"

"Since I got the upgrade?" Certain already that he knew the answer, he squirmed in his seat. "Let me think. Yes, once. In a restroom in the Globnet Building. I was looking at the new stars in my screen, though. Not at my own face."

"You will have seen your face, though," the woman said thoughtfully. "I'd like to know if they broadcast that. In a toilet? Maybe not."

"I'd like to watch the news tonight. I know how silly this sounds, but I can't visualize it." Apologetically he added, "I haven't watched much holovid."

"I'd like to, too," the woman said, "because I haven't seen this either, just had people tell me. I'll fix it."

"Thanks."

"What about this carbine? Do you want it?"

"I don't know. Perhaps I'd better take it, if there's nothing else. No rifles."

"They're harder to hide, so the Feds have about cleaned them out, and there's not much call for them. Later I might be able to find one for you."

"Later I won't be here. What caliber is it?"

"Forty. Same as a forty-caliber pistol is what he says, and uses the same magazine." She pressed more buttons. "It folds up, too."

"A folding stock?"

"Doesn't say. Just that it's thirty inches long to shoot and sixteen folded. What are you grinning about?"

Jay patted the duffel. "I was afraid this wouldn't be long enough to hold the rifle I was hoping to get."

She grunted. "Well, you could carry this under that coat. Put a loop of string over your shoulder and fold it over the string. It wouldn't be as handy as a pistol, but you could do it."

"I'd rather hang it by the butt, if it will stay folded." Jaw was silent for a moment, thinking. "I'll have to see it first. I don't suppose that gadget gives an effective range?"

More buttons. "A hundred and fifty meters is what he says."

"Huh."

"Probably got a lot of barrel. Twelve, fourteen inches. Something like that, and even out of a pistol barrel a forty travels pretty fast."

"I imagine he's stretching it," Jay said slowly, "even so, most of the shots I get are under a hundred yards, and those that are longer aren't a lot longer."

"Going to take it?"

He nodded. "I've been using a bow. A bow I made myself and arrows I made myself, too. Did I tell you?"

"I don't think so. I thought maybe you had a shotgun already. You hunt a lot."

He nodded again. When ten minutes had passed, and they were crawling along steadily, he asked, "Where are we going?"

"Dump I got. You know that address? Greentree?"

"There were people there, you said."

"We're not going there. I just wanted to say I don't live there. It's a place

I got where I make sales sometimes, that's all. Where we're going now's like that, only uptown."

The sunroof slid smoothly back, and a woman in an orange jumpsuit dropped into the rear seat. Jay released his seat harness to turn and look at her, and the vanette said, "I am required by law to caution you that your chance of survival in a high-speed crash has been reduced by seventy percent."

The woman who sold guns snapped, "Shut your sunroof!"

The woman in the orange jumpsuit had cleared a space for herself on the seat. She removed her helmet, shook out long, dark hair, and smiled at Jay. "I'm sure you know who I am."

He tried to return the smile. "I have no idea."

"Who I represent, I mean. My name is Hayfa, Hayfa Washington." She ran her finger down the front seam of her jumpsuit, reached inside, and produced a sparkling business card. "Look at this, please. Read it carefully."

CAPTAIN H. WASHINGTON

Fifth Airborne Brigade

Federal Revenue & Security Services

0067 5667-1339

www.hayfawings.gov

"You may keep the card, of course."

"I'd like to," Jay told her. "I've never seen such a beautiful one."

She smiled again. "You have a great deal of money belonging to our Federal Government. One hundred thousand, if not more."

The other woman said, "He thinks it belongs to him."

"I do," Jay said. "It was paid me by Globnet."

"Which didn't own it either," Hayfa Washington told him.

Jay said, "They ran advertisements, as I understand it, and included it in a lot of their news broadcasts. I was at a friend's house and saw one. My rifle's broken, and I need a new ax and—" For a moment, her expression silenced him. "And other things. You don't care about that, do you?"

"Not really."

"So I wrote a letter and my friend emailed it, with some pictures of me and my cabin. They said that if I'd come here and talk to them, they might give me the money."

"A hundred thousand."

"Yes, one hundred thousand. I borrowed money for bus fare, and I came. And they talked to me and gave it to me."

"No, they didn't." The woman in the orange jumpsuit looked sincere and somewhat troubled; she leaned toward Jay as she spoke. "They couldn't, you see. It didn't belong to them. All money belongs to the Federal Government, Jay. People—people who own small businesses, particularly—speak of making money. Quite often they use those exact words. But if you'll think about it, you'll see that they are not true. All money is made by Government, and so all money belongs to Government, which allows citizens like you and me to have some, sometimes, so we can buy the things we need. But Government keeps title to all of it, and by the very nature of things it can't lose title to any of it. I've most of last month's pay on me right now." She paused, extracting a hard plastic portemoney from an interior pocket of her jumpsuit.

"You're saying that what they paid isn't mine at all."

"Correct. Because no money really belongs to anyone except Government, which issued it." The woman in the orange jumpsuit opened her portemoney, took out bills and fanned them. "Here's mine. You see? Eleven five-hundreds, three one-hundreds, and some twenties, tens, fives, and singles. This is what our Government lets me have, because my taxes were already deducted from my check."

The other woman said, "Except sales tax."

"Correct, although sales tax is actually paid by the seller. There's a pretense that the buyer pays, but we needn't get into that. The point is that I have this money, although it's not mine, and I'm showing it to you. This is what I've got, Jay. Now will you, in an act of good faith, show what you have to me?"

"No," Jay said.

"I'm sorry to hear that, very sorry." The woman in the orange jumpsuit paused as though expecting her expression of regret to change his answer. He said nothing more; neither did the other woman.

"There's an easy, painless way to handle this," the woman in the orange jumpsuit said. "You could turn the money over to me now. I'd count it and give you a receipt for it that would be backed by the full faith and credit of the Federal Government. When the Government had decided how much should be returned to you, it would be sent to you. I'm sure there would be enough for a new ax. Not for a rifle, though. The danger a rifle would pose to you and your family would far outweigh any possible benefit to you."

"They're against the law," the other woman remarked a little dryly.

"Yes, they are, for that very reason." The woman in the orange jumpsuit spoke to Jay again. "You wouldn't have to do prison time. I think I can promise you that. There probably wouldn't even be a trial. Won't you please hand that money—the Government's money—to me to count? Now?"

He shook his head.

"You want to think it over. I understand." The woman in the orange jumpsuit tapped the other woman's shoulder. "Where are we? Ninety-fifth? You can let me out now. Just stop anywhere."

The vanette stopped, causing several vehicles behind it to blow their horns, and the woman in the orange jumpsuit opened its sliding door and stepped out. "You've got my card, Jay. Call anytime."

He nodded and shut the door, the vanette lurched forward, and the woman driving it said, "Thank you for appearing on our show tonight."

Jay nodded, although he could not be sure she was looking at him. "That was for the holovid, wasn't it? She was so pretty."

"Prettier than me?" There was a half-humorous challenge in the question.

"I don't know," Jay told her. "You don't want me to look at you."

"Well, she was, and she wasn't just pretty, she was beautiful, the way the Government wants you to think all the Feds look, beautiful women and good-looking men. She'll make the next news for sure. I wouldn't be surprised if they run everything she said. You still want to see it?"

"Yes," he said. "Certainly."

"Okay, we will. I've got a place a couple of blocks from here."

"What about my carbine? I'd like to buy it tonight."

"He's got to get it from wherever he's got it stashed. Ammo, too. I said fifty rounds."

"More," Jay told her. He considered. "Five hundred, if he has them."

"Okay, I'll tell him." The vanette pulled into an alley and the laptop returned to the steering wheel. When the woman who sold guns had closed it again, she said, "Ten years ago I could have stood up to her. I was a knockout. You don't have to believe me, but I was."

He said he believed her.

"But I had two kids. I put on some weight then and I've never got it off, and I quit taking care of my complexion for a while. You haven't been looking at me."

"No," he said.

"That's good, but now don't look at anything else either, okay? I want you to shut your eyes and keep them shut. Just lean back and relax."

He nodded, closed his eyes, and leaned back as she had suggested, discovering that he was very tired.

As if it were in another room, her fingers tapped the instrument panel. Softly she said, "Hey you. Open your sunroof."

Cold poured over him like water, and he shivered. She grunted, the vanette shook, and the seat he had shared with her sagged; after a little thought, he decided that she was standing on it with her head and shoulders thrust up through the open sunroof.

Sometime after that, the sunroof closed again and she left the vanette, got into the rear seat, and rummaged among her possessions there.

"Okay," she said. "Only don't open your eyes."

He said that he would not.

"I figured she might have planted some sort of bug, you know? Something to tell the Feds where we went. Only it would have to be on the roof or in back, and I couldn't find it, so probably they figure you're all the bug they need. We're going to drive around some now, and I want you to keep your eyes shut the whole time. We'll be turning corners and doubling back and all that, but don't look."

They "drove around" for what seemed an hour; but though there were indeed a number of turns, Jay got the impression that the point at which they stopped was miles from the one at which he had closed his eyes.

"All right." She tapped the instrument panel. "No lights." The engine died; the soft *snick* he heard was presumably the ignition key backing out. It rattled against other keys as she removed it and dropped it into her purse. "You can look around. Just don't look at me."

He did. "It's dark."

"Yeah. Well, it gets dark early this time of year. But it's about eight o'clock. You don't have a watch."

"No," he said.

"Me neither. There's the dash clock if I'm driving, and the holovid will give it if I'm inside. Come on."

There was no doorman, but the lobby into which she led him was fairly clean. He said, "You don't really live here."

"Hell no. But sometimes I sleep here, and I'm going to sleep here tonight. We both are."

He wondered whether she meant together. Aloud, he said, "You don't really live in Greentree Gardens, either. That's what you told me."

"Nope."

"I would think it would be horribly expensive to rent so many places."

The doors of an elevator shook and groaned, and at last rattled open. They stepped inside.

"It costs, but not nearly as much as you'd think. These old twentieth-century buildings are all rent-controlled."

He said, "I didn't know that."

"So what it is, is the grease you've got to pay the agent to get in. That can be quite a chunk. You don't understand grease, do you?"

"No," he said.

"I could see you didn't. It's under-the-counter money, money the agent can put in his pocket and not pay taxes on. Money's like three, four times more without taxes."

The elevator ground to a halt, and they got out.

"So I pay that—I've got to—and the first month's rent. I buy used furniture, not very much, and move in. Then I don't pay anything else for as long as I can get by with it."

The keys were out again, jangling in her hand.

"That could be six months. It could be a year. When I get the feeling they're about ready to take me to court, I pay another month, maybe, or half a month. It's rent-controlled, like I said, so it's not much."

She opened a door that had long ago been damaged by water. "My utility bills aren't much because I'm hardly ever here, and I don't complain or cause trouble. See? And they know if they go to court the judge will find out I just paid something and tell them to give me more time. So they don't. You want to turn that thing on? It's almost time for the nine o'clock."

He did, fumbling with the controls until he found the right control.

"It's an old one," she said apologetically.

A shimmering beach half filled the stale air of the dingy room; on it, young women with spectacular figures tossed a multicolored ball, at last throwing it into the ocean and swimming out to retrieve it.

"You were expecting voice control, right? I got it at the Salvation Army store. They fixed it up so it would work again."

He nodded. A brunet with flashing eyes had gotten the ball. She threw it to a blonde, tracing a high arc of red, green, and yellow against the clear blue sky.

"This's a commercial," the woman who sold guns told him. "See how their makeup stays on and their hair stays nice even in the water? That's what you're supposed to be looking at."

He nodded again.

An elderly sofa groaned as she sat down. "You want the sound? It's the next knob up, only they're going to be talking about hair spray and stuff."

He shook his head.

"Fine with me. Only we better turn it on when the news comes on."

He did, and by the time he had taken a seat next to her, a handsome black man and a beautiful Chinese woman faced them across a polished double desk. Both smiled in friendly fashion. "Thank you for inviting us into your living room," the black man said.

The Chinese woman added, "There's a lot of news tonight. What do you say we get to it, Phil?"

Phil nodded, abruptly serious. "There certainly is, Lee-Anne. Johns Hopkins has a new artificial heart so small you can have it implanted before your present heart gives out."

Lee-Anne said, "There's the cat in the mayor's Christmas tree, too. I like that story. The firemen way up on their little ladders look like ornaments."

Phil smiled. "You're right, they do. We've got a review of the new Edward Spake film, too. *The Trinidad Communiqué.* It got raves at Cannes."

"Aunt Betsy's going to show us how to make cranberry flan for the holidays."

"Almost live coverage of the big parade in Orlando."

"And a peek in on the Hundred Thousand Man. He's had a little visit from FR&SS."

"That's you," the woman who sold guns told Jay. "It's going to be a while before they get to you, though. You want something to eat?"

"Yes." He had not realized how hungry he was.

"I don't keep much besides beer in these places. Usually I just phone out. Pizza okay?"

He had not eaten pizza since college. He said it was.

"You've got to get out of here, 'cause I'll have to give the address. Why don't you go in the kitchen?"

A plastic model of a large artery enclosing a very small artificial heart stood in the middle of the room. He nodded and went into the kitchen.

"Bring me a beer, okay?"

The refrigerator was white, as his mother's had been; he knew vaguely that no one had white refrigerators now, though he did not know why. It held beer in squat plastic bulbs and a deli container of potato salad. He opened a bulb over the small and dirty sink, afraid that the foam might overflow the bulb. When he could no longer hear her voice, he called, "Can I come back in?"

"Sure."

He brought her the beer, and she said, "Pepperoni, hot peppers, and onions, okay? You can have a beer too."

He shook his head. "Not until the food gets here."

"Don't you think it's coming?"

It had not even occurred to him. He said, "Of course it is," and returned to the kitchen to get a beer for himself.

"I need to make another call. I got to call my babysitter and tell her I won't be back tonight. But I'll wait till we see you."

He nodded, careful not to look at her. A towering Christmas tree, shrunken by distance, disappeared into the ceiling. Little firemen in yellow coveralls and Day-Glo red helmets clambered over it like elves.

"I turned off the sound so I could call. All right?"

"Sure," he said.

"Maybe you'd better turn it back on now."

He did, getting it too loud then scaling it back. Reduced to the size of a child's battery-powered CUV, an immense float trundled through the room, appearing at one wall and disappearing into the other while doll-sized women feigned to conceal their nakedness with bouquets from which they tossed flowers to the onlookers. Lee-Anne's voice said, ". . . la tourista fiesta queen and her court, Phil. They say the fiesta is worth about three hundred million to the city of Orlando."

Phil's voice replied, "I don't doubt it. And speaking of money, Lee-Anne, here's a lady trying to collect some."

A good-looking woman in a skintight orange jumpsuit rappelled down a mountain of air, bouncing and swaying. Jay said, "I didn't see that."

"They were shooting from a helicopter, probably," the woman who sold guns told him.

It took about half a second for him to realize that by "shooting" she intended the taking of pictures; in that half second, the swaying woman on the rope became the helmetless woman he recalled, shaking out her hair in the rear seat of the vanette. "You have a great deal of money belonging to our Federal Government. One hundred thousand, if not more."

The other woman said, "He thinks it belongs to him." Then his own voice, just as he heard it when he spoke: "It was paid me by Globnet."

Their conversation continued, but he paid little attention to what they said. He watched Hayfa Washington's face, discovering that he had forgotten (or had never known) how beautiful she had been.

Too soon it was over, and a woman in a spotless gingham apron coalesced from light to talk about lemon custard. The woman who sold guns said, "You want to turn that off now?" and he did.

"I'm going to call my sitter, okay? You can stay, though. I won't tell her where I am."

"I'll go anyway," he said, and returned to the kitchen. Faintly, through the tiny dining nook and the door he had closed behind him, he heard her tell someone, "It's me, Val. How are the kids?"

The card was in his shirt pocket, under the hunting coat he had been careful not to remove. "Captain H. Washington, Fifth Airborne Brigade." He turned it over, and discovered that her picture was on the reverse, and that her soul was in her huge dark eyes.

"Hey!" the other woman called from the living room. "The pizza's here. Bring out a couple more bulbs."

He did, and opened hers for her while she opened the pizza box on the rickety coffee table, then returned to the kitchen for plastic knives and forks, and paper napkins.

"If we eat in there we'll have to sit facing," she said. "So I figured in here. We can sit side by each, like in the car. It'll be easier."

He said that was fine, and asked about her children.

"Oh, they're okay. My girlfriend is sitting them. She's going to take them over to her house till I get back. Ron's eight and Julie's seven. I had them right together, like. Then we broke up, and he didn't want any part of them. You know how that is."

"No," he said. "No, I don't."

"Haven't you ever been married? Or lived with a woman?"

He shook his head.

"Well, why not?"

"I've never been rich, handsome, or exciting, that's all." He paused, thinking. "All right, I'm rich now, or at least have something like riches. But I never did before."

"Neither was he, but he got me."

Jay shrugged.

"He was nice, and he was fun to be with, and he had a pretty good job. Only after the divorce his company sent him overseas and he stopped paying support."

"I've never had a job," Jay said.

"Really?"

"Really. My friends call me a slacker." He found that he was smiling. "Dad called me a woods bum. He's dead now."

"I'm sorry."

"So am I, in a way. We seldom got along, but well . . ." He shrugged and drank beer.

"I know."

"He sent me to college. I thought I was a pretty good baseball player in those days, and a pretty good football player, but I didn't make either team. I tried hard, but I didn't make the cut."

She spoke with her mouth full. "Tha's too bad."

"It was. If I had, it would have been different. I know it would. The way it was, I worked hard up until I was close to graduation." The pizza was half gone. He picked up a square center piece that looked good, bit into it, and chewed and swallowed, tasting only the bitterness of empty years.

"What happened then?" she asked.

"When I was a senior? Nothing, really. It was just that I realized I had been working like a dog to acquire knowledge that nobody wanted. Not even me. That if I did everything right and aced my exams and got my master's I'd end up teaching in the high school in the little Pennsylvania town where we lived, or someplace like it. I'd teach math and chemistry, and maybe coach the baseball team, and it would be kids who were going to work on farms or get factory jobs when they got out of school. I said to hell with it."

"I don't blame you."

"I went back home and told my folks some story. They didn't believe it, and I don't even know what it was now. I got my camping stuff together and went out into the woods. I had a little tent, an air mattress and a sleeping bag. The first winter was rough, so I built a cabin about as big as this room in a place where nobody would ever find it." He paused, recalling Hayfa Washington and the helicopter that had let her down on a rope and somehow made their sunroof open. "It's Federal land, really. National forest. I don't think about that much, but it is."

The woman shrugged. "If all the money's theirs, all the land is too, I guess."

"I suppose you're right." He put his half-eaten piece of pizza back in the box.

"You just live out there? Like that?"

"It was always going to be for a little while."

"But you never came back in?"

"Oh, sometimes I do. For my father's funeral, and then for Mom's. She died about a month after he did."

"I'm sorry."

"I was too. But they left everything to me—I was the only kid. The house and so on. The car and a little money. I sold the house and the car, and I don't spend much. I hunt deer and snare small game, and that's what I eat, mostly. Wild plants in the summer." He smiled. "I use dead leaves for toilet paper."

"Do you want to know about me?"

"If you want to tell me."

"Well, I never got to go to college. I was a clerk in a store and a waitress. Then I got married and had the kids, and you know about that. You want to know how I got started selling guns? A friend wanted to know where she could buy one, so I asked this guy I knew, and he sent me to somebody else. And that guy said he'd sell to me only not to her, because the guy that sent me didn't know her. So I said, okay, sell it to me, and I paid him, and I told him I'd get my money back from her. And he said you ought to charge her about a hundred more, I would. So I charged her fifty over. And after a couple weeks, I guess it was, she sent somebody else to me, another woman in her building that was scared worse than she was. Now here I am."

Softly he said, "I steal from campers, sometimes. From hunters, too. That's how I got this coat. A hunter got hot, and hung it on a tree."

She nodded as though she had expected no less. "You want to get me another beer?"

The telephone buzzed as he rose; a thin-lipped man who wore a business suit as though it were a uniform said, "You still haven't called Captain Washington."

"No," Jay admitted. "No, I haven't."

"We don't like to arrest people over tax matters. You may have heard that."

Jay shook his head.

"We don't. Yet more than half the prison population is made up of tax offenders." The thin-lipped man vanished.

the musty little bedroom hid the stains on the wallpaper and let him look at her face.

Next morning she said, "I want to have breakfast with you. Isn't that funny?"

Not knowing what else to do, he nodded.

"I never used to have breakfast with Chuck. I'd have to get up early to see about the kids, and he'd sleep till ten or eleven. After he left me I'd have a boyfriend sometimes. Only we'd do it and he'd get up and go. Back to his wife, or where he lived. They weren't ever around for breakfast."

"All right," Jay said, "let's eat breakfast."

"We don't have to take the car. You don't mind walking three or four blocks?"

He smiled. "No."

"Okay. We've got a couple things to settle, and maybe the safest way is while we're walking. I don't know how serious they are, but if they're serious at all they'll have bugged this place while we slept. The café'd be better, but out on the street's probably as good as it gets. Keep your voice down, don't move your lips a lot when you talk, and if it's serious hold your hand in front of your face."

He nodded and, seeing blowing snow through a dirty windowpane, pulled the reversible coat he had bought the day before out of his wheeled duffel and put it on over the hunting coat that still (almost to his dismay) held his money.

Out in the cold and windy street she murmured, "They'll figure we're going back, so first thing is we won't. If they have a man watch it and maybe another guy watch the car, they could get a little shorthanded. We can hope, anyway."

He nodded, although it seemed to him that if there were a homing device in the vanette it would not be necessary to have anyone watch it.

"When we go out of the café we'll split up, see? I'll give you the address—where to go and how to get there. Don't look to see if they're following you. If they're good you won't see them. Just lose them if you can."

"I hope I can," he said.

The little restaurant was small and crowded and noisy. They ate waffles in a tiny booth, he striving to keep his eyes on his plate.

"The way you lose a tail is you do something unexpected where the tail can't follow you," she said. "Say there's a cab, but just the one. You grab it and have him take you someplace fast, all right? Only not to the address I'm going to give you. Someplace else."

He nodded.

"I thought maybe you were going to say there's got to be a thousand cabbies, and they can't talk to them all. Only every cab's got a terminal in it, and it records when fares get picked up, and where they're going. Like if they know you caught the cab at eleven oh two, all they've got to do is check cabs that picked up somebody right about then. It's maybe a dozen cabs, then they can find out where you went."

"I understand," he said.

"Or maybe you go to the john. He's not going to come in the john with you because you'd get too good a look at him. He'll wait outside. Well, if it's got two doors you duck in one and out the other. Or climb out the window, if there's a window. It gets you ten or fifteen minutes to get away."

"Okay," he said.

She had taken a pen and a small notebook from her purse; she scribbled in it, tore out the page, and handed it to him. "Where we're going to meet," she said. "Don't look at it till you're almost there."

He was too stunned to say anything.

"You're finished."

He managed to say, "Yes, but you're not."

"I'm awfully nervous, and when I'm nervous I don't eat a lot. I look at you and see the two dots, and I know they're seeing what you do, your sausages or whatever. Let's go."

Out on the street again, in the cutting wind, she squeezed his hand. "See that subway entrance up ahead? Maybe you can see the escalator through the glass."

"Yes," he said.

"We're going to walk right toward it. When we get there, I'll go in and down. You keep walking."

He did, badly tempted to watch as the moving steps carried her away but staring resolutely ahead.

Soon traffic thinned, and the sidewalks grew dirtier. The vehicles filling every parking space were older and shabbier. He went into a corner store then and asked the middle-aged black man behind the counter for a package of gum. "This a bad neighborhood?"

The counterman did not smile. "It's not good."

"I heard it was really bad," Jay said. "This doesn't look so bad."

The counterman shrugged. "One and a quarter for that."

Jay gave him a hundred. "Where would it be worse?"

"Don't know." The counterman held Jay's hundred up to the light and fingered the paper. "You pushin' queer? I knows what you looks like now."

"Keep the change," Jay said.

The counterman stared.

"Where does it get really bad? Dangerous."

For a second or two, the counterman hesitated. Then he said, "Just keep on north, maybe six blocks?"

Jay nodded.

"Then you turns east. Three blocks. Or fo'. That's 'bout as bad as anythin' gits."

"Thanks." Jay opened the gum and offered a stick to the counterman.

The counterman shook his head. "Gits on my dentures. You goin' up there where I told you?"

He did, and once there he stopped and studied the shabby buildings as though searching for a street number. Two white men—the only other whites in sight—were following him, one behind him with a brown attaché case, the other on the opposite side of the street. Their hats and topcoats looked crisp and new, and they stood out in that neighborhood like two candy bars in a brushpile. He turned down an alley, ran, then halted abruptly where a rusted-out water heater leaned against a dozen rolls of discarded carpet.

Often he had waited immobile for an hour or more until a wary deer ventured within range of his bow. He waited so now, motionless in the wind and the blowing snow, half concealed by the hot-water tank and a roll of carpet, a sleeve breaking the outline of his face; and the men he had seen in the street passed him without a glance, walking purposefully up the alley. Where it met the next street they stopped and talked for a moment or two; then the attaché case was opened, and they appeared to consult an instrument of some kind. They reentered the alley.

He rose and ran—down that alley, across the street and into the next, down another street, a narrow and dirty street on which half or more of the parked cars had been stripped. When he stopped at last, sweating despite the cold, he got out Hayfa Washington's card and tore it in two.

Threadlike wires and their parent microchips bound the halves together still.

He dropped both halves down a sewer grating, pulled off his reversible coat, turned it green-side-out and put it back on, then unbuttoned his hunting coat as well and transferred the hunting knife his father had given him one Christmas to a pocket of the now-green raincoat, sheath and all.

An hour later—long after he had lost count of alleys and wretched streets—he heard running feet behind him, whirled, and met his attacker with the best flying tackle he could muster. He had not fought another human being since boyhood; he fought now as the bobcat had fought him, with the furious strength of desperation, gouging and biting and twice pounding the other's head against the dirty concrete. He heard the bottle that had been the other's weapon break, and felt the heat of the blood streaming from his ear and scalp, and by an immense effort of will stopped the point of the old hunting knife short of the other's right eye.

The other's struggled ended. "Don' do that, man! You don' want to make me blind."

"Give up?"

"Yeah, man. I give up." The jagged weapon the bottle had become clinked on the pavement.

"How much did you think I'd have on me?"

"Man, that don't matter!"

"Yes, it does. How much?"

"Forty. Fifty. Maybe credit cards, man, you know."

"All right." The point of the knife moved a centimeter closer. "I want you to do something for me. I want you to work. If you'll do it, I'll pay you a hundred and send you away. If you won't, you'll never get up. Which is it?"

"I'll do it, man." The other at least sounded sincere. "I'll do whatever you says."

"Good." Jay rose and dropped the knife back into his pocket. "Maybe you can pull me down. I don't know, but maybe you can. Whenever you want to try . . ." He shrugged.

"You bleedin', man."

"I know. It will stop, or I think it will." Jay got out a hundred. "You see this? It'll be all yours." He tore it in two and gave half to the other. "You get the other half when you've done what I'm hiring you to do."

"Okay if I gets up, man?"

Jay nodded, and the other got slowly to his feet. His Jeens and plastic jacket were old and cracked, his Capribuk athletic shoes nearly new.

"Listen carefully. If you don't do exactly what I tell you, our deal is off. I'm going to give you a piece of paper with an address on it."

The other gave no indication that he had heard.

"I want you to read that address, but I don't want you to tell me what it is. Don't say it, and don't let me see the paper."

"What is this shit, man?"

"Do you watch the news?"

"I got no time for that shit, man. I listens to music."

For two or three seconds Jay stared at the blank screen on the other's forehead, recalling that his own was—or had been—equally blank. "There's no point in explaining. Do you understand what you're got to do?"

"Look at the address. Not tell you. Not let you look, even. You want me to tear it up?"

Jay shook his head. "I want you to keep it, and I want you to take me there. If we have to spend money to get there, I'll pay."

Reluctantly, the other nodded.

"When we get there, you give me the paper so I can see you took me to the right place. When you do, I'll give you the other half of that hundred and you can go."

He had expected the subway, but they took a bus; the ride lasted over an hour. "'Bout two blocks now," the other said when they left it at last. "You wants to walk?"

Jay nodded.

"You going to turn me in, man?"

"No," Jay said. They were walking side by side. "I'm going to give you the other half of that hundred, and shake hands if you're willing to shake hands, and say good-bye."

"You a pretty fair scrapper, you know? Only you catches me by surprise. I wasn't expectin' you to turn 'round like what you done."

"Wasn't that what you were trying to do to me? Take me by surprise?"

"Sho'!" The other laughed.

"So that's all right. Except that right and wrong really don't count in things like this. I hunt a lot. I hunt animals to eat."

"Do tell?"

"And for hide and bone to make things out of. Generally I try to give the animals a fighting chance."

"Uh-huh."

"But when I'm hungry, really up against it, I don't. I kill any way I can."

"We here." The other waved at one of several squat concrete buildings. "Got a number on it 'n' everythin'. You don' want to look at that?"

"I don't think it matters now," Jay said, and looked.

"Number eighteen." The other fished in his pockets and pulled out the page of notebook paper, now much folded, that the woman who sold guns had given Jay in the café. "All right. It says here Greentree Gardens. An' it says buildin' eighteen. Then it says number eight. Have a look."

Jay did.

"Now this here's Greentree Gardens, all right? You look right over there 'n' there's a sign on top of that buildin'. What do it say?"

"Greentree Gardens."

"Right on, man. Right over there's buildin' number eighteen, like you sees. Number eight will be ground flo', mos' like, or maybe next up. Places like this ain't bad as some other places, you know? Only they ain't real safe neither. You wants me to go in there with you? Be glad to if you wants it."

Jay shook his head, took out the remaining half of the torn hundred, and handed it to the other. Then he offered his hand, which the other accepted after putting the torn half bill into one of his pockets.

Abruptly his grip tightened. Jay tried to jerk away, but the other's fist caught him under the cheekbone.

He went down, rolling and trying to cover his head with his arms. A kick dizzied him, its shock worse than its pain. Another missed, and another must have struck his forearm, because his arm felt as though it had been clubbed.

Somehow he got to his feet, charged the other and grappled him. *I killed that buck like this,* he thought; the buck had an arrow in its gut, but that had hardly seemed to matter. His knife was in his hand. He stabbed and felt it strike bone.

Then it was gone.

At once the other had it, and there was freezing cold where his shirt pocket should have been, cold followed by burning heat, and he was holding the other's wrist with both hands, and the blade was wet and red. The other's fist pounded his nose and mouth. He did not hear the shot, but he felt the other stiffen and shudder.

He pushed the other's body from him, insanely certain that it was only a trick, only a temporary respite granted so that he might be taken by surprise again in a moment or two. Rising, he kicked something.

It was the knife, and it went clattering over the sidewalk. He pulled it out of some snow, wiped the blade with his handkerchief, returned it to its sheath and the sheath to his pocket.

Then the woman who sold guns was tugging at his sleeve. In her other hand she held a short and slender rifle with a long box magazine. "Come on! We've got to get out of here."

He followed her docilely between the hulking building that was eighteen Greentree Gardens, and a similar building that was probably sixteen or twenty. Two floors down in a dark underground garage, she unlocked a blue CUV. As he climbed in he said, "Borrowed from another friend?"

"This's mine, and if I didn't sell what I do I couldn't afford it."

It reeked of cigar smoke; he said, "In that case, I'd think they'd know about it—the plate number and so forth."

She shook her head. "It's registered under a fake name, and these aren't my plates."

He considered that while she drove eight or ten blocks fast, then up a winding ramp and onto the interstate.

When they were in the leftmost lane, he said, "Why are we running away?"

She turned her head to look at him. "Are you crazy? Because I killed that guy."

"He was going to kill me." He looked down at his wound, and was mildly surprised to find that it was still bleeding, his blood soaking the two-sided raincoat and, presumably, the hunting coat under it.

"So what? Look, I can't even defend myself, according to the law. Say you were going to rape me and kill me."

"I wouldn't do that."

"Just suppose. I couldn't shoot you or stab you or even hit you, and if I did you could sue me afterward."

"Could I win?"

"Sure. What's more, I'd be defending your suit from a cell. And if I hurt you worse'n you hurt me, you'd be out."

Jay shook his head. "That doesn't make sense."

"Not for us it doesn't." The interstate sloped sharply down here, but she kept pedal to the floor; for a moment the CUV shook wildly. "For them it does—for the Feds. If we got used to the idea of going after somebody who went after us, we'd go after them. Capeesh?"

"We should."

"Sure. Only for me it's a lot worse. For you, too. I killed that guy. Don't say maybe he's not dead. I saw him when I hit him, and I saw him afterward. He's gone."

"How did you know we were out there?"

"Saw you out the window, that's all. It'd been a while, so I kept looking outside, hoping you were just looking for the right number. I'd stopped off and picked up your gun on the way home, and I was afraid you'd come and gone before I got there. You want to see it? It's on the back seat. Only be careful, it's loaded. I think I put the safety on."

Jay took off his seat belt and picked up the carbine, careful not to touch its trigger.

"Keep it down so the other drivers can't see it."

He did. "This car doesn't talk to us."

"I killed that bastard as soon as I got it. It's pretty easy."

Sensing that she was about to cry, Jay did not speak; he would have tried to hold her hand, perhaps, but both her hands were on the wheel.

"And now I've killed the bastard that was trying to kill you. There's tissues in back somewhere."

He got them, heard her blow her nose.

"I told you how bad that is. It's murder one. He was trying to kill you, but that doesn't make a damned bit of difference. I should have called the cops and showed them your body when they got there. That would have been when? Two or three o'clock. My God, it's lunchtime."

He looked at the clock on the instrument panel. It was nearly one.

"You hungry?"

"No," he said.

"Me neither. Let's skip lunch. We'll stop somewhere for dinner tonight."

He agreed, and asked where they were going.

"Damned if I know."

"Then I'd like you to take Eighty."

"We need to get off the interstate before too much longer," she said.

He nodded. "We will."

"Listen, I'm sorry I got you into this."

"I feel the same way," he said. "You saved my life."

"Who was he, anyway?"

"The man I'd gotten to read your note. You didn't want Globnet to get it on the air before we'd left, so I had to have somebody who would look at it for me and take me there. I tried to find somebody who wouldn't call the police as soon as we separated. Clearly that was a bad idea." Jay paused. "How did you think I'd handle it?"

"That you'd guess. That you'd go there and look at my note and see that you were right when you got there."

"No more crying?"

"Nope. That's over. You know what made me cry?"

"What?"

"You didn't understand. You can't kill people, not even if they're killing other people, and I did it with a gun. If they get me I'll get life, and you didn't understand that."

"Who'd take care of your kids?" He let his voice tell her what he felt he knew about those kids.

She drove. He glanced over at her, and she was staring straight ahead, both hands on the wheel.

"I'm going back into the woods. Maybe they'll get me in there, but it won't be easy. If the holovid company can't help you, maybe you'd like to come with me."

"You had it all doped out." She sounded bitter.

He shook his head. "I don't think I understand it all even now, and there's a lot of it that I just figured out a minute ago. How much were you supposed to get for this?"

"A couple thousand."

He thought about that. "You're not an employee. Or at least, you don't work for Globnet full-time."

"No." She sniffled. "They did a documentary on the gun trade last year, and I was one of the people they found—the only woman. So I was on holo with this really cool mask over my face, and I thought that was the end of it. Then about a month ago they lined me up to do this."

He nodded.

"They figured you'd want women or drugs, mostly, and they had people set for those. I was kind of an afterthought, okay? Stand by for a couple hundred, or a couple thousand if you called. Another thousand if I sold you a gun. I did, but I'll never collect any of it."

"The bot must have called you after he gave me your number."

"Kaydee Nineteen? Sure. That's how you knew, huh? Because you got it from him."

Jay shook his head. "That was how I should have known, but I didn't.

It was mostly the phone call you made last night to somebody who was supposed to be sitting your kids. Real mothers talk about their kids a lot, but you didn't. And just now it hit me that you'd called your friend Val, and James R. Smith's secretary was Valerie. Then I thought about the bot. He took his security work very seriously, or at least it seemed like he did. But he had given me the number of a gun dealer as soon as I asked, and he had been friendly with Valerie."

"So I was lying to you all the time."

He shrugged.

"Don't do that! You're going to get that thing bleeding worse. What happened to your ear?"

He told her, and she pointed. "There's a truck stop. They'll have aid kits for sale," and cutting across five lanes of traffic, raced down an exit ramp.

That night, in an independent motel very far from Interstate Eighty, he took off his reversible raincoat and his hunting coat, and his shirt and undershirt as well, and sat with clenched teeth while she did what she could with disinfectant and bandages.

When she had finished, he asked whether she had been able to buy much ammunition.

"Eight boxes. That's four hundred rounds. They come fifty in a box."

He nodded.

"Only we don't have it. It's back in that place in Greentree Gardens."

He swore.

"Listen, you've got money and I've got connections. We can buy more as soon as things quiet down."

"A lot of the money's ruined. It has blood on it."

She shook her head. "It'll wash up. You'll see. Warm water and a little mild detergent, don't treat it rough and let it dry flat. You can always clean up money."

"I thought maybe I could just give it to them," he said. "Show them it wasn't any good anymore."

She kissed him, calling him Skeeter; and he shut his eyes so that Globnet and its audience would not see her kiss.

———

He had been after deer since before the first gray of dawn; but he had never gotten a shot, perhaps because of the helicopters. Helicopters had been flying over all morning, sweeping up and down this valley and a lot of other valleys. He thought about Arizona or New Mexico, as he sometimes did, but concluded (as he generally had to) that they would be too open, too exposed. Colorado, maybe, or Canada.

The soldiers the helicopters had brought were spread out now, working their way slowly up the valley. Too few, he decided. There weren't enough soldiers and they were spread too thin. They expected him to run, as perhaps he would. He tried to gauge the distance to the nearest.

Two hundred yards. A long two hundred yards that could be as much as two hundred and fifty.

But coming closer, closer all the time, a tall, dark-faced woman in a mottled green, brown, and sand-colored uniform that had been designed for someplace warmer than these snowy Pennsylvania woods. Her height made her an easy target—far easier than even the biggest doe—and she held a dead-black assault rifle slantwise across her chest. That rifle would offer full or semiautomatic operation, with a switch to take it from one to the other.

Less than two hundred yards. Very slowly Jay crouched in the place he had chosen, pulled his cap down to hide the stars of his upgrade, then raised his head enough to verify that he could keep the woman with the assault rifle in view. His wound felt as hot as his cheeks, and there was blood seeping through the bandage; he was conscious of that, and conscious too that it was harder to breathe than it should have been.

A hundred and fifty yards. Surely it was not more than a hundred and fifty, and it might easily be less. He was aware of his breathing, of the pounding of his heart—the old thrill.

Thirty rounds in that black rifle's magazine, possibly. Possibly more, possibly as many as fifty. There would be an ammunition belt too, if he had time to take it. Another two or three hundred rounds, slender, pointed bullets made to fly flatter than a stretched string and tumble in flesh.

For an instant that was less than a moment, less even than the blink of an eye, a phantom passed between him and the woman with the black assault rifle—a lean man in soiled buckskins who held a slender, graceful gun that must have been almost as long as he was tall.

A hallucination.

"They know where we are," Jay told the woman.

"Yeah. Get me that beer, will you?"

"Shouldn't we leave?"

She did not speak, and after half a minute or so he brought her another beer from the kitchen.

"Here's how I see it," she said when he (with face averted) held out the beer. "Let me go through it, and you tell me if you think I'm wrong.

"To start with, how do they know we're here? Answer—that FR&SS woman put a bug on our car, I just didn't find it. That means that if we take the car we might as well stay here. And if we don't take the car, we'll have to go on foot. They'll have people all around this building by now waiting to tail us, and with the streets pretty well empty it would be a cinch."

"Where would we go?" he asked.

"Damned if I know. We might end up walking all night. Next question. Are they about to break down the door and bust us? Answer—no, because they wouldn't have called first if they were. The FR&SS woman made the news, she was good-looking, it was dramatic and blah blah. It was meant to. Now they'll be watching to see if that phone call makes it. I think what they'll do is get a little rougher every time, because every time they come around the chance that it'll make Globnet's news show gets slimmer. The woman was really pretty nice, on purpose. The guy on the phone wasn't so nice, and next time's going to be worse. Or that's how it looks to me."

"You're probably right. But you're leaving something out. They knew that we were in this apartment, and not in some other apartment in this building."

"Piece of cake. The guys staking it out talked to the pizza man. 'Who paid you?' 'Well, she was a middle-aged woman with red hair.' 'Anybody else in there?' 'Yeah, I could hear somebody moving around in back.' 'Okay, that's them.' They got a look at me when we talked on the phone, and the Fed that got into our car probably described us."

Jay said, "You're not middle-aged."

She laughed. "When you've got two kids in school, you're middle-aged. How old are you?"

"Forty-one."

"See, you're middle-aged, too. You're older than I am." To his amazement, her hand had found his.

They kissed, he with his eyes shut; an hour later, turning off the lights in

Jay smiled to himself. Had they seen that, back at Globnet? They must have, if they still saw everything he did. Would they put it on the news?

A scant hundred yards now. The little carbine seemed to bring itself to his shoulder.

Seventy yards, if that.

Jay took a deep breath, let it half out, and began to squeeze the trigger.

Rattler

with BRIAN HOPKINS

◆

We heard this in a truck stop in Oklahoma. Two men in the next booth were talking about dogs, and one said that he had trained pointers and setters of several breeds, and that it was much easier to train a bird dog if you had a trained dog that would hunt at the same time—that the trained dog taught the untrained one.

It don't (the other man said), or not so's you could notice. I've hunted with dogs all my life, and I ain't never noticed no dog teaching but one. That German shorthair you got now learns, sure enough. But the other don't teach it. It just sees what the other's doin' and sees you like it. That's all. That pup wants to please, so it does like the other dog.

No, sir, I never seen nor heard of but one dog that taught like a regular teacher would, and that was a ol' coonhound I used to have. Bud his name was. Ol' Bud taught sure enough, only it wasn't no other dog he taught. I reckon he thought that would be too easy for him. Or else maybe he never wanted to see another dog smarter than he was. That there was the smartest dog ever made. I could tell you—well, you wouldn't believe it. And it ain't to the point anyways, you know.

You seen my ol' pickemup what we rode out here in? I parked it in the barn back then like I do now, and Bud was always feered he'd miss a ride, so he slept in the back so I couldn't go off without him 'less I chased him out first. It got so anytime I nailed up a coonskin, Bud would tear it down and carry it back there to sleep on. He had quite a pile there before long. I'd nail 'em higher and higher, and I never did figure out how he moved the ladder.

Oh, sure, he could climb it all right. Any coon dog worth a biscuit can climb, you bet! They'll climb trees and such if there's limbs for 'em, to get at the coon.

Bud got hisself a nice pile of coonskins in the back of my pickup, and he'd sleep back there just about every night. If I had to put hay bales or somethin' in the back I'd have to chase him out, and throw all them coonskins out, too, 'fore I could do it. Only if I was just goin' into town to pick up fixin's and maybe some beer, I'd leave him and his coonskins right where they was and ride him into town to watch my truck.

Well, sir, one day I drove that ol' pickemup into town 'cause I had to go to the bank, and when I come out there was a kid hangin' around it, you know, and I heard Bud growl. "You get away from there," I says, and he growls at the kid again. I took three or four more steps, and it hit me that Bud was dead. He'd died the week before, and I'd buried him out in the back of my wood lot and read over him, too, changing a couple words so it was dogs 'stead of people, you know how you do, and put up a marker for him that I'd cut his name in.

It was his ghost was what I thought. He'd loved that ol' truck and come back to it, and I went goosefleshed all over. Felt like my skin was goin' to crawl right off me. Only when I started up the engine I heard the growl just like before. That same exact growl, you know. It was the starter motor, and it was my ol' pickemup that had been growlin'.

After that I noticed a few things. Like if I'd parked by a tree or the light pole or somethin', there'd be a little puddle of gas when I pulled out. I put newspaper under, you know how you do, to see where it was leakin', only it wasn't. Bone dry. Then I was ridin' a feller and he said what a nice truck, and it lost the back like it was on ice. Just a teeny little it was, but I noticed. It quit pretty quick but I got to thinkin' why'd it do that, and by-'n-by it come to me—he'd been waggin' his tail.

So I called him Bud awhile, you know, thinkin' he was hauntin' it, only that truck never did cotton to the name. After that I tried various names that didn't none of 'em work. And he give me some trouble, always wantin' to chase coons. You know how you'll drive at night and see a coon in your headlights? I always try to miss 'em. I been a coon hunter all my life, and the more coons the better the huntin' is, is the way I see it. Only that ol' pickemup had been learned by Bud real good and he'd chase after 'em. Took me right through a bobwire fence once and 'bout a half a mile over the prairie 'fore I could get him stopped. I killed the lights and drove out quiet as I could, you bet!

Well, sir, one time he took off after a coon and I was wrestlin' the wheel and stompin' the brake tryin' to get him back on the road. You know how you do. And I hollered out, "Stop! Stop you derned ol' rattler!"

And he done it. So I knew then what his name was do you see, and I call him Rattler when I got to get his attention or quiet him down when I take him to the vet—the mechanic's what I mean, that OK Auto Repair place in town. Only Rattler, he likes vet better, and if you'll just quit interruptin', I'll let you have your say.

(The first man, the one who trained bird dogs, spoke at some length at this point. We will not give his entire argument word for word, but he was skeptical.)

Well, sir (the other man said), you're just like to Junior. He's my brother-in-law, the dumb fat one. He seen Rattler and rode in him and all, and he just kept on sayin' how'd you get him to do that? I tol' him just like I tol' you, but it took a heap of tellin' 'fore he'd believe me. Then he said whatever a dog could do he could do. Dumbest thing I ever heard a man say. I says can you scratch your neck with your back foot, Junior? Everybody laughed—this was at the Baptist social, you know—and he got mad and shut up, which was what I wanted.

'Bout a month after, he let drop that he'd been teachin' hisself. Had a big green pickemup with a crew cab he cared the world about, you know, and he said he'd talk to it while he was drivin'. What's its name? I says. He tells, and it wasn't the truck's name but the company that made it. Dumbest thing I ever heard. So I asks if he's taught it to fetch. He says not yet, how's it goin' to do that? You watch I says.

So right there's where I took a big chance. I'll be square with you like I always am, and say if I had it to do over again probably I wouldn't. But I was mad and wanted to show Junior, and I got ol' Rattler and I says, "You see that calf with the white blaze? Fetch!"

Well, sir, Rattler hadn't had a lot of practice workin' cattle back then but he made me proud. He never blowed his horn or nothing that would get the calf stirred up. No, sir! And he never bent. You can't with cattle. You bend, and they'll walk all over you. He showed that calf what he wanted, and he let down his tailgate and sort of pulled in the back shocks so his back set so low his tailgate dragged.

The calf, he turned and went off, you know how they do, only Rattler was out in front of him fast, still low, still got his tailgate down and talkin' quiet with his engine. That went on for about five minutes. Coulda been ten. Then the calf give in and walked up into the back. Rattler shut his tailgate—you know how you do when you're headin' back home? He just shut it and shut it pretty quiet, but there was a world of satisfaction in it. He'd done the job, and he knew he'd done it. He come back to where we was waitin', and he showed off a little then. Flashed his headlights at us, you know. It was broad daylight, too. I reckon he couldn't help it, he just felt so good.

And so'd I. I turned to Junior and I says that's fetch, and it's pretty easy to teach. He went off without another word, and that suited me fine. Every time he opens his mouth I hear more than I want to, even if it's just hello.

So that was that for about a month. Only one day I had to ride Junior into town to get his truck back from the OK Auto Repair place. He got to talking about how tough them pickemups was to train. "Junior," I says, "we got to face the facts, and the fact is you don't know nothin'. You get you a good truck, and it's instinct. It's born in a good pickemup, and you oughter know that. All you got to do is get a good 'un to start and bring the instinct out. I never seen a good coonhound that would point birds, and neither have you. Neither has anybody. Now you take ol' Rattler here." And then I leaned back like I was a passenger, you know, and laced my hands behind my head the way you do.

He kept right on a-goin' about ten miles, and then he come to where a coon'd crossed the road, and he got the scent. He follered it off into the woods, and you could hear that gearbox bayin' and then the muffler comin' in deep where the J-B Weld had got scraped off. It was as pretty a music as you ever heard.

Ol' Rattler treed that coon, too, and right there I would say is where the real trouble come in. I oughter have stopped him right there and me and Junior got out and had a look at the coon—from the ground is what I mean—and got back in and drove away. Only I wanted to show off. I never touched the wheel nor the brake nor the clutch. I give him his head, you know.

And he started up the tree after that coon, goin' to run him over even if it was fifty feet up in the air.

It ain't easy for a pickemup to climb a tree, no more than for a hound, and they got the same trouble—their tires ain't sharp. Rattler'd get up a ways, and hook his front bumper on a limb, you know how they do, probably. And he'd feel around with his front wheels trying to get traction. He's got front-wheel drive, naturally. If he hadn't had that we'd still be tryin' to get up that tree. Front-wheel drive and all it still took quite a time.

Finally he got pretty close and I got out my ol' Ruger Bearcat and put a long rifle in the coon where it would hurt, and he fell out of the tree. Rattler come down then, a lot faster than what he went up. Junior was a mite shaken up, you know.

I got out and threw the coon in the back and off we went, me feelin' right proud and Junior sort of lookin' out the window and swearin' to hisself. I wouldn't let him do it where I could hear. It's bad luck to hear a fool cuss—I guess you know.

I'd pretty much forgot about all that when Midge phoned me up. Midge's Junior's wife and a nice girl. I never did figure out why she married him 'less she felt sorry for him, and after that the rest of us felt sorry for Midge. "You got to do somethin'," she says. "He's tore up his truck three times since the picnic. He keeps gettin' it fixed and there's no money for anythin'."

Well, sir, that picnic had been on the fourth of July, it wasn't August by a week, so I could see the thing was serious. I phoned up Junior that night and I says I'd heard he'd been teachin' his truck and maybe he could come by and show me. He hemmed and hawed just like I'd been scared he would, and we went 'round a few times on it, him talkin' five to my one like usual. I'd hol' the phone away from my ear, you know how you do, till it got quiet, then I'd come back. And all the time I was thinkin' how I could hook him. Them that won't go for a night crawler will bite on a shiner sometimes. You know how that is.

Pretty soon it come to me that what with Midge not gettin' the house money the table was likely pretty poor over there. So I says why don't you and her come for dinner? Sarah's baked, and we'll barbecue and have us a slap-up good feed. So he come just like I knew he would and Midge too.

After we et I got him in the truck, said I wanted to go into town and get more ice cream. I knew that'd fetch him, which it did; he jumped into that new truck of his and strapped hisself in like he was going to the NASCAR. Soon's we were out on the county road I says, I hear you been learnin' this pickemup of yours, Junior. What does it do?

Well, he just shook his head.

Maybe you got it to sit up and beg, I says. That's a real pretty trick when a truck does it, and lets you get the oil filter off easy, too.

"I been talkin' and talkin'," he says—which I believed, you bet!—"and showin' it how every which way, and the only thing I've learned it is to roll over."

That's a good trick too, I says, only if you don't mind I'm going to get out before you show it, and I'm sure you'll get out too 'cause you're a big man and that seat belt you're wearin' can't take but just so much.

"It won't do it unless I'm inside and hol'in' the wheel," Junior says, "and I ain't goin' to do it anyhow 'cause it tears up the cab too bad."

That had me scratchin' and whistlin'. Not that I didn't know what was wrong. I'd knew before we ever got off my property. Midge was the puzzler, do you see? I'd promised I'd help out all I could, so I couldn't just tell Junior flat out,'cause it'd probably make him worse. I thought and thought, and finally I says, you know, it ain't only the student that learns. I noticed that myself and probably you have too. Sometimes the teacher learns as much as he does. More, now and then. Have you learned anything from teachin' this here pickemup, Junior?

"I have," he says. "I've learned that this here is the dumbest derned truck ever come off a assembly line."

I keeps my voice real gentle when I says, now that ain't so. This here truck has a automatic transmission, Junior. You don't have to tell it what gear. It *knows.* Can't nobody say a truck like that's dumb.

"You mean it's teachin' me," he says.

That's for you to say, Junior, I says real gentle-like. Only I don't believe anybody's ever goin' to teach a pickemup that has a automatic anythin'.

We got the ice cream real quiet and come back real quiet, too, and I kept tellin' myself how nobody'd ever got anythin' through that thick skull of Junior's but I'd promised Midge and done the best I could.

Well, sir. Come Thanksgivin' we had the whole family over, and Junior, he got to talkin' about a cattle auction that was coming up in about a week and what might be good to buy now, and what might be good to sell, and what to look for dependin' on who came. For a while he was flappin' along pretty fair like always. Then he sort of spaced out the words more and give a little time between orations where somebody else might speak a word if they was inclined, which he never done before. I noticed pretty quick, and I seen there was somethin' in his eyes that I'd never seen there before in the whole time since I started courtin' his sister. It took me a while to read the brand, you know, 'cause I kept thinkin' I had to be wrong. Then he said somethin', and I knew for certain sure. It was thoughts. There was somethin' goin' on behind those eyes, and the eyes knew it like they always do.

Junior, I says, that's plumb smart, and I notice you're takin' your time with it more than usual, if you don't mind me sayin' it.

"Well," Junior says, "that auction's a long grade and a steep 'un, and sometimes a feller needs to shift down."

That was all the other man said, and the bird-dog man held his peace, trying to digest everything just as we were. Soon the waitress brought checks to both booths. We paid—and so did they—and started out.

"To see a world in a grain of sand, and a heaven in a wild flower."

Brian looked around at Gene and said, "Did you say that?"

"No," Gene said, "I think it was Robert Blake."

When we got outside, the two men who had been in the next booth were already there. One shouted, "Here, Rattler!" and we heard an engine start in the parking lot.

A small pickup truck, old and red, drove up to the door and stopped.

"Not like that you derned fool," one man said, "I got to get behind your wheel."

The truck pulled away, and returned with its left side toward the curb. The door opened, and the driver got in. "You'll have to open your own door," he told his friend. "He ain't learned that yet."

We stood watching until the small red truck pulled out onto the highway, and it appeared to us that when it did the driver was still fumbling in his pocket for his keys.

In Glory like Their Star

✦

We dined last night before seven skun of natives who had built a stone table for us. They heaped it with wood, set the wood ablaze, and cooked our food by throwing it into the fire. We pulled out the parts we wanted and in the end ate nearly all of it, though it was scorched here and raw there. (The hard, white parts are rich in calcium.) How is it that we can eat their food when it is not vegetable in origin? I must ask the others.

They revere our ship and us. We talked with them about it. They speak for a very long time when they have begun (and do not like to be interrupted), saying the same things over and over in the same words, or at times with changes in wording. They want us to be kind to them, to destroy their enemies, and to make their crops grow. It seems senseless to me, and I do not believe the others understand better than I. Why should we be kind to them when they are unkind to each other? If we are to understand them—and they, us—we must act as they. So much is manifest. Are not their enemies in no regard different from themselves? If we were to destroy these natives instead, the same result would ensue with less difficulty and less chance of error. I may propose it. Of what benefit are the crops to them? This place swarms with food untended. The desert people, who grow none, eat as well as they and with less trouble. These crops they ask us to encourage only encourage their own gluttony. If there is another result, it can be but small.

When they had sung and talked and sung and talked until they and we were tired, we spoke together for a time almost sensibly. We told them something of our home, and though we told them very little it was more than they could understand. Our long voyage through space impressed them. I doubt they grasped its length, for their concepts of the five they call "time" are muddled, and so erroneous that they cannot be termed primitive with any precision. They will be primitive, perhaps, when sunlight reaches them on this place.

Someone told them that I was in the scout first sent from our ship. That impressed them too, although they can have had little notion what my mission was or why I chose to perform it. They asked many questions, of which a few were sensible. They could not understand (I cite an example where I might cite many) why I went alone. Even the youngest soon grasps that where there are two they must often look at each other and not at the place they have been sent to see, and that three will be worse than two, and four worse than three. That those in a crowd see nothing, save its other members. Some may be acute observers. Often some are. But they will observe (acutely) those before and behind, and to one side and the other, and the crowd as a whole will always see less than any member has.

I told them how I had landed in the desert lands. I was unable to control my loquacity once I had begun and tried to tell them how those lands had appeared to me. The wind that was never still, and the sand that whispered and whispered under my foot, speaking of great trees and beasts, and fair meadows that had vanished only a moment before we came. The flaming lights that filled the night sky, the cold of night and the heat of day. Cities and forests and mountain ranges and vast lakes of tossing water that seemed not so far away that a shout might not reach them, but vanished too as I approached them on my machine. No matter how swiftly I rode. They nodded, as I had expected, and looked at one another; but they did not understand. Less even than those who share our ship did they understand me.

Perhaps I said also how lonely a place the desert is. Perhaps it was my saying it that prompted them to ask why no one had come with me. That would be logical and so must be true—or as the pedants would have it, must be accepted as true until the truth be found.

Was it for truth's sake that I rode across the desert? Was it for truth's sake that I pursued my melting cities and the lakes that evaporated as I approached them? Inarguably. Across that desert—I will never forget it, and because I will not, I will never forget this place, which the large subspecies (that is, those without tails) call Earth—I rode for truth, rising before their star and riding onward, always on so long as I could be certain my way was clear, after it had fallen beneath the horizon.

In that desert the horizon is larger than a place of this size can produce. I think it clear that this place is not a true sphere (though most are) but has a flat spot: its desert. I must mention this to the others. Some may agree.

If it is so, the level desert must appear to one near its center to rise all around, so that he moves only with augmented effort in every direction, since each step carries him farther from the center. Walking upon level ground, he nonetheless ascends its gravity pit. A flat pit, this, which tires and bewilders. That is exactly how it seemed to me, and if my theory does not embrace the physical facts (though I am sure it does) it embraces the subjective ones. This in itself may be a new discovery.

Every theory is true in some discipline.

The beauty of this is that it carries its own confirmation. It ravishes me.

When I had begun to tell of my time alone, some of the others tried to explain what knowledge is, and how it is to be valued. The natives could not understand, saying again and again in many different ways that knowledge is a thing one uses. We sought to explain by the Great Disciplines that such things have nothing to do with its value. We spoke much of our ship, because they themselves had spoken of it again and again, saying (with many voices) that our great knowledge had permitted us to build it. That is so, but who would labor to gain knowledge for such a purpose? It is the interior change that suffices, the transformation that rewards. I know that you know this, but they could not understand.

At last I spoke again of the desert. Not because I felt I could add to their understanding, but because I myself had understood that they would have to gain much more knowledge than they possessed, and undergo many interior changes by its power, before they themselves could understand. The little ones with tails would never. Of that I am certain. But the larger subspecies may, in time.

It is not easy for me to speak of the desert. Still less easy is it for me to scribe it as I do. There is so much that might be said; and yet no one who reads this will have understanding of the desert. Not even those who share this ship with me have it. One must go.

I say again: one must go. I went.

Perhaps there can be too much understanding. I have so much now, and that is why I will never forget this place. My companions understand nothing of that. The whisper of the sands, and the night silence when the sands no longer spoke. Although I had homeair, I found it difficult to breathe when the sands fell silent.

Yet the homeair never failed me. If it had I would be dead. I would be dead and not he.

So much failed me. My companions first of all. The people of this place were correct tonight. One must not see too much, and never is that more true than it is when sight shows only how little there is to be seen. The emptiness. The sand, mountains of sand that move like water animals. The black rocks, uncovered by the wind. Covered by the wind. Uncovered by the wind once again. The wind itself, a thing that spins and strides.

My navigator failed. I do not mean that it would no longer indicate a direction for the scout that had carried me down. It did. I rode and rode. I would sleep on the couch, I told myself. I would eat from the little cold-closet under the work flat. At last, when I was so weary that I feared I would strike a rock and fall, I stopped and ate the last of the food I had carried, and slept (as I had before) upon the sand. When I woke the navigator indicated a direction for the scout indeed, but it was a new direction. My machine no longer pointed as the navigator pointed. They had come for me, I thought. They had come for me, and for some reason—no doubt for the best of reasons—they had moved the scout to a new location. To a better landing place, and a place nearer me than the place where I had at first landed, for the distance was very short now. I rode as the navigator directed, and the distance increased. When I rode as I had the previous day, it increased also. I endeavored to find a direction in which it would decrease, and the direction indicated by my navigator changed again.

Of the next days, I will not speak. On the third, I found a person of this place. My reflector deceived him, and he made the beast he rode halt for me and lie upon the sand. He gave me water; and I told him of my plight, the useless navigator, my machine broken when it collided with a stone. He told me where he was going. I begged to accompany him, for he had water.

That night we camped at a spring, a tiny place but very beautiful, where plants grew green. Dried fruits were his food, with another food like small stones that grew soft when boiled. I could eat none of it, but was glad to see him eat of it, for I knew I would perish if he died. He told stories of desert spirits that night, stories filled with knowledge though none were true. I heard him in awe, and begged that he speak on, until at last it came to me that he believed me one. I turned off my reflector then, and he abased himself.

Eight days we searched the desert for my scout and found it on the ninth. I leaped from the back of his beast and would have run to it ahead of him; but he lashed it to a gallop, though it was so near death, and we arrived together. I had promised him that he would live forever if we found my scout. This I told tonight to those who had burned beasts on the stone table for us, at which their eyes grew wide.

He would be taller than other men, I had promised, and stronger than the beast he rode. He had believed me, and the others, tonight, believed me too.

For a time at least.

The truth is that I believed it myself. In the scout I would be able to correct or alter my own nucleic acids. The tiny machines I inserted beneath my shin for that purpose could, I thought, be inserted beneath his also. So inserted, they would achieve the changes I directed. There in the desert it had seemed so easy.

He questioned me once more when we reached the scout. How hard he tried to ingratiate himself! How many times he touched his face to the sand! I would not cheat him. No, not I. I would never cheat him, who had saved my life in the desert. He waited for me to assert (I could see this) that he had not. But it was true, and I acknowledged it.

The natives who fed us nodded to themselves when I recounted this. The larger sort cover their faces with hair as he did. They remind me of him, and the memory is not wholly unpleasant. How much I learned from him!

I pledged myself again and I took his body fluid. Have I already scribed this? I repeated all the promises I had made before. Better, more, and stronger, for I was starved and shrunken then and feared he would prevent me from boarding the scout. He sensed it, for he severed the head of his beast, and we cooked its flesh and ate it before I went into the scout. I had explained that he could not breathe inside, and I let him stand by me when I opened the lock. He coughed and backed away, and I—I!—achieved the goal of so many empty days.

It was a triumph, and I inspected every part of the scout glorying, and tested every instrument in every possible way, recalling my navigator. They functioned without a flaw, all of them. I was ecstatic.

And then, having grown so greatly in my own estimation, I attempted to reprogram the tiny machines. I would make my promises turn to truths.

The natives who had fed us grew restless when I spoke of this, and looked one to another. They are strange creatures, too simple for their own good; but because they are very simple, it is not easy to guess what they think or what they feel. Their thoughts will be simple thoughts, but without logic and without knowledge. Who can say where they will run? Their feelings know no truth.

It could not be done. I told them so again and again, that they might understand. For three days I labored, though by the third I knew. There was no hope.

And when this star had set (this I made as plain as I could) I restarted the engines and returned to this ship. He, waiting for the promises that could never come, died swiftly and in glory like their star.

I repeated it many times and in many ways, and it seemed to me they understood.

Calamity Warps

✦

Calamity Jane is our dog, and she warps though space. I suppose I should say space-time, though that implies a level of expertise I haven't actually got.

Still, she does. I told Bob Smith next door and he said, "Yep, she's really, really fast." And he may be right. Maybe that's all it is. Maybe the laws of physics say that if a thing—a dog, in this case—moves a whole lot faster than other things of the same kind, she warps though space. I don't know, and to tell you the truth, I don't think anybody else does either.

I ought to go back to the beginning. Our old dog died, and my wife decided we should have a new dog. I didn't think so. It wasn't that I don't like dogs. I do. It was just that I know how much trouble they can be and how much responsibility is involved. If it had been up to me, I would have contacted the breeder and gotten another cairn terrier. But I told my wife I didn't think we ought to, and if she really wanted a dog she would have to get it herself.

So she did. Being on the frugal side, she went to Save-A-Pet and got one for the price of the shots. That was Calamity Jane; she had been spayed and was housebroken, and that was all we really knew about her. The people at Save-A-Pet think she's about eighteen months old.

My wife has various ideas about what kind of dog she might be, some kind of Belgian shepherd one day, and half this and half that the next.

What's for sure is that if you dropped her in a pack of coyotes the coyotes would roll out the welcome mat, and brag afterward about their new member. She's the color of sand, her legs are so long it looks like she's walking on stilts, and she has big, stiff wolf ears. She also has a long, long muzzle with teeth. Lots of them, and the big ones are really, really big. She knows who got her from Save-A-Pet and is my wife's dog. She tolerates me except for late at night. Late at night she thinks I'm sneaking up with some villainous purpose in mind, like giving her a rabies shot, and she lets me know there's no guarantee I'll always have two arms. Boy, I hope she's wrong about that.

Because she warps, like I said.

At first I thought she was just fast. Like, she'd be out in the back yard, and I'd go to the gate, and when my hand touched the latch she'd be right beside me—without ever having gotten there, if you know what I mean.

Then there was the rabbit. We're pretty far out in the burbs, and we get deer and coons and whatnot now and then. It's kind of nice, but the deer will eat your rosebushes unless Calamity's around.

So here was this big cottontail, and the first thing I knew Calamity wasn't in the back yard anymore. She was out in the street after that rabbit. Her legs are really, really long, like I told you, and she just flew.

But the rabbit could turn quicker. She would be snapping at its hind feet and it would make a hard right or a hard left and she'd overshoot it. She'd turn, of course, but the rabbit would have gotten a couple of yards. (I mean like Dawson's yard or Smith's.) When she caught up again, the rabbit would make another hard turn.

Then it did, but she didn't overshoot. Or turn, either. They had been running straight downhill toward Hillside Drive, and the rabbit made a sharp right toward the house on the corner. And Calamity was running that way, too. It wasn't that she had turned, she still had all her momentum, just a sandstorm. The rabbit turned again, and she was right on top of it and bit it in the neck.

She brought it to me after shaking it pretty good, and dropped it at my feet. Then she sort of stepped back and said, *I know you don't like me much, but look what I can do.* Right there's where I made my second big mistake. (My first one was not getting a cairn terrier.) I should have said bad dog and all that, but I picked up the rabbit and said thank you, good dog, and a lot more. What would you have done? Would you want a dog like Calamity mad at you?

Afterward I asked my wife why she'd named her Calamity Jane, and she said she hadn't, the people at Save-A-Pet had. That's when I called them up. And the woman I talked to said they called her that because she was always getting into things and getting out of her run and showing up in places where she shouldn't have been.

I'll bet. I think they knew. They just didn't want to tell us.

So that was that, and I tried chaining her up, but that didn't work either. I think it really made things worse, because she got into the habit, if you know what I mean. She'd see another dog or something, and run to the end of her chain and be with that other dog. And her collar lying on the ground with the chain still on it. So I quit doing it.

Then she started bringing stuff home, and she would give it to me. Mostly it was stuff she could have gotten anywhere, but once it was a wallet with Japanese money in it and Japanese ID. I sent that to the Japanese consulate.

The next I remember was just a stick. Only it was heavy, and the harder you looked at it, the funnier it looked, if you know what I mean. The bark was kind of like skin, and warty, and the wood inside wasn't really bone, but it made you think of that. Polished bone, and that hard and heavy.

After that a little animal, still alive. It was sort of cute, but Calamity had hurt it pretty bad catching it, and it had trouble breathing. It had pink fur. I read one time that they used to take white rabbits and dye them all sorts of colors for Easter and sell them for pets, and I thought maybe it had been dyed like that. But it looked really strange, and after it was dead and couldn't bite I took it down in the basement and cut into it.

I took biology in high school, and it was about the only time in my life I ever got a B. But I had been good at that, and we had cut up dead frogs and studied the heart, the stomach, and so forth, and I thought I would just have a look inside that little pink animal. So I laid it on my workbench down there and put a new blade in my utility knife, and opened it up.

You talk about a shock. It wasn't a vertebrate. It had fur—that pink fur—but it didn't have a backbone. Maybe there's something on this planet that has fur but no backbone, but I don't know what it is. Even fish are vertebrates, and so are birds. Its blood was pink, too. So right then I was starting to get an inkling of what was going on.

Only I didn't know where Calamity was going to get this stuff. I thought Mars, so I read up on Mars and it could be there were little pink animals there, but the stick didn't fit, and neither did some of the other stuff.

After that came the real mindblower. There's no way I can make you believe it, so I'll just tell it. She brought home a shadow.

I don't mean her own shadow. I mean another shadow that she carried in her mouth and dropped at my feet. Of course it tried to stick onto me then. I jumped away and kicked at it, and for a while it was off by itself.

If you shine a light on it, it sort of disappears, and if there are a bunch of lights all around, like in the living room with all the lights on, you can't see it very good at all. But if you take it outside late in the day, when the sun's pretty low, you can see it really well. It's the shadow of a big man with wide shoulders and four arms. He's got on a helmet with horns on it, too, or that's what it looks like—the kind of thing you see in pictures of Vikings.

It would try to stick to me, and I'd get rid of it by jumping and kicking, and at first that worked pretty well. Or I thought it did. And I would try to get rid of it by losing it or shining lights on it, which didn't work at all.

Then I noticed I didn't have my regular shadow anymore. I could stand right beside my wife in the sunshine, and she'd have a shadow, and you could see the shadow of the birdbath or whatever as plain as day. But not mine. You couldn't see my shadow at all. So I thought, pretty soon somebody's going to notice this.

And I let the shadow Calamity had brought stick to my feet the way it wanted. Now I can't get rid of it when I try, and it's a man a lot bigger than I am, with horns and four arms.

Which is fine if we're standing in high grass or something that breaks the shadow up. I look perfectly normal then. But if we're on concrete, like the driveway, and the sun is low and bright. Well, you can imagine.

A lucky thing is that I work in an office where there are a lot of bright fluorescent lights up in the ceiling. Nobody notices. But the other thing is that we've got these emergency lights that come on if the power fails. That happened about two years ago, and they were really bright. Everybody was casting hard, sharp shadows. If it ever happens again, I'm going to hide under my desk until everybody else has left.

So that's pretty bad. But what really worries me is this new thing Calamity's given me. It's not exactly like a sword, and it's not exactly like an ax, and there's little dashes of other stuff in there, too, maybe a baseball bat with a big nail through it and a machine gun. Stuff like that. If you saw it, you'd say, "What's that?"

You're supposed to hold it with two hands. Or maybe three. It's hard to tell. It's pretty, too.

No, let me be up front here. Mrs. Smith's an art teacher and I showed it to her yesterday. It was a cloudy day and she was weeding her annuals. I just carried it over and said, "Have a look at this."

She said, "My God, how ugly!" Then, "No. No . . . Yes, it is. It's terribly ugly, but it's beautiful, isn't it? It's too beautiful to be bothered with looking pretty. Can I hold it?"

So I gave it to her, and she almost dropped it, it was so heavy. Only it doesn't feel heavy to me. It feels about like a broom handle. I guess it feels like that to Calamity, too. But I set the sharp end on the bathroom scale and sort of balanced it, and the scale said thirty-seven pounds.

The funny thing is that when I hold it, my shadow holds it, pretty much the same as me. I can pick up a book or my attaché case and my shadow doesn't have it. But when I pick up the sword or whatever it is, it does. Sometimes with three hands.

Now it's started talking to me at night. Is that what they call runes? It whispers, late at night when I'm in bed, and that's why I'm telling you this now.

Graylord Man's Last Words

✦

T ell us a story," the young said, and so the old one downloaded this tale of his youth. But for you to understand it as they did, I must cast it in our own terms. Think of them gathered about a fire, although they were not gathered about a fire. Think of the old one as an old man, although he was not, and the young as so many children, although they were not. He stretches out his legs, puffs the charred old briar he has not got thoughtfully, and begins.

I was new made in those days, boys and girls, and there wasn't much for me to do up on AT-111 where I was born. My family was long on children and short on money, somethin' I've heard of a time or two even in this enlightened period we got right now.

Well, sir, a relation that I'd never seen back on E-1 wrote to my ma. Said you send him and we'll feed him and give him a place to sleep. Even doctorin' if he needs it. No money now, you understand, but there might be some later. Only you got to send him first.

She had to borrow. I never did know what she found to take to the hock shop, but she raised the money somehow, and kissed me, and pushed me onto the next shuttle for E-1. And me only just learnin' to use my jets, so to speak.

Well, sir, we didn't go in E-1 at all like I was expectin'. Set her down on the hull, and you never seen the like. Big yellow star right up overhead, and nothin' but space between you and it. Space and gas, I ought to have said, for there was a world of gas there. Nitrogen, mostly. Nitrogen and water vapor. I won't tell you about the trees there was, because you wouldn't believe me. You look in a book and you'll see.

"I got to go to Area Nine Hundred," I told a man in the terminal. "You're there," he says. "This right here's Area Nine Hundred, and smack-dab in the middle, too."

"Then I got to go to Mr. Graylord Man's place," I says.

I showed him the address, and he looked it up for me in his big book. "You got to take a plane," he says. "I got no money," I tells him. "Then you got to walk," he says, "or else beg a ride."

Well, I tried. Every time I saw a pilot I'd stop him and explain. And he'd say he wasn't goin' anywhere near there, every time. Boys and girls, that went on for a lot longer than it's taken me to tell you about it. Sky'd get dark, then bright. Bright, then dark. But I kept tryin'.

Finally one said he was goin' pretty close, only he wouldn't let me ride without payin'. It was contrary to regulations, he said. When I heard that, I was about ready to shut down for good. He seen it, and sort of got me off into the corner.

"Now I'm not supposed to," he says, "but I'll tell you a little somethin' that might help. They're expectin' you where you're goin'?"

My aunt Esmerelda was. It was her that had wrote Ma, and I said so.

"Then here's what you do. You go down to Level Neg Twelve, you hear? There's boxes down there, plenty of them if you'll just scout around. Pick out one big enough to hold you good, only not so big you'll rattle inside. Or else get some nice soft packin' to put in there with you. Address it to your aunt, and figure out some way you can close and seal it from inside. Or else find somebody to help you."

I says, "I got stapler capability built right in. Triple-O to Number Fifteen."

"Them big ones will do fine," he says. "There's a UPX up on Level Five Fifty-five. You carry your box up there. Soon as you're there, 'fore anybody sees you, you climb inside and seal her up. They'll stick you on my plane, and once you're delivered, UPX'll get your aunt to pay."

You may guess I did it. Fast too. Sure I was scared in there in the dark, and got pretty cold. But I turned everythin' down, you know how you do, and waited. Suppose I was driftin' out in space, I said to myself. Waitin' for somebody to see me and pull me down. That might go on for quite a while, so . . .

About then she ripped the old box open and seen me. Well, she was fit to be tied. She'd had to pay, you see, to get me delivered. I owed her, she said, and I admitted I did.

"You'll work, Youngone. You'll wash and scrub and fetch and carry. Cook and clean and anythin' I say. Or you're out of this house. First time you shirk, you're out, and good riddance, whatever becomes of you."

Well, there was a big old woman there about the age I am now, boys and girls. Mrs. Brassbound, her name was. "Don't be so hard on the boy," she says. "Just kick him when you need to get him movin'." They were good-hearted women, both of 'em, and thought they had to lay the law down or else I wouldn't lift a finger, you know. Only I was eager to work, and earn a upgrade if I could.

They set me to washin' windows, and I did that for a while. It was a little old house, and there isn't one of you ever seen anythin' like it. That kind was what the Biologicals built for themselves, way back when. There was still quite a few houses sort of like it left in them days, and had a sight of windows.

Finally I was doin' the fifth level, which was the top, and wonderin' what I'd have to do when I finished it. I got to one particular window, a big one with a world of little panes, and lookin' in through the one I started on I could see Aunt Esmerelda sittin' by a sort of big booth with curtains all around, embroiderin'. After a minute or two she seen me, too, and come over to the window and opened it told me to come in.

"I got a hundred things to do, Youngone," she says, "and you can watch him good as me. He's in bed." She pointed to the booth I'd seen. "And quiet as a nut, for he hasn't got power, hardly, to kiss his hand. You set in the chair, and don't you dare open them curtains. Only if he asks for anythin', you bring it quick. And if he tells you to do somethin', you do it quick. Do you understand every word I've said to you, Youngone?"

Course I said I did.

"You better. And if there's anythin' you can't handle, you run for me or else Mrs. Brassbound."

I said I would.

"His great-great-grandson, Mr. Oberman, he don't look in more than once a hundredtime. But he's due, or about due, and if Mr. Man ain't satisfied, there's hell to pay. So you do exactly like I said."

She went, and I sat, and time wore on. Turnin' up the gain on my hearin', I could hear Mr. Man on the other side of the curtain, you know, takin' in gases and blowin' them out. Takin' 'em in and blowin' them out, like it was a game he was playin' with himself that never got over and nobody won. And I got curious, the way boys will.

I was thinkin' about home a lot, too. My ma, and the other youngones, you know, boys and girls like you. The old compartment, with the colored wires runnin' up and down the walls home-like. The room I was in had paper on the walls—you don't have to believe this, but it did. Paper with pictures, like in a book. Thinkin' about all that, I forgot what Aunt Esmerelda had said about not pullin' the curtain back.

And I did.

There he lay. There was white cloth cut to fit his arms and legs, only not tight on. His hair was as white as that cloth, and spread all around. His eyes was shut.

Well, I was startin' to put the curtain back, and they opened. Wide! I tell you, I never been so scared in my life. He sat up, and I seen his mouth work. He was tryin' to tell me somethin', I knew he was, only he couldn't get it out. Just noise was all it was. Sound waves, you know.

I backed away mighty fast.

He swung his feet over the edge of the bed. I had seen him and I was pretty sure he wouldn't have enough power to get up, even. Well, he had some trouble with it, but he did, and he come at me, makin' noises all the time. I backed off till my back was to the wall, and so scared I might have gone right through it.

Then he fell on his face. Broken, you see. Broken so bad he couldn't be fixed. Dead's what Mrs. Brassbound called it.

Well, sir. I waited quite a while for him to move again, or make more noise, only he never did. So I lifted him up and laid him in the booth where he belonged, and closed that curtain again. And when Aunt Esmerelda came back, I lied. I'm not proud of it, but I did. I told part of all that had happened, only I said it had been him that had pushed back the curtain. She pushed back the curtain herself and got Mrs. Brassbound, and she come and that's when I heard about "dead." They said they'd have to tell Mr. Oberman, which they did. Only he was out on A-1117, and couldn't come. He said to burn him and save the ashes, which we did, and he'd come as soon as he was able. Meantime we was to stay right where we was and take care of the place.

So we did, and it was quite a while, too. One day I was told to go into the library and dust the books and readers. I did it and got to lookin' around, and there was a little thing there that would take noises and turn them into readin', you know. Like a book. I tried to think of noises I had heard that might be interestin', like the gas made in the trees sometimes, or the water that dripped on the house. I put them in, and it was fun. So then I remembered the noises Mr. Man had made before he broke, and I put them in. When I read that, I thought I had to tell Aunt Esmerelda, and I did.

"He said to look in the bottom drawer of the biggest bureau," I told her, "and to be really, really careful of what was in there."

"He said this to you?"

I remembered that I had not opened the curtain. "He just said it," I told her. "I heard him makin' noise in there, and just now I put that noise in the machine, and that's what it said."

"I could've given you software." She went back to her dustin', lookin' thoughtful. "Only I'm not sure there's room enough in that little head for it."

"But what about the drawer?" I asked. "He said to look in there."

"It's locked," she said. "I used to straighten out everythin' and put the clean clothes away. That one was always locked."

I said that he probably had a key, but maybe we burned it with him.

She shook her head. "I washed him and dressed him. That was the last time, so I wanted to do it. It must be around somewhere. We'll find it when Mr. Oberman comes, never fear."

"Maybe we ought to find it now."

She shook her head again. "I don't want Mr. Oberman to think I've been thievin'," she said, and wouldn't talk any more about it.

"What happened next, Grandpa?" one of the children asked. The old man smiled, but soon his face grew serious.

All the leaves fell off the trees—that's the green part you see in pictures. It all fell away, and left only the brown part. Solid water came out of the sky in little chips and flakes, pullin' the branches down and breakin' some, and everythin' out there looked white.

Mr. Oberman came. I thought he'd be a Biological like Mr. Man, but he looked like everybody. He talked for a long time with Mrs. Brassbound, then for a long time with Aunt Esmerelda, and then for a long time with both of them together. I was scared even to talk to him, but when he was about to go out into the white, I did. I said, "What about the drawer?"

Aunt Esmerelda had forgotten to ask him. He seemed kind of interested and got out a big bunch of keys. Later I found out that Mrs. Brassbound had given them to him. All four of us went upstairs to the room that had been Mr. Man's, and Aunt Esmerelda, Mrs. Brassbound, and I watched while he found the key to the drawer, unlocked it, and pulled it open. Inside was a lot of paper, written like in a book. He wadded it up so it wouldn't scatter around and laid it on the carpet. Under the paper was a old, old set of disks, probably five or six in the box. I can't be sure. Big letters on the box said THE HISTORY OF HUMANKIND. Underneath that in smaller letters was: From the Stone Age to the Present Moment.

Mr. Oberman put it back into the drawer, and the papers, too. The next time he came, he burned a lot of stuff out back where Mrs. Brassbound had grown special plants for Mr. Man for fuel. The things that had been in that drawer were only a little bit of it.

"What happened to you then, Grandpa?" the same child inquired.

"Oh, ever so many things," the old man said, "some you might hear 'bout tomorrow."

After that he left them to their beds, and turned out the lights.

Shields of Mars

✦

Once they had dueled beneath the russet Martian sky for the hand of a princess—had dueled with swords that, not long before, had been the plastic handles of a rake and a spade.

Jeff Shonto had driven the final nail into the first Realwood plank when he realized that Zaa was standing six-legged, ankle-deep in red dust, watching him. He turned a little in case Zaa wanted to say something; Zaa did not, but he four-legged, rearing his thorax so that his arms hung like arms (perhaps in order to look more human) before he became a glaucous statue once again, a statue with formidable muscles in unexpected locations.

Zaa's face was skull-like, as were the faces of all the people from his star, with double canines jutting from its massive jaw and eyes at its temples. It was a good face, Jeff thought, a kind and an honest face.

He picked up the second Realwood plank, laid it against the window so it rested on the first, and plucked a nail from his mouth.

Zaa's gray Department shirt ("Zaa Leem, Director of Maintenance") had been dirty. No doubt Zaa had put it on clean that morning, but there was a black smear under the left pocket now. What if they wanted to talk to Zaa, too?

Jeff's power hammer said *bang* and the nail sank to the head. Faint echoes from inside the store that had been his father's might almost have been the sound of funeral drums. Shrugging, he took another nail from his mouth.

A good and a kind face, and he and Zaa had been friends since Mom and Dad were young, and what did a little grease matter? Didn't they want Zaa to work? When you worked, you got dirty.

Another nail, in the diagonal corner. *Bang.* Mind pictures, daydream pictures showed him the masked dancers who ought to have been there when they buried Dad in the desert. And were not.

Again he turned to look at Zaa, expecting Zaa to say something, to make some comment. Zaa did not. Beyond Zaa were thirty bungalows, twenty-nine white and one a flaking blue that had once been bright. Twenty-eight bungalows that were boarded up, two that were still in use.

Beyond the last, the one that had been Diane's family's, empty miles of barren desert. Then the aching void of the immense chasm that had been renamed the Grand Canal. Beyond it, a range of rust-red cliff that was in reality the far side of the Grand Canal, a glowing escarpment lit at its summit by declining Sol.

Jeff shrugged and turned back to his plank. A third nail. *Bang.* The dancers sharp-edged this time, the drums louder.

"You're closing your store."

He fished more nails from his pocket. "Not to you. If you want something I'll sell it to you."

"Thanks." Zaa picked up a plank and stood ready to pass it to Jeff.

Bang. Echoes of thousands of years just beginning.

"I've got one in the shop that feeds the nails. Want me to get it?"

Jeff shook his head. "For a little job like this, what I've got is fine."

Bang.

"Back at the plant in a couple hours?"

"At twenty-four ten they're supposed to call me." Jeff had said this before, and he knew Zaa knew it as well as he did. "You don't have to be there. . . ."

"But maybe they'll close it."

And I won't have to have to be the one who tells you. Jeff turned away, staring at the plank. He wanted to drive more nails into it, but there was one at each corner already. He could not remember driving that many.

"Here." Zaa was putting up another plank. "I would have done this whole job for you. You know?"

"It was my store." Jeff squared the new plank on the second and reached to his mouth for a nail, but there were no nails there. He positioned his little ladder, leaning it on the newly nailed one, got up on the lowest step, and fished a fresh nail from his pocket.

Bang.

"Those paintings of mine? Give them back and I'll give you what you paid."

"No." Jeff did not look around.

"You'll never sell them now."

"They're mine," Jeff said. "I paid you for them, and I'm keeping them."

"There won't ever be any more tourists, Jeff."

"Things will get better."

"Where would they stay?"

"Camp in the desert. Rough it." *Bang.*

There was a silence, during which Jeff drove more nails.

"If they close the plant, I guess they'll send a crawler to take us to some other town."

Jeff shrugged. "Or an orthopter, like Channel Two has. You saw *Scenic Mars.* They might even do that."

Impelled by an instinct he could not have described but could not counter, he stepped down—short, dark, and stocky—to face Zaa. "Listen here. In the first place, they can't close the plant. What'd they breathe?"

Even four-legging, Zaa was taller by more than a full head; he shrugged, massive shoulders lifting and falling. "The others could take up the slack, maybe."

"Maybe they could. What if something went wrong at one of them?"

"There'd be plenty of time to fix it. Air doesn't go that fast."

"You come here."

He took Zaa by the arm, and Zaa paced beside him, intermediate arm-like legs helping support his thorax and abdomen.

"I want to show you the plant."

"I've seen it."

"Come on. I want to see it myself." Together, the last two men in the settlement called Grand Canal went around the wind-worn store and climbed a low hill. The chain-link fence enclosing the plant was tall and strong still, but the main gate stood open, and there was no one in the guard shack. A half mile more of dusty road, then the towers and the glassy prisms, and the great pale domes, overshadowed by the awe-inspiring cooling stack of the nuclear reactor. On the left, the spherical hydrogen tanks and thousands upon thousands of canisters of hydrogen awaiting the crawler. Beyond those, nearly lost in the twilight, Number One Crusher. It would have been a very big plant anywhere on Earth; here, beneath the vastness of the russet sky, standing alone in the endless red-and-black desert, it was tiny and vulnerable, something any wandering meteor might crush like a toy.

"Take a good look," Jeff said, wishing Zaa could see it through his eyes.

"I just did. We might as well go now. They'll be wanting to call you pretty soon."

"In a minute. What do you suppose all that stuff's worth? All the equipment?"

Zaa picked his teeth with a sharp claw. "I don't know. I guess I never thought about it. A couple hundred million?"

"More than a billion. Listen up." Jeff felt his own conviction growing as he spoke. "I can lock the door on my store and board up the windows and walk away. I can do that because I'm still here. Suppose you and I just locked the gate and got on that crawler and went off. How long before somebody was out here with ten more crawlers, loading up stainless pipe, and motors, and all that stuff? You could make a better stab at this than I could, but I say give me three big crawlers and three men who knew what they were doing and I'd have ten million on those crawlers in a week."

Zaa shook his head. "Twelve hours. Eight, if they never took a break and really knew their business."

"Fine. So is the Department going to lock the door and walk away? Either they gut it themselves—not ten million, over a billion—or they'll keep somebody here to keep an eye on things. They'll have to."

"I guess."

"Suppose they've decided to stop production altogether. How long to shut down the pile and mothball everything? With two men?"

"To do it right?" Zaa fingered the point of one canine. "A year."

Jeff nodded. "A year. And they'd have to do it right, because someday they might have to start up again. We're pretty well terraformed these days. This out here isn't much worse than the Gobi Desert on Earth. A hundred years ago you couldn't breathe right where we're standing."

He studied Zaa's face, trying to see if his words were sinking in, if they were making an impression. Zaa said, "Sure."

"And everybody knows that. Okay, suppose one of the other plants went down. Totally. Suppose they lost the pile or something. Meltdown."

"I got it."

"Like you say, the air goes slow now. We've added to the planetary mass—covered the whole thing with an ocean of air and water vapor three miles thick, so there's more gravity." Jeff paused for emphasis. "But it goes, and as it goes we lose gravity. The more air we lose, the faster we lose more."

"I know that."

"Sure. I know you do. I'm just reminding you. All right, they lose one whole plant, like I said."

"You never lose the pile if you do it right."

"Sure. But not everybody's as smart as you are, okay? They get some clown in there and he screws up. Let's take the Schiaparelli plant, just to talk about. How much fossil water have they got?"

Zaa shrugged.

"I don't know either, and neither do they. They could give you some number, but it's just a guess. Suppose they run out of water."

Zaa nodded and turned away, four-legging toward the main gate.

Jeff hurried after him. "How long before people panic? A week? A month?"

"You never finished boarding up."

"I'll get it later. I have to be there when they call."

"Sure," Zaa said.

Together, as they had been together since Jeff was born, they strode through the plant gate upon two legs and four, leaving it open behind them. "They're going to have to give us power wagons," Jeff said. "Suppose we're at home and we have to get here fast."

"Bikes." Zaa looked at him, then looked away. "In here you're the boss. All right, you had your say. I listened to everything."

It was Jeff's turn to nod. He said, "Uh-huh."

"So do I get to talk now?"

Jeff nodded again. "Shoot."

"You said it was going to get better, people were going to come out here from Elysium again. But you were boarding up your store. So you know, only you're scared I'll leave."

Jeff did not speak.

"We're not like you." To illustrate what he meant, Zaa began six-legging. "I been raised with you—with you Sol people is what I mean. I feel like I'm one of you, and maybe once a week I'll see myself in a mirror or someplace and I think, my gosh, I'm an alien."

"You're a Martian," Jeff told him firmly. "I am too. You call us Sols or Earthmen or something, and most of my folks were Navahos. But I'm Martian, just like you."

"Thanks. Only we get attached to places, you know? We're like cats. I hatched in this town. I grew up here. As long as I can stay, I'm not going."

"There's food in the store. Canned and dried stuff, a lot of it. I'll leave you the key. You can look after it for me."

Zaa took a deep breath, filling a chest thicker even than Jeff's with thin Martian air that they had made. "You said we'd added to the mass with our air. Made more gravity. Only we didn't. The nitrogen's from the rock we dig and crush. You know that. The oxygen's from splitting water. Fossil water from underground. Sure, we bring stuff from Earth, but it doesn't amount to shit. We've still got the same gravity we always did."

"I guess I wasn't thinking," Jeff conceded.

"You were thinking. You were scraping up any kind of an argument you could to make yourself think they weren't going to shut us down. To make me think that too."

Jeff looked at his watch.

"It's a long time yet."

"Sure."

He pressed the combination on the keypad—nine, nine, two, five, seven, seven. You could not leave the door of the Administration Building open; an alarm would sound.

"What's that?" Zaa caught his arm.

It was a voice from deep inside the building. Zaa leaped away with Jeff after him, long bounds carrying them the length of the corridor and up the stair.

"Mr. Shonto? Administrator Shonto?"

"Here I am!" Panting, Jeff spoke as loudly as he could. "I'm coming!"

Undersecretary R. Lowell Bensen, almost in person, was seated in the holoconference theater; in that dim light, he looked fully as real as Zaa.

"Ah, there you are." He smiled; and Jeff, who was superstitious about smiles, winced inwardly.

"Leem, too. Good. Good! I realized you two might be busy elsewhere, but good God, twenty-four fifteen. A time convenient for us, a convenient time to get you two out of bed. Believe me, the Department treats me like that too. Fourteen hours on a good day, twice around the clock on the bad ones. How are things in Grand Canal?"

"Quiet," Jeff said. "The plant's running at fifteen percent, per instructions. We've got a weak hydraulic pump on Number One Crusher, so we're running Number Two." All this would have been on the printout Bensen had undoubtedly read before making his call, but it would be impolite to mention it. "Zaa Leem here is making oversized rings and a new piston for that pump while we wait for a new one." Not in the least intending to do it, Jeff gulped. "We're afraid we may not get a new pump, sir, and we want to be capable of one hundred percent whenever you need us."

Bensen nodded, and Jeff turned to Zaa. "How are those new parts coming, Leem?"

"Just have to be installed, sir."

"You two are the entire staff of the Grand Canal plant now? You don't even have a secretary? That came up during our meeting."

Jeff said, "That's right, sir."

"But there's a town there, isn't there? Grand Canal City or some such? A place where you can hire more staff when you need them?"

Here it came. Jeff's mouth felt so dry that he could scarcely speak. "There is a town, Mr. Bensen. You're right about that, sir. But I couldn't hire more personnel there. Nobody's left besides—besides ourselves, sir. Leem and me."

Bensen looked troubled. "A ghost town, is it?"

Zaa spoke up, surprising Jeff. "It was a tourist town, Mr. Bensen. That's why my family moved here. People wanted to see aliens back then, and talk to some, and they'd buy our art to do it. Now—well, sir, when my folks came to the Sol system, it took them two sidereal years just to get here. You know how it is these days, sir. Where'd you take your last vacation?"

"Isis, a lovely world. I see what you mean."

"The Department pays me pretty well, sir, and I save my money, most of it. My boss here wants me to go off to our home planet, where there are a lot more people like me. He says I ought to buy a ticket, whenever I've got the money, just to have a look at it."

Bensen frowned. "We'd hate to lose you, Leem."

"You're not going to, Mr. Bensen. I've got the money now, and more besides. But I don't speak the language or know the customs, and if I did I wouldn't like them. Do you like aliens, sir?"

"I don't dislike them."

"That's exactly how I feel, sir. Nobody comes to Grand Canal anymore, sir. Why should they? It's just more Mars, and they live here already. Me and

Mr. Shonto, we work here, and we think our work's important. So we stay. Only there's nobody else."

For a moment no one spoke.

"This came up in our meeting, too." Bensen cleared his throat, and suddenly Jeff understood that Bensen felt almost as embarrassed and self-conscious as he had. "Betty Collins told us Grand Canal had become a ghost town, but I wanted to make sure."

"It is," Jeff muttered. "If you're going to shut down our plant, sir, I can draw up a plan—"

Bensen was shaking his head. "How many security bots have you got, Shonto?"

"None, sir."

"*None?*"

"No, sir. We had human guards, sir. The Plant Police. They were the only police in Grand Canal, actually. They were laid off one by one. I reported it—or my predecessor and I did, sir, I ought to say."

Bensen sighed. "I didn't see your reports. I wish I had. You're in some danger, I'm afraid, you and Leem."

"Really, sir?"

"Yes. Terrorists have been threatening to wreck the plants. Give in to their demands, or everyone suffocates. You know the kind of thing. Did you see it on vid?"

Jeff shook his head. "I don't watch much, sir. Maybe not as much as I should."

Bensen sighed again. "One of the news shows got hold of it and ran it. Just one show. After that, we persuaded them to keep a lid on it. That kind of publicity just plays into the terrorists' hands."

For a moment he was silent again, seeming to collect his thoughts; Zaa squirmed uncomfortably.

"Out there where you are, you're safer than any of the others. Still, you ought to have security. You get supplies each thirty-day?"

Jeff shook his head again. "Every other thirty-day, sir."

"I see. I'm going to change that. A supply crawler will come around every thirty-day from now on. I'll see to it that the next one carries that new pump."

"Thank you, sir."

"But you'll be getting a special resupply as quickly as I can arrange it. Security bots. Twenty, if I can scrape that many together. Whatever I can send."

Jeff began to thank him again, but Benson cut him off. "It may take a while. Weeks. Until you get them, you'll have to be on guard every moment. You're running at fifteen percent, you said. Could you up that to twenty-five?"

"Yes, sir. To one hundred within a few days."

"Good. Good! Make it twenty-five now, and let us know if you run into any problems."

Abruptly, Bensen was gone. Jeff looked at Zaa, and Zaa looked at Jeff. Both grinned.

At last Jeff managed to say, "They're not shutting us down. Not yet anyhow."

Zaa rose, two-legging and seeming as tall as the main cooling stack. "These terrorists have them pissing in their pants, Jeff. Pissing in their pants! We're their ace in the hole. There's nobody out here but us."

"It'll blow over." Jeff found he was still grinning. "It's bound to, in a year or two. Meanwhile we better get Number One back on line."

They did, and when they had finished, Zaa snatched up a push broom, holding it with his right hand and his right intermediate foot as if it were a two-handed sword. "Defend yourself, Earther!"

Jeff backed away hurriedly until Zaa tossed him a mop, shouting, "They can mark your lonely grave with this!"

"Die, alien scum!" Jeff made a long thrust that Zaa parried just in time. "I rid the spaceways of their filth today!" Insulting the opponent had always been one of the best parts of their battles.

This one was furious. Jeff was smaller and not quite so strong. Zaa was slower; and though his visual field was larger, he lacked the binocular vision that let Jeff judge distances.

Even so, he prevailed in the end, driving Jeff through an open door and into the outdoor storage park, where after more furious fighting he slipped on the coarse red gravel and fell laughing and panting with the handle of Zaa's push broom at his throat.

"Man, that was fun!" He dropped his mop and held up his hands to indicate surrender. "How long since we did this?"

Zaa considered as he helped him up. "Ten years, maybe."

"Way too long!"

"Sure." Sharp claws scratched Zaa's scaly chin. "Hey, I've got an idea. We always wanted real swords, remember?"

As a boy, Jeff would have traded everything he owned for a real sword; the spot had been touched, and he found that there was still—still!—a little, wailing ghost of his old desire.

"We could make swords," Zaa said. "Real swords. I could and you could help." Abruptly, he seemed to overflow with enthusiasm. "This rock's got a lot of iron in it. We could smelt it, make a crucible somehow. Make steel. I'd hammer it out—"

He dissolved in laughter beneath Jeff's stare. "Just kidding. But, hey, I got some high-carbon steel strip that would do for blades. I could grind one in an hour or so, and I could make hilts out of brass bar stock, spruce them up with filework, and fasten them on with epoxy."

Though mightily tempted, Jeff muttered, "It's Department property, Zaa."

Zaa laid a large, clawed hand upon his shoulder. "Boss boy, you fail to understand. We're arming ourselves. What if the terrorists get here before the security bots do?"

The idea swept over Jeff like the west wind in the Mare Erythraeum, carrying him along like so much dust. "How come I'm the administrator and you're the maintenance guy?"

"Simple. You're not smart enough for maintenance. Tomorrow?"

"Sure. And we'll have to practice with them a little before we get them sharp, right? It won't be enough to have them, we have to know how to use them, and that would be too dangerous if they had sharp edges and points."

"It's going to be dangerous anyhow," Zaa told him thoughtfully, "but we can wear safety helmets with face shields, and I'll make us some real shields, too."

The shields required more work than the swords, because Zaa covered their welded aluminum frames with densely woven plastic-coated wire, and wove a flattering portrait of Diane Seyn (whom he had won in battle long ago) into his, and an imagined picture of such a woman as he thought Jeff might like into Jeff's.

Although the shields had taken a full day each, both swords and shields were ready in under a week, and the fight that followed—the most epic of all their epic battles—ranged from the boarded-up bungalows of Grand

Canal to the lip of the Grand Canal itself, a setting so dramatic that each was nearly persuaded to kill the other, driving him over the edge to fall—a living meteor—to his death tens of thousands of feet below. The pure poetry of the thing seemed almost worth a life, as long as it was not one's own.

Neither did, of course. But an orthopter taped them as it shot footage for a special called *Haunted Mars*. And among the tens of billions on Earth who watched a few seconds of their duel were women who took note of their shields and understood.

From the Cradle

A woman hath nine lives like a cat.
—JOHN HEYWOOD

The boy's name was Michael, but his father called him Mike. His mother called him Mickey, and his teacher (who was both humorous and devout) The Burning Bush in her thoughts and Mick when she called on him in class. His principal said "that redheaded boy," a memory for boys' names not being among his principal accomplishments.

He was in back straightening up a shelf, tickling Eppie Graph (at which Eppie smiled and purred), and looking for another book as good as *Starfighters of the Combined Fleets* when the old lady came in. She wore a navy-blue suit and shiny black shoes with heels not quite so high as his mother's, and a big gray coat that looked warm; but none of those things were of interest to Michael just then. What was of interest was the bag she carried, which was old and large and real leather, bound all the way around with straps, and plainly heavy. She tried to lift it onto the counter to show Mr. Browne, but could not raise it that high until Michael helped her, scrooching down and pushing up on the bottom.

She thanked him and smiled at him; and though her hair was white, she had the brightest blue eyes he had ever seen; her smile seemed to last a long time, but not long enough. When it was over she unbuckled the straps, big black ones that made Michael think of horses. He stood up very straight then, trying hard to look like a grownup nobody would even think of chasing away.

From her big leather bag, she took a book of ordinary size with a dark brown cover and light brown pages. Unlike real books, it seemed to have no pictures; but there was a great deal of writing on all the pages; and Michael was at that age at which one begins to think that it might be better if there were fewer pictures after all, and more print.

Mr. Browne whistled.

The lady nodded. "Yes, it's very old."

"You don't want me," Mr. Browne said slowly. He fingered the pages in a way that said he was afraid she would tell him not to. "I'd try Kalmenoff and Whitechapel."

"I have," she said. "They don't want it. Not on the only terms I could offer it. Don't you want it either?"

"I don't know your terms." Mr. Browne hesitated. "But no, I don't. It's not the sort of thing I handle. I'd want to give you a fair price." He stopped talking to rub his jaw. "I'd have to borrow most of it, and it might be years before I found a buyer."

The lady had money in her hand, although Michael was not sure she had taken it from a purse or pocket. It might have been in the black leather bag with the brown book.

"This is for you," she said. She laid it on the counter. "So you'll want it. On my terms."

Mr. Browne looked at it, and blinked, and looked again. And after Michael had just about decided that he was not going to talk anymore, he said, "What are your terms?"

"This old book"—he had shut it, and she tapped the scuffed brown cover with a long fingernail as she spoke—"was my late husband's most prized possession. He loved it."

"I understand," Mr. Browne said. "I'm something of a collector myself, in a much smaller way."

"And it loved him. He said it did." The lady's voice fell. "He wasn't making a joke. Oh, yes, he made jokes often. But this wasn't one of them. We were married for almost fifty years. Trust me, I knew when he was serious."

Mr. Browne nodded. "I'm sure you did."

"He told me that if he died—he was in some danger for years, you understand. He wasn't morbid about it, but he was realistic. We both were. We'd talked about the things that might happen, and what I ought to do if they did."

Mr. Browne said he was sure that had been wise.

"Take the money. Now. I mean it. It's your money, and I don't like seeing it lying there."

Mr. Browne did.

"He said that if he died, I was to put this book up for sale. He said that it would choose its new owner, and that I was to trust its judgment." She hesitated. "He didn't say *how* I was to put it up. I've thought of running ads on vid, but there would be a thousand cranks."

Mr. Browne nodded, though Michael was not sure that he agreed.

"So I thought I'd better enlist the help of a dealer—someone who has a shop and can display it. Someone like you. My name's Caitlin Higgins. Here's a card for your terminal."

A little too late Mr. Browne nodded again, his head not moving much.

"Only you must warn them I might not sell. It will tell me when the right one comes along." Caitlin Higgins bit her lips in a way that made Michael sorry for her. "Or I hope it will," she said.

When she had gone, Mr. Browne put the brown book, open, in the window farthest from the door, with a sign that he had made over it. And when Mr. Browne (after half a dozen nervous glances at the book) had gone as well—gone into his office above the shop—Michael went out into the street and read the sign:

INCUNABULUM
On Consignment
Make Offer

It stood open, as has been said, upon a small stand that looked very much like real wood; and Michael was happy to see that it was open to a story.

The Tale of the Dwarf
and the Children of the Sphinx

A certain dwarf who wandered from place to place, at times begging and at others stealing, was driven forth from the last, a town that beholds the desert and is itself beheld by mountains far away. Not daring to return until the wrath of the townsfolk had abated, he walked very far, and when night stole over the land taking far more than he ever had, he laid himself down upon the sand and slept.

In dream, he was a tall young man, and handsome, and owned five fine fields of barley and three of millet. For long hours of the night he walked among them, seeing barley as high as his waist and millet higher even than the lofty stature that sleep had bestowed upon him.

Chancing to look toward the desert, he beheld with alarm a great spinning wind that drew sand and stones up by its force, and so had become visible, a wind that moaned and roared as it rushed toward him. His first thought was to conceal himself; but he soon noticed that it grew smaller as it advanced, so that when it reached him it scarcely exceeded his own height.

For a moment only it stood before him. Dust, sand, and stones fell to the ground, revealing a beautiful young woman, naked save for her hair. "You must force me," this woman said to him. "We yield only when forced." In his dream he seized her, smothered her with kisses, and bestowed his love upon her while she writhed in ecstasy—not once, not twice, but three times.

Then he woke, and found that he was but a dwarf, and that a great beast lay beside him. When he tried to rise, it held him; and the paw upon his chest was soft as thistledown, big as a saddle, and strong as iron.

A woman's face bent above him, and it was a face much larger than that of any true woman. "O my lover, I have had my way three times with you. Ask a gift, and if it be in my power you shall have it."

Through chattering teeth he said, "I am small and stunted."

She laughed, and her laugh was deeper than the thunder. "Not in every part."

"Spare my life!"

"I will never take it, but what boon is that once I have kissed you, and you me? Will you not ask another?"

"Then make me g-great and p-p-powerful," the poor dwarf stammered, "and small and stunted no more."

"I will," she told him, "for this night only. Suckle at my breast."

The breast she presented to him was like to that of a human woman, though greater by five. He gave suck, and at the first drop felt his back straighten. At the second he knew himself as large as she, and at the third— ah, at the third strength filled him; his thews grew thick as pythons, his body supple as a whip.

He rose, a lion with the head and shoulders of a man. He roared, and the earth shook. Roaring still, he returned to the town that had driven him forth, and his mate went with him. It was a small place now, a little cluster of wretched houses of sun-dried brick. A dozen blows from his paw would have left no brick upon brick, but he swept the roof from one such house and saw the trembling man within: a man too weak with fear to hold his spear, and his moaning wife, and the wailing children she clasped.

And he pitied them, and went away.

Then he and his mate bounded whole leagues, and raced across the desert, and reaching the mountains bounded from rock to rock there, glorying until the sun rose.

But when the sun rose, he found himself a man again, and but a dwarf, and wept.

The great sphinx who for one night had been his mate then told him how it would be with him, and left him.

He returned to the town that had cast him out, weary still, and dizzied with the memory of the night. There they told him of the storm that had so terrified them, and showed him the house whose roof had been blown away. He laughed at them for that, and because he laughed they stoned him and he fled into the fields.

Long he wandered, through many a town and down many a long road; and at length the days were complete, and in a marsh beside the great slow north-flowing river he knelt in mud and water and was sicker than he had ever been, coughing and retching until at last, with a great heave that seemed that it must take his bowels with it, he coughed out an infant, a baby boy who lay howling in the dirty water and opened amber eyes. This boy the dwarf named Kalam, "pen," because his birth had been foretold, and of what has been foretold his people say, "It was written."

He would have picked Kalam up and fled with him, for he feared the crocodiles; instead he retched again, and from jaws almost burst asunder spat another infant, also a boy. This second child he named Wahl, for as he came forth he spattered his brother with mud, and it seemed to the dwarf that *Wahl!*, which means "mud," was the child's first cry.

Then would he have picked up both brothers if he could; but that affliction with which he had been afflicted held him there, and he coughed forth a third infant, a girl, whom he called Jamil, "beauty," because he saw her mother's face in hers.

Then rose he from the marsh, holding his sons and his daughter in arms scarce long enough for the task, as some other might hold a litter of kittens; and he returned to the plowlands and the grazing lands, where he found, or begged, or stole, the milk and the blood on which he fed them.

How he brought them up, and how he took them on his wanderings—how Wahl climbed the wall of the pasha's palace and returned with the pasha's roast in his mouth—how Jamil, lovely as new-minted gold though her hair was matted with dung, was pitied by the Rani, who gave her a ruby—and how Kalam, the eldest, wrote this tale with his forefinger in the dust—any one of these would make a story too long for we who must end this one.

We leave them to others. The day came when they stood at the right hand of the dwarf, with their feet upon sand and millet at their backs, and all three stood much taller than he. And upon that day he called across the desert to their mother. Small though he was, his voice was large, and held the pain of a thousand beatings and the pain of a lover who knows that love is past. All the people of all the towns that border on the desert heard him, and spoke in awe, one to another; and some said that a storm approached, and some that the earth groaned, and more than a few muttered of ghosts and ghouls and worse.

But the dwarf said, "Now, my children, you will see whether your father be mad or no. Your mother, I say, will come to my call as I have oft told you. You will see what manner of creature she is, and if you are wise you will join her, for it is the finest life in the world." His voice broke at the last word, and he fell silent.

Then Kalam, the eldest said, "How are we to join her, Father? You have told us many times that she has the feet of a lioness."

The dwarf affirmed that it was so.

"You have said also," Wahl remarked, "that she is large as many a mountain. How then can we join a creature so huge? We will be as ants to her."

"She is of that great size when she wills it," the dwarf explained, "but scarcely larger than an ox when she wills otherwise. Did you imagine she was of mountain size when we lay together?"

At this, Jamil said, "How could we join her, Father, when to join her we must leave you? It is you, not she, who has fed, and taught, and cherished us through all our lives. If our blood is hers, is it not yours also?"

"It is," the dwarf affirmed.

"I cannot speak for my brothers," Jamil told him, "but for myself, dear Father, I will remain with you."

"The time for choosing is not yet," the dwarf told her.

"I make no pother of it," Wahl declared. "But I will remain with you as well—should the monster come. How could I, a man, join in the frolics of such a creature?"

"And I," announced Kalam, "go. Not with the monster-mother, but out into the world of men. I have been a beggar and a thief, but there are better things. The ships in Abu Qir are always wanting crew, and it would be a rare captain who could find no use for a crewman well able to wield the pen. I wish you well . . ." His eyes softened.

"As I, you," said the dwarf, his father.

"And if you wait here all night, I will wait too with my sister and you. But when the sun rises, I go north to the docks."

"I may follow you, in time," said his brother. "I have not decided."

"If our father waits here for a year," declared Jamil, "I will wait with him, save when I go to fetch him food and drink."

"But I—" began Kalam. And fell silent, for far off, he heard the howl of a wild wind among the desert peaks. Louder it grew, and louder. The millet bowed and stood straight and bowed again.

And she came.

Kalam stepped forward. His features changed, becoming those of a man more noble than any man, though his own still. His first bound carried him so far that he was almost lost to sight; he turned and grew, so that they saw him still, and the power that was in him, and the glory. When he smiled, the love that went out from him washed over them like a wave.

Wahl passed him to stand beside their mother; and, oh, but he was terrible and great! Even as she, and the strength of him was like the strength of the river, irresistible.

"Go," dwarf said, and he gave Jamil a push.

"I will stay with you, Father."

"But not obey me? Go!"

She did as he bid, though with many a backward glance. Ten steps, twenty, a hundred. She has not changed, the dwarf thought. Yet she had. Taller and more graceful, with hair black as storm cloud and tawny skin. "Go!" he said again.

She stopped instead, turned, and beckoned to him.

And he bounded after her.

———————

Michael thought about this story all the way home, for it had made clear to him certain things about which he had wondered, but raised questions, too. At home he went to his link and called his teacher.

Her face appeared in his screen. "What is it, Mick?"

"Have I seen you anyplace else?"

"I don't know. Have you?"

"I don't know either," Michael admitted.

"I'm a simulation, Mick. There was a real teacher once, a very good teacher who looked about like this."

Michael nodded.

"Many of my programs and subroutines are based upon her. So is my face."

Michael thought a long time about that, and at last he said, "What's an incunabulum?"

in-cu-nab-u-lum in-kyoo-'nab-ya-lam (in + cunabula L. infancy, origin) A book printed in the second millennium.

Michael was working part-time at the bookstore when R. T. Hurd came in. A friend, R. T. Hurd explained, had mentioned the brown book. He wanted to make an offer, but he would have to examine the book first. Michael switched off the motion alarm and took the brown book from the window. R. T. Hurd opened it reverently and turned its pages with care, and at length wrote his offer on a kneeboard keyboard and signal-signed it.

When he had gone, Michael replaced the brown book in its window and switched the motion detector back on. R. T. Hurd's offer he carried upstairs and left on the owner's desk. It was not until he and Michael had locked the store for the day that Michael realized he had left the brown book open at a new place. And it was not until he came to work the next day that he read the pages he himself had freshly exposed.

The Tale of Prince Know-Nothing

When the world was young, there lived a certain prince who did not know he was a prince. Two thousand years before, his many-greats-grandfather had been a glorious king, renown for courage and wisdom throughout all the world. Many sons and daughters had he fathered; and although some had perished without issue, others had as many children as he, and two had more. Because they had been the sons and daughters of the king, they had been men and women of wealth, masters of great houses and broad lands and coffers of gold and jewels. But as the years turned to centuries, and generations were born and aged and died, the wild thyme grew up around all these things, which vanished from the sight of men; so that when Prince Know-Nothing was born, his mother did not know he was a prince or that she herself was a princess. Nevertheless the blood royal ran strong in his veins, because his father had been a prince also, though neither of them knew it. (But someone did.)

Thus the young prince lived as other boys lived. He was strong and brave, but there were many other boys who were stronger and braver than he—or if they were not, they were at least louder in their boasts, which is much the same thing among boys. And although he was wiser than they, at his age wisdom consists largely in honoring one's parents and careful listening to the counsel of those older than oneself; thus his wisdom, though it made him well-liked and kept him from harm in a hundred ways, brought him only mockery whenever it became apparent.

"Once upon a time," said his teacher, "there was a king who had but a single child, the princess, and twelve golden plates. They were very beautiful, with knights and dragons and elves around their borders—"

"What is a princess?" asked Prince Know-Nothing, and the other children all laughed.

"If everyone else knows," said his teacher, "everyone else can tell you." And she asked the girl with the pink hair ribbon to tell Prince Know-Nothing what a princess was.

"It's a girl that's very pretty on Halloween and has a pretty white dress with a big skirt," explained the girl with the pink hair ribbon.

Their teacher agreed that was a good definition, but she was afraid that it wasn't quite rigorous enough, so she asked the smartest boy in the whole class to tell Prince Know-Nothing what a princess was, too.

"It's the one the knight marries," the smartest boy in the whole class said at once.

"That's a good definition, too," the teacher agreed. "But princesses don't always marry knights. Sometimes they marry princes."

———

Here the page ended, and since the book was locked away in its window again, Michael was unable to turn it. He went home, and when the book remained in its window day after day and week after week, he knew that R. T. Hurd's offer had been refused.

Years passed, and there came a year in which he, and not the old owner, took inventory; and when it was nearly done, he got out the brown book so that he might look at it again. He was listing books by their UAISBN numbers, and he hoped to find one on it, although he did not. He considered listing it by title, but he knew only too well that there were often half a dozen books with a single title. He was puzzling over this when a young woman with bright blue eyes came in and remarked that she would like to look at the book, since it was out of its window.

"I generally leave it there, where it's secure," Michael explained. "It's alarmed, you know, and the glass filters out the ultraviolet. But I had to take it out now, or anyway I thought it did. Maybe I just wanted to touch it again." And he explained about inventory, and looking for a UAISBN in the brown book.

"You have a lot more books here than most bookstores I've been in," the young woman said. "Usually they want you to look on the screen. And then they'll print up one for you if you want it. But till you want one, they don't actually have many books."

"We can print anything you want, to order," Michael explained, "but we find we sell more books when the customer can handle an actual copy. I don't mean that we keep copies of ephemera—best-sellers, and that sort of book. We don't have to. But there are a lot of very good books most people have never heard of, and we like to have copies of those, of the books we recommend."

The young woman looked thoughtful.

"Then too, we do a good deal of business in used books. You can often buy a used copy more cheaply, for one thing."

"Aren't there old editions that are nicer?"

Michael nodded. "Sometimes. Quite often, in fact. There are different papers, and for art books . . ." He shrugged. "When the plates have been produced under the supervision of the artist, that's something stores can't duplicate. Though we try."

"Can you make me a copy of this?" The young woman indicated that brown book.

Michael shook his head. "There's no number. That's the problem."

When she had gone, he returned the brown book to its window and went back to his inventory, feeling empty in a strange, sad way, and very much alone. *I should get a cat,* he thought. *We used to have a cat. A lot of stores have cats.*

It was time to close, or nearly; and yet the inventory remained not quite finished. In the end he entered "Browne's Book—Wonders of " for the book in the window, and did the rest, turned off the lights, and pulled shut the big front door, hearing it lock behind him. Deep within the store ALARM—ALARM—ALARM flashed dimly and slowly, indicating that the system was powered, and on guard. How many times had he come out of this door?

It was not that he did not love the store; he did, just as he had loved his parents. And yet . . .

He would get a cat—a nice cat with white paws and an interesting name. (But a cat would not be enough either.)

The bus floated by. He had missed it, and there would be no more for half an hour. He inspected his windows. *The Race for Saturn's Moons* was no longer selling. It should be relegated to a shelf and replaced. Perhaps with *Fear of the Future* or *The Fall of the Republic.*

Here was the brown book again, opened at a new place.

The Tale of the Boy and the Bookshop

Long, long ago in a faraway land, there was a boy we will call Wishedfor. He had been born late in his parents' lives, after many years in which they had prayed devoutly for a son, and they treasured him above all else. One might think such a boy would be spoiled. He was not, for Allah had blessed them with a poverty not too great. He grew, and as he grew, showed himself wise and generous, strong of limb and clear of eye. He helped his mother wash and cook and sweep, and when he was old enough to assist his father, he did not cease to do so, but turned his labors from the amendment programs to household tasks as soon as he and his father returned from the archives, for his mother was not strong.

At length she died, and his father called him to his side. "O my son," quoth his father, "thou art the light of my eyes. Not a day passes but I thank Allah for what he gave. Which is noblest, my son? Is it the gifts Allah gives to us, or the gifts we miserable mortals give to Allah, who has given us life? Consider well."

For some minutes the boy sat deep in thought; at length he said, "Gold and silks, skimmers and golights are but muck. The value of a gift cannot be reckoned from the price the giver gave or the price his gift might fetch in the market. Is that not so, O my father?"

Sadly, the old man nodded. "Proceed."

"How then is the value of a gift to be reckoned? It must be according to the heart of its giver. The most valuable gift is that given with unbounded love from a pure heart. Mere mortals, alas, are never pure of heart. Nor is our love boundless, though we may think so. Allah is pure of heart, as we are not. Allah's love is without bound, as ours cannot be. Therefore it seems to me, O my father, that the gifts Allah gives to mortals must ever be greater than those we mere mortals present to Allah."

At this the old man looked more doleful than ever. "By what means, O my son, can we poor mortals offer Allah a gift equal to those he has given us?"

Now the boy thought again, scratching his head as if he feared his mind slept there, rubbing his chin and pulling his ear; and at last he said, "O my father, I do not know. Is it possible? Tell me."

"It is, my son." The old man's gaze, which had been upon the boy's face until that time, was now upon the dust before him. "When we return to Allah a gift he has given us, we make him a gift as fine as that he gave, do we not?"

"Ah!" said the boy, and his eyes flashed like sunlight on dark pools. "Thou hast cut the knot, O my father! In all the world, is there any like to thee?"

"Many, many. My son, I would give such a gift to Allah. In the city to the north there stands a mosque like no other, the Madrasa of Sultan Hasan. Here the wisest gather to speak of the will of Allah, and His knowledge, and the knowledge of all the world. Young men come there to hear them, that they may become wise in their turn, and when they have sat long, they may question them, and so become wiser still."

At this the boy's eyes grew very wide.

"O my son, for seven years I give thee to Allah. Thou shalt go to the mosque I have named, and my blessing go with thee. Learn there. Betimes thou must labor, even as I labor at my keyboard, for the belly must be fed. As thou strain and sweat, thou must repeat in thine own ear that thou hast come to learn, and not to labor. And in seven years, if Allah grant seven years more of life, I will come for thee. If thou hast learned well, I shall die full of joy. But if thou has not, tears and sorrow will be my lot in this life and in paradise."

"I will learn, O my father," the boy promised. And before the sun rose again, he had set out for the city; and though his heart was sad when he recalled his mother, it leaped for joy to think of the learning that would be his.

A year passed, and another, and another. The old man labored, recalling often the son he had given to Allah. Now it seemed to him that his son would surely grow discouraged upon the path of wisdom; he himself had not traveled far along it, yet he well knew how steep were its slopes and how rock-strewn the way. And now it seemed to him that within a day or two the boy would surely return, making some excuse, and he told himself ten score times that he must have hard words for the boy if it were so—and knew in his heart that they could never pass his lips. On such days he watched the road for hours. But the boy never came.

And again he imagined his son sitting at the feet of the wisest of the wise in that great mosque, the Madrasa of Sultan Hasan; and he was happy, and went about his work with increased vigor. In this way, year followed year.

At last it seemed to him that seven had passed, and more than seven, and he went to his neighbor and spoke of the boy; and when his neighbor had praised him, as all did, the old man said, "How long has it been since we have seen the light of his face? Five years, I think? I have lost track of the reckoning. Six? Has it been as many as six?"

"More," declared his neighbor. "Long and long. Behold! My picktruck that is old shone like a jewel when thy son left us."

The old man could scarcely speak, his voice shook so. "Seven? Has it been seven?"

"What is seven years to a picktruck?" replied his neighbor.

The old man left, confessing in his heart that he himself was but another such laboring machine and begging forgiveness for it. On the next day he dug up the fifteen milpiasters he had buried in his floor, and set out. The road was not short, nor was it gracious to poor travelers; yet he reached the city at last, and asking directions of those who bore kind faces, he made his way to the Madrasa of Sultan Hasan, and sat of a long afternoon hearing the wise discourse on Al Qur'an and much more, and was greatly improved thereby. Ever he looked for the boy, but he did not see him.

Betimes the light faded, and the wise departed one by one, and the old man also, to seek a place in which to lay his head.

Down one street he went, and up another, and chancing to look into a bookshop beheld one tall and lean and of serious mien, whose beard was touched with gray. Their eyes met, and both knew.

Of their embraces and the many things they said, a long tale might be made; but at last they sat together with coffee between them. Then quoth he who had been the boy, "O my father, I thought thee dead when the seventh year passed. Had I known thou still lived, I would have returned to the south long ago, and carried thee to my house in this city—the house in which thou shalt repose this night. Thou came not, and I thought, *surely he is dead.*"

"O my son," said the old man, "as each year passed I resolved to let thee remain a little longer, that thou might grow in wisdom yet more at the feet of the wise. Another year, and another year, until this. Now I feel the hand of death upon me, and I would not die as a frog in a well, by all forgotten."

"Thou shalt not die at all," he who had been the boy declared, "but bide here full many a year. But, O my father, I have sinned against thee."

"It cannot be!" the old man declared.

"It is." And he who had been the boy sat in silence while the traffic of the street clamored on all uncaring.

Until at last the old man said. "Thou canst not speak, my son. I see it. Do not speak. Let us rather rejoice, and talk of thy mother, and the days when thou wert small."

"I will not deceive thee more, O my father." He who had been the boy lifted the fragrant cup yet left it untasted. "I have betrayed thee, my father. Betrayal atop betrayal I shall not set. To this city I came worn and hungry, and thus before going to the mosque as thou had instructed me I looked first for employment that I might be fed. In this street, I beheld an old man unloading a flitter. Hastening to him, I said, 'Grandfather, thou art of years, and the boxes weighty. Permit me to assist thee.' For I hoped that he would give that with which I might eat when the task was done.

"He stood aside, and while I worked we talked. And when the last had been unloaded, he bid me carry them into this shop, and when I had carried the last, he bid me open them. They held books, such as thou seest."

He who had been the boy sighed, and the old man nodded.

"I put them in their places, as he directed me, and as I labored he discoursed upon their contents. Some came from Baghdad, some from Damascus, some from Frankish lands even to the other side of Earth, some from the stars of heaven. All were wondrous in my sight, and he saw it. He bid me sleep in the shop that night, as many a night thereafter, with a cudgel by my side to protect our wares."

The old man sipped his coffee, hot, strong, and very sweet. "There is nothing shameful in this, O my son."

"My master died. It was my loss, and all the world's, for he was both learned and compassionate. I took his shop in charge, and delivered all profit therefrom, which was never great, to her who had been his wife. Too soon she followed him. His shop became mine, and the house that had been his also. It is not large, but thou will ever find a place there, O my father."

"Nor is there dishonor in that," the old man declared, "but the contrary."

"O my father, thou sent me to this city that I might sit at the feet of the wise in the mosque. I have been there to worship many times. But I have never done as thou wished, my father. When the call to prayer came, I went—or oft times went not. And when my prayers were done, I returned to this shop in which thou discovered me. I have done wrong, and it is no childish matter, I know. What is thy judgment? That punishment which thou decree, I will accept without murmur. It will be less than I deserve."

The old man did not speak again until he had drunk the last drop, and eaten the grounds as well, for he followed the old ways. And when the last were gone, he said only, "O my son, I must think on this."

Next morning he rose early and made his way to the Madrasa of the Sultan Hasan. All morning he sat in silence, harkening to the wise as he had the day before; but when the sun neared its zenith, "O my uncle," quoth one, "thy beard is gray. Thou hast seen much of life. Is it not so?"

The old man acknowledged that it was.

"And yet thou harken to us, and never speak. Whether thou hast come to teach us or to learn, we would hear thee."

"O revered sheikh," quoth the old man, "know that I am sorely troubled. I am a simple man. To mere compilers and codes, to interrupts, subroutines, and iterations has my life been given. Now I must judge a weighty matter, and know not the way."

"Speak on," quoth the one to whom he had spoken.

"Upon the one hand, my son has disobeyed, O revered sheikh," quoth the old man. "Upon the other, he has done well and is deserving of approbation. Upon the first hand, I sought to honor Allah, to whom all praise. Upon the second, he confesses his fault."

"Thy voice breaks," observed he to whom the old man had spoken.

"I love him dearly, O revered sheikh, and no man ever had a better son. Yet he did wrong, and I know not which way to turn."

Others had fallen silent to listen as the old man spoke, and for a time they discussed the matter. Then came the call to prayer. All prayed, and when the prayer was done, he to whom the old man had spoken declared, "This is a troubled matter, O my uncle. Thy son hath transgressed."

The old man nodded.

"And his transgression was against Allah and thee. Is it not so?"

The old man nodded as before.

"Yet he is true of tongue, contrite of heart, and a good Moslem?"

The old man nodded a third time, and while others spoke he to whom he had spoken sat stroking his beard. Ere long, the speech of those others turned to other topics, and when that time came, quoth he, "O my uncle, there is one in this city whom we reckon wisest of the wise. Matters of great difficulty are brought to him. Let us bring thine, thou and I."

And they went, down one street and up another, and so came to a certain shop. He to whom the old man had spoken entered first, and the old man after him.

And behold!

It seemed to Michael that this story had been intended for him from the beginning. It was true that he had not remained long at the university. Money had been in short supply, and he was a member of no prioritized group. During his long wait at the bus stop, he turned the story over and over in his mind, with all that he could recall of the first two, which he had read years before.

Next morning, the young woman returned to the store. Michael looked at her, then looked again and snapped his fingers. "What is it?" she asked.

"I've been trying to think who you reminded me of," he explained. "It's my teacher, the teacher I had when I was a kid. I mean, she was really a machine, and she was older than you are, and the principal was the machine, too, like for everybody, but—but—"

"I understand." She grinned at him. "Were you sent to the principal a lot? You must have been a bad boy."

"Well, sometimes." He discovered that he was blushing, something he had not done in years. "He could never remember my name until I told him, but she called me Mick. I never could understand that. I mean, since it was all the same machine, really."

The young woman's grin had softened to a smile. "I do, Mick. May I have some of your coffee?"

"Yes. Certainly." He hurried over to show her. "There are nice chairs, and reading lights, and—and everything. Sweetener and sugar and real cream. So people can sit down and look at the books, you know. And—and everything."

"But not the big book in the end window." She was still smiling. "The brown one."

"I'd have to stay and watch." Michael decided he could use some coffee too; his mouth felt dry. He poured a cup for her and another for himself.

"Do you eat the grounds, Mick?"

"Do I . . . ? That story. You read it."

"Uh-huh." Her smile had become impish.

"It's been bothering me." He smiled in return. "It bothers me more than the teaching machine ever did. Or Junior Teacher Huggins or Principal Maxwell. Will you—I feel silly saying it here, but won't you please sit down?"

She did, and accepted the coffee he had poured for her.

"Would you like sweetener? Cream?"

"Honey, Mick. I see you have honey over there."

He got it for her, and sat beside her on the sofa. "Do you really want to see that book? Are you thinking of buying it?" He tried to gauge the cost of her clothing and jewelry, and failed.

"No," she said.

"Then I can't. I mean I shouldn't. It really is a very valuable book. But just for a minute or two, while I watch."

She sipped her coffee, and smiled, and added more honey, and smiled again.

"If you read that story, it sounds like me. Like my life. Not exactly, of course, but . . ."

"Uncomfortably close."

"That's it. That's it exactly."

"The book does that, you see. That's what makes it so valuable. It's not just its age. It knows, somehow, and we were never sure whether it was just opening itself to the right place—that's what a man I knew thought—or whether it created the stories. Made them to order, so to speak, the way you print your books. I think it does both."

He was speechless for a moment, then remembered to sip his coffee, and spilled a little, and winced. At last he said, "It seems to be saying that what I'm doing—this bookstore—is right. But it doesn't feel right. Or not as right as it ought to. I think the man in the story . . . That he didn't feel right either, until his father came."

She nodded.

"So I thought of getting a cat or something. But I don't know." He sighed, and ran his free hand through his hair. "Only what you said about the stories, that can't be right. There was one I read a long time ago, about a boy in class, and what was a princess? Only it wasn't all there. I could never read the end."

"Tell me," she said, and he recounted as much as he could remember of "The Tale of Prince Know-Nothing."

When he had finished, she said, "I can tell you how it ended. Prince Know-Nothing decided he should go in search of a princess; but a thousand things conspired to stop him, and he never did. At the end, a very plain girl in a very plain dress kissed him, and after the wedding he discovered that she was a princess who had gone forth in search of a prince."

"You read that one, too," Michael said.

She nodded. "Did you read any more?"

"Just one other one." He paused, not sure he remembered it at all. "It was about a dwarf and a sphinx. They had children—he gave birth to them, which used to puzzle me. And he wanted to be a sphinx like her, and at the end his children made him one, and it was wonderful."

"It was saying you ought to have children." For a moment she looked pensive. "I've never had any," she said.

"I haven't either. I mean, I'd like some, but I've never been married."

"I'd like some too, Mick." Quite suddenly she kissed his cheek; and when he turned his head in surprise, his lips. "There," she said when they parted, "and now I'm through fooling you. You've never been married."

He shook his head.

"I have. I was married for almost fifty years, Mick, but we never had children. There were reasons, but the reasons don't matter anymore, and the children do. We had love, and the love was enough, but now that's gone too, and I want love again. I want it back."

"You—you're . . ." Michael felt as though the whole world had dropped from under him.

"I'm eighty-seven now, Mick, and I used to be a teacher before I married. Don't tell me you haven't heard of cell therapy. They go in and clean up the nuclei, and your cells start dividing again, and you grow younger instead of older."

Michael managed to nod. "I've read about it. It's terribly expensive."

"It was. Fortunately, I'm terribly rich. Does it bother you that I'm so much older than you are?"

He shook his head desperately.

"It doesn't bother me, either." Her hand found his. "Because I'm not. I mean biologically. And I don't want to buy that book because I own it already. My name's Caitlin Higgins. It should be in your files."

He could not speak.

"But please don't call me Caitlin, or something awful, like Junior Teacher Huggins."

She had smiled, and he felt that he could look at that smile forever, and it would always be new, and always magic.

"My friends call me Kitty," she said.

Black Shoes

✦

I *heard this story from an old college acquaintance, a man I had not spoken to for twenty years. I do not vouch for its veracity, but I do—I will—vouch for his: he believed every word of it. My questions, of which there were many, I will omit for brevity's sake. His answers and explanations I will insert in his narrative.*

You left the university and went to work as soon as you got your undergraduate degree, he said. I did not. I got a master's—two, actually—and my Ph.D. Once I had it, I was able to get a tenure-track job teaching. I got tenure, and I'm still there. As I will be for the rest of my life. This happened just before my ex-wife and I went on vacation. Most of it the day I left the hotel to come back, really, but it started a day or two before we left.

I described our trip—she felt I needed a rest—to the class, and told the students Mr. Durkin would take over while I was gone. That was Gelt's opportunity. I'd learned not to call on him when he waved his hand with enthusiasm, but I'd been softened up by thoughts of a little time off, and I did. He presented the theory that our ancestors were aquatic in all its preposterous detail, just as he had read it in some crank book, and challenged me to refute it.

I had to, of course. As I did, presenting the overwhelming case for the arboreal background of pre-humans and ending, rather generously, by conceding that all life originated in the sea.

That set Gelt off on folklore—selkies, swan-maidens, mermen, and the rest. I let him go on longer than I should have because some of his ideas about the Rhinemaidens were new to me and interesting.

Finally Morgan raised his hand. It was the first time that hand had gone up all semester; so I silenced Gelt—which wasn't easy—and called on Morgan.

He rose. He's tall and as lanky as a rake, straight black hair like a Native American, swarthy and hatchet-faced. "All those things," he said, "those mermaids and all, they're nothing but the ghosts of people that drowned."

It started an uproar, everybody laughing and talking. I got them quiet and explained to Morgan as kindly as I could that there are no such things as ghosts. When I finished, he said, "Okay, but that's what they are. My grand-dad was a fisherman all his life, and he talked to them. He knew."

The bell rang soon after, and long before I carried our suitcases out to the car I had forgotten the whole incident, though I shouldn't have. Gelt was contradicting and arguing because he loved to contradict and argue, but Morgan was as sincere as only a man his age can be. His belief was deeply held. I should have thought more about that.

My ex and I did all the things we'd planned to do. We slept late, ate big meals, lay on the beach, lay beside the pool, swam a bit, and did a little sightseeing. It was the end of the season, you understand. The very end. Our hotel would close its doors the week after we checked out.

On the last day, the weather turned bad. Not raining, but dark and chill, with a north wind blowing. My ex took one look and said she was going shopping. I could do whatever I liked, but no more bathing suits for her. No beach and no pool. I can't stand shopping, you understand. I made that plain years ago. She could shop all she wanted wherever she wanted, and try on a hundred pants suits. But I wouldn't go with her. Not for one minute, not for one hour, and certainly not for all day. I wished her good luck and read for half the morning before I started feeling restless. One can read at home, after all.

I'd had the foresight to bring a wool sweater. I pulled it on and went outside. The whole place was deserted. The beach chairs, the tables, and the umbrellas were still there, but the people had gone. All of them. Well, well, I thought to myself, this is really quite nice! I went down to the water's edge and breathed the sea air, and began to walk.

Have I mentioned that I was wearing shoes? I was. These shoes here.

He stood up and came forward to let me see them better. They were ordinary black oxfords, laced tight and a good deal worn.

They got sand in them, he said, and I decided to take them off. I stuffed my socks into them and put them up on some rocks where I would be sure to find them, and went on, hiking down the beach, barefoot over the sand.

Not that it was all sand, not after the first mile or so. There were rocks and sea oats and so on, and several times I wished I had brought my shoes. But I persevered. I'm not a hiker and I'm not telling you this to boast about my walking prowess, but I went a hell of a long way.

Now here's my first confession, and you have to accept it: I got lost. Doesn't that sound ridiculous? I went out of the hotel, turned left, and started walking down the beach. How could anybody get lost like that? But I did. I turned around to go back, you know, and nothing was familiar. Nothing. There were rocks I'd have to climb, and I had no memory of having climbed them before. None. Finally I convinced myself that I'd been wrong in thinking that the ocean had been to my right—that it had actually been on my left.

It wasn't foggy, but it was dark, as I said, with the sea kicking up and the wind blowing spray. I stopped a dozen times to watch the big combers rolling in, while an old poem ran through my head.

> *Where run your colts at pasture?*
> *Where hide your mares to breed?"*
> *'Mid bergs about the ice-cap*
> *Or wove Sargasso weed;*
> *By chartless reef and channel,*
> *Or crafty coastwise bars,*
> *But most the ocean-meadows*
> *All purple to the stars!*

So I tried to see the white horses. Sailors have been seeing horses—and a lot of other things, too—in the sea for thousands of years. Poseidon was the god of horses as well as the sea god, although I didn't know that then. I've been reading up on these things since.

Well, I didn't see any horses, but I started seeing people. Men. Fish-like men with white hair and white beards, hiding in the waves. They wait underneath, you know, hiding in the water, and looking out at us through the foam when they think they can't be seen.

I was frightened, and I'm not ashamed to admit it. I was alone out there, and there were hundreds of them. Perhaps as many as a thousand, men with brutal shark faces, little eyes, slit mouths, and wide, flat cheeks. Oh, I saw them better later on, believe me. I saw them up close. I wish to God I hadn't.

The smart thing would have been to get up and walk inland, fast. I knew that, but for a time I didn't do it. I froze like a rabbit, staring at them while all sorts of things ran through my head. One was that they would think me afraid, and of course I was, very much so. Another was that I would have to turn my back on them and they would jump me, dragging me into the water. There were more, but I'll spare you the rest. Finally, I suppose the actual time was no more than half a minute, I jumped up and ran straight inland, terrified that I was going to fall and knowing I was a middle-aged man now, and a sedentary one. I couldn't run far or fast.

When I couldn't run any more I stopped and leaned against a little stunted tree, gasping for breath. I was out of sight of the sea, in a sort of scraggly wood, and there was nothing behind me. Nothing chasing me.

I sat down and cried. That's my second confession. There are more coming, I warn you.

It was very slow walking through that woods. There were sticks and briars and all sorts of things, and my feet were tender and bleeding. I kept telling myself that there would be a road soon. Another step, another step. Another hundred, perhaps, and there would be a road. I would wait there beside the road for a car, and flag it down, and explain that I was lost and offer the driver a hundred dollars (I had more than that in my wallet) if he'd take me back to my hotel.

But there was no road. There were open spaces of sand and sea oats, and rocks, and stunted trees, but no road, no cars, no food, and no water. I was hungry by that time, tired and ready to drop, and terribly, terribly thirsty. It seemed to me that I ought to be in the middle of town, the town where my wife was shopping. It hadn't been all that far from the hotel, and I had walked for miles and miles.

Finally I came to a big dune, much too big to see over. I will never forget it. Never. I climbed to the top, which wasn't easy at all. Can you guess what I saw?

No, not the hotel. I wish it had been. I saw the ocean. I had curved around like any fool, thinking that the wind was veering, so that the north wind that ought to have been to my right was behind me, then to my left. I was back at the beach. They knew it and were coming up out of the water.

They are dwarfs, I suppose, really. Perhaps we ought to say that our dwarfs are throwbacks to them. They are bullet-headed, and have no more shoulders than a seal; but their short thick arms and legs are as strong as iron. Their skin is very white. I don't imagine that they would come up out of the water any time the sun was bright and hot. Just on days like that, you know. And at night.

I got away from them. That's all I'm going to say. I'd like to tell you I laid five low with devastating punches or something. The kind of thing you see in movies. I didn't. I didn't outrun them, either. I was so tired by then that I couldn't have run two steps. I bargained my way out, all right? I did them a certain favor and promised to do certain things. Don't ask any more. I'm not going to confess that.

What difference does it make to you what language they spoke? We communicated. Trust me, we did. I knew what they wanted, and I did it. I understood the other thing they wanted me to do, and I promised to do that too.

And they let me go. No, I didn't ask them to point the way to the hotel. I doubt that they would have, and I never thought of it. I just wanted them to go away, which they did.

Maybe I could have just walked down the beach in safety after that. I probably could have. But I didn't, and I would have given everything I've got in this world not to. I never wanted to see the ocean again. I still won't go near it.

So I told myself not to be a fool this time. Remember that the wind is in the north. Keep it on your right, and you'll be walking inland, and if you walk inland far enough you'll come to a road. I don't know how far I walked. Maybe it was ten miles, but as tired as I was already, it was probably a lot less, just trudging along with my head down, and thinking about what I had promised, you know, and getting back to the hotel and resting, and eating a lot, and drinking all the ice water in the place, maybe with some vodka in it.

Then I came to water—an inlet, sort of a little river or something. I screamed when I saw it. Would you believe that? I did. I thought they were going to come right up out of it.

But after that it hit me. I had to be pretty far inland. It was probably fresh water, and if it was I could finally get a drink. I ran to it and knelt there in the mud, and put my face down into it, and it was warm and muddy and tasted absolutely wonderful. I drank and drank, taking deep breaths in between, until finally I'd drunk enough. I straightened up and had a look around, and there she was smiling up at me through the water.

Her name had been Jo Ann. Two words: Jo Ann. I saw her, and I knew that I had loved her a long, long time ago. I started crying again, and that's when she came up out of the water, bare breasts, you know, and long hair, and the fresh, beautiful face of seventeen. She called my name and told me not to cry, and motioned for me to come to her. Finally I did, wading out into the water.

We hugged and kissed and hugged again, and I said—this is exactly what I said, the exact words, "Oh, God, Jo. I loved you so much." She only smiled, but when she smiled, it hit me.

I had drowned her.

I had murdered her and gotten away with it, and I had been fooling myself all these years, my unconscious mind deceiving my conscious mind entirely successfully.

No, I want to tell somebody. Why do you think I'm here? It's eating me alive. I've got to tell somebody, so listen.

It was our junior year. Some kid's parents went away and gave him the run of the house. Henry something. I don't remember, and it really doesn't matter. He threw a big party and asked everybody in the class. Jo Ann and I had been going steady, and I just assumed, you know, that she would go with me. I went over to her house to get her that night, and her mother told me she had gone with somebody else. I know how childish it sounds now; but then, that night, it was the end of the world. I decided I wouldn't go and went home, but after a while I went anyhow. I was going to find Jo Ann and have it out with her.

So I got there late, and everybody was pretty tight. I looked all though the party without finding her and drank a couple of beers, more or less by myself, and then I went out to the pool again. Henry's folks were rich, and they had a big pool. Some of the kids were skinny-dipping, some had brought swimsuits, and some were swimming in their underwear or cutoffs or whatever. I thought it looked like fun, so I stripped and jumped in.

Some of the guys were ducking each other and ducking girls and splashing them, and some girls were ganging up to duck guys. Some guy ducked a girl and let her go, and when she came up I grabbed her.

You know who it was.

I got her back under and I held her under. She fought me at first, then went limp; but she wasn't fooling me, I knew she was still alive and I kept her under for another five minutes or so. Then I let go and just let her drift away.

And I got out of the pool and went home. Nobody saw her body at the bottom of the pool until the next day.

So it was an accidental drowning, and nobody even talked to me about it. Nobody asked me anything. They talked to the guy she had gone to the party with, and a couple of other kids, and that was it.

Did you like hearing the truth?

Maybe you're thinking of calling the police. You can if you want. I'll say it never happened and I never told you anything, and my doctor will tell them about me. They'll write you off as vindictive and ethically challenged, so go right ahead.

That's good. Maybe I'm just making it up. You can't really know, can you? Maybe I am. All right if I tell you what happened next?

Jo Ann, there in the water—both of us waist-deep in that little river—said, "I really loved you. I want you to know that. I loved you and I thought you were getting bored with me, and I wanted you back."

Then we talked, and she showed me the direction and said that if I'd walk that way, straight, I'd come to some rocks. If I'd climb the rocks and look to my right, I'd be able to see the hotel. After that we kissed again and she swam away.

Under the water.

So I did what she said. I swam across the little river—oh, I was wet already. It didn't matter. I swam across and walked like she had said, and climbed the rocks.

He paused and pointed to his feet.

And there they were. These shoes, exactly where I had left them, with my socks still stuffed into them. I sat down on the rocks and pulled the socks on again just like I had that morning, and put on these shoes and tied them.

Everything changed when I did that. It started to change when I first put my foot into a shoe, and by the time I had tied the second shoe it was complete. I knew that none of it had really happened. There were no brutal pre-humans living under the sea. There had been no mermaid Jo Ann in the river. It was all nonsense, and I climbed off the rocks and went back to the hotel.

I'll make the rest short and sweet. I've gone on too long already, and I know it. My ex came back to the hotel with eight or ten packages and shopping bags, and I said I was tired too and we'd just stay in and order room service, which is what we did. I put off undressing for bed as long as I could, because I knew my feet had been bleeding in my shoes and it would upset her. So I let her take the first bath and get into bed, and then I went into the bathroom to undress.

When I untied my left shoe I felt something. I can't describe it, but I did. Something was terribly, terribly wrong. By the time I had that shoe off—it had stuck, like I thought it would, and it was torture to get it off—I knew. It had all been real. I'd promised what I'd promised, and if I didn't keep my promise they'd come for me. Someday. Some way. They would come for me, those sea devils, and they would own me body and soul. Of course you can guess what I did next.

You can't? Well, you should have. I put the shoe back on. I put it on, and everything was all right. Back in the bedroom I got my bag, very quietly, and went down to the lobby. I told the woman at the desk I'd received an important call, and I had to go home at once. I paid our bill and said my ex knew and she was going to sleep tonight and take a plane home in the morning.

I got a place of my own the day after I landed, a little apartment. I couldn't tell her, you see. I simply couldn't, and naturally she would want to know why I slept with my shoes on.

Which is the only way I can sleep. Oh, yes, I take them off sometimes. I have to. Maybe once a week, and then I wash my feet very carefully, and put iodine on the ulcers, and put on clean socks. While I'm doing that, the whole time, I'm shaking with fear. The sweat runs down my face, and my hands tremble, and I know that this is a more terrible world then you can possibly imagine. Do you sleep barefoot? I thought so. I used to do it too.

Other shoes? Yes and no. Sometimes they work for a while and quit. Sometimes they don't work at all.

You're right. The law is just a bunch of made-up rules created for the benefit of those who have power. It has nothing to do with justice. Besides, I never really confessed to—well—anything. I'm a bit challenged, you know. Reality-challenged. Ask my students.

He smiled as he turned to go, and when I saw his smile I knew there was no point in trying to have him punished for the murder he had committed so many years ago. He has been punished already, punished by his own mind, and he will live in Hell for as long as he lives. It is worse here than anything any judge could ever do.

You can trust me on that. I know.

Has Anybody Seen Junie Moon?

✦

The reason I am writing this is to find my manager. I think her name is really probably June Moon or something, but nobody calls her that. I call her Junie and just about everybody else calls her Ms. Moon. She is short and kind of fat with a big wide mouth that she smiles with a lot and brown hair. She is pretty, too. Real pretty, and that is how you can be sure it is her if ever you see her. Because short fat ladies mostly do not look as good as Junie and nobody thinks boy I would really like to know her like I did that time in England when we went in the cave so she could talk to that crabby old man from Tulsa because Junie believes in dead people coming back and all that.

She made me believe it too. You would too if you had been with Junie like I have.

So I am looking for a Moon just like she is, only she is the Moon that I am looking for. The one she is looking for is the White Cow Moon. That is an Indian name and there is a story behind it just like you would think, only it is a pretty dumb story so I am going to save it for later. Besides I do not think it is true. Indians are nice people except for a couple I used to know, but they have all these stories that they tell you and then they laugh inside.

I am from Texas but Junie is from Oklahoma.

That is what started her off. She used to work for a big school they have there, whatever it says on that sweatshirt she wears sometimes. There was this cranky old man in Tulsa that knew lots of stuff only he was like an Indian. He would tell people, this was when he was still pretty young I guess, and they would never believe him even if it was true.

I have that trouble too, but this cranky old man got real mad and did something about it. He changed his name to Roy T. Laffer and after that he would tell things so they would not believe him or understand, and then laugh inside. Junie never said what the T. stood for but I think I know.

Do you know what it says on the tea boxes? The ones with the man with the cap on them? It says honest tea is the best policy. I know what that means, and I think that cranky old Roy T. Laffer knew it too.

He gave big boxes full of paper to the school Junie worked for, and Junie was the one that went through them and that was how she found out about White Cow Moon. He had a lot of stuff in there about it and Junie saw her name and read it even if his writing was worse even than mine. He had been there and taken pictures and she found those too. She showed me some.

It goes slow. Junie said that was the greatest secret in the world, so I guess it is. And there were pictures of a big old rock that Roy T. Laffer had brought back.

One picture that I saw had it sitting on a scale. The rock was so big you could not hardly see the scale, but then another picture showed the part with numbers and that big old rock was only about a quarter ounce. It was kind of a dirty white like this one cow that we used to have.

Maybe that was really why they call it that and not because a cow jumped over it like those Indians say. That would make a lot more sense only I did not think of it till just now.

I ought to tell you things about me here so you understand, but first I want to tell more about Junie because I am looking for her but I know where I am already, which is here in Florida at the Museum of the Strange and Occult. Only it is all big letters like this on our sign out front, THE MUSEUM OF THE STRANGE AND OCCULT ADMISSION $5.50, CHILDREN $2, CHILDREN IN ARMS FREE, SENIORS $3 OR $2 WITH ANOTHER PAID ADMISSION. The letters are gold.

Junie had been to college and everything and was a doctor of physic. When she got out, she thought she was the greatest since One Mug. That is what she says it means only it is German. I do not remember the German words.

So she went to work at this big laboratory in Chicago where they do physic, only they had her answer the phone and empty the wastebaskets and she quit. Then she went back home to Oklahoma and that is why she was at the big school and was the one that went through Roy T. Laffer's papers. Mostly I do not much like Oklahoma people because they think they are better than Texas people, only Junie really is.

So if you see her or even just talk to somebody that has, you could come by and tell me, or write a letter or even just phone. I will be glad any way you do it. Dottie that works in our office here is putting this in her computer for me and printing it, too, whenever I have got a page done. She says you could send email too. That would be all right because Dottie would tell me. I would be very happy any way you did it. Dottie says www.Hercules@freaky.com.

My name is not really Hercules that is just the name I work under. My name is really Sam and that is what Junie calls me. If you know her and have talked to her and she said anything about Sam that was me. If you want to be really formal it is Sam Jr. Only nobody calls me that. Most people I know call me Hercules. Not ever Herk. I do not like it.

Let me tell you how bad I want to find Junie. Sometimes there is a man in the tip that thinks he is stronger. I really like that when it happens because it is usually fun. I will do some things that I figure he can do too, like bending rebars and tearing up bottle caps. Then if I see the tip likes him, I will say something hard and let him win.

A week ago maybe there was this one big guy that thought he was really strong, so I did him like I said. I threw him the two-hundred-pound bell and he caught it, and when he threw it back to me I pretended like I could not catch it and let it fall when I had my legs out of the way and everybody was happy. Only yesterday he came back. He called me Herk and he said I was afraid to go up against him again. The tip was not with him then. So I said all right, and when he could not lift my five-hundred-pound iron I did it with one hand and gave it to him. And when he dropped it I picked him up by his belt and hung him on this high hook I use for the pulley. I left him up there until everybody was gone too and when I took him down he did not say a word. He just went away.

Well I want Junie back so bad that if he was to tell me where she was I would let him win anytime he wanted.

I do not make a lot of money here. It is just five hundred a month and what I make selling my course, but they have got these trailers out back for Jojo and Baby Rita who is a hundred times fatter than Junie or anybody. So I have one too and it is free. I eat a lot but that is about all I spend much on. Some fishing gear, but I have got a real good reel and you do not need much else.

Well, you do, but it does not cost the world.

So I have a lot saved and I will give you half if you tell me where Junie Moon is and she is really there when I go look.

This is the way she got to be my manager. I was in England working at a fair that they had at this big castle where King Arthur was born and Junie was in the tip. So when it was over and they were supposed to go see Torchy Junie would not go. The steerer said she had to but she kept saying she wanted to talk to me and I could tell she was American like me. So after a while I said she probably knew that if she really wanted to talk to me all she had to do was meet me out back. So then she went.

When I went out back which was where the toilets were I did not expect to see her, not really, even if I had let her feel my arm which is something I do sometimes. But there she was and this is what she said, with the little marks around it that you are supposed to use and all of that stuff. Dottie help me with this part.

"Hercules, I really need your help. I don't know whether I was really one of the daughters of King Thespius, but there were fifty of them so there's a pretty good chance of it. Will you help me?"

That was the first thing Junie ever said to me, and I remember it just like it was a couple days ago. Naturally I said I would.

"You will!?! Just like that????"

I said sure.

"I can pay you. I was going to say that. A hundred pounds right now, and another hundred pounds when I'm over the fence. I can pass it to you through the fence. Look." She opened her purse and showed me the money. "Is that enough?"

I explained how she did not have to.

"You'll be in danger. You might be arrested."

Junie looked really worried when she said that, and it made me feel wonderful, so I said that was okay. I had been arrested once already in England besides in America and to tell the truth in England it was kind of fun, especially when they could not get their handcuffs to go around my wrists, and then they got these plastic strap cuffs and put those on me and I broke six pairs. I like English people only nothing they say makes any sense.

Junie said, "Back there, you threw an enormous barbell up in the air and caught it. How much did you say it weighed?"

I said, "Three hundred. That was my three-hundred-pound bell."

"And does it actually weigh three hundred pounds?"

I said sure.

"I weigh only a little more than half that. Could you throw me, oh, fifteen feet into the air?"

I knew I could, but I said I did not know because I wanted to get my hands on her.

"But you might? Do you really think you might be able to, Hercules?"

I sort of raised up my shoulders the way you do and let them drop.

"We—if you failed to throw me high enough I would get a severe electric shock." She looked scared.

I nodded really serious and said what we ought to do was try it first, right now. We would measure something that was fifteen feet, and then I would throw her up, and she could tell me if I got her up that high. So she pointed to the temporary wires they had strung up for the fair, and I wanted to know if those were the ones. She said no. They were not fifteen feet either. Ten or twelve maybe. But I said okay only do not reach out and grab them or you might get killed, and she said okay.

So I got my hands around her which was what I had been wanting to do and lifted her up and sort of weighed her a couple times, moving her up and down, you know how you do, and then I spun around like for the hammer throw, and I heaved her maybe ten feet higher than those wires, and caught her easy when she came down. It made her really scared, too, and I was sorry for that, but I got down on my knees and hugged her and I said, "There, there, there," and pretty soon she stopped crying.

Then I said was that high enough? And she said it was.

She was still shaky after that, so we went back inside and she sat with me while I waited for the next tip. That was when she showed me the pictures that Roy T. Laffer had taken up on the White Cow Moon and the pictures of the rock that he had brought back, a great big rock that did not hardly weigh anything. "He let a little boy take it to school for a science show," Junie told me, "and afterward the science teacher threw it out. Mr. Laffer went to the school and tried to reclaim it the following day, but apparently it had been blown out of the Dumpster."

I promised her I would keep an eye out for it.

"Thank you. But the point is its lightness. Do you know why the moon doesn't fall into the Earth, Hercules?"

I said that if I was going to throw her around she ought to call me Sam, and she promised she would. Then she asked me again about the moon and I said, "Sure, I know that one. The moon beams hold it up."

Junie did not laugh. "Really, Sam, it does. It falls exactly as a bullet falls to Earth."

She went and got a broom to show me, holding it level. "Suppose that this were a rifle. If I pulled the trigger, the bullet would fly out of the barrel at a speed of three thousand feet per second or so."

I said okay.

"Now say that you were to drop that weight over there at the very same moment that the rifle fired. Your weight would hit the ground at the same moment that the rifle bullet did." She waited for me to argue with her, but I said okay again.

"Even though the bullet was flying along horizontally, it was also falling. What's more, it was falling at virtually the same rate that your weight did. I'm sure you must know about artificial satellites, Sam."

I said I did, because I felt like I could remember about them if I had a little more time, and besides I had the feeling Junie would tell me anyhow.

"They orbit the Earth just as the moon does. So why doesn't the bullet orbit it too?"

I sail it probably hit a fence post or something.

She looked at me and sort of sucked on her lips, and looked again. "That may be a much better answer than you can possibly be aware of. But no. It doesn't orbit Earth because it isn't going fast enough. A sidereal month is about twenty-seven days, and the moon is two hundred and forty thousand miles away, on average. So if its orbit were circular—that isn't quite true, but I'm trying to make this as simple as I can—the moon would be traveling at about three thousand five hundred feet a second. Not much faster than our rifle bullet, in other words."

I could see she wanted me to nod, so I did.

"The moon can travel that slowly." Slowly is what she said. Junie is always saying crazy stuff like that. "Because it's so far away. It would have to fall two hundred and forty thousand miles before it could hit the Earth. But the bullet has to fall only about three feet. Another way of putting it is that the closer a satellite is the faster it must move if it is to stay in orbit."

I said that the bullet would have to go really fast, and Junie nodded. "It would have to go so fast that the curve of the Earth was falling away from it as rapidly as the bullet itself was falling toward the Earth. That's what an orbit is, that combination of vertical and horizontal motions."

Right then I do not think I was too clear on which one was which, but I nodded again.

Then Junie's voice got sort of trembly. "Now suppose that you were to make a telephone call to your wife back in America," is what she said. So I explained I did not have one, and after that she sounded a lot better.

"Well, if you were to call your family, your mother and father, your call would go through a communications satellite that circles the Earth once a day, so that it seems to us that it is always in the same place. It can do that because it's a good deal lower and going a great deal faster."

Then she got out a pen and a little notepad and showed me how fast the bullet would have to go to stay in orbit just whizzing around the world over and over until it hit something. I do not remember how you do it, or what the answer was except that it was about a jillion. Junie said anything like that would make a terrible bang all the time if it was in our air instead of up in space where stuff like that is supposed to be. Well about then is when the tip came in for the last show. I did my act and Junie sat in the front row smiling and cheering and clapping and I felt really swell.

So after it was all over we went to Merlin's cave under the big castle and down by the water, and that was when Junie told me how King Arthur was born there, and I told her how I was putting up at the King Arthur, which was a pub with rooms upstairs. I said they were nice people there, and it was clean and cheap, which is what I want anywhere, and the landlord's name was Arthur, too, just like the pub's. Only after a while when we had gone a long ways down the little path and got almost to the water I started to sort of hint around about why are we going way down here, Junie, with just that little flashlight you got out of your purse?

Maybe I ought not say this right here, but it is the truth. It was scary down there. A big person like I am is not supposed to be scared and I know that. But way up on the rocks where the fair was the lights kept on going out and you could see the fair was just sort of like paint the old walls of that big castle. It was like somebody had gone to where my dad was buried and painted all over his stone with flowers and clowns and puppies and kitties and all that kind of thing. Only now the paint was flaking away and you could see what was underneath and he had run out with his gun when the feds broke our front door and they killed him.

Here is what I think it was down there and what was so scary about it. King Arthur had been born there and there had been knights and stuff afterward that he was the head of. And they had been big strong people like me on big strong horses and they had gone around wearing armor and with swords and for a while had made the bad guys pay, and everybody had loved them so much that they still remembered all about them after a hundred years. There was a Lancelot room in the pub where I was staying, and a Galahad room and I was in the Gawain room. And Arthur told me how those men had all been this king's knights and he said I was the jolly old green giant.

Only it was all over and done with now. It was dead and gone like my dad. King Arthur was dead and his knights were too, and the bad guys were the head of everything and had been for a long, long time. We were the paint, even Junie was paint, and now the paint was getting dull the way paint does, with cracks all over it and falling off. And I thought this is not just where that king was born, this is where he died too. And I knew that it was true the way I meant it.

Well, there was a big wire fence there with a sign about the electricity, only it was not any fifteen feet high. I could have reached up to the top of it. Ten feet, maybe, or not even that.

"Can you pick me up and throw me over?" Junie said.

It was crazy, she would have come down on rocks, so I said I could only she would have to tell why she wanted me to so much or I would not do it.

She took my hand then, and it felt wonderful. "People come back, Sam. They come back from death. I know scientists aren't supposed to say things like that, but it's true. They do."

That made me feel even better because it meant I would see my dad again even if we would not have our farm that the feds took anymore.

"Do you remember that I said I might have been one of the fifty daughters of Thespius three thousand years ago? I don't know if that's really true, or even whether there was a real King Thespius who had fifty daughters. Perhaps there was, and perhaps I was one of them—I'd like to think so. But this really was Merlin's cave and Roy T. Laffer was Merlin in an earlier life. There were unmistakable indications in his papers. I know it with as much certainty as I know Kepler's Laws."

That got me trying to remember who Kepler was, because I did not think Junie had told anything about him up to then. Or after either. Anyway I did not say much.

"I've tried to contact Laffer in his house in Tulsa, Sam. I tried for days at a time, but he wasn't there. I think he may be here. This is terribly important to me, and you said you'd help me. Now will you throw me over?"

I shook my head but it was really dark down there and maybe Junie did not see it. I said I was not going to be on the other side to catch her and throw her back, so how was she going to get out? She said when they opened in the morning. I said she would get arrested and she said she did not care. It seemed to me that there were too many getting arrested when she said that, so I twisted on the lock thinking to break the shackle. It was a pretty good lock and I broke the hasp instead. Then I threw the lock in the ocean and Junie and I went inside like she wanted. That was how she found out where White Cow Moon was and how to get on it, too, if she wanted to.

It was about two o'clock in the morning when we came out, I think. I went back to the King Arthur's and went to bed, and next day Junie moved in down the hall. Hers was the Lancelot room. After that she was my manager, which I told everybody and showed her off. She helped me write my course then, and got this shop in Falmouth to print it up for us.

Then when the fair was over she got us tickets home, and on the airplane we got to talking about the moon. I started it and it was a bad mistake, but we did not know it for a couple of days. Junie had been talking about taking pictures and I said how can you if it goes so fast?

"It doesn't, Sam." She took my hand and I liked that a lot. "It circles the Earth quite slowly, so slowly that to an observer on Earth it hardly seems to move at all, which was one of the things Roy T. Laffer confided to me."

I said I never had seen him, only the lady with the baby and the old man with the stick.

"That was him, Sam. He told me then, and it was implied in his papers anyway. Do you remember the rock?"

I said there had been lots of rocks, which was true because it had been a cave in the rocks.

"I mean the White Cow Moon rock in the picture, the one he lent to the science fair."

I said, "It didn't hardly weigh anything."

"Yes." Junie was sort of whispering then. "It had very little weight, yet it was hard to move. You had to pull and pull, even though it felt so light when you held it. Do you understand what that means, Sam?"

"Somebody might have glued it down?"

"No. It means that it had a great deal of mass, but very little weight. I'm sure you haven't heard of antimatter—matter in which the protons are replaced by antiprotons, the electrons by positrons and so on?"

I said no.

"It's only theoretical so far. But current theory says that although antimatter would possess mass just as ordinary matter does, it would be repelled, by the gravitational field of ordinary matter. It would fall up, in other words."

By the time she got to the part about falling up Junie was talking to herself mostly only I could still hear her. "Our theory says a collision between matter and antimatter should result in a nuclear explosion, but either the theory's mistaken or there's some natural means of circumventing it. Because the White Cow Moon rock was composed of nearly equal parts matter and antimatter. It had to be! The result was rock with a great deal of mass but very little weight, and that's what allows the White Cow Moon to orbit so slowly.

"Listen to me Sam." She made me turn in my airplane seat till I was looking at her, and I broke the arm a little. "We physicists say that all matter falls at the same rate, which is basically a convenient lie, true only in a hard vacuum. If that barbell you throw around were balsa wood, it wouldn't fall nearly as fast as your iron one, because it would be falling in air. In the same way, a satellite with great mass but little weight can orbit slowly and quietly through Earth's atmosphere, falling toward the surface only as fast as the surface falls away from it."

"Wouldn't it hit a mountain or something, Junie?"

"No, because any mountain that rose in its path would be chipped away as it rose. As light as the White Cow Moon must be, its mass has got to be enormous. Not knowing its orbit—not yet—we can't know what mountain ranges it may cross, but when we do we'll find it goes through passes. They are passes because it goes through them."

Junie got real quiet for a while after she said that, and now I wish she had stayed quiet. Then she said, "Just think what we could do, Sam, if we could manufacture metals like that rock. Launch vehicles that would reach escape velocity from Earth using less thrust than that of an ordinary launch vehicle on the moon."

That was the main trouble, I think. Junie saying that was. The other may have hurt us some too, but that did for sure.

We were flying to Tulsa. I guess I should have written about that before. Anyway when we got there Junie got us a bunch of rooms like an apartment in a really nice hotel. We were going to have to wait for my bells to come back on a boat, so Junie said we could look for the White Cow Moon while we were waiting, and she would line me up some good dates to play when my stuff got there. We were sitting around having Diet Cokes out of the little icebox in the kitchen when the feds knocked on the door.

Junie said, "Let me," and went, and that was how they could push in. But they would have if it had been me anyway because they had guns. I would have had to let them just like Junie.

The one in the blue suit said, "Ms. Moon?" and Junie said yes. Then he said, "We're from the government, and we've come to help you and Mr. Moon."

My name never was Moon but we both changed ours after that anyway. She was Junie Manoe and I was Sam Manoe. Junie picked Manoe to go with JM on her bags. But that was not until after the feds went away.

What they had said was we had to forget about the moon or we would get in a lot of trouble. Junie said we did not care about the moon, we had nothing to do with the moon what we were doing mainly was getting ready to write a biography about a certain old man named Roy T. Laffer.

The man in the blue suit said, "Good, keep it that way." The man in the black suit never did say anything but you could see he was hoping to shoot us. I tried to ask Junie some questions after they went away, but she would not talk because she was pretty sure they were listening, or somebody was.

When we were living in the house she explained about that, and said probably somebody on the plane had told on us, or else the feds listened to everything anybody said on planes. I said we were lucky they had not shot us, and told her about my dad, and that was when she said it was too dangerous for me. She never would tell me exactly where the White Cow Moon was after that, and it traveled around anyway, she said. But she got me a really good job in a gym there. I helped train people and showed them how to do things, and even got on TV doing ads for the gym with some other men and some ladies.

Only I knew that while I was working at the gym Junie was going out in her car looking for the White Cow Moon, and at night I would write down the mileage when she was in the living room reading. I figured she would find the White Cow Moon and go there at least a couple of times and maybe three or four, and then the mileage would always be the same. And that was how it worked out. I thought that was pretty smart of me, but I was not going to tell Junie how smart I had been until I found it myself and she could not say it was too dangerous.

I looked in her desk for moon rocks, too, but I never found any, so that is why I do not think Junie had been up there on the White Cow Moon yet.

Well for three days in a row it was just about one hundred and twenty-five on the mileage. It was one hundred and twenty-three one time, and one hundred and twenty-four, and then one hundred and twenty-six. So that was how I knew sixty-three miles from Tulsa. That day after work I went out and bought the biggest bike at the big Ridin' th' Wild Wind store. It is a Harley and better for me than a car because my head does not scrape. It is nearly big enough.

Only that night Junie did not come home. I thought she had gone up on the White Cow Moon, so I quit my job at the gym and went looking for her for about a month.

A lot of things happened while I was looking for her on my bike. Like I went into this one beer joint and started asking people if they had seen Junie or her car either. This one man that had a bike too started yelling at me and would not let me talk to anybody else. I had been very polite and he never would say why he was mad. He kept saying I guess you think you are tough. So finally I picked him up. I think he must have weighed about three hundred pounds because he felt about like my bell when I threw him up and banged him on the ceiling. When I let him down he hit me a couple of times with a chain he had and I decided probably he was a fed and that made me mad. I put my foot on him while I broke his chain into five or six pieces, and every time I broke off a new piece I would drop it on his face. Then I picked him up again and threw him through the window.

Then I went outside and let him pick himself up and threw him up onto the roof. That was fifteen feet easy and I felt pretty proud for it even if it did take three tries. I still do.

After that, two men that had come out to watch told me how they had seen a brown Ford like Junie's out on this one ranch and how to get there. I went and it was more than sixty-three miles to go and Junie's brown Ford was not there. But when I went back to our house in Tulsa it was sixty-eight. A lot else happened for about two weeks, and then I went back to that ranch and lifted my bike over their fence real careful and rode out to where those men had said and sat there thinking about Junie and things that she had said to me, and how she had felt that time I threw her higher than the wires back in England. And it got late and you could see the moon, and I remembered how she had said the feds were building a place for missiles on the other side where nobody could reach it or even see it, and that was why they were mad at us. It is supposed to be to shoot at other countries like England, but it is really to shoot at us in case we do anything the feds do not like.

About then a man on a horse came by and said did I want anything. I told him about the car, and he said there used to be a brown car like that parked out there, only a tow truck cut the fence and took it away. I wanted to know whose truck it had been, but he did not know.

So that is about all I have got to say. Sometimes I dream about how while I was talking to the man on the horse a little white moon sort of like a cloud came by only when I turned my head to look it was already gone. I do not think that really happened or the little woman with the baby and the old man with the stick in the cave either. I think it is all just dreams, but maybe it did.

What I really think is that the feds have got Junie. If they do, all they have got to do is let her go and I will not be mad anymore after that. I promise. But if they will not do it and I find out for sure they have got her, there is going to be a fight. So if you see her or even talk to anybody that has, it would be good if you told me. Please.

I am not the only one that does not like the feds. A lot of other people do not like them either. I know that they are a whole lot smarter than I am, and how good at telling lies and fooling people they are. I am not like that. I am more like Roy T. Laffer because sometimes I cannot even get people to believe the truth.

But you can believe this, because it is true. I have never in my whole life had a fight with a smart person or even seen anybody else have one either. That is because when the fight starts the smart people are not there anymore. They have gone off someplace else, and when it is over they come back and tell you how much they did in the fight, only it is all lies. Now they have big important gangs with suits and guns. They are a lot bigger than just me, but they are not bigger than everybody and if all of us get mad at once maybe we will bring the whole thing crashing down.

After that I would look through the pieces and find Junie, or if I did not find her I would go up on the White Cow Moon myself like Roy T. Laffer did and find her up there.

Pulp Cover

✦

My name does not matter. You have the name of the man I have gotten to tell my story. That's all you need to know. I'm an American, and I live in a town big enough to call itself a city.

I worked for Mr. Arthur H. East, as I'm going to call him. Furniture was our business—Mr. East owned three stores, two in our town and one in a neighboring town. We carried good quality and sold it at reasonable prices. Mr. East was sufficiently well off to have a big house in town and a vacation cottage on a good fishing lake. He hired me as a sales clerk, but promoted me to manager after six years. The promotion included an invitation to dinner, which I of course accepted. Up until that time, I knew no more of Mr. East's family than that he had a plump and pretty daughter I will call Mariel. I knew that only because she had come into the store I called mine looking for her father, and smiled at me.

I fell in love with Mariel at dinner that night. And she with me? I'd like to think so, but I don't know. Since this is my story, let's assume what I want so much to be true: she fell in love with me, but was too young to know it.

She was only fifteen—ten years younger than I was. That was one of the things I learned that night. Others were that she had no brothers or sisters, and that her mother had been dead about eight years.

"You're wondering," Mr. East said, "whether I plan to remarry. I won't until my daughter marries. After that I might."

I tried to say something noncommittal.

"I was raised by a stepmother," he told me. "I will not let that happen to my daughter."

"It will be quite a while," I said, "before Mariel finishes college." I assumed, of course, that the daughter of such a wealthy man would go to college.

Mr. East leveled his finger at me. "You didn't finish college yourself."

I'd had to drop out at the end of my freshman year, when my parents could no longer afford it. I had been taking night classes ever since, switching my major from pre-law to business administration; it is a slow process.

"Finishing college has nothing to do with getting married," Mr. East declared. "Not for Mariel, and as far as I can see, not for anybody. There are plenty of married students, and plenty of successful people who never graduated."

By that time I realized, as you will have faster than I did, that I was under consideration. I got home that night without so much as bending a fender, although I haven't the least idea how I did it or what route I followed. I would marry lovely Mariel. We might or might not inherit her father's stores—it did not matter. Lovely Mariel would marry me. If her father left them to a second wife, she'd need somebody to run them, and I would be that somebody. Lovely Mariel and I would soon be married.

If her father left them to us, we would be rich. If he did not, it would hardly matter. I'd have a good, secure job, doing work I liked and running a business I understood.

And I would have Mariel.

My whole life opened out before me, and it was a life of love and success. I was walking on air.

A few days later a note from Mariel was in my mail. You will sneer when I say that my hands shook as I opened it, but that is sober fact. They did.

She told me she had found out my address without asking her father, who wouldn't have wanted her to write. She said she thought I might want to write to her, and gave me the address of a friend at school. If I would write to the friend enclosing an envelope with "Mariel" on it, the friend would pass it to her in study hall.

I wrote, of course. I must have torn up a dozen letters before I finally wrote the one I sent. I told her how beautiful she was and (I will never forget this) I said that any man on earth would be attracted to her. I said that she could count on me to be a loyal friend and a protector whenever she needed one, and that I would never do anything to hurt her.

After I had sealed the envelope, I wrote a note to her friend, thanking her for what she was doing for us and asking her to write whenever she had news of Mariel.

Here I'm going to try to put three or four years into a couple of minutes. We wrote back and forth like that, generally two or three times a week. As often as she could, Mariel came by the store to see me, trying to time things so that she could stay until closing. I would drive her home, and she would tell Mr. East that she had been shopping at the mall and I had given her a ride home. That was all true. We held hands, and sometimes we kissed. She was more beautiful every time I saw her.

She dated various boys at school. I knew none of them meant much to her because they changed every few weeks. I knew that I meant a lot to her because she told me all her deepest feelings in her letters. Her father was dating a woman from the town where our third store was. Sometimes he brought her home, and she stayed the night. Mariel didn't think she was good enough for her father, and wrote a lot about her. Mariel herself wanted to get married right away—or didn't want to get married until she was thirty. (I think "thirty" was forever to her, although I was near that age.)

She wanted children. She wanted to be an actress who was a famous singer and dancer, and she wanted to be an astronomer and spend her whole life looking up at the stars—or else go to South America and study monkeys. All that stuff changed and changed, and pretty soon I saw that what she really wanted was pretty simple. She wanted security. She wanted people who would love her and take care of her, people who would love her always, no matter what happened. After that I knew what I had to bear down on, and I did. I told her over and over that what I wanted was a good marriage and children, and that I would always be faithful and loving. Even if my wife did things I did not like, I would always love her and be faithful to her I said, and I meant every word of it.

It was early in May. I know that because my mother bought pansies and violas in early May every year, and I was digging a new bed for them when my father came to tell me my boss was on the phone.

Mr. East asked me to meet him at Wheeler's for dinner, and I could tell from the way he said it that he had a lot on his mind. When we had eaten dinner together before it had always been at his house. He had a housekeeper, and she would make a company dinner for Mr. East, Mariel, and me. So this was different, and it was pretty obvious why: he wanted to talk to me without Mariel around or even knowing that we were talking. I was scared.

He was already in a booth with a drink and a cigarette when I got to Wheeler's. We ordered steaks, and after the waiter had gone, Mr. East said, "This isn't about business, and I like to keep my office business-like. Besides, there are always phone calls. Here we won't be interrupted."

I suppose I nodded.

"You know my daughter Mariel. You've given her a lift a couple of times. Do you like her?"

"Yes," I said. "Very much. She's a wonderful girl."

"She's still just a kid."

I waited for him to go on.

"She'll do whatever I tell her to. I might have to jaw at her a little first, but she'll do it. It's a heavy responsibility."

I said that I realized that, and realized he would have to carry it until Mariel was twenty-one.

"Or until she gets married," he said.

You can guess how I felt when he said that.

"Oscar Pendelton was my roommate in college. We were close then, though we haven't kept in touch the way we ought to. He's been very successful—a lot more successful than I have. I founded a company and ran it. He's founded half a dozen and sold them out. He has millions. You remember that big piece *Furniture Trade* did on us?"

I certainly did, it had been a cover story with a lot of color photographs.

"Oscar saw that and showed it to Jack. Jack's his oldest, and the only son he's got. I think there are a couple of girls, too."

I suppose I nodded.

"Oscar sees a lot of business magazines because he's been into and out of a lot of businesses. Naturally he was interested in a story about his old roommate's success. There were two pictures of Mariel in there, remember? One of us outside the house, and another in my study talking to her. Jack got very, very interested in Mariel as soon as he saw her. One of those crazy things, you know? Like falling for a girl you saw on TV."

That was when the waiter came with our steaks, and I'll tell you I was damned glad of it.

"So Oscar wrote to me. Would it be okay if Jack came for a visit? He would stay at our house and take Mariel to shows and so on. I suppose he'll play tennis with her too. I'd be there, and if things looked like they might go too far, I could break it up."

I nodded and pretended I was busy eating.

"Jack's a Yale man. He'll graduate this year. Mariel will graduate from high school, too. I doubt that you knew that, but it's true. She's been looking at colleges. Just fooling around with it, really. You know how kids are."

"Sure."

"So four years difference in their ages. That's not a lot, and she's mature for her age. When Jack's forty, she'll be thirty-six."

I said a difference that small hardly mattered.

"Right. Just what I've been thinking myself. Now listen, I want a favor and a big one. Jack's plane lands at nine twenty. United Airlines. I'd like you to meet him at the airport. You can drive out as soon as we finish here. Jack Pendelton. I want you to size him up for me, and I want you to meet me for lunch at noon tomorrow. Tell me what you think of him. Tell me everything the two of you said, and exactly how he seemed to you. I'll have formed my own impressions by that time, but I want to check them against those of a man I can trust who's closer to his own age. Can I count on you?"

Out at the airport, I didn't have to ask which passenger was Jack Pendelton. He was six-foot-two and something about him made you think he was even bigger. He was plenty handsome enough for the movies, and he had on a Yale sweater. We shook hands. I explained that I worked for Mr. East; I said an important business matter had come up, and he was too busy to come in person, but he would probably be home by the time we got there. Jack nodded. He didn't smile. I don't think I ever saw him smile, except at Mariel; and I couldn't get a dozen words out of him the whole time.

Here it is going to sound like I want to make myself out to be a lot smarter than I am. Riding back into town and then out to Mr. East's it seemed to me that there was only one person in the car: me. And there was something else in there with me that wasn't really an animal or a machine or even a plant or a rock—something else that wasn't any of those things. We went into Mr. East's and the two of them shook hands, and he introduced Jack to Mariel. I could see that Mariel was attracted to him and scared of him, both at once. I wasn't attracted and I wasn't scared, either, but I had the feeling I'd be scared half to death if I knew more.

Next day Mr. East and I had lunch at a little French place he liked. He asked what I thought of Jack, and I said he was big and strong and tough, from what I'd seen of him, and as hard as nails. But he wasn't human.

"I know what you mean. Oscar says his IQ is in the stratosphere."

"Maybe," I said, "and maybe not. But what I mean is there's nothing warm there. Suppose I had stopped the car, and we got out and fought."

(I said that because I had been thinking of it during the drive.) "He could have killed me and thrown my body in the trunk and never turned a hair."

I pointed to my salad. "That stuff is alive. That's why it's nice and fresh and green. When I chew it up and swallow it, I'm killing it. Killing me would bother Jack about as much as killing this stuff bothers me."

"I think he's a fine young man," Mr. East told me, and after that he changed the subject.

I had hoped that Mariel could go to a college in the town where Ellie Smithers lived. Ellie was the woman Mr. East was dating. So did Mariel, and she had said so in her letters. She went to a famous girl's college in upstate New York instead. I won't tell what it was, but if I said the name you'd recognize it. You could have gotten the best car at Bailey's Cadillac & Oldsmobile for what it cost to go there for just one year.

I think it was around Christmas when Mr. East told me about the double wedding. It would be in June, and I was invited. The couples would be Jack Pendelton and Mariel, and Mr. East and Ellie Smithers. It would be a garden wedding "with five hundred guests, if Ellie has her way," and Jack's father, mother, and sisters would fly out.

Mr. East cleared his throat and leaned back. "I'm telling you this in confidence. I want that understood. Oscar's settling a portfolio of investments— stocks and bonds—on Mariel. I'll manage it for her until she's of age. I've checked out those investments, checked them very thoroughly, then had my broker check them over again for me. Two million, three hundred thousand and change if you sold everything today. The income should be around two hundred thousand a year. It could be more. Growth twelve percent or so. Mariel will always be taken care of."

I came to the wedding, but Oscar Pendelton, his wife, and his daughters didn't. Later I found out that Mr. East had gotten a phone call. The woman who called said she was Sara Pendelton, and he had no reason to doubt her. Oscar'd had a heart attack. He was in intensive care. She knew the wedding was all set, and couldn't be postponed. But only Jack would be there.

After it was all over, and Jack and Mariel had flown to Boston to see Jack's father in the hospital, supposedly, I did something I felt a little guilty about at the time. I phoned every last hotel and motel in the area. Nobody'd had reservations for an Oscar Pendelton and family. Nobody'd had reservations for a Sara Pendelton, either. Mr. East and Ellie were honeymooning then, so I went out to the house and talked to the housekeeper. She didn't know where the Pendeltons were going to stay, but she hadn't been told to expect five house guests and there was no way in hell she wouldn't have been.

"It wouldn't be regular, anyway, would it? The groom in the house the day before the wedding? Him and his folks would put up at the Hyatt or something, I'm pretty sure." So I checked with the Hyatt again, this time in person. Nothing. It wasn't "I don't know"; it was "absolutely not."

By that time I was so worried I couldn't eat. And I was fighting mad. It took a hell of a lot of doing, but I got Oscar Pendelton on the phone, long-distance. Certainly he remembered his old friend Art East. How was Art doing? Jack? No, he didn't have a son with that name. Two sons, Donald and Douglas. Don and Doug, their friends said. Nobody ever called either one of them Jack. He had no daughters. His wife's name was Betty.

You're going to say that I should have told Mr. East before he got back from his honeymoon. I've told myself that about a thousand times. Only I kept thinking it might be some kind of silly mistake. By that time the honeymoon was nearly over; I told myself I would tell him when he got back.

But I didn't. The thing was that I had called his broker. I told him Mr. East had put me in charge of his financial affairs while he was gone, and I wanted to make sure Mariel's trust fund was in order. It was. The brokerage was holding everything, but they would not sell or buy, or make any other changes, without a signed authorization from Mr. East. I explained that I didn't want to change anything, I just wanted to make sure everything was straight. It was. They'd had the whole trust portfolio in their hands two weeks before the ceremony. There was nothing to worry about.

After I hung up the phone I felt like I ought to laugh, but I didn't. On the one hand I was damned sure something was terribly, terribly wrong. On the other it was a couple of million. Suppose the man I'd talked to hadn't been Oscar Pendelton at all. Suppose it had been some joker, and he had been stringing me?

A few days later Mr. East got back all happy and tanned, and I asked as casually as I could where Mariel had gone on her honeymoon, and whether he had heard from her. They were going to tour Europe, he said, for a month. (He had taken two weeks, not wanting to be away from the business any longer than that.) He hadn't heard from her, but then he hadn't expected to.

I said I was worried, and he told me to forget it.

You can probably guess what I did next. I got hold of the girlfriend who had passed my letters to Mariel. She had heard nothing. She had been a bridesmaid, and she gave me the names of the other bridesmaids, and told me where they lived. None of them had heard from Mariel. I talked to every one of them in person, and if they had been lying I would have known it. They weren't. None of them had heard a word from the girl who had liked writing letters enough to write me two and three times a week.

I went to Mr. East and gave it to him straight. I said I was sure something had happened to Mariel, and he had damned well better get in touch with his friend Oscar and find out where Jack was. He got in touch with Oscar Pendelton all right, and you know what he found out: no Jack, no heart attack, no plans that had been canceled, no anything.

He hired a detective agency. All they were able to tell him was that there was no such person as Jack Pendelton. Yale had never heard of him. Neither had Social Security. And a lot more of that. They told Mr. East he'd better go to the police and have them list Mariel as a missing person. By that time Jack and Mariel should have been back from Europe for a couple of months, so Mr. East did. Nothing came of that either.

Years passed.

Oscar Pendelton had never had a heart attack, but Mr. East did. It was bad.

He'd had enough time in the hospital to write a will; and when his lawyer read it the audience was the housekeeper, Ellie, and me. The housekeeper got ten thousand. Ellie got the house, the cabin, the cars, and the rest of his money, and she was to administer Mariel's trust fund. If Mariel could not be found, the trust fund went to charity.

Mariel got the business, which I was to run in trust for her, with a nice raise. If Mariel could not be found, the business was to be sold and the money given to charity.

All nice and neat. My folks died, and I sold the house and moved into an apartment.

Seven years after her wedding, Mariel was declared legally dead. And that was that.

I had an M.B.A. A night-school M.B.A., but still an M.B.A. I knew the furniture business backward and forward, and I had a lot of contacts in that business; I moved to a bigger town when a company there offered me a good job. I was thirty-six, going bald but not too bad-looking. All right, I wasn't Jack. But Jack hadn't been Jack either. I dated maybe half a dozen girls, but the more I saw of them the less I liked them.

One night my bell rang. I pushed the button to let my visitor in and went to the door to see who it was.

It was Mariel.

She was only twenty-five, but she looked like hell. Her cheeks had fallen in and you could see the fear in her eyes. (You still can.) I told her to come in and sit down, and said I was damned glad to see her—which I was—and I had wine and beer and cola, and could make coffee or tea if she'd like that. What did she want?

And she said, "Everything."

Just like that.

She had no money and no place to stay. She couldn't remember the last time she had eaten, but she couldn't chew anything much because her back teeth were gone. She needed a bath and clean clothes.

I asked her how she'd found me, and I expected her to say Ellie'd told her, or at least somebody in the town where we were born. She didn't. She had been wandering from city to city for months, hitchhiking, begging, doing time in jail for shoplifting canned soup from a supermarket. She couldn't remember the town we had lived in or where it was. All she could remember was three names: Mary East, Arthur East, and my name. Mary East had been her mother. She had repeated those names a hundred times to people she met, and finally someone had pointed out my building, and of course my name had been on the plate beside the bell button. As if all that wasn't bad enough, she kept switching to a foreign language, and I'd have to stop her and get her to speak English again. I can recognize quiet a few languages when I hear them, and it wasn't remotely like Spanish or German or even Chinese or Arabic, and it certainly wasn't Polish or Russian.

I got milk and soup into her, and crackers she soaked in her soup so she could eat them. She handed her clothes to me out the bathroom door, and I put them in the little washing machine off my kitchen. When she came out, all wrapped up in one of my robes, she asked me who I was, saying she had remembered my name and knew my face, but didn't know how she had known me. I said I was the guy who wanted to be her husband, and she screamed.

We're married now, Mariel and me; so I got what I had wanted so badly years ago. Eleven months after we were married, she had Een. She said he had to be named Een, and got hysterical when I argued; so I guess it's a name from the place where she was. She won't tell me where that is, and says she doesn't know. She let me pick Een's middle name, so his name is Een Richard and my name, and most people think it's Ian Richard. Lauri and Lois came after that, and I know they're mine.

Okay, you're going to say it's not possible, that human women carry children for nine months and that's that. But when I look into Een's eyes, I know.

He's a good kid. Don't get me wrong. He's bright, and when you tell him to clean up his room he does it. He doesn't play with other kids, but they respect him. Or else. In two more years, he's going to be one hell of a high-school football player.

That's almost all I have to say. One night I woke up, and Mariel wasn't in the bed. I happened to look out the back window, and she was out there with Een pointing out stars and stuff.

So I thought I ought to warn people, and now I have. While I was telling all this, the man who's going to write it showed me one of his old pulp magazines. It has a monster with great big eyes and tentacles on it, and this monster is chasing a girl in a one-piece tin swimsuit. But it's not really like that.

It isn't really like that at all.

Of Soil and Climate

✦

I have been looking into the crystal and have seen myself. I am tempted to put quotation marks about that last word, but I shall not. Is the self I have seen in crystal NOT the self I feel myself to be? Very likely it is. Very likely this second dubious self is someone else, an accessory to nothing—or so I would like to believe. But really now? There is no evidence for that.

I wonder what Jung would say. How I would love to know! Might it be possible? Hummm! Could I summon up his spirit and question him? I may well attempt the experiment, although it would be dangerous.

What my dear Estar says—what Her Royal Highness the Most Puissant Princess Plenipotentiary says—I know already. "That's not you."

And yet, the face. It's the face I shaved for years, and my prison hospital office.

I cannot hear through the crystal, yet I know what is being said. It is all so terribly, awfully familiar.

Me (motioning toward the couch): "We don't have to use that. To tell you the truth, they only let me have it in here because so many patients expect it. If you'd rather sit the way you are now and just tell me, that's fine."

He (squirming): "I'll stay here."

Me: "Good. It's actually very comfortable, though. That leather's as soft as a glove, and it's nicely upholstered. To confess, I have napped there sometimes. Now let's begin. What's troubling you, Jim?"

Jim: "When I was a kid . . . I think you ought to know this to start with, Doc. I always felt like everybody was, you know, shutting me out. . . ."

Me: "Yes?"

Jim: "I wasn't, you know, very good at anything. Baseball or anything."

Me: "Neither was I."

Jim: "I—I watched a lot of TV."

Me: "You feel that led you to your present difficulties?"

Jim: "Uh . . . No. Maybe it really would be better if I could lay down."

And so on. It will not do to be contemptuous of these men, and now that I find myself as I am, a head taller than anyone, with a sword at my side, I find myself less tempted to contempt.

Which is good. If I watch the crystal long enough will I not see myself in the office of some other psychiatrist? Perhaps my patients—but no. I am here. A stroke, perhaps?

Later. The bird has returned. The Armies of Night are mobilizing. We were fools not to attack while the sun was up—but we were such fools, and there is no point in denial. I could have ridden. With what? Half the Palace Guard, twenty or thirty other men-at-arms, and a few boys. Or a dozen men-at-arms. Half a dozen. We would have been wiped out in the Pass of Tears if not before. Perhaps after this . . .

If there is any "after this."

The light had awakened him. He had yawned and stretched, blinked in the sunshine, and wondered where he was. Wondered with the comforting certainty that he would soon remember.

A certainty that had proved entirely unfounded. There were no bars, and there was no cot. The horrors of imprisonment had vanished, and with them the certainty of regular meals, books, and the net. He had slept in fern, in a cool and shadowy place where a beetling cliff held off the sun. The sun was setting. . . .

He squinted up at it: half down the sky. It might, he told himself, be midmorning instead; he knew that it was not. There was a warm, sleepy feel to the air that could not have come before late afternoon.

How did you tell time save by looking at the sun? He glanced at his wrist. Numbers? Why weren't there numbers there?

There were none, and he began to walk. Surely numbers were attached, somehow, to the gauging of time.

A tree of a species he did not know stood at the edge of the clearing, a graceful tree with light gray bark and leaves that turned copper when the wind blew. He paused to admire it.

"You'll need a sword."

Who had spoken? He saw no one until a slender girl in russet silk stepped from behind the tree. "You'll need a sword," she repeated. "I know of one. I'd better not leave my husband to show you where it is, but I can tell you."

"How do you know I'll need a sword?" The question amused him because he had never expected to say anything of the sort.

There was no slender girl, only the slender tree. I'm hallucinating, he thought. I've never done that in my life, always been less interested in patients' hallucinations than I should have been. This is fascinating.

He walked for miles, south as well as he could judge. His clothes, he discovered, had no pockets (like the orange jumpsuits) but the purse on his belt held two small coins, and there was a knife on his belt as well, a short, single-edged knife with a broad, thick blade.

A phallic symbol? He had never really given much credence to those.

It was a good, sharp phallic symbol in any event; he used it very carefully to open nuts he brought down by throwing sticks. The nutmeat was small but good; the nuts large and satanically hard. He nicked a finger in spite of all his care, and walked on.

The sun was almost down when he found the road, a faint dirt road such as men make for themselves where the county will not make a road for them, a single, narrow, dusty track. It revived his optimism, and he followed it with enthusiasm, up a low hill and into a deep valley where the declining sun was lost behind wilder, more ragged hills, so that his own steps brought evening.

For hours after that he followed the road still, by starlight and moonlight. The moon, a small and pearl-like moon as round as a button, set; another rose, larger and holding a leering face. Leering or not, it shed more light and he resolved to press on.

Animals that were not wolves howled and bellowed in the forest to either side. As he passed a lightning-blasted tree, he heard a roar he felt certain had come from the throat of a tiger.

At last there came a time when he could walk no longer. He sat down, careless of where he sat, and pulled off the soft boots and sodden woolen stockings. His feet had blistered. They hurt, and were infinitely tired. His legs ached and throbbed so that, exhausted though he was, whole minutes passed before he slept.

The light woke him, or nothing. Twilight—nearly night, he thought. Or dawn, perhaps. Dawn seemed more likely. The sun was out of sight behind the hills. He began to walk again, saw a lightning-blasted tree and turned about. He had been that way, and there was nothing save big trees robed in moss.

Far away, a tiger roared.

The road wound deeper and deeper into the valley, and it was night. Very near, just around the next bend, a woman screamed.

He was running toward it even as he told himself that he must run away from it. She screamed again, stirring an instinct he had not known he possessed. A dark form bent above—what? A bundle of rags? A mossy trunk? He saw the flash of fangs, plunged the short blade into something that was not quite a boar, and was thrown backward. He kicked with both feet and somehow managed to regain those feet.

A half-clothed, frantic woman thrust a cudgel at him. He seized it and struck the beast, great blows with a four-foot stick as heavy as iron, blows each of which would have killed a man. It fled at last, but not before he had felt its claws.

It was twilight when he woke again, and a woman held his head in her lap and sang, the wordless crooning of wind in treetops. He sat up, weak, sore, and sick.

"I heal," she told him. "There is a spring whose waters give strength." With her help he got to his feet, steadying himself with the broken limb with which he had beaten the beast. She wept beside him; he longed to comfort her and tried to as clumsily as any other man.

The spring rose among rocks; it was deep, or at least the light of a small and pearl-like moon made it appear so. He drank and drank, and it was cold and pure and good, and it did indeed make him stronger, as she had promised. "I lost some blood, I think," he said.

She nodded without speaking. Her robe of green velvet left a shoulder bare.

"Did it hurt you?"

"She killed my husband." The woman in the green velvet robe shrugged, and he knew her sorrow was too deep for words.

"We'll bury him," he said.

She shook her head. "He would not have wanted that. What he would have wanted is what he now has, to lie in the forest until Nature returns him to the soil. In time, new growth may spring from his root. I hope so."

He stared at her for a moment, then recalled that David had sprung from the root of Jesse. "What will you do now?"

"Follow you." She glanced at the heavy limb with which he had routed the beast. "As long as you have that, and longer. If I try to go with you, will you drive me away? Throw things?"

"Of course not." He picked up the limb and examined the ragged breaks at its ends; he could scarcely see them, so deep was the twilight, and his fingers told him more than his eyes. "This could use trimming," he said. "I think I left my knife in that animal, whatever it was, but it may have fallen out. If you'd rather stay here while I go back to look for it . . . ?"

She shook her head, putting her arm through his. She smelled earthy and sweet, he thought, an odor he associated with Boy Scouts and camping out. It was a clean perfume he had not smelled in a long, long time and was happy to greet again.

He could not have found the place without her, a fact he admitted to himself long before they found it. "It might be better if we wait 'til sunup," he said. "I doubt that we can find my knife in the dark, even if it's here."

"If you want to lie down, I will lie with you gladly," she told him, "but the sun will not rise for many rains."

"Then I want to lie down," he said. "I'm so tired I've stopped being hungry."

"Rest. I will weep for my husband first."

He did not, but followed her to a fallen tree a few steps away.

She knelt beside it. "They strip away the bark to eat," she said, "and when the tree is ringed, he dies."

A tear fell on his hand, and he put his arm around her. She was—she has been, he told himself—a holy woman in some strange cult in which girls who had been taught to accept such things were married to trees. That seemed plain enough, but he found it hard to imagine a place where such things happened. Where was he, in California? And how had he gotten here?

"We will rest now," she said at last.

"And I'll comfort you," he told her, to which she only nodded and wept.

She spread her gown on the ground. They lay upon it together, and it was soft, furry, and warm. When they were cuddled as one, spoon-fashion his mother would have said, her gown folded itself over them; that covering, too, was warm, furry, and soft.

For a time she wept on, but he kissed her shoulders and the back of her neck and drew her to him, and her weeping ceased.

The beast woke him, looming above him, huge and dark, not with a sound (for it was terribly silent) or the brute, dull claws that caressed his torn face, but by the animal stink of it. It was, he decided later, half ape and half bear.

"I have your knife," the beast said, "and I've cleaned it for you. I thought you'd like to have it back."

He froze, certain that he was about to receive it in the chest; half a minute, perhaps, passed until he realized that the beast we holding it out to him in darkness.

Too numb to speak, he accepted it, pulled it gingerly below the strange stuff covering him, and returned it to its sheath.

"I was starving," the beast said. "You have to understand that. Starving, and I attacked a tree. That was all."

He spoke without thinking. "If you attacked me now, there wouldn't be much I could do."

"No," the beast said, "but you don't have to worry. I killed farther down." It paused. "We kill only when we have to eat. We're not like the Night People. Not even like you Sun People."

He was about to say that it had attacked the woman, but it vanished into the shadows before he could speak.

He slept again until the woman awakened him. They made love, and washed afterward in a small, cold creek. "Is it always night here?" he asked her.

"No," she said.

She had brought the broken limb with which he had beaten the beast; he carried it as they walked deeper into the valley. He had lost the road in the night, and they went by almost invisible forest paths.

"I don't suppose you know where we could get some breakfast?" he asked her.

She only shook her head.

"What are Sun People?"

"You are," she told him.

"Then you must be a Sun Person too."

"I am a Tree Person," she said.

A long while after that, while they were looking for a place where they could ford the river, she asked where he had come from.

"I'm not even sure," he said, and then, as if a fact that explained nothing explained everything, he added, "I'm a psychiatrist."

She nodded encouragingly; the trees were beginning to drop their leaves. One blew past her face.

"I had an office in the Brighton Hills Mall," he said. "It was very upscale. Everything there was very upscale. Orthodontists and furriers, and so on. Saks. Gucci. I charged—well, it doesn't matter."

Memories flooding back.

"I went to prison. I remember now. That's what happened."

"What is prison?" she asked.

They forded the river. It seemed darker than ever on the other side, but they were going toward the light, which cheered him. Three men attacked them; he fought with the desperate courage of a man who knows he must win or die, killing two with shattering blows of the severed limb. The third fled.

He picked up the sword one had drawn against him. "A woman was going to get me a sword like this a while ago," he said, "and I didn't want it. I want it now."

"I don't like it," the woman with him told him.

He searched the dead men, finding soft, thin cakes that were not quite tortillas, and dried meat. "I don't eat that," she said when he tried to give her half.

"For Sun People?"

"They were Night People."

He ate everything, learning in the process that he was ravenous. His meal finished (it had not taken long) he picked up the sword once more and examined it. "Yesterday . . ."

Had it really been yesterday? Two days before? Three? He had gone from a changeless afternoon to an unchanging twilight.

"You said you didn't like them," he told the woman. "I didn't either. To tell you the truth, I thought they were silly. When you've needed something and not had it, you don't think it's silly anymore, I suppose. If I had a gun, I don't think I'd know what to do with it. I have a pretty good idea of what to do with this."

"I am of trees," the woman said, "that wars on trees."

"I'm flesh," he told her, "flesh is what this war's on, not wood. I want it just the same."

The blade was somewhat discolored save where it had been whetted sharp, as long as his arm and three fingers wide. He tried to think what that would be in inches and failed.

He made cuts in air.

"Don't," she said. "Please."

"Then I won't," he promised her. The grip was bone, the guard and pommel iron. "Do you know," he said, "I don't think I've ever told you my name, or asked yours. I'm Tuck."

"Nerys." She hesitated. "I am called Nerys. Is that a good name?"

He smiled. "Of course." She seemed to expect something more, so he held out his hand. "Pleased to meet you."

She took it, clearly uncertain as to what she was to do with it. "May I see your sword, Tuck?"

"Certainly." When she released his hand, he held out the sword, hilt-first.

She took it, holding it level between them. "Have I been a good friend to you, Tuck?"

"A very good friend," he said.

"I am going to ask a favor. It is a small thing, and only one favor—the only one I will ask. Will you promise, before you hear it, to do me this favor?"

He nodded. "You have my word, Nerys. If I can do it, I will."

"You can. That club you have borne was my dead husband's arm. I have loved you doubly because you bore it, even as he. Should the bone of this sword fail, you must replace it with wood from his arm."

He was about to say that it was not likely a bone hilt would fail when he noticed that fine dust was cascading from the hand that gripped the hilt. He said, "I will—trust me," instead.

She returned the sword to him, and he looked down at the grip. It had been smooth and polished, he felt sure; it was rough now, and hairy with splinters. He rubbed it, and bone dust fell. He drew his knife, and the bone split and crumbled under the edge, falling away until nothing remained save the steel spike that held the iron pommel.

When he looked up, she had gone. He called her name and searched for her in a hundred places, and at last he sat down with the club that had served him so well and cut away the smaller end. The pommel was screwed tightly to its steel spike; he had to carve a sort of wrench of the tough wood before he could unscrew it. But he did at last, and managed, with his knife, the end of the spike, and the sharp point of the sword itself, to bore a passage for the spike through the rough wooden grip he had carved.

When the work was done and the iron pommel back in place, he felt that a full day had passed—this though the twilight seemed neither deeper nor lighter than it had been. "I must go on for a few more miles today at least," he told himself. "If I don't reach civilization soon, I'll starve." He was about to throw aside his shortened club when he felt (a deep and somehow peaceful emotion he could never have put into words) that it wished to remain.

He picked it up and ran his hands over the smooth bark, seeing it for the first time as it saw itself: a mutilated tree. He dug a hole in the soft forest loam with the blade of a larger and coarser knife the other dead man had borne, and planted the big end of the club that was no longer his in it; then he dug shallow graves for the two men, one to either side of the thick cutting he had planted, and laid them in their graves and covered them with earth, and the earth with leaves and fallen branches. When all that was accomplished (and it seemed neither darker then nor lighter) he felt that he should pray. He had never been a religious man, but he did his best.

He had dusted his hands as well as he could and was on the point of leaving when he caught sight of the larger, coarser knife and realized that he had neglected to inter it with its owner. Unwilling to undo much of what he had only just finished, he put it through his belt.

Which was well. The beast had said it had killed; he found its kill by the odor of rotting flesh—a child, a girl, he decided, of perhaps fourteen. Save for her eyes, her head was largely intact. Little remained of the rest but scattered bones. He collected as many as he could, and began to dig, muttering, "Poor kid," over and over.

"Are you going to bury those here?" The voice was a girl's.

He looked behind him and saw her half concealed by shrubs.

"I can show you a place," there was a long pause, "that she'd like better."

"You can?" He had not looked at her as he spoke, and there was no reply. When he looked around at last, she was gone.

A dress that had once, perhaps, been ankle-length had been reduced to a bloodstained rag. He gathered the bones and the head into it as well as he could, though he had been unable to find one thighbone and the other protruded no matter what he did.

Then he was ready to leave, but the girl had not returned. He decided to press forward carrying the bones and the head in the hope of finding her, but to bury them when he came upon a particularly suitable spot.

The land rose, and some light returned. At last he found a hut that was almost a small house, with three plots of vegetables on three bits of almost-level land. There were roots he did not know, and beans like no beans he had ever seen that most certainly could not be eaten raw. He tasted two of the roots, and decided that he could eat the second, which he did, scraping the dirt away with his coarse knife.

Behind him, the girl's voice said, "This is where."

She stood at the door of the hut, starved and insubstantial—"Like a bad hologram" was the way he put it to himself. "There?" he said. "Right where you are now?"

"At my feet."

He nodded, knelt at her feet, and began to dig. "Did you know her?"

"I thought I did."

A hole a foot by two feet would be sufficient, he decided. He roughed it out with the knife blade and began to deepen it. "It's cold here."

"That's me," the girl said. She sounded sad.

"You're cold?" He looked up.

"Maybe you'd give me a little blood?"

She had sounded serious. "If you mean a transfusion . . . ?"

"You could just scratch a little line on your arm." She paused, and in a moment he realized that she was trying to take a deep breath but could not breathe. "A few drops? Please?" (Another deep breath that would not come.) "I'll be your friend forever. I swear it!"

He paused, sickened by realization that he had lost utterly the life he had once known. This was a new life, in a new place; and no child—not even she—could have been more hapless and forlorn. "Friends answer questions for their friends," he said slowly. "Will you answer questions for me? Not just one question, or two, but a great many?"

"Yes!"

"I need help," he continued, "figuring out who I am and where I am. You'll help me? As much as you possibly can?"

"*Yes!*"

"Okay." He stood up and took the short, broad-bladed knife from its sheath on his belt. "This isn't sterile, I'm sure." He wiped it on his sleeve. "I wish we had some way to sterilize it. But we don't, and clean steel will have to do." Carefully and slowly, he reopened the cut in his finger.

Seconds passed before the first drops of blood appeared. When they did, she bent over the cut eagerly, not licking or sucking it as he had expected but wetting a finger and smearing her nostrils again and again. "Deeper? Please? Just a little deeper? It won't hurt you."

It stung, but he ran the sharp blade down the cut again.

She drank now. Her lips were frigid when they pressed his hand, but grew warmer—as she herself grew more real, an actual and even ordinary girl, far too thin but very much alive, just entering womanhood.

At length she straightened up. "It's stopped," she said. "I'd ask you to do it again, but I know you wouldn't. Would you?"

He shook his head.

"But you'll bury me? Please?"

"Those are your bones?"

"Of course. I—we—it's hard to explain,"

He knelt to dig again. "Try."

"It's like not being able to sleep. Well, it's really not like that. It's not being able to rest. If you could dig, and walk around and talk to people, and maybe plow, or hoe the garden. But you could never just sit in the shade and fan yourself, or shut your eyes."

He looked up. "You're her ghost? This was you?"

"Of course."

"You live here?"

"I lived here," the ghost said. "It got to be nearly night, and the Night People started. Night comes really soon to this valley. Everybody left when the sun did except me. I had to bury Mama and get the roots in before they rotted. I never did get them all in."

"You're a Sun Person," he said, still digging. "Like me."

"No," the ghost told him, "I'm a Dead Person."

He hesitated. "You look real."

"Because of your blood. If it was sunshine here like it used to be, you'd see. I think I'll fade pretty fast anyway. But I'm grateful. It feels really good, even if it won't last."

He judged the hole deep enough, picked up her head and bones and lowered them into it, then began to replace the earth, mostly by pushing it back into the hole with his hand and the broad blade of the coarse knife. "What's your name?" he asked.

"It was Mej."

"That's short. Maybe I could put up a marker."

The ghost shook her head. "That's just so somebody can find them and dig them up again. I was born here and I died here, and this is where I stay."

"Will you disappear when I finish filling the hole?" Within himself he added, "Will I?"

"Do you want me to?"

He shook his head.

"Then I'll stay awhile, but pretty soon I'll want to go someplace warmer. I don't think you will either. Why should you?"

"I used to be a psychiatrist." He stopped shoving dirt into the hole to think. "Do you know what that is?"

"Someone like you."

"Yes," he said. "Yes, that's it exactly. May I tell you?"

She nodded.

"I treated people who had sick minds. I tried to make them well. Or if I couldn't make them well, I tried to get them better, help them just a little. It was hard, very hard, but I tried hard, too, and sometimes I could make a real difference. People who had hardly been able to function at all were able to function normally sometimes. Oh, they had quirks, moments of intense fear and so on. But they functioned better than many others, and were happy now and then. That's the most any of us can hope for, to be happy now and then."

"I was happy here," the ghost said.

He had finished filling the hole. He piled the rest of the earth on it, forming a mound that he would later tamp down. "Before your mother died, you mean."

"No, after. While I was burying her and getting in the roots. I wasn't happy when she was so sick. I couldn't be. But afterward it was just me. I could do anything I wanted. I went to bed and listened to the owls, when I woke up I lay in bed and listened to the wren and the song sparrow." She laughed, a strange but almost a living sound. "Once I put bread beside the bed, so I could eat before I got up. When I got it in the morning the mice had nibbled out a place." She laughed again.

"I went to prison," he told her, "because I helped a patient too much, and my records were very important to me. My notes. I had to know what my patients had told me, so I could review it. I couldn't remember everything, so I had to write it down. My patients had to know those records would never be made public." He tried to remember what those patients had called him, Dr. Something, and finished weakly by saying, "I'm Tuck, by the way." His mother had called him Tuck.

"I'm Mej. Are you going to step on that, Tuck?"

"No," he said, "I don't believe that would be right. I'm going to pat it down with my hands."

"Thank you. I think I'll get a little sleep."

When he looked around for her again, she was no longer there. He shrugged, selected a likely vegetable from the small garden, and walked on, eating as he walked. "There are no such things as ghosts," he told himself, "yet I'm nearly sure patients see ghosts frequently. From those two facts, two more emerge readily. The first is that things which do not exist are frequently visible. The second: I myself am a patient.

"If I am a patient, I must assist in my own cure; but how can I, if I do not understand the nature of my disease? Answer: by examining the symptoms, I can deduce the nature of my disease.

"First symptom: I frequently mutter to myself when my mouth is full." He chewed vigorously and swallowed, grinning.

"That symptom is disposed of. My disease remains, of course. Second symptom: I have lost all contact with reality. Presumably I am in the prison hospital in a vegetative state. To return to reality, I must comprehend the nature of my delusions. This darkness presumably represents the ethical desert of the penitentiary. It is less now than it was because I have been taken to the hospital where things are somewhat better. The vertical trees reflect the vertical bars on windows and doors. Take that one." He directed his own attention toward an inoffensive sapling. "It's even the right thickness."

Seizing it with both hands, he shook it until its dying leaves rattled. "Just so, Dr. Tuck. I cannot effect my escape by shaking the bars. I am still in prison. What if I take my sword to it?"

He drew his sword and slashed halfheartedly at the sapling, scarring the bark. "No result. But what about a serious attack?" He cut, right and left and right again. Chips flew, and soon the sapling fell.

"Listen!" said a familiar voice at his elbow.

Tuck spun around. "Nerys?"

"Here I am." She stepped out of the shadows. "Did you believe I had left you?"

He nodded.

"I was with you. Where else should I be? Weeping among the living while I watched my husband's body rot?" She pointed to the sword he held. "There is my man."

"This?" He held the sword up.

"There." Her finger slipped between his to touch the wooden grip he had made. "Your hand warmed that. Thus you see me."

"When I carried the club . . ." He let the sentence trail away.

"Again! Listen!"

Screams, he thought.

Silence succeeded the screams; he visualized another Tree Woman like Nerys in the grip of a second beast, and dashed away.

Before he had run far he struck another road, the first real road he had seen, a road of pounded red clay wide enough for horsemen to ride four abreast. The man thundering toward him rode alone, and if he had ever had three companions it seemed likely they were dead—his clothing was bright with blood, which streamed from his head and shoulders.

Tuck stood aside panting and let him pass, receiving two drops of blood on his face for his trouble, and three on his shirt.

Jogging now, he topped a rise. Dead men lay in the road; not far from one lay a horse too badly wounded to rise, with blood pulsing from its nostrils. A second horse shied as soon as it caught sight of him, its reins dragging, its head up, and its eyes wide.

He stopped, careful not to meet its gaze. "You are mistaken," he said. "I don't hate horses or want to hurt them. I love horses." It was not true, and he felt obliged to amend it. "I like horses. Before Sally left me, we had three horses, two geldings and a beautiful little Arabian mare. You're a stallion, right? You would have loved her." He edged closer, careful not to look directly at the brown stallion with the trailing reins. "Sally loved her a lot more than she ever loved me, but I liked her anyway. She was as affectionate and gentle as any animal could ever be."

At the word, he had gotten a foot on the trailing reins. He picked them up, still careful not to look directly at the brown stallion. "You're a fighting horse," he said. "I'm not a fighting man, but I'm a man who'll fight when he has to. For the present that may be good enough. It may have to be."

Mounted, he wheeled the stallion and trotted up the slope.

They were nearer than he would have guessed, one covering the woman while six more watched. Those six turned at the drumroll of the stallion's hooves, and one managed to raise a javelin before he was ridden down. The sword with the wooden grip split the skull of another. Frantic with victory Tuck dropped the reins and threw the coarse knife at the man separating himself from the woman. The pommel struck his eye, and in a moment more he was ridden down as well.

The woman was naked and weeping, and for an hour or more unwilling to rise. Tuck found the ruin of a silk gown, covered her with it, and sat beside her stroking her hand. "It was terrible," he said. "I know how bad it was. Believe me, I know. Now it's over, and it won't happen anymore. For the rest of your life you'll know that nothing you face will be as terrible as what happened here today, and that you lived through this and came out of it better and stronger." He said this and much more again and again, perhaps a score of times.

At last she said, "Will they come back?"

He shrugged. "You would know better than I."

After that he lifted her onto the brown stallion's saddle and mounted behind her. "Where are we going?" she asked.

"Wherever you want to."

"It will be more dangerous if we go back," she told him, "but I would like to go back."

She had pointed as she spoke. He turned the brown stallion, holding it to a rapid walk. "Where are we?"

"This is the Valley of Coomb. You must be a stranger here. Are you from the west?"

"From a far country," he said, and to himself added, "I think."

"You are a brave man, if you are rushing to meet the night, O my husband. But I knew you for a brave man when you slew those who had slain my guards."

"I'm not your husband," he said.

"You have seen my nakedness. Do you not know the law?"

"More than I want to now," he told her, "but I don't think I've come across this one."

"If a man beholds the nakedness of a maid, he must restore her honor by wedding her, if he himself is unwed. That is the law for common women. But if a man beholds the nakedness of a royal maiden, he must put away his wife, and he has one, to wed the royal maiden and restore her honor, O my husband. Had you a wife?"

"Not anymore."

"Indeed. Indeed." She looked over her shoulder, smiling. "You that saved me are harmed the worse. Though I am most grateful for the hand which braces my waist in your saddle, might it not perhaps be some trifle higher?"

The light failed as they followed the road into the Valley of Coomb.

"Here our poor folk left a hundred-eatings gone," she told him, "for this valley is the very Herald of Night."

"I'm surprised you wanted to come back here."

She wiggled closer, although they were already very close. "I have you to protect me. Besides, we met their group as we were about to leave the eastern side, thus they had only entered. Had there been others in deeper night, they would have attacked us sooner."

"I met bandits deeper in," he told her.

"Our own people?" She turned to look at him over her shoulder.

"Not my people," he said, "but Night People, which I suppose must be what you mean."

"My people are the Sun People," she said, "and because they are mine, yours as well, O my husband. Do you not know me?"

"No, but I should introduce myself first."

She nodded.

"I'm Tuck, at your service."

"You are Prince Tuck, my consort. My own name is Estar." She coughed apologetically. "Princess Estar. Please do not grovel."

"I'll avoid it if at all possible."

The smile she directed at him was almost a grin. "Thank you. I have met others, now and then, who did not know me. They groveled, and I hate that. That is a poor man's sword you wield so well. You are not rich?"

"I have nothing," Tuck said.

She dimpled. "Except me."

"No, you have me. You're the loveliest woman I've ever seen. I'm afraid that I'll wake up any minute and you'll be gone."

"You," she said, "are going to make a most satisfactory husband."

There was a farm at the western edge of the valley. He left her some distance from it and explained to the farm wife that she must sell a gown.

"Sacking," Estar said as she pulled it down, "at least you will no longer see that my hips and legs are fat."

"I've seen your hips, and your legs, and they are perfect. Both of them."

"Both legs you mean, and you are looking very far down. You have no money?"

"Nope. I paid the woman for your dress with what I had."

"You could have become rich by searching the bodies of those you killed back there. They took my jewels."

Tuck shrugged.

"You are right. Swords, not jewels, make a king. It was a saying of my father's."

"He's passed away? I'm sorry to hear it."

"Died?" Estar shook her head. "He seldom speaks. He is old, and . . . Sometimes he will not eat."

"I see."

"If he were dead, I would be queen. You, my husband, would be our king until I bore an heir and he reached the age of maturity. But I do not want my father to die. Does that surprise you?"

"No. Certainly not."

"That is well. Look above those trees."

She pointed, and he discovered an unexpected pleasure in the slenderness and whiteness of her arm. His lips brushed the shoulder that held it in the lightest and swiftest of kisses.

"Do you see—" For an instant she seemed to choke, and coughed. "The flag? It is green and yellow, and so not easily seen above the trees."

"I think so."

"It flies from Strongdoor Tower. There is yellow stone beneath it. Perhaps you cannot see it."

"I'll take your word for it," he said.

"The baron's name is Blaan. He is my most loyal vassal, or says loudly that he is, and would wed me if you would step aside for him. Will you?"

"No." A woman—this woman—was much too precious.

She dimpled. "You have not seen how large and strong he is. You will shake with fear, O my husband."

He smiled back. "I doubt it."

"We must see. I cannot ride back to Cikili in this gown. Thus we must ask his aid. He has, I should think, three hundred men, if not more. Will you kill them all for me?"

"I doubt that it'll prove necessary."

The guard at the portcullis looked incredulous when Tuck said that the woman who shared his saddle was Princess Estar, and gawked when he recognized her. Baron Blaan welcomed her, ignored Tuck, and turned her over to a housekeeper and a bevy of maids. He was, as she had said, a tall, beefy, and quite muscular man.

Tuck seated himself in the best chair in the Great Hall and stared at the fire, which was larger than any summer evening could have required.

He had refused to turn over someone's records. Who had she been?

Records showing he had helped with what? Bit by bit he pictured a dozen patients and former patients. A woman accused of killing a child—accused on slender evidence, presumably, since they would not have wanted her psychiatrist's notes if they had a strong case. He himself had been psychoanalyzed ten years ago, as all analysts were at the beginning of their careers. Could it have been those notes they wanted?

Could he have murdered a child?

He decided that he could not, but that he could certainly have been accused of having done it and worse. Anyone these days—any man, particularly—could be accused of anything by anyone.

"That's my chair you're sitting in," Blaan said.

"Sorry." Tuck rose and moved to another.

"That's my chair, too."

Tuck sighed. "No doubt it is. This is your castle and you own all its furniture. I thank you for allowing me, a mere prince and your guest, to use it. But if you want me to vacate it, you need stronger arguments."

"A prince? You don't look it. Of what nation?"

"Yours."

The word hung there for perhaps half a minute. At last Blaan said, "You're a dreamer. I can tell that—a dreamer with a torn cheek! What do you dream of as you peer into my fire, dreamer?"

He had been thinking of the prison wood shop to which he had initially been assigned, his practice in the prison hospital, and his fill-in work in the library. "Stevenson," he said. "Blinking embers, tell me true, where are those armies marching to, and what the burning city is, that crumbles in your furnaces?"

Blaan blinked too; he was saved by Estar, who swept into the room, resplendent in cloth-of-gold, with two maids to carry her train.

Blaan rose, and Tuck with him.

"My husband is not obliged to bow save on the most ceremonial occasions." Estar's voice would have frozen seawater. "You, Baron, are not thus exempt."

"You have married this—this . . ." For a moment Blaan could only stare, at a loss for words. "This *vagabond!*"

Tuck laid a friendly hand on Blaan's shoulder. "Bow."

Blaan spun to face him. His sword was in his hand so quickly it seemed impossible that he had actually drawn it. *"Guards!"*

Estar screamed.

Tuck dodged behind the chair. "I think you need to consider what you're doing. Will you listen to reason? Just for a minute?"

"I will not only listen to it," Blaan told him, "I will voice it. The princess has wed a vagrant, a decision she must deeply regret. I will free her from her miscegenation. In gratitude, she will accept me and obey me as a good wife should. Or suffer the consequences."

The last word was nearly drowned in the pounding footfalls of the guards, a score of big men with helmets and spears.

"Wait!" Estar raised both her hands. "I am your Princess Plenipotentiary, the Regent of our King."

Tuck kept his eyes on Blaan. "Your lord's following a suicidal policy," Tuck said.

Estar's voice rose above the hubbub. "Hear the Prince Consort!"

"True loyalty lies in saving him from it."

Blaan lifted his sword for an overhand cut, edging to his right.

"That will preserve your own lives too. Obey him now and you'll die as traitors, and quickly."

"Die!"

Tuck got the chair up in time to block the swift sword cut, though the edge bit deep into its back. He grabbed one end of the wide sword guard, and Blaan jerked to free it.

Estar spoke again. "Do none of you wish this barony? Not one?"

As if by magic, the blade of a spear emerged from Blaan's chest. His blood followed it, his eyes glazed, and he fell.

With all the poise she might have exhibited at her coronation, Estar approached the guardsman while her maids scurried behind her, trying to snatch up the cloth-of-gold train they had let fall. "Congratulations, my lord." She smiled. "A good cast!"

The king lay in bed staring at the embroidered canopy eight feet above his snowy head. "He will speak at times," Estar whispered. "Let us hope this will be one." More loudly she said, "This is my husband, Father. The ceremony will be at sunset—we're hoping that will cheer the city as well as giving our warriors a new leader."

There was no response.

"Already, he wears the seal, Father. Don't you see it?" She touched the heavy gold seal suspended from Tuck's neck. "The seal you wore for so many years?"

There was nothing to indicate that the old man in the huge bed had heard her.

"He is wise, and certainly much too wise not to listen to the advice of a man much older than he who has devoted his life to statecraft. A few words from you, now, might help him shape a better path for our whole nation."

"No," the old king said distinctly. "Go, Estar. Leave me."

"Better," Tuck muttered to her.

"Is it really?" She scarcely breathed the words. "I would have said worse."

"It's better," Tuck's tone was conversational, "because it doesn't point to Alzheimer's, which is what I was afraid of. I can't treat that with what we've got here. This is senile depression, I would say, and I may be able to do something."

"Really?"

"Really. Will you trust me alone with him for half an hour or so? I won't hurt him, I promise, or demean him in any way. But this will be tricky and may not work."

When she had kissed him lightly and gone out, he took off the seal and pulled a chair up to the bed. Seated, he held the seal by its chain, letting it swing gently. "I wanted to give you a better look at this, Your Majesty. Do you see it? Look carefully, please. I know you wore it for years, but you were very busy during all those years. Did you notice how beautiful it is? See how it catches the light as it swings back and forth. See how it turns as it swings. It's bright gold, pure gold, and my valet polishes it every time I change clothes."

There was no response.

"I'm going to try something to take away the pain, or make it lighter if I can't take it away entirely. The thing I'm going to do here this warm afternoon is called hypnotherapy. Hypnos is one of the names of sleep. Did you know that? That's why it's called hypnotherapy. It's sleep therapy, sleep healing. You're old now. You can no longer grasp a sword, and you hate that. It hurts you inside, I know. You can no longer walk like you used to, and that hurts too. I understand. But there's so much pain, so much pain like that. I'm sure you would like to get away from it for a while, even if it was only a little while. Haven't you noticed that it no longer hurts when you sleep? It doesn't. You're warm and comfortable then, and those things no longer matter, do they? It's so much better to sleep, and not hurt.

"To sleep and wake up better and stronger with no pain. Are you still watching the seal? That's fine, but I can see your eyelids are getting heavy. Close them if you want to. Rest your eyes. Get away from the pain while the seal swings back and forth."

When Tuck left the king's bedchamber, the king was holding his arm. He did not grip it tightly, and with its slight help walked almost as well as Tuck himself. The crimson velvet retiring robe he wore was trimmed with ermine and positively regal. He greeted half a dozen courtiers by name, while they bowed almost to the rich carpet of the corridor, or gaped open-mouthed.

"I am feeling better," he told Estar when they found her in the music room of the suite she now shared with Tuck. "It has been a great help to have you and this prince, a loving couple I can trust with everything, as my regents. I hope that you will consent to continue in your service to our nation."

"We will, Your Majesty," Tuck said.

Still too astonished to speak, Estar nodded agreement.

Later, in a curtained room, Tuck sat before the crystal watching the golden seal he had hung above it swing. "Wake," he murmured. "Wake up. This is a dream, a good dream, but only a dream. Awake. Awake. Awake . . ."

It took much longer than that. But a moment came when he realized he was no longer watching the seal—that he was sitting on a small, hard stool with his eyes shut.

He opened them and saw the stacks of the prison library. A cart showed that he had been reshelving books. He rose from the gray metal stool and went back to work.

That night a whistle shrilled in Cell Block Seven. "Lockdown!" a guard shouted. Two or three voices echoed him derisively: *Lockdown. Lockdown.* Thirty seconds later, every door in the block that was not closed already slammed shut and every bolt in every door shot home.

"Wish it didn't make such a racket," the other man in the cell said, and sat up.

"We are the Night People." Tuck gripped the bars and looked out, wondering vaguely what the other man's name was, and whether he would ever recall it.

"What you mean by that, Doc?"

He turned and looked at the other man—at Clark. "You have to kill the Night People or lock them up. If you don't they will murder and rape and burn. It's the same everywhere, 'in spite of differences of soil and climate, of languages and manners, of laws and customs.' We are the Night People, and they are safe from us now."

"You're quotin' again, ain't you?"

Tuck nodded. "Wordsworth."

"My granny used to talk about them," Clark said, "them dime stores."

Murder, rape, and burn. And hide evidence.

There were patients next day, both alcoholics. When he had finished with them, he went to the library; secreted once more in the stacks, he tried by every method he knew to return to his dream.

Next morning he was in the library again. He ate lunch and endeavored to treat a man who fantasized—only fantasized, he insisted—about doing horrible things to women with long dark hair.

The next day there were no psychiatric patients and he filled in at the hospital, looking at sore throats and sprained ankles. In that fashion day followed day. And evening after evening he read while Clark watched TV. Had a book guided him to the dream? He hoped one had and searched his mind in spare moments, for if such a book existed it might be found again; found, it might guide him back. Might guide him home.

Once Clark asked him what he would do when he got out, and he said, "Lead those who'll follow me to blunt the next incursion." Clark asked him no more questions after that.

So one year passed, and another, until at last a patient explained that his sleep was haunted by a plaintive girl. "She's real skinny, Doc, and looks real poor. She keeps tellin' me and tellin' how I promised something, only I never done it."

Tuck nodded. "Something in your unconscious mind is trying to enter your consciousness. Have you any idea what it might be?"

The patient nodded. "Yeah, I do. That's why I acted crazy until they let me in to see you." He held out a scrap of wood. "A guy asked me to give you this, a long time ago. I promised I would, only I never did. You can just pitch it out if you want to."

Tuck examined it. It was a simple cylinder with a clumsily cut hole down its axis.

"Thing is, he got your old bench when they moved you up here out of the wood shop, and he found it in a drawer. He thought it might be a piece of somethin' you'd been workin' on, and you might like to have it."

"It's a wooden grip for a sword," Tuck told him.

When the patient had gone, he rubbed it between his palms, pressed it to his cheek, shut his eyes, and (feeling not at all foolish) kissed it.

There were hands upon his shoulders; he knew at once whose hands they were. "The Sun People have need of you," Nerys said, and somewhere a tiger roared.

He rose, wrapped in crystalline mist, and took three steps.

Escaped the crystal. He paused, brushing his lips with the end of the quill. *Half the city has burned. I have rallied the survivors. We must free Estar, and because we must, we shall. The Armies of Night are scattered, expecting no concerted attack. With luck and guts we'll teach them a lesson that will last a long, long time.*

The Dog of the Drops

✦

Not long ago, my duties took me to the lands beyond the bombed cities. They are a different kind of people there, poor, lonely, loquacious, and insular. There are no cook-shops in their wretched villages, and no accommodations for travelers. Someone told me to apply at a farm in the next valley. I did, and was welcomed by a beautiful, very quiet young woman and five noisy boys who called her "Ma."

I had scarcely left her door the next morning when I was stopped by an elderly man; he was stooped and weatherworn, but his handclasp proved he was still strong. I have no great ear for dialect, but I will attempt to give his tale as he did, while omitting my own questions and promptings.

'E know wat a doog be, sar? Well, sar, I knowt it ter, er thought I done. My pa, he showt me a picture, do 'e see, an' 'twar smallish. Had years like ter sma' rugs, it did, er else yearmuffs on ter keep its biddy years cozied. On'y somebody'd had ter put 'em on it, do 'e see, an' somebody'd had ter make 'em fer it ter. Fer it couldn't do sich for itself, nae havin' nae hands. Pa tolt me. 'Em doogs cud talk, sar, like ter a man er ter a lady dependin'. Do sma' errants fer 'em wat owned 'em, they wud. Go ter th' neebors an' tell wat 'e tolt it ter say. Flush coneys, ter, an' fetch hum wat 'e shot wat got inter th' bush, sar. Watch th' hoose when 'e was gun, if 'e kin swaller sich.

On'y th' Life Man wat were, he didna fancy 'em, fer they didna care fer his taxers, sar, on'y fer 'em wat fed 'em, an' if we's all so 'twud be better fer us all, do 'e see. So he kilt 'em. An' said they brought th' sickness, wich no-body'd took no note o' afore, sar, an' hung 'em wat kept 'em. So they's all gun, sar. Dead as cats, sar, is wat Pa tolt me.

On'y there's a neebor name o' Pet, do 'e see. An' he went inter th' drops, sar, wat th' awld folks calt th' barbs, sar, ware folk used ter live 'round th' fallinwalls. We calls 'em drops 'cause there's holes ever'where, do 'e see, most wi' water in 'em an' dint go nowheres nohow. On'y a man drops inter 'em, do 'e see, an' 'e don't look sharp. Holes an' holes. They et dirt in 'em times, it do seem, fer there's none 'round wear they dug.

Pet were out huntin' do 'e see, an' a good place fer it.

Well, sar, he shot a wolf, sar, an' follered it, wantin' th' hide fer his miz. On'y he never caught oop. Dark coom, an' him way inter th' drops, sar, an' nae wolf.

Oh, he knowed he hit it, sar. A blud trail, do 'e see, an' he'd seen it ramp wen his bullet hit. On'y he lost th' trail an' thrashed aboot tryin' ter find it, do 'e see, an' dark coom. They's bad places, th' drops is, wear them awld folk was in th' awld time 'fore Bigkill, 'round th' glass an' fallinwalls. On'y Pet were a brave 'un an' he made ter spend th' night there, like.

He got a fire goin' an' cookt an' et th' way 'e do, sar. He laid down, an' 'fore he got ter sleep he hert a biddy gal, like, talkin' ter him. He sat up spry, he said, an' well I believt him. He had ter think it were a ghast, do 'e see. Wanted grub, she done, an' said her ma were dead an' none left ter feed her. Pet, he says, "You coom set by th' fire." On'y she never would, sar. Said he weren't ter see her. Not never. Said ter throw her food an' lay doon, an' she'd fetch it. Wich she done, sar, an' he hert her eatin' wen he lay.

"Wat 'e goin' ter do wen I'm awa'?" says Pet. "An' 'e wi' none ter see ter 'e?"

"Die, sar," says she.

"I'll coom back tomorrer," says Pet, an' he thought, sar, he'd learn her ter trust him an' take her home an' find a gal ter do fer her, do 'e see, for he'd th' five boys o' his ain at hum an' dint want nae mair kits.

Well, sar, it went on sae fer a yar an' soom. Pet, he wud coom an' stay if it were fine wetter, an' leave a barley caike 'er wat he had an' go an' it were none. On'y she growed oop that yar, sar. Dinna soond but a bitty kit wen she coom ter Pet's fire, sar, on'y ready fer a rin' wen th' yar coom 'round agin.

Gud thin' it were, fer he passed. In th' medder, do 'e see, an' bull gored him. On'y wen his miz, wat were sae kind ter 'e, coom lookin' fer him th' bull's gun an' somethin' standin' o'er Pet wat wudnae let her coom near. She went fer me, sar, an' ter mair wat had been his neebors. We coom, an' 'twere dark er near dark, an' there were somethin' big an' black wat watcht o'er him. I knowt. I made 'em wi' me down th' guns. "He's gone," I says, "an' we got ter put him under right, do 'e see. I know 'e'd nae harm him, Doog." An' she went, sar, like ter a shadder.

We fetcht him hoom, an' laid him in th' kitchen on th' big table, sar, an' it's wen we seen it were th' bull. He were gored an' tossed, sar, an' neck broke.

'Tis been hard, sar, fer her, feedin' five kits. On'y coom dark, there mawt be a fawn er coney on th' step fer 'em, sar. Or nae. There's nae tellin'.

'E seen Pet's miz, sar. On'y a yonker herself, sar, fer it was Pet's first wat carryt his boys. A gud woman, sar, an' a kinder, neater gal never I seen, an' there's Sut, sar, wat tuk ter her like wat 'e done.

Him, sar? She lykt him well enough till he thumpt her, sar, an' she had ter run ter me. Dinna 'e fret 'bout Sut, sar, fer a wolf kilt him the night after, sar. Neck tore, do 'e see, and a leg took ter eat or fer th' kits. A wolf 's wat they say, sar, an' dinna ast me wat 'ud tell 'em different.

'E take care, do 'e see, sar? 'E treat her gud, an' Pet's kits, ter, sar. Er else gae hum.

He turned at the last word, fearful perhaps that he had offended me. I stood and watched him go until his broad, bent shoulder and old gray coat vanished in the furze and the mist. Then I turned to look back at the lonely, noisy cottage I had left, to which I hope soon to return.

And I wondered where she lay, she who watched it with me.

Mute

✦

Jill was not certain it was a bus at all, although it was shaped like a bus and of a bus-like color. To begin with (she said to herself) Jimmy and I are the only people. If it's a school bus, why aren't there other kids? And if it's a pay-when-you-get-on bus, why doesn't anybody get on? Besides there was a sign that said BUS STOP, and it didn't.

The road was narrow, cracked and broken; the bus negotiated it slowly. Trees closed above it to shut out the sun, relented for a moment or two, then closed again.

As it seemed, forever.

There were no cars on the road, no trucks or SUVs, and no other buses. They passed a rusty sign with a picture of a girl on a horse, but there were no girls and no horses. A deer with wide, innocent eyes stood beside a sign showing a leaping buck and watched their bus (if it really was a bus) rumble past. It reminded Jill of a picture in a book: a little girl with long blond hair with her arm around the neck of just such a deer. That girl was always meeting bad animals and horrible, ugly people; and it seemed to Jill that the artist had been nice to give her this respite. Jill looked at the other pictures with horrified fascination, then turned to this one with a sense of relief. There were bad things, but there were good things too.

"Do you remember the knight falling off his horse?" she whispered to her brother.

"You never saw a knight, Jelly. Me neither."

"In my book. Most of the people that girl met were awful, but she liked the knight and he liked—"

The driver's voice cut through hers. "Right over yonder's where your ma's buried." He pointed, coughing.

Jill tried to see it, and saw only trees.

After that she tried to remember Mother. No clear image would come, no tone of voice or remembered words. There had been a mother. Their mother. Her mother. She had loved her mother, and Mother had loved her. She would hold on to that, she promised herself. They could not bury that.

Trees gave way to a stone wall pierced by a wide gate of twisted bars, a gate flanked by stone pillars on which stone lions crouched and glared. An iron sign on the iron bars read POPLAR HILL.

Gate, sign, pillars, and lions were gone almost before she could draw breath. The stone wall ran on and on, with trees in front of it and more trees behind it. Alders in front, she decided, and maples and birches in back. No poplars.

"Did I ever read your storybook?"

She shook her head.

"I didn't think so. I was always going to, but I never got around to it. Was it good?"

Seeing her expression, he put his arm around her. "It's not gone forever, Jelly. Okay? Maybe they'll send it."

When she had dried her eyes, the bus had left the road and was creeping up a narrow winding drive between trees. It slowed for a curve, slowed more. Turned again. Through the windshield she glimpsed a big house. A man in a tweed jacket stood in what seemed to be its back doorway, smoking a pipe.

The driver coughed and spat. "This here's your papa's place," he announced. "He'll be around somewhere, and glad to see you. You be good kids so he's not sorry he was glad, you hear?"

Jill nodded.

The bus coasted to a stop and its door opened. "This's where you get out. Don't you forget them bags."

She would not have forgotten hers without the reminder. It held all the worldly goods she had been allowed to take, and she picked it up without difficulty. Her brother preceded her out of the bus carrying his own bag, and the door shut behind them.

She stared at the back door of the house. It was closed. "Dad was here," she said. "I saw him."

"I didn't," her brother said.

"He was standing in the door waiting for us."

Her brother shrugged. "Maybe the phone rang."

Behind them the bus backed up, pulled forward, backed a second time, and started down the drive. Jill waved. "Wait! Wait a minute!"

If its driver heard her, there was no sign of it.

"We ought to go in the house." Her brother strode away. "He might be in there waiting for us."

"Maybe it's locked." Reluctantly, Jill followed him.

It was not, and was not even closed enough to latch. There were leaves on the floor of the big kitchen, as though the door had stood open for hours while the wind blew. Jill pushed it solidly shut behind her.

"He might be" (her brother's voice cracked) "in front."

"If he was talking on the phone, we'd hear him."

"Not if the other person was talking." Her brother had already seen enough of the kitchen. "Come on."

She did not. There was an electric stove whose burners glowed crimson then fiery scarlet, a refrigerator containing a pound of cheese and two bottles of beer, and a pantry full of cans. There were dishes, pots, pans, knives, spoons, and forks in plenty.

Her brother returned. "The TV's on in the front room, but there's nobody there."

"Dad has to be around somewhere," Jill said. "I saw him."

"I didn't."

"Well, I did."

She followed her brother down a wide hall with high, dark windows on one side, past the big door to a big dining room where no one sat eating, and into a living room in which half a dozen drivers might have parked half a dozen buses, full of sunshine. "A man did this," she said, looking around.

"Did what?"

"In here. A man picked out this furniture, the rugs, and everything."

Her brother pointed. "Have a look over there. There's a chair made out of horns. I think that's hot."

She nodded. "So do I. Only I wouldn't have bought it. A room is—it's a frame, and the people in it are the pictures."

"You're crazy."

"No, I'm not." She shook her head in self-defense.

"You're saying Dad got this stuff to make him look good."

"To make him look right. You can't make people look good. If they don't, they don't. That's all there is to it. But you can make them look right, and that's more important. Everybody looks right in the right place. If you had a picture of Dad—"

"I don't."

"If you did. And you were going to get a frame for it. The man in the frame store says take any of these you want. Would you take a pretty black one with silver flowers?"

"Heck, no!"

"There you are. But I'd like a picture of me in a frame like that."

Her brother smiled. "I'll do it someday, Jelly. Did you notice the TV?"

She nodded. "I saw it as soon as we came in. Only you can't hear what that man's saying, because it's on mute."

"So he could talk on the phone, maybe."

"In another room?" The telephone was on an end table near the television; she lifted the receiver and held it to her ear.

"What's wrong? Could you hear him?"

"No." Gently, she returned the receiver to its cradle. "There's no noise at all. It's not hooked up."

"He's not on a phone in another room, then."

It was not logical, but she felt too drained to argue.

"I don't think he's here at all," her brother said.

"The TV is on." She sat down in a chair, bare waxed wood and brown-and-orange cushions. "Did you turn on these lights?"

Her brother shook his head.

"Besides, I saw him. He was standing in the door."

"Okay." Her brother was silent for a moment. He was tall and blond, like Dad, with a face that was already beginning to discover that it had been made for seriousness. "I'd have heard the car if he went away. I've been listening for something like that."

"So have I." She sensed, although she did not say, that there was a presence in this empty house that made you listen. Listen, listen. All the time.

MUTE, said the screen, and made no sound.

"I'd like to know what that man on the TV's saying," she told her brother.

"It's on mute, and I can't find the remote. I looked."

She said nothing, snuggling back against the brown-and-orange cushion and staring at the screen. The chair made her feel that she was enclosed by some defense, however small.

"Want me to change the channel?"

"You said you couldn't find the changer."

"There's buttons." He swung back a hinged panel at the side of the screen. "On and off. Channel up and channel down, volume up and volume down. Only no Mute button."

"We don't need a Mute button," she whispered, "we need an Unmute button."

"Want to change the channel? Look."

The next channel was a gray screen with wavy lines and the yellow word MUTE in one corner, but the next one after it had a pretty, friendly looking woman sitting at a table and talking. The yellow MUTE was in the corner of her screen, too. She had a very sharp yellow pencil in her hands, and she played with it as she talked. Jill wished that she would write something instead, but she did not.

The next channel showed an almost empty street, and the yellow MUTE. The street was not quite empty because two people, a man and a woman, were lying down in it. They did not move.

"You want to watch this?"

Jill shook her head. "Go back to the man Dad was watching."

"The first one?"

She nodded, and channels flicked past.

"You like—" Her brother froze in mid-sentence. Seconds crept past, fearful and somehow guilty.

"I—" Jill began.

"*Shhh!* Someone's walking around upstairs. Hear it?" Her brother dashed out of the room.

She, who had heard nothing, murmured to herself, "I really don't like him at all. But he talks slower than the woman, and I think maybe I can learn to read his lips if I watch him long enough."

She tried, and searched for the control between times.

There had been no one upstairs, but there was a big bedroom there with two small beds, one against the east wall and one against the south, three windows, and two dressers. Her brother had wanted a room of his own; but she, terrified at the thought of lying alone in the dark, promised that the room would be his room and she would have no room—that she would sweep and dust his room for him every day, and make his bed for him.

Reluctantly, he consented.

They ate canned chili the first night, and oatmeal the next morning. The house, they found, had three floors and fourteen rooms—fifteen, counting the pantry. The TV, which Jill had turned off when she had left the room to heat their supper, was on again, still on mute.

There was an attached garage, with two cars. Her brother spent all afternoon hunting for the keys to one or the other without finding them. Indeed, without finding any keys at all.

In the living room, the man who had been (silently) talking talked silently still, on and on. Jill spent most of her time watching him, and eventually concluded that he was on tape. His last remark (at which he looked down at the polished top of his desk) being followed by his first.

That evening, as she prepared Vienna sausages and canned potato salad, she heard her brother shout, "Dad!" The shout was followed by the banging of a door and the sound of her brother's running feet.

She ran too, and caught up with him as he was looking through a narrow doorway in the back hall. "I saw him!" he said. "He was standing there looking right at me."

The narrow doorway opened upon darkness and equally narrow wooden steps.

"Then I heard this slam. I know it was this one. It had to be!"

Jill looked down, troubled by a draft from the doorway that was surely cold, dank, and foul. "It looks like the basement," she said.

"It *is* the basement. I've been down here a couple times, only I never could find the light. I kept thinking I'd find a flashlight and come down again." Her brother started down the steps, and turned in surprise when a single dim bulb suspended from a wire came on. "How'd you do that, Jelly?"

"The switch is here in the hall, on the wall behind the door."

"Well, come on! Aren't you coming?"

She did. "I wish we were back at that place."

Her brother did not hear her. Or if he heard her, chose to ignore her. "He's down here somewhere, Jelly—he's got to be. With two of us, he can't hide very long."

"Isn't there any other way out?"

"I don't think so. Only I didn't stay long. It was really dark, and it smelled bad."

They found the source of that smell in back of a bank of freestanding shelves heaped with tools and paint cans. It was rotting and had stained its clothing. In places its flesh had fallen in, and in others had fallen away. Her brother cleared scrap wood, a garden sprayer, and half a dozen bottles and jugs from the shelves so that the light might better reach the dead thing on the floor; after a minute or two, Jill helped him.

When they had done all they could, he said, "Who was it?" and she whispered, "Dad."

After that, she turned away and went back up the stairs, washed her hands and arms at the kitchen sink, and sat at the table until she heard the basement door close and her brother came in. "Wash," she told him. "We ought to take baths, really. Both of us."

"Then let's do it."

There were two bathrooms upstairs. Jill used the one nearest their room, her brother the other. When she had bathed and dried herself, she put on a robe that had perhaps been her mother's once, hitching it up and knotting the sash tight to keep the hem off the floor. So attired, she carried their clothes downstairs and into the laundry room, and put them in the machine.

In the living room, the man whose lips she had tried to read was gone. The screen was gray and empty now save for the single word MUTE in glowing yellow. She found the panel her brother had shown her. Other channels she tried were equally empty, equally gray, equally muted.

Her brother came in, in undershorts and shoes. "Aren't you going to eat?"

"Later," Jill said. "I don't feel like it."

"You mind if I do?"

She shrugged.

"You think that was Dad, don't you? What we found in the basement."

"Yes," she said, "I didn't know being dead was like that."

"I saw him. I didn't believe you did, that time. But I did, and he closed the basement door. I heard it."

She said nothing.

"You think we'll see him any more?"

"No."

"Just like that? He wanted us to find him, and we did, and that was all he wanted?"

"He was telling us that he was dead." Her voice was flat, expressionless. "He wanted us to know he wouldn't be around to help us. Now we do. You're going to eat?"

"Yeah."

"Wait just a minute and I'll eat with you. Did you know there isn't any more TV?"

"There wasn't any before," her brother said.

"I guess. Tomorrow I'm going out. You remember that gate we passed on the bus?"

He nodded. "Poplar Hill."

"That's it. I'm going to walk there. Maybe it will be unlocked to let cars in. If it isn't, I can probably get over the wall some way. There were a lot of trees, and it wasn't very high. I'd like it if you came with me, but if you won't I'm going to anyhow."

"We'll both go," he said. "Come on, let's eat."

They set out next morning, shutting the kitchen door but making very certain that it was unlocked, and walking down the long, curving drive the bus had climbed. When the house was almost out of sight, Jill stopped to look back at it. "It's sort of like we were running away from home," she said.

"We're not," her brother told her.

"I don't know."

"Well, I do. Listen, that's our house. Dad's dead, so it belongs to you and me."

"I don't want it," Jill said; and then, when the house was out of sight, "but it's the only home we've got."

The drive was long, but not impossibly so, and the highway—if it could be called a highway—stretched away to right and left at the end of it. Stretched silent and empty. "I was thinking if there were some cars we could flag one down," her brother said. "Or maybe the bus will come by."

"There's grass in the cracks."

"Yeah, I know. This way, Jelly." He set out, looking as serious as always, and very, very determined.

She trotted behind. "Are you going into Poplar Hill with me?"

"If we can flag down a car first, or a truck or anything, I'm going with them if they'll take me. So are you."

She shook her head.

"But if we can't, I'm going to Poplar Hill like you say. Maybe there's somebody there, and if there is, maybe they'll help us."

"I'll bet somebody is." She tried to sound more confident than she felt.

"There's no picture on the TV. I tried all the channels."

He was three paces ahead of her, and did not look back.

"So did I." It was a lie, but she had tried several.

"It means there's nobody in the TV stations. Not in any of them." He cleared his throat, and his voice suddenly deepened, as the voices of adolescent boys will. "Nobody alive, anyhow."

"Maybe there's somebody alive who doesn't know how to work it," she suggested. After a moment's thought she added, "Maybe they don't have any electricity where they are."

He stopped and looked around at her. "We do."

"So people are still alive. That's what I said."

"Right! And it means a car might come past, and that's what *I* said."

A small bush, fresh and green, sprouted from a crevice in the middle of the highway. Seeing it, Jill sensed that some unknown and unknowable power had overheard them and was gently trying to show them that they were wrong. She shuddered, and summoned up all the good reasons that argued that the bush was wrong instead. "There were live people back at that place. The bus driver was all right, too."

The iron gates were still there, just as she had seen them the previous day, graceful and strong between their pillars of cut stone. The lions still snarled atop those pillars, and the iron sign on the iron bars still proclaimed Poplar Hill.

"They're locked," her brother announced. He rattled the lock to show her—a husky brass padlock that looked new.

"We've got to get in."

"Sure. I'm going to go along this wall, see? I'm going to look for a place where I can climb over, or maybe it's fallen down somewhere. When I find one, I'll come back and tell you."

"I want to go with you." Fear had come like a chill wind. What if Jimmy went away and she never saw him again?

"Listen, back at the house you were going to do this all by yourself. If you could do it by yourself, you can stay here for ten minutes to watch for cars. Now *don't follow me!*"

She did not; but an hour later she was waiting for him when he came back along the inside of the wall, scratched and dirty and intent on speaking to her through the gate. "How'd you get in?" he asked when she appeared at his shoulder.

She shrugged. "You first. How did you?"

"I found a little tree that had died and fallen over. It was small enough that I could drag it if I didn't try to pick up the root end. I leaned it on the wall and climbed up it, and jumped down."

"Then you can't get out," she told him, and started up a road leading away from the gate.

"I'll find some way. How did you get in?"

"Through the bars. It was tight and scrapy, though. I don't think you could." Somewhat maliciously, she added, "I've been waiting in here a long time."

The private road led up a hill between rows of slender trees that made her think of models showing off green gowns. The big front door of the big square house at the top of the hill was locked; and the big brass knocker produced only empty echoes from inside the house no matter how hard her brother pounded. The pretty pearl-colored button that she pressed sounded distant chimes that brought no one.

Peering though the window to the left of the door, she saw a mostly wooden chair with brown-and-orange cushions, and a gray TV screen. One corner of the gray screen read MUTE in bright yellow letters.

Circling the house they found the kitchen door unlocked, as they had left it. She was heaping corned beef hash out of her frying pan when the lights went out.

"That means no more hot food," she told her brother. "It's electric. My stove is."

"They'll come back on," he said confidently, but they did not.

That night she undressed in the dark bedroom they had made their own, in the lightless house, folding clothes she could not see and laying them as neatly as her fingers could manage upon an invisible chair before slipping between the sheets.

Warm and naked, her brother followed her half a minute later. "You know, Jelly," he said as he drew her to him, "we're probably the only live people in the whole world."

Petting Zoo

✦

R oderick looked up at the sky. It was indeed blue, but almost cloudless. The air was hot and smelled of dust.

"Here, children . . ." The teaching cyborg was pointedly not addressing him. "—*Tyrannosaurus rex*. Rex was created by an inadequately socialized boy who employed six Build-a-Critter kits . . ."

Sixteen.

"—which he duped on his father's Copystuff. With that quantity of GroQik . . ."

It had taken a day over two weeks, two truckloads of pigs that he had charged to Mother's account, and various other things that had become vague. For the last week, he had let Rex go out at night to see what he could find, and people would—people were bound to—notice the missing cattle soon. Had probably noticed them already.

Rex had looked out through the barn window while he was mooring his airbike and said, "I'm tired of hiding all day."

And he himself had said . . .

"Let's go for a ride." One of the little girls had raised her hand.

From the other side of the token barrier that confined him, Rex himself spoke for the first time, saying, "You will, kid. She's not quite through yet." His voice was a sort of growling tenor now, clearly forced upward as high as he could make it so as to seem less threatening. Roderick pushed on his suit's AC and shivered a little.

It had been cool, that day. Cool, with a little breeze he had fought the whole way over, keeping his airbike below the treetops and following groundtrucks when he could, pulled along by their wake.

Cold in the old barn, then—cold, and dusty—dust motes dancing in the sunbeams that stabbed between its old, bent, and battered aluminum panels.

Rex had crouched as he had before, but he was bigger now, bigger than ever, and his smooth reptilian skin had felt like glass, like ice under which oiled muscles stirred like snakes. He had fallen, and Rex had picked him up in the arms that looked so tiny on Rex but were bigger and stronger than a big man's arms, saying, "That's what these are for," and set him on Rex's shoulders with his legs—*his* legs—trying to wrap around Rex's thick, throbbing neck . . .

Had opened the big doors from inside, had gone out almost crawling and stood up.

It had not been the height. He had been higher on his airbike almost every day. It had not been his swift, swaying progress above the treetops, treetops arrayed in red, gold, and green so that it seemed that he followed Rex's floating head over a lawn deep in fallen leaves.

It had been—

He shrugged the thought away. There were no adequate words. Power? You bought it at a drugstore, a shiny little disk that would run your house-bot for three or four more years or your drill forever. Mastery? It was what people had held over dogs while private ownership had still been legal.

Dogs had four fangs in front, and that was it, fangs so small they did not even look dangerous. Rex had a mouthful, every one as long as Roderick's arm, in a mouth that could have chewed up an aircar.

No, it had not been the height. He had ridden over woods—this wood among them—often. Had ridden higher than this, yet heard the rustling of the leaves below him, the sound of a brook, an invisible brook of air. It had been the noise.

That was not right either, but it was closer than the others. It had been the snapping of the limbs and the crashing of the trees falling, or at least that had been a lot of it, the sound of their progress, the shattering, splintering wood. In part, at least, it had been the noise.

"He did a great deal of damage," the teaching cyborg was saying, as her female attendant nodded confirmation. "Much worse, he terrified literally hundreds of persons. . . ."

Sitting on Rex's shoulders, he had been able to talk almost directly into Rex's ear. "Roar."

And Rex had roared to shake the earth.

"Keep on roaring."

And Rex had.

The red-and-white cattle Rex ate sometimes, so short-legged they could scarcely move, had run away slowly only because they were too fat to run any faster, and one had gotten stepped on. People had run, too, and Rex had kicked over a little pre-fab shed for the fun of it, and a tractor-bot. Had waded hip deep through the swamp without even slowing down, and had forded the river. There were fewer building restrictions on the north side of the river, and the people there had really run.

Had run except for one old man with a bushy mustache, who had only stood and stared pop-eyed, too old to run, Roderick thought, or maybe too scared. He had looked down at the old man and waved; and their eyes had met, and suddenly—just as if the top of the old man's head had popped up so he could look around inside it—he had known what the old man was thinking.

Not guessed, known.

And the old man had been thinking that when he had been Roderick's age he had wanted to do exactly what Roderick was doing now. He had never been able to, and had never thought anybody would be. But some-body was, that kid up there in the polka-dot shirt was. So he, the old man, had been wrong about the whole world all his life. It was much more won-derful, this old world, than he, the old man, had ever supposed. So maybe there was hope after all. Some kind of a hope anyhow, in a world where things like this could go on, on a Monday right here in Libertyberg.

Before the old man could draw his breath to cheer, he had been gone, and there had been woods and cornfields. (Roderick's suit AC shuddered and quit.) And after lots of corn, some kind of a big factory. Rex had stepped on its fence, which sputtered and shot sparks without doing any-thing much; and then the aircar had started diving at them.

It had been red and fast, and Roderick remembered it as clearly as if he had seen it yesterday. It would dive, trying to hit Rex's head, and then the override would say, my gosh, that's a great big dinosaur! You're trying to crash us into a great big dinosaur, you jerk! The override would pull the aircar up and miss, and then it would give it back to the driver, and he would try the same thing all over.

Roderick had followed it with his eyes, especially after Rex started snapping at it, and the sky had been a wonderful cool blue with little white surgical-ball clouds strolling around in it. He had never seen a better sky—and he never would, because skies did not get any better than that one. After a while he had spotted the channel copter, flying around up there and taking his picture to run on everybody's threedeevid, and had made faces at it.

Another child, a scrubbed little girl with long, straight, privileged-looking yellow hair, had her hand up. "Did he kill a whole lot of people?"

The teaching cyborg interrupted her own lecture. "Certainly not, since there were no people in North America during the Upper Cretaceous. Human evolution did not begin—"

"This one." The scrubbed little girl pointed to Rex. "Did he?"

Rex shook his head.

"That was not the point at issue," the teaching cyborg explained. "Disruption is disrupting, and he and his maker disrupted. He disrupted, I should say, and his maker still more, since Rex would not have been in existence to disrupt had he not been made in violation of societal standards. No one of sensitivity would have done what he did. Someone of sensitivity would have realized at once that their construction of a large dinosaur, however muted in coloration—"

Rex interrupted her. "I'm purple. It's just that it's gotten sort of dull-lookin' now that I'm older. Looky here." He bent and slapped at his water trough with his disproportionately small hands. Dust ran from his hide in dark streaks, leaving it a faded mulberry.

"You are not purple," the teaching cyborg admonished Rex, "and you should not say you are. I would describe that shade as a mauve." She spoke to her female attendant. "Do you think that they would mind very much if I were to start over? I've lost my place, I fear."

"You mustn't interrupt her," the female attendant cautioned the little girl. "Early-Tertiary-in-the-Upper-Eocene-was-the-Moeritherium-the-size-of-a-tuber-but-more-like-a-hippopotamus."

"Yum," Rex mumbled. "Yum-yum!"

A small boy waved his hand wildly. "What do you feed him?"

"Tofu, mostly. It's good for him." The teaching cyborg looked at Rex as she spoke, clearly displeased at his thriving upon tofu. "He eats an air-truckload of it every day. Also a great deal of soy protein and bean curd."

"I'd like to eat the hippos," Rex told the small boy. "We go right past them every time I take you kids for a ride, and wow! Do they ever look yummy!"

"He's only joking," the teaching cyborg told the children. She caught her female attendant's left arm and held it up to see her watch. "I have a great deal more to tell you, children, but I'll have to do it while we're taking our ride, or we'll fall behind schedule."

She and her female attendant opened the gate to Rex's compound and went in, preceded, accompanied, and followed by small girls and boys. While most of the children gathered around him, stoking his rough, thick hide with tentative fingers, the teaching cyborg and her female attendant wrestled a stepladder and a very large howdah of white pentastyrene Wickedwicker from behind Rex's sleeping shed. For five minutes or more they struggled to hook the howdah over his shoulders and fasten the Velcro cinch, obstructed by the well-intended assistance of four little boys.

Roderick joined them, lifted the howdah into place, and released and refastened the cinch, getting it tight enough that the howdah could not slip to one side.

"Thank you," the female attendant said. "Haven't I seen you here before?"

Roderick shook his head. "It's the first time I've ever come."

"Well, a lot of men do. I mean it's always just one man all by himself, but there's almost always one."

"He used to lie down so that we could put it on him," the teaching cyborg said severely, "and lie down again so that the children didn't have to use the ladder. Now he just sits."

"I'm too fat," Rex muttered. "It's all that good tofu I get."

One by one, the children climbed the ladder, the teaching cyborg's female attendant standing beside it to catch each if he or she fell, cautioning each to grasp the railings and urging each to belt himself or herself in once he or she had chosen a seat. The teaching cyborg and her female attendant boarded last of all, the teaching cyborg resumed her lecture, and Rex stood up with a groan and began yet again the slow walk around the zoo that he took a dozen times a day.

It had been a fall day, Roderick reminded himself, a fall day bright and clear, a more beautiful day than days ever were now. A stiff, bright wind had been blowing right through all the sunshine. He had worn jeans, a Peoria White Sox cap, and a polka-dot shirt, had kept his airbike low where the wind wasn't quite so strong, had climbed on Rex's shoulders and watched as Rex had taken down the bar that held the big doors shut. . . .

"Now," the teaching cyborg said, "are there any additional questions?" and Roderick looked up just in time to see the corner of the white Wicked-wicker howdah vanish behind Rex's sleeping shed.

"Yes." He raised his hand. "What became of the boy?"

"The government assumed responsibility for his nurturing and upbringing," the teaching cyborg explained. "He received sensitivity training and reeducation in societal values and has become a responsible citizen."

When the teaching cyborg, her female attendant, and all the children had gone, Rex said, "You know, I always wondered what happened to you."

Roderick mopped his perspiring forehead. "You knew who I was all the time, huh?"

"Sure."

There was a silence. Far away, as if from another time or another world, children spoke in excited voices and a lion roared. "Nothing happened to me," Roderick said; it was clearly necessary to say something. "I grew up, that's all."

"Those reeducation machines, they really burn it into you. That's what I heard."

"No, I grew up. That's all."

"I see. Can I ask why you keep lookin' at me like that?"

"I was just thinking."

"Thinkin' what?"

"Nothing." With iron fists, stone shoulders, and steel-shod feet, words broke down the doors of his heart and forced their way into his mouth. "Your kind used to rule the Earth."

"Yeah." Rex nodded. He turned away, leaving Roderick his serpentine tail and wide, ridged back, both the color of a grape skin that has been chewed up and spit out into the dust. "Yeah," he mumbled. "You too."

Castaway

✦

We picked him up on some dead world nobody ever goes to. We did because we had a field problem that required a lot of tests, and that stuff is easier if you can just dodge in and out of the ship without worrying about the airlocks and how much air you're dumping every time you go outside. Bad as this place was, you could breathe—the air turned out to be real good, in fact—so we set down in a warm belt around the middle.

Warm's one of those words, you know? It was still cold enough for hightherms, and even with hightherms I blew on my fingers a lot. The sun was red and real close, but there didn't seem to be a lot of heat in it.

Anyway, he had been there twenty-seven years, he said, and I said, standard years or world years? and he said they were so close it didn't make any difference. World years were half an hour shorter now, he said, and I should've asked why *now*, had they been longer a while back? Only I didn't think of it right then.

"We got hit by the Atrothers," he said, so it had been back during the war all right, back before I was born. "We tried to get home, but we could see we couldn't make it. This place was close and we landed here."

We're not there anymore, I told him, we took off. Well, that shut him up for the rest of the week. So next time I tried not to say things like that. I know they had him up to Debriefing three times. So you know they never got much out of him, didn't get what they wanted, or they wouldn't have talked to him so much. Somebody said his mind was blown, and I guess that was sort of right.

Only he used to open up to me sometimes in the break area, and that's what I want to tell about. Then maybe I can stop thinking about him.

"There were only three of us," he said, "and Obert died the first year and Yarmouth the second year. I thought we were dying off one by one and I'd go next year if nobody came. But I didn't. We'd hung up the distress buoy. It didn't do a bit of good, but I stayed tough."

He looked at me then like I wanted to argue. I just said sure.

"The rations ran out," he said. "I had to eat whatever I could find. There's still a few plants. They're not good, but you can eat them if you boil them long enough and keep changing the water."

I said you were there all alone, huh? It must've been double duty.

Of course that shut him up again, but next day he came in about ten minutes after I got off shift. He sat down right where he'd sat before. All the tables are white and so are the chairs, so it doesn't make any difference where you sit, it's all the same. Only he knew somehow, and that's where he sat. I carried my caff over and sat down across from him and waited.

About ten minutes after that he said, "There was a woman. A woman was there with me. I wasn't alone. No. Not really. Not with her there."

I said you should have told us. We'd have taken her off too.

He just shook his head.

Later he said it was too late for her. "She's old," he said. "Old and ugly, and she can't think anymore. She tries to think of new things, but nothing comes. Nothing works now, and sometimes she can't think at all. She told me. You've got a good medpod. That's what they say."

I guess I nodded.

"I've been spending a lot of time in there. Maybe it's helping. I don't know. But it wouldn't help her."

Then he reached over and grabbed my wrist—his hand was like a vise. "We could have saved her. Earlier. We could have made her young again. We could have taken her away. We could have done it. Nothing stopping us."

Next day he wouldn't talk at all, or the day after that either. I guess I should have just let him alone, but I was sick of talking to the other guys in the crew. I'd been talking to them ever since I signed on, and I knew what they were going to say and the games they wanted to play, and what all their jokes were.

So I tried to figure out a way to get him going again. Everybody likes to brag, right? Especially when you can't check up on them. The next time he was in the break room I sat down next to him and said tell me some more about this woman that was dirtside with you. I guess you got plenty, huh?

He just looked at me for maybe two minutes. I knew he was talking in his head. He'd been alone for so long. I ran into a guy once who had tended a navigation beacon way out on the Rim for ten years. You do that, and the severance pay's a fortune. Go in at thirty—you've got to be at least thirty—and come out at forty, rich for life. What they don't tell you is that most of them go crazy. Anyway, he said you get to talking to yourself. When they finally pull you out you try to stop and you don't talk to anybody, just in your head. You haven't talked to anybody for so long that talking out loud is the same as talking to yourself as far as you're concerned.

Finally he said, "She was old. Terribly old and dying. I thought I told you."

I said, yeah, I guess you did.

"Millions and millions of years old, and used to think she'd never die. But it was all over for her, and she knew it. We never wanted to help her. We never wanted to save her, and now we couldn't if we wanted to. It's too late. Too late . . ."

After that he started to cry. I listened to it and sort of tapped his shoulder and talked to him for as long as it took to finish my caff. But he didn't say anything else that day.

The next day he sort of motioned to me to come over and sit with him. He'd never done that before. So I did.

"She could make pictures in your head." He was whispering. "Show you things. Did I tell you about that?"

He never had, and I said so.

"They're trying to make me forget the leaves. Billions and billions of leaves, all sizes and shapes and shades of green, and the rising sun turning them gold. Sometimes the bottom was a different color, and when the wind blew the whole tree would change."

I wanted to ask what a tree was, but I figured I could just look it up and kept quiet.

"She used to show me birds, too. Wonderful birds. Some that could sleep while they flew. Some that sang and flew at the same time. All kinds of colors and all kinds of shapes. You know what a bird is?"

Naturally I said I didn't.

"It's a kind of flying animal. Some of them made music. A lot of the little ones did. Singing, you know, only they sounded more like flutes. It was beautiful!"

I said, did they know "Going to Bunk with You Tonight," because that's my favorite song. He said they didn't play our music they played their own, and he sang some of it for me, looking like he was going to kiss somebody. I didn't like it much, but I pretended I did. I wanted to know how she had showed him all this and made him hear it, because I think it would be really nice if I could do that, and useful, too. He said he didn't know, and after that he was pretty quiet till I'd finished my caff.

Then he said, "You know how a man puts part of himself into a woman?"

I said sure.

"It's like that, only in the brain. She puts part of herself into your brain."

Naturally I laughed, and I said was it as good for you as it was for her, and did you feel the ship jump?

And he said, "It wasn't good for her at all, but it was wonderful for me, even the time I watched the last bird die."

There was a lot of other stuff, too, some of it happy and some really, really sad. I will remember it, but I don't think you would want to hear about all of it. Finally he told me how sick she had been, and how he had sat beside her night after night. He would pick up her hand and hold it, and try to think of something he could say that would make her feel better, only he could never think of anything and every time he tried it was just so dumb he made himself shut up. He would hold her hand, like I said up there, and sort of stroke it, and after a while it would melt away and he would have to look for it and pick it up all over. I didn't understand that at all. I still don't.

But finally he thought of something he could say that didn't make him feel worse, and he thought maybe it had even made her feel better, a little. He said, "I love you." It seemed like it worked, he said, and so he said it again and again.

And that is all I remember about him except for when we set down and he left the ship. Only I want to say this. I know he was crazy, and if you read this and want to tell me I was crazy too to hang out with him in the break area like I did for so long, that's all right. I knew he was crazy, but he was somebody new and it was kind of fun to pull it out of him like I did and see what he would say.

Besides, he was a lot older than I am and his face had all these lines because of being down there so long and practically starving, so he was fun to look at, and the other thing was the color. The ship is all white, the walls and ceilings and floor and everything else. That makes it easy to spot fluid leaks and sometimes shorts that start little fires someplace. But all that white and the white uniforms and so on seem like they just suck the color out of everything except blood.

Only it never sucked the color out of him, and that made him special to me. Nice to look at, and fun, too. I remember seeing him walking along Corridor A the last time. He was headed for the lock and going out, and I knew it from the old, old dress blues and the little bag in his hand. And I thought, oh shit that's the last color we had and now he's going and this really licks.

And it did, too.

So I ran and said good-bye and how much I was going to miss him and called him Mate and all that. You know. And he was nice and we talked a little bit more, just standing there in Corridor A.

Of course I put my elbow in it, the way I always did sooner or later. I said about the woman that had been dirtside with him, was she still alive when we took him off, because he'd said how sick she was and I thought he wouldn't go off and leave her.

He sort of smiled. I never had seen a smile like that before, and I don't ever want to see another one. "She was and she wasn't," he said. "There were things inside her, eating the corpse. Does that count?"

I said no, of course not, for it to count they would have to have been part of her.

"They were," he said, and that was the real end of it.

Only he turned to go, and I wanted to walk with him at least till he got to the lock. Which I did. And talking to himself I heard him say, "She had been so beautiful. Just so damned beautiful."

All right, his mind had blown, like everybody says. But sometimes I can almost see him again when I'm in my bunk and just about asleep. He smiles, and there's somebody standing behind him, but I can't quite see her.

Not ever.

The Fat Magician

✦

May 3, 2000
Franklin A. Abraham, Ph.D., Chair
Comparative Religion and Folklore
U. of Nebraska Lincoln
Lincoln NE 68501
Amerika

Dear Frank,

I have quite a tale to tell. It is not exactly folklore. Not yet, but it is fast becoming folklore. It is a mystery story if you will, and centers about a man in league with the Devil, who was on the side of the angels. It is also a story of murder, though there is no mystery about the murder. Most signally, it is a horror story, by far the most horrible I have ever been made aware of.

And it is a ghost story, on top of everything else. You will have to accept my own testimony as regards the ghost; so let me say here that everything I am about to tell you is true to the best of my knowledge. I am going to stretch nothing, because there is nothing that requires stretching. I am not, however, going to tell you the *whole* truth. I cannot do that without betraying the pledge I gave this morning to a most attractive woman who has been exceedingly kind to me. I know, Frank, that is not a thing you would wish me to do.

As you will probably be able to tell from the postmark, I am not yet in Vienna. Trains do not break down—or so I have always thought. It turns out I was wrong. I am not sorry, but I am very glad that I allowed myself a few days in Vienna before the opening of the WFC.

In brief, I woke up this morning and found my train at a dead stop between two flower-spangled mountain meadows when it ought to have been in the Vienna station. I have my demotic, as you know, and fair command of Spanish. My German, I fear, is merely amusing. Amusing to me, I mean. Actual Germans and Austrians are inclined to burst into tears.

By jumping up and down and shouting, I was able to make the conductor ("Herr Schaffner") understand that I wished to know why we were not in Vienna. Herr Schaffner, by shouting back, stamping, spitting in my face, and wiping his own with his handkerchief, was able to convey to me that ein gross Herr Shaft (I suppose the crankshaft) of our engine had broken. In all fairness, I must admit Herr Schaffner's English is better than my German. Say, about ten percent better.

Soon we were joined by a handsome young guy called Heinz, a grad student who speaks English a good deal better than I shall ever speak German. Heinz conferred with Herr Schaffner, and explained to me that the Austrian State Railway would not be able to spare us a new engine for a day or so. We were welcome to stay on the train until the new engine arrived, eating such food as there was in the dining car. Or we could walk three kilometers down the tracks to R——, where there would be restaurants and so forth. When the new engine arrived, the train would pull into the station at R——and stay there for an hour or more collecting its passengers.

Heinz and I conferred and decided to walk to the village and perhaps take rooms there, I promising to buy his breakfast if he would interpret for me. We fetched the overnight bags that were all we were permitted to have in our compartments and off we went, hurrying along before the rest of passengers (they were still yawning and dressing for the most part) came along to overwhelm the village facilities.

"I myself am living not so far from this place when I was a child in Freistadt," Heinz informed me. "This R——, it is where the famous and terrible Ernst S——lived."

Naturally I wanted to know what made Herr S——famous and terrible.

"He is a Hexenmeister." Heinz grinned and made magical gestures.

"A master of bad luck?"

Heinz laughed. "He will make you a dog or a toad, Herr Cooper. This is bad luck enough, ja? Only we do not worry now. He is dead. When I am little, the older kinder scare us with him, the big children."

After that I wanted to know a great deal more, as you can imagine; but Heinz could only tell me that "Fat Ernst" (this was the name used to frighten children, apparently) had been a giant, that he had disappointingly boasted but a single head, and most surprisingly that he had been a living, breathing man in Heinz's grandparents' time. Heinz's great uncle, a traveling salesman, had met him more than once; Heinz thought that he had died during World War II, and that he had probably been killed by a bomb.

We got to the village and soon found a snug das Café, where Heinz quizzed our waitress on my behalf. She called "Fat Ernst," Ernst the Great (which interested me), agreed that he had been a bad man, but seemed to feel a secret sympathy for him. An older man with a bristling mustache stopped at our table on his way out and snapped something in German that I could not understand, at which our waitress colored. When she had gone, Heinz explained in a whisper that the other patron had called Fat Ernst a liar and a thief.

Our Frühstücks came (bread, butter, pastries, cold cuts, three kinds of cheese, and the wonderful Austrian coffee), and with all the other things an old man who had been drinking his coffee at a table in the back, speaking a German so slow and simple that even I could understand most of what he said: Fat Ernst had been a friend of the Devil's. It was better not to talk, or even think, about such people.

Properly chastened, Heinz and I confined our conversation to the excellence of the food and the length of our delay for the remainder of the meal.

When I paid our bill, the owner of the cafe said in halting English. "Quick you will want das Mittgassen, ja? In R——we have ein fine Gasthaus." He pointed. "Der Romantik Hotel S——. Sehr alt. Sehr in-ter-es-ting. Gutes Speise."

Well, Frank, I have never claimed to be the sharpest knife in the drawer; but even I could not help noticing that he was—yes, earnestly—recommending a place other than his own, and that the name of the "Romantic Hotel" he recommended was also that of Fat Ernst.

In retrospect, we should have found a cab. As it was we assumed that der Romantik Hotel S——was in the village; and when we found out (by asking directions on a street in which all the houses seemed to be been modeled on cuckoo clocks) that it was not, that it was nearby. As, alas, it was not. Frank, the Chinese are right. Uphill miles *are* longer. So are uphill kilometers. By the time we had gone wrong, and found the right road again, and stopped a couple of times to rest and hold lengthy conversations concerning job opportunities in American universities, and Austrian folklore, and American folklore (poor Heinz thought that Pecos Bill and Paul Bunyan were legitimate, but had never heard of the Boss in the Wall), and German and Russian and Polish folklore, to say nothing of the opportunities awaiting an unmarried man in Vienna . . . Well, it was nearly lunchtime when got there; and I honestly think I could have sat down, taken off my shoes, and eaten Heinz's lunch as well as my own.

Now I'm going to describe Gertrun's hotel. Pay attention, Frank. This stuff is important.

Although the setting is lovely, the building itself is not. What it is, is old. It was built (Gertrun says) in 1757 as a hunting lodge. Her family, the S——s, took it over in 1860 and have operated it as a hotel ever since. It is of weathered gray stone, is as square as a bouillon cube, and has three stories, with one of those high, pointed roofs you see everywhere here and (I suppose) a good-sized attic underneath it. Parlor, dining room, kitchen, hotel office, et cetera on the ground floor, with a wine cellar and other cellars underground. High ceilings in all the rooms. Go up the stairs and you find a square landing on which you might drill troops, with a massive carved railing. This landing gives access to the twelve rather old-fashioned bedrooms on the floor. The stair continues to the floor above where there are more rooms; I did not bother to count those, but Gertrun says those are smaller, so sixteen up there, possibly.

Gertrun owns and runs the place. Picture a substantial woman between thirty-five and forty, very blond, with a round, smiling face, a toddler's complexion, and truly beautiful clear blue eyes. She showed us into a dark-paneled dining room ornamented with the antlers of deer that had died before any of us were born, assured us that lunch would be ready in a minute or two, and stayed to chat with us. At first I supposed, as I think anybody would, that she was an employee; I asked if there were any members of the owner's family about.

"I am here, Mein Herr. I am Gertrun S——."

I apologized, and we introduced ourselves and explained about the train.

When I mentioned Ernst S——, I unleashed a flood of information. He had been Gertrun's grandfather. A giant? Oh, ja! She rose on tiptoe and stretched a hand as high as she could reach to indicate his height, and embraced an imaginary barrel show his girth. Three hundred kilos—four hundred. She did not know, but he had been sehr gross, huge.

Heinz asked several questions I was too dense to understand; Gertrun replied in German, but I caught the word *Jude.*

Heinz turned to me, smiling. "He hid people from the Nazis when they took power in our country, Herr Doktor. Jews—"

Gertrun interrupted in German.

"She says he had a Jew, a priest, and a man that wore dresses in his secret room at the same time once." Heinz roared with unfeigned delight. "What a rumpus that must have been!"

"They wished to send them to the camps," Gertrun explained. "Mein Grossvater did not like." She shook her head violently. "He was before on die stage, ein performer."

I said that I had thought the Nazis sent only Jews to their concentration camps, at which Gertrun became very somber. "It does not matter what they say, Herr Doktor Cooper. When such mans have authority, they send to their camps what they do not like. They send Jews und the priest does not like that, und so they send the priest. A man which does Lippenstift." Her finger signaled lipstick. "He . . ." (She groped for a word, one hand on her own soft stomach.) "They grow sick from seeing it. So him auch. Him also. Mein Grossvater hides him like those other mans."

I asked whether the Nazis had found them.

"Nein! To Schweiz they go." Gertrun's eyes, which were very round already, became rounder still. "Again und again der Nazis come! All night almost for many, many . . . Mein vater ist a little boy, Herr Doktor. He hears them up und down die steps, in den cellars, everywhere. Into his room they come, und under his bed look. If him they frighten, mein Grossvater will show wo ist das Geheimzimmer. This they think, but they make der mistake."

"The secret room," Heinz translated.

"Never! Never his secret room he shows! Kommen mit, I show you his chair."

She led us back into the parlor. It was an enormous chair, like a throne. The seat was as high as a table and four feet across, and the legs looked sturdy enough to support a small house. " 'Search!' he tells them. 'I sit till you are done. You leave, you close mein door.' So they think the secret room it is he sits on. They make him get up. They move his chair." She showed us a nick in the sturdy oak back that the Nazis had supposedly made. "They take up der carpet. They drill through our floor, but ist der Weinkellar they searched every night. There they find ein klein Judsch Mutze," she touched the back of her head, "und mein Grossvater laughs."

Naturally Heinz and I wanted to know where the secret room was.

Gertrun's face went blank. "I do not know, Herr Doktor. Nobody knows but mein Grossvater. I see in die Kuche. You will be hungry, ja?" She hurried away.

"She knows," Heinz told me.

"Of course she does," I said. "What I'd like to know is why she doesn't want us to."

From that time until our lunches arrived, Heinz tapped panels and moved pictures, and ran up the stairs to the floors on which the guest rooms were located, without finding anything. He went back to the train after lunch, but I decided to rent a room at the Romantik Hotel S——, enjoy a good dinner (there is excellent food all over Austria, but our lunches had been superb) and a good breakfast today before I re-boarded.

"In Juni will be full," Gertrun told me. "Ist when young people ist married. They come then to hike und climb. Now you have mein best."

It was indeed a large room, and beautifully furnished with antiques. I have seen more dramatic views than the one afforded by its four wide lace-curtained windows, but few if any that were lovelier.

"There und there ist dem doors for des rooms next door." Gertrun pointed them out to me. "Sometimes two ist rented together. For this die Hotelrechnung for number two ist half. But you have die Bolzen. Chains mit locks die handles of them both holds, you see?" She demonstrated, shaking the handle of one of the bolts. "Here ist keys to der locks for dem chains. So you know nobody comes und bother you. You must give back to me mit der key of das room when away you go. If you not, I must telfonieren der Schlosser from R——." She pantomimed cutting the shackle.

I promised that I would certainly return all her keys, and asked whether she had been in show business like her grandfather, praising her appearance and melodious voice.

She laughed. "Nein! Nein! But I have picture. You would like to see?"

I thought she meant a picture of herself, but she led me to her office, a small room off the parlor, and showed me a framed theatrical poster on which rabbits bounded, rings flew, and maidens floated about an imposing man in evening dress—a man already portly, although from what Gertrun told me he must have been quite a bit younger in those days than his waxed mustache and full beard made him appear. Behind him a shadowy, Mephistophelian figure taller even than he stooped as though to whisper some dreadful confidence. Fat Ernst had been a conjurer!

"Till his vater ist no more," Gertrun explained. "Then he comes home to take care of mein hotel."

"With the secret room in which he hid the Jew and those others."

"Ja, ja." Gertrun looked a trifle flustered. "Many more also, Herr Doktor."

"No doubt. The room that the Nazis were never able to find, even though they searched this building repeatedly and no doubt systematically, since Austrians are every bit as systematic as Germans."

"Ja. Never." She was at ease now, and smiling. She has good teeth and is very attractive when she smiles.

"You said that they found a yarmulke in the wine cellar?"

Gertrun nodded. "In die attic, too, they find something once. I do not remember."

"A rosary or a crucifix, I'm sure. A breviary, perhaps. Something of that kind." I took her hand, "Frau S——, I don't know why you're so anxious to keep the location of your grandfather's secret room a secret, but I want you to know that whatever harm others may intend to you or your family, I intend none. I like you—more than I should, perhaps. And yet I can't help being curious. Would it trouble you if I had a look at your wine cellar? And the attic?"

"Nein!" She shook her head violently. "I take you myself, Herr Doktor."

I told her she need not bother and went up to my room, where I immersed myself in thought as well as hot water.

Fat Ernst's having been a conjurer had given me the clue. When I had dried myself and changed my underwear, shirt, and socks, I unlocked the heavy wrought-iron bolt on one of the connecting doors and tried to move it. It traveled a sixteenth of an inch, perhaps, but no farther.

Let me interrupt myself here, Frank. On the first page of this letter, I promised you a mystery. It is the location of Fat Ernst's secret room. You have all the facts that I had now. Where was it?

Gertrun and I breakfasted together the next morning in her private apartment—a meal large enough to last me all day. Over coffee, I asked her whether her grandfather himself had ever spoken of a secret room. Had he said, for example, that there was one?

She shrugged. "Gone he was before I am here to hear him, Liebling."

"I doubt that he did, although he may well have said that no one would ever find it. In that he was quite correct. No one ever will, because it does not exist."

She stared without speaking.

"Allow me to tell you, so you'll know I'm not bluffing. Then I will give you my word that I will never reveal the name or location of this hotel, or the name of your family. Never. Not to anyone."

"Danke." I had taken her hand as I spoke, and she managed to smile. "Danke schön."

"There's only one kind of secret room that can't be found no matter how thorough the search, Gertrun. It's a secret room that does not exist. Your grandfather put the people he was hiding into the ordinary rooms of his hotel. Many hotels have connecting doors between rooms, as yours does. And all of those I have ever seen have sliding bolts on both sides of the doors; I cannot enter my neighbor's room unless his bolt is drawn back as well as my own, and he cannot enter mine. In this hotel, however, those bolts are connected by a slot through the door. I don't know the word in German, but an American conjurer would say they were gimmicked. Or gaffed. That's why you think it necessary to chain and padlock them."

I waited for her to speak, but she just stared; I saw her lower lip tremble.

"When the Nazis put their room key into the lock, the person hiding in that room had only to slip into the next and hold the bolt of the connecting door closed until he heard the searchers leave and he could return. When the Jew's room was being searched, he could slip into the priest's, and when the priest's was searched he could slip into the Jew's. Or both could slip into the room occupied by the transvestite. I would imagine that they were careful to sleep on the floor, and so on—not to leave any indication that the room had been occupied that could not be snatched up and carried away. As for the yarmulke in the wine cellar, and whatever may have been found in the attic, they were false clues planted by your very clever and very brave grandfather to throw the searchers off the track."

She nodded and gave me a shaky smile.

"How did he die? Was it an Allied bomb? That's what Heinz thought."

"Nein. These Nazis here take him."

That puzzled me. I said, "But they can have had no evidence if they never found—"

"For ein trial, Herr Doktor?" Gertrun's smile was bitter then. "Evidence they do not need. They take him, und he ist dead."

It required some time to digest. That immense body sprawled in a gas chamber. Half a dozen Storm Troopers to drag it out and get it on the truck. Then I said, "You keep his secret—"

"For nachst, Herr Doktor. For next time."

There you have it, Frank. But my train has not come yet, so let me tie up a few details. I promised you a mystery, and I think you will agree that I gave you one.

A murder, as well. Was not Fat Ernst murdered by his government? If not, how did he die?

That seems to me the greatest of all horror stories. When the millennium now ending began, government meant a king; and that king, whatever else he might be, was his nation's leader. He might wage war upon his neighbors, but he would have been thought mad if he had waged war upon his followers. Bandits and cutpurses abounded, and they constituted a very real and present danger to everyone except the strongest; but the king was the sworn foe of all such criminals. In the century we are just now closing out, we ordinary men and woman have been in much greater danger from our own governments than from all the criminals in the world.

In Nazi Germany, and not long afterward here in beautiful, smiling Austria, the government declared that Jews must die. The priest objected, so the priest had to die too. The man who cross-dressed disgusted the government's functionaries, and he was added to the list.

Which is more disgusting, a man in a dress or a government that murders the people who created it to protect them? Which is more horrible, Frank? Is it the werewolf of our folklore, or this soulless monster squatting over the corpse of its nation, its hands running with innocent blood?

Sincerely,
Sam Cooper

PS. Still no train, although I spent nearly an hour sipping coffee in das snug Café. Thus I have time to tell you that last night about one thirty I woke to the sound of footsteps, footsteps slow and so heavy that the timbers of the landing creaked and groaned. Very distinctly, I heard the door open and saw a vertical bar of very bright-seeming light from stairwell. Somebody standing not more than a step from the bed in which I lay said softly but unmistakably, "Ist gut," and the door closed again. I got out of bed and turned on a light, but the only other person in the room was sleeping soundly. All three doors were securely fastened, as we had left them.

I intend to return here to R——for a week or so after the conference to investigate this and other matters.

Hunter Lake

✦

"You'll get arthritic eyes," Susan declared, "if you keep watching that thing. Turn it off and listen a minute."

Ettie pressed Mute.

"Off!"

Obediently, Ettie pressed the red button. The screen went dark.

"You know what Kate told us. There's a lake here—a beautiful lake that isn't on anybody's map."

"I did the Internet search, Mom. Remember?"

"And you sit watching an old TV with rabbit ears in a rented cabin." Susan was not to be distracted. "You know what your father says—people who get eyeball arthritis see only what they're supposed to see, like that TV screen. Their eyes stiffen—"

Ettie turned off the TV and brought out the artillery. "If Dad's so smart and such a good father, why did you divorce him?"

"I didn't say he was a good husband. Come on! Get your coat. Don't you want to look for a haunted lake?"

Thinking it over, Ettie decided she did not. For one thing, she did not care for ghosts. For another, she was pretty sure this was a dream, and it might easily turn into a bad one. A haunted lake would give it entirely too much help. Aloud she said, "You're going to write a magazine article and get paid. What's in it for me?"

"I'll take pictures, too," Susan declared. "Lots of pictures. It's supposed to be very scenic. If a ghost shows up in one of my pictures, the sale will be a . . ."

"Snap," Ettie supplied.

"Foregone conclusion."

The car door slammed, and the car pulled smoothly away from the one-room log cabin that had been their temporary home. Ettie wondered whether she had left the TV on and decided she had. Would Nancy Drew have remembered to turn it off? Absolutely.

"The Indians performed unspeakable rites there," Susan continued. Studying Ettie from the corner of her eye, she concluded that more selling was in order. "They tortured their white prisoners, gouging out their eyes and scalping them while they were still alive. Isn't that exciting?"

"Native Americans never did anything like that." Ettie sounded positive, even to herself.

"Oh yes, they did! A hunter found the lake hundreds of years afterward, and took his family there for a picnic because it was so pretty. His little daughter wandered away and was never seen again."

"I knew I wasn't going to like this."

"Her spirit haunts it, walking over the water and moaning," Susan declared with relish.

"You can't possibly know that."

"It's what everybody says, Kate says. So today we'll find it—you and me, Ettie—and we'll stay out there all night and take lots and lots of pictures. Then I can write about how a sudden chill descended at midnight, a chill our struggling little fire could not dispel, seeming to rise from the very waters that—"

"*Mother!*"

"Harbor the ghosts of hundreds of Mohicans massacred by the Iroquois and thousands—no, innumerable—Iroquois massacred by white settlers, waters said to harbor pike of enormous size, fattened for centuries upon—ah! There's the farmhouse."

It looked horrible, Ettie decided. "Burning that down would be an improvement."

"They're old and poor. It's not polite to make fun of old people. Or poverty." A wrench at the wheel sent the car gliding into a farmyard from which no chicken fled in terror.

"They're dead, if you ask me." Ettie pointed toward the little cemetery that should have been the front yard. Its cast-iron fence was rusting to pieces, and its thin limestone monuments leaned crazily.

Susan took her key from the ignition. "Just a private burying ground, Ettie. Lots of old farms have them."

"Right in front of the house?"

"I think that's touching. They cared about their dead." They were climbing broken steps to a ramshackle porch innocent of paint. "Probably they sat out here on rockers and talked to them."

"Cozy."

"It is, really. The dead are nearer the living than you know, Ettie."

You're dead yourself, Ettie thought rebelliously, and ohmyGod how I miss you.

Susan knocked. The knocks echoed inside the old farmhouse. There was no other sound.

"Let's go," Ettie suggested.

"I'm right here, dear."

"I know you are," Ettie said. "I'm scared anyway. Let's go. Please?"

"Kate says there's an old man here who knows precisely where Hunter Lake is. I'm going to question him and tape everything he says. I'm going to take his picture, and take pictures of this house."

Somebody behind them said, "No, you're not."

Ettie found that she had turned to look, although she had not wanted to. The woman behind them was old and bent, and looked blind.

Susan smiled, laid a hand on Ettie's shoulder, and tried to grasp that shoulder in a way that would make it clear to Ettie that she, Susan, was counting on her not to misbehave. "Mrs. Betterly?"

"Ain't no business of yours, young woman."

"My name's Susan Price," Susan continued bravely, "and my daughter and I are friends—good friends—of Kate Eckert's. We're looking for Hunter Lake—"

The old woman moaned.

"And Kate said your husband would help us."

"He won't talk to no women," the old woman declared. "He hates women. All of us. Been fifty years since he spoke civil to a woman, he tolt me once."

Susan looked thoughtful. "My daughter isn't a woman yet."

"*Mother!*"

"Really now, Ettie. What would Nancy Drew say?"

" 'I'm getting out of here,' if she had any sense."

"He won't hurt you. How old is he, Mrs. Betterly?"

"Eighty-seven." The old woman sounded proud. "He's ten year old'n me, and won't never die. Too mean."

Susan gave Ettie her very best smile. "You see? What are you afraid of? That he'll hit you with his walker? He might call you a name, at worst."

"Or shoot me."

"Nonsense. If he shot little girls for asking polite questions, he'd have been sent to prison long ago." Susan turned to the old woman. "All right if Ettie tries?"

"Door's not locked," the old woman said. After a moment she added grudgingly, "That's a brave little gal."

As though by magic, Ettie found that her hand was on the doorknob.

"He'll be in the parlor listenin' to us. Or if he ain't, in the sittin' room. If he ain't in the sittin' room, he'll be in the kitchen for sure."

The hinges are going to squeak, Ettie told herself. I just know it.

They did, and the floorboards creaked horribly under her feet. She closed the door so that her mother would not see her fear and pressed her back against it.

Outside, Susan endeavored to peep through several windows, returned to her car, and got her camera. "All right for me to take your picture, Mrs. Betterly?"

"Just fog your film," the old woman said. "Always do."

"Then you don't mind." Susan snapped the picture, being sure to get in a lot of the house.

In it (it appeared immediately on the back of her camera) the old woman was holding a bouquet of lilies. "Where did you get the flowers?" Susan asked.

"Picked 'em," the old woman explained. "Grow wild 'round here. Buttercups, mostly."

"Where did they go?" Susan tried to hide her bewilderment.

"Threw 'em away once your picture was took."

Inside, Ettie was poking around the parlor, pausing every few seconds to look behind her. The carpet, she noticed, was too small for the room, torn and moth-eaten. Dust covered the bare floor, and there were no footprints in the dust save her own.

He isn't here, she thought. He hasn't been here for a long, long time.

And then: I could take something. A souvenir. Anything. None of this stuff is doing anybody any good, and I've earned it.

There was a glass-topped case at the end of one of the divans. It held old coins and arrowheads, and the top was not locked. She selected a worn little coin with a crude picture of a Native American on it, and slipped it into her pocket. It had not looked valuable, and she would have it always to remember this day and how frightened she had been.

There was no one in the sitting room and no one in the kitchen. No one in the dining room, either.

A crude stair took her upstairs as effortlessly as an escalator. He's old, she thought, I'll bet he's sick in bed.

There were three very old-fashioned bedrooms, each with its own small fireplace. All were empty.

He's gone, Ettie told herself happily. He's been gone for years and years. I can tell Mother anything.

Outside again, speaking to Susan from the porch, she said, "Do you want everything, or just the important parts?"

"Just the important parts."

"Where's the old lady?"

"She went away." For an instant, Susan forgot to look perky. "I turned around, and she wasn't there. Did her husband call you names?"

That was easy. Ettie shrugged. "You said you just wanted the important stuff. Here it is. He said for us to go home."

Susan sighed. "That's not what I sent you in to find out."

"Well, that was the important thing." Ettie did her best to sound reasonable.

"All right, everything. But leave out the names."

"Okay. He said, 'Little lady, that lake's a real bad place, so don't you ever forget you're a grown woman and got a Ph.D. and a daughter of your own.' Am I supposed to do the dialect?"

"No."

"Fine. He also said, 'If you got to go there, you time it so your alarm goes off before anything bad happens. You go home. One way or the other. That's all I'm going to tell you. Get on home.' "

Curious, Susan asked, "Did he really call you little lady?"

"Heck no. You said to leave out the names so I did."

Susan sighed. "I suppose it's better that way. How did he say to get to the lake?"

"He didn't." Ettie shrugged. "Want me to go in and ask him again?"

"Will you?"

"Not unless you tell me to."

"All right. Ettie, you get yourself back in there and tell him we *must* find Hunter Lake. Don't take no for an answer. You have to be firm with men, and you might as well learn now."

Nodding, Ettie went back inside. It would be smart, she told herself, to spend quite a bit of time in there. She pulled a book off the shelf in the parlor and opened it. *The Alhambra,* by Washington Irving. It looked as though it had never been read.

After a minute or two, she realized that her mother was trying to peer through the very dirty windowpane and the filthy curtains, and went into the sitting room. There was a nice old rocker in there. She sat in it and rocked awhile, reading Washington Irving.

Outside again, blinking in the sunlight, she realized that she had never really decided what to say when she came out. To buy time, she cleared her throat. "You really want to hear this?"

"Yes. Of course."

"Okay, first he asked me all about you. That was after I had said you kept sending me back in. He said you sounded like a real bitch, and if you came in he'd get the chamber pot and throw shit at you."

"Ettie!"

"Well, you said you wanted to hear it. After that he explained to me about Hunter Lake. He said didn't I know why they called it that? I said because a hunter found it. He said that was wrong. He said it was 'cause it hunted people. He said it could move all around just like a bear and climb trees—"

Susan stamped her foot. "We want directions."

"What do you mean, 'we'?"

"Did he give you any directions? Any directions at all?"

"Just go home. I told you that the first time."

"We need directions, not stories. Go back in there and tell him so."

Ettie walked through the empty house, slowly, stopping to stare at things and open drawers, until she felt that something was following her. When she did, she hurried back outside, slamming the door and running down off the porch. "I'm not going back in there! Never! Never any more. You can ground me forever! I won't!"

Susan studied her, her lips pursed. "That bad, huh?"

"*Yes!*"

"Did he give you directions?"

Mutely, Ettie went to the car and got in. Two minutes passed before Susan slipped into the driver's seat next to her. "Ettie?"

Ettie said nothing, and Susan started the engine.

"Get out of here," Ettie told her. "Pull out onto the road again. Turn left."

"That's away from the cabin. I thought you wanted to go home."

"Home-home," Ettie said. "Not away-home. Turn left."

"Our bags are back at the cabin."

"Left."

Susan turned left.

"Go down this road," Ettie said, "till you see a road off to the right through the cornfield. There's no sign and it's easy to miss."

Wanting to do more than glance at her, Susan slowed instead. Twenty miles an hour. Fifteen. Ten.

"Slower," Ettie told her. "Follow it to the woods. Stop the car and get out. Look for the path. Follow the path to the house. A Injun named George Jones lives in the house. He knows. Give him ten dollars."

"You said 'Injun,'" Susan muttered. "You never even say *Indian*."

Ettie said nothing.

Half a mile later, Susan saw the road, braked too late, backed up, and turned down it—a red dirt road barely wide enough for a farm truck, two ruts flanking a strip of grass and weeds.

When the road would take them no farther, she and Ettie got out.

"Please don't lock the car," Ettie said. "I've got a feeling we might want to get in and get away quick."

Susan stared, then shrugged. "I think I see the path. I'm going down it. You can wait in the car if you want to, but it may be quite a while."

"You won't leave the keys?"

"No."

"Two will be safer than one," Ettie said.

The house was a shack, perhaps ten feet by fifteen. An Indian woman was tending a tiny plot of vegetables. Susan said, "We're looking for George Jones," and the Indian woman straightened up and stared at her.

"We need his help. We'll pay him for it."

The Indian woman did not speak, and Ettie wanted to cheer.

Susan opened her purse and took a ten-dollar bill from her wallet. She showed it to the Indian woman. "Here it is. Ten dollars. That's what we'll pay him to guide us to Hunter Lake."

Something that was no expression Susan had ever seen before flickered in the Indian woman's eyes. And was gone. "He fish," she said.

"In Hunter Lake?"

Slowly, the Indian woman nodded.

Susan breathed a sigh and gave Ettie one triumphant glance. "Then take us to him, or tell us how to find him."

The Indian woman held out her hand, and Susan dropped the ten into it. The Indian woman clutched it, wadding it into a tiny ball.

"How do we get there?"

The Indian woman pointed. The path was so narrow as to be almost invisible even when they were on it. A game trail, Susan decided. "Deer made this," she told Ettie.

If Ettie spoke, twenty or thirty feet behind her, she could not be heard.

"They need water," Susan explained, "just like us. They must go to Hunter Lake to drink." Privately, she wondered how far it was, and whether her feet would hold up. She was wearing her jogging shoes, but she rarely jogged more than a couple of blocks. Ettie, in jeans, T-shirt, and loafers, was probably worse off still. But younger, Susan told herself. Ettie's a lot younger, and that counts for a lot. "Ettie?" She had stopped and turned.

"Yes, Mother?"

"Am I going too fast for you? I can slow down."

"A little bit."

Susan waited for her to catch up. "What are you thinking about?"

"Nothing."

Susan bent and kissed her. "Really, dear. I love you. You know that. I'll always love you."

Ettie shook her head. "That's not how it will be. Not really. I'll always love you, Mom."

Susan kissed her again. "Now tell me what's troubling you."

"I was wondering if I'd turned off the TV before we left."

"Really, dear?"

Ettie nodded.

"Is that all?"

"Why I'd told you that stuff. About the Native American. All this. I could have just said he wouldn't tell, only I didn't."

"Because you're an honest, decent person, Ettie."

Ettie shook her head. "Because he made me. I don't know how he did it, but he did."

"Well, come on." Susan turned and began to walk again. "It's probably right over the next hill."

"It's a long, long way," Ettie said despondently. "Besides, this path doesn't even go there. We'll walk until we're too tired to walk any more, and be lost in the woods. Nobody will ever find us."

In point of fact, Susan was right. The path skirted the crest of the hill and descended sharply through close-packed hardwoods. For almost twenty minutes Susan and Ettie picked their way through these, Susan holding up branches for Ettie, who hurried under them, waving away mosquitoes.

As abruptly as the explosion of a firework, they emerged into sunlight. Water gleamed at the bottom of a steep hillside thick with ferns. On the other side of the gleam, water like molten silver cascaded down the face of a miniature cliff.

Susan raised her camera. A hundred yards or so down to the water—from here, she could only suggest that by showing a few fern fronds at the bottom of the picture. Then the water, then the cliff with its waterfall, then white clouds in the blue sky, and thank God for sky filters.

She snapped the picture and moved to her left.

"Are we really going to stay here?" Ettie asked.

"Only overnight, dear. We'll have to carry some gear from the car—not the tent, just the sleeping bags and a little food. It won't be all that hard. Will you want to swim?"

Ettie shook her head, but Susan was looking through her viewfinder and did not see her. It wasn't really a hundred yards, she decided. More like fifty. She snapped the picture, and decided the next should be taken at the water's edge.

"Mom . . ."

She stopped and turned. "Yes, Ettie? What is it?"

"I wish you wouldn't go down there."

"Afraid I'll fall in? I won't, and I doubt that it's very deep close to shore." Susan turned and began walking downhill again. She was a little tired, she decided; even so, walking down a gentle slope over fern was remarkably easy.

"Mom!"

She stopped again.

"Where's the Native American man, Mom? Where's George Jones? He was supposed to be down here fishing. I can see the whole lake. There's nobody here but us."

Suddenly, Ettie was tugging at her arm, "It's coming up! Get back!"

It was, or at least it seemed to be. Surely the lake had not been that large.

"It's a natural phenomenon of some kind," Susan told Ettie, "like the tide. I'm sure it's harmless."

Ettie had released her arm. Ettie was running up the slope like the wind. A loafer flew off one foot as Susan watched, but Ettie never paused. She walked up the slope to the spot, found the loafer, and looked back at the water.

In a moment more it would be lapping her feet.

She turned and ran, pausing for a moment at the highest point of the path to watch the water and take another picture. That was probably a mistake, as she realized soon after. The water had circled the hill, not climbed it. She ran then, desperately, not jogging but running for all that she was worth, mouth wide and eyes bulging, her camera beating her chest until she tore it off and dropped it. The Indian shack was nowhere in sight; neither was her car. Woods gave way to corn, and corn to woods again, and the water was still behind her. When the land over which she staggered and stumbled rose, she gained on the water, when it declined, the water gained on her with terrifying rapidity.

Ettie had turned back to look for her, limping on tender feet. She met the water before she had gone far, and thereafter ran as desperately, leaving a trail of blood the water soon washed away. Twice she fell, and once crashed straight though a tangle of briars whose thorns did nothing at all to hold back the water behind her.

"Here, Ettie! Over here!"

She looked to her left, and tried to shout *Mom*. There was precious little breath left for Mom.

"It's our cabin! Over here!"

It was not. The cabin they had rented had been of logs. This was white clapboard.

"Get in!" Susan was standing in the doorway. (Behind Susan, Ettie glimpsed the flickering television screen.) Ettie stumbled in, and fell.

Susan slammed the door and locked it. "It'll try to get in under it," she said, "but we'll pack it with towels. Clothes. Anything." She had thrown her suitcase on the bed. She opened it.

Ettie raised her head. "I've got to wake up, Mom."

"We'll beat it!" Briefly, Susan bent to kiss her. "We've got to!"

Then Ettie faded and was gone, and Susan was alone in the clapboard cabin. Water crept past the towels and her terry-cloth robe to cover the cabin floor. When the water outside had risen higher than the windowsills, it crept under and around the sashes to dribble on the floor.

Henrietta woke sweating, terrified of something she could not name. Through the closed door, Joan said, "Everything's ready, Mom. You want to have your Mother's Day breakfast in bed?"

"No," Henrietta whispered. More loudly, "No. I don't want to stay in here. I'll be out in a minute, honey."

There were two robes in her closet, terry-cloth and silk. Henrietta put the silk one on over her nightgown and tied its belt with a sudden violence she could not have explained.

The bed was a mess, sheet and blanket twisted and half on the floor. As she paused to straighten it up before she left the bedroom, her eyes caught the dull red of old copper. Once the worn little coin was in her hand, memories came flooding back.

Bacon and waffles, real butter and almost-real maple syrup in the sunshine-yellow breakfast nook, and Joan spraying Pam on the waffle iron. "Coffee's on the stove," Joan announced.

Henrietta sat, put the penny on her plate, and stared at it. A minute passed, then two. At last she picked it up and dropped it into a pocket of her robe.

"Do you know," she told Joan, "I've just recalled how your grandmother died, after being wrong about it all these years. She drowned."

"Sure." Joan held the steaming coffeepot. She filled Henrietta's cup. "Fluid in her lungs. Uncle Ed told me."

The Boy Who Hooked the Sun

✦

On the eighth day a boy cast his line into the sea. The sun of the eighth day was just rising, making a road of gold that ran from its own broad, blank face all the way to the wild coastline of Atlantis, where the boy sat upon a jutting emerald; the sun was much younger then and not nearly so wise to the ways of men as it is now. It took the bait.

The boy jerked his pole to set the hook, and grinned, and spat into the sea while he let the line run out. He was not such a boy as you or I have ever seen, for there was a touch of emerald in his hair, and there were flakes of sun-gold in his eyes. His skin was sun-browned, and his fingernails were small and short and a little dirty; so he was just such a boy as lives down the street from us both. Years ago the boy's father had sailed away to trade the shining stones of Atlantis for the wine and ram skins of the wild barbarians of Hellas, leaving the boy and his mother very poor.

All day the sun thrashed and rolled and leaped about. Sometimes it sounded, plunging all the earth into night, and sometimes it leaped high into the sky, throwing up sprays of stars. Sometimes it feigned to be dead, and sometimes it tried to wrap his line around the moon to break it. And the boy let it tire itself, sometimes reeling in and sometimes letting out more line; but through it all he kept a tight grip on his pole.

The richest man in the village, the moneylender, who owned the house where the boy and his mother lived, came to him, saying, "You must cut your line, boy, and let the sun go. When it runs out, it brings winter and withers all the blossoms in my orchard. When you reel it in, it brings droughty August to dry all the canals that water my barley fields. Cut your line!"

But the boy only laughed at him and pelted him with the shining stones of Atlantis, and at last the richest man in the village went away.

Then the strongest man in the village, the smith, who could meet the charge of a wild ox and wrestle it to the ground, came to the boy, saying, "Cut your line, boy, or I'll break your neck," for the richest man had paid him to do it.

But the boy only laughed at him and pelted him with the shining stones of Atlantis, and when the strongest man in the village seized him by the neck, he seized the strongest man in return and threw him into the sea, for the power of the sun had run down the boy's line and entered into him.

Then the cleverest man in the village, the mayor, who could charm a rabbit into his kitchen—and many a terrified rabbit, and many a pheasant and partridge too, had fluttered and trembled there, when the door shut behind it and it saw the knives—came to the boy saying, "Cut your line, my boy, and come with me! Henceforth, you and I are to rule in Atlantis. I've been conferring with the mayors of all the other villages; we have decided to form an empire, and you—none other!—are to be our king."

But the boy only laughed at him and pelted him with the shining stories of Atlantis, saying, "Oh, really? A king. Who is to be emperor?" And after the cleverest man in the village had talked a great deal more, he went away.

Then the magic woman from the hills, the sorceress, who knew every future save her own, came to the boy, saying, "Little boy, you must cut your line. Sabaoth sweats and trembles in his shrine and will no longer accept my offerings; the feet of Sith, called by the ignorant Kronos son of Uranus, have broken; and the magic bird Tchataka has flown. The stars riot in the heavens, so that at one moment humankind is to rule them all, and at the next is to perish. Cut your line!"

But the boy only laughed at her and pelted her with the shining stones of Atlantis, with agates and alexanderites, moonstones and onyxes, rubies, sardonyxes, and sapphires; and at last the magic woman from the hills went away muttering.

Then the most foolish man in the village, the idiot, who sang songs without words to all the brooks and boasted of bedding the white birch on the hill, came to the boy and tried to say how frightened he was to see the sun fighting the line in the sky; though he could not find the words.

But the boy only smiled and let him touch the pole, and after a time he too went away.

And at last the boy's mother came, saying, "Remember all the fine stories I have told you through the years? Never have I told you the finest of all. Come now to the house the richest man in the village has given back to us. Put on your crown and tell your general to stand guard; take up the magic feather of the bird Tchataka, who opens its mouth to the sky and drinks wisdom with the dew. Then we shall dip the feather in the blood of a wild ox and write that story on white birch bark, you and I."

The boy asked, "What is that story, Mother?"

And his mother answered, "It is called 'The Boy Who Hooked the Sun.' Now cut your line and promise me you will never fish for the sun again, so long as we both shall live."

Ah, thought the boy, as he got out his little knife. *I love my mother, who is more beautiful than the white birch tree and always kind. But do not all the souls wear away at last as they circle on the Wheel? Then the time must come when I live and she does not; and when that time comes, surely I will bait my hook again with the shining stones of Uranus, and we shall rule the stars. Or not.*

And so it is that the sun swims far from earth sometimes, thinking of its sore mouth; and we have winter. But now, when the days are very short and we see the boy's line stretched across the sky and powdered with hoarfrost, the sun recalls earth and her clever and foolish men and kind and magical women, and then it returns to us.

Or perhaps it is only—as some say—that it remembers the taste of the bait.

Try and Kill It

◆

His name was Tom, Tom Hunter. He had gone to bed early the night before and risen at three, having enjoyed six and a half hours' sleep, which was about as much as he ever got. His bow and his quiver of broadheads had been in the van already, along with his hunting knife and most of his other stuff. He had put on coffee that perked while he fooled around with the rest, mostly looking for the silver flask Bet had given him on his birthday four years ago, so he could fill it with rock-and-rye. At about the same time the coffee perked, he woke up for real and remembered that he'd filled it the night before and put it in a hip pocket of his hunting pants.

He'd washed his face again (no shave today), put on the pants, and filled his thermos with fresh hot coffee—light cream, no sugar.

Now here he was, and the sun not up. He got out of the van, shutting the driver's-side door as quietly as he could, switched on his flashlight, and got his stuff from in back, shutting that door quietly, too, and making sure the van was locked.

The night wasn't even getting gray, the stars obscured by an overcast and the moon already down. Padding along in crepe-soled boots, he jogged down the little path and turned onto the game trail nobody else knew about. It was possible—not likely, but possible—that his light would spook the deer, though he'd taped over most of the lens and was careful to aim the beam low. Noise would spook them sure, so he moved as quietly as he could, which was not quietly enough to satisfy him.

The tree looked different at night. Alive, somehow. It was a live tree, of course, with green leaves and even little winged seeds early that summer. He had always known it was alive, but it had looked no more alive when he had built his blind on the big limb than the plastic trees that would appear in Wal-Mart in another week or two. It was different now, a placid thing that stood in the night like a huge horse and let him touch it and even climb it using the spikes he had driven into its rough hide in June, not because it liked or was afraid of him, but because it didn't care.

He thought about Rusty then, whether he ought to have taken Rusty hunting, was Rusty too young or what? He had decided no, not this year, not this Saturday which would be today when the sun came up to make a new day. Rusty was too young, would whine at being awakened so early and wake up Bet, who would insist on oatmeal. And it would be seven o'clock before they got into the woods, maybe eight, and the best part of the day wasted.

But he had been wrong, and knew it as he eased into the blind, gripping the familiar handholds. He could have, should have, carried Rusty out to the van and let him sleep a little more on the drive out. Waked him before they got to the woods so he could get dressed, and brought him to the tree so he could feel this, feel it standing here in night waiting for a rider who might not come this year or the next. Who might not come at all but who was worth waiting for in rain and wind and snow, because waiting for the rider (who was certainly not himself, no, never Tom Hunter) was the only worthwhile thing anybody could do. And if Rusty could just once be made to feel that, Rusty would be all right forever, good and decent at the core even if he gave them trouble sometimes or got in trouble with the law, even.

So he should have brought Rusty, and perhaps next year it would be too late. Bow season was only a week, but there would be rifle season after. They could do it next Saturday, maybe.

He stood and took his bow out of the bow case as quietly as he could, then pulled out a broadhead quietly too, nocked it, and drew the bow just to satisfy himself (as he had so often before) that there was room enough up here, letting the bowstring go straight again without letting fly. The broadhead's razor-sharp blades gleamed dully in the night, and he realized with a little start that the night was not quite so black as it had been. Soon—

very soon, now—the sun would peep above the horizon and bow season would begin officially.

There was talk of having a black-powder season, too, a week for black-powder hunters after regular deer season. It meant he would have to get a black-powder gun, a good one, just as he'd gotten the Ruger Redhawk for handgun season. Learn to load and shoot it before next year, to be safe. If there was overtime this winter, maybe he could, a long Kentucky rifle to get the highest possible velocity out of the feeble propellant. He'd—

A thump. Not exactly loud but not soft either, not near and not far—middle distance and very, very impressive. Impressive enough to spook every deer in the county.

He gnawed his lip as he tried to think what had made it so impressive, why he'd known at once that it was an important and a significant thump—that something big had happened not very far away. Without training in logic or any other science, he was of an analytical turn of mind, getting to the roots of things when he could, and when he couldn't returning to them again and again to paw at the earth and sniff (he smiled to himself) like Dad's coonhound. This one wasn't too hard for him though, not nearly. Not rooted too deep for him at all.

It had been because he'd felt the thump as well as hearing it. It had shaken the ground, if only a little, and the ground had shaken the tree, which might even have acted as an amplifier or a sounding board, like the back of the fiddle he'd built from a kit about the time he met Bet but never learned to play. The old fiddle collecting dust in the basement, not a very good fiddle really though something might be made of it now, stripped and refinished after some sanding and regluing. He was a whole lot more patient these days, a better worker.

A craftsman.

A supervisor had called him a craftsman back in July, and Dean and Juan had kidded him about it; but he had felt at the time that it was the greatest compliment he could ever get or would ever get, and if he died after that it would not really matter—would matter to Bet and Rusty, no doubt, but not to him.

It had worn off a little since. He had come to realize in his analytical way that it didn't really matter much whether the supervisor thought he was a craftsman, or what the supervisor said. What mattered was whether he was; and he had worked more carefully than ever after that, taking no more time than was needed to do the job, but always taking the time to do the job right, fixing any little thing he came across so nobody would have to come back and do it later, and leaving each machine clean and tight, running as much like new as he could make it.

Dad. . . . He hadn't thought of his father much in probably a year, but here he was again. Dad had bought a used pickup and said later that if only the guy who'd sold it had told him what the little scraps of wire in the box under the seat were for it would have saved him a hundred dollars. But he didn't like the kind of fixes you did with little scraps of wire. There was magic in the first drop of oil, and magic in a good, clean oily rag. Out past that it was what you knew and how much you were willing to think, making your mind go like the parts, not just replacing stuff and walking away.

But what had the thump been? What could it have been? Trucks hitting out on the highway?

Trucks hitting out on the highway couldn't possibly have shaken the earth in which this tree stood on a wooded hillside three valleys away; but maybe he had been wrong about that.

An explosion at the plant; but this had been closer, he felt sure. He tried to think whether there was another plant closer, or whether it could have been a truck blowing up; and decided it had not been an explosion at all. More like a tree falling, but that wasn't quite it either.

Now he could see the ground below, and the place where the game trail turned, the place where he would take his shot—twenty-two yards, he had measured it in July. An easy shot for a compound bow as powerful as his, a bow that could send an arrow straight and true a hundred yards easy.

The little wind that had brushed his cheek once or twice in the dark could be seen playing all around now, shaking leaves and stirring the few dead leaves that had already dropped, leaves red and yellow or brown, sometimes with green patches on them, alive in death.

Like Mom. Dad had been old and tired and dead, that was all, dressed up in his coffin in a fashion that would have embarrassed him if he had been alive; but some part of Mom had still been alive, had not given up until they had closed the lid and screwed it down, so that he had half expected to hear her rapping on it when they lowered her into the grave. Although she was dead, of course, and only some small part of her that death had not yet claimed still living in his mind, a green patch that worried about him and Bet and Rusty, and planned to bake more pies, to teach Bet stuff she already knew or did not want to learn, make another quilt with Dora Skinner, because a real cold winter might come someday when he and Bet would be grateful for a nice—

Something was moving away down the slope, down where the little creek barely trickled along the valley. Something bigger than a deer but just about as quiet. Another hunter, probably. Not driving deer toward a partner, because anybody trying to drive deer would make more noise. Just prowling through the woods with his bow, pretty quiet, hoping to get a shot.

It was too bad he wasn't driving, whoever he was, because if he had been the deer might have run up here along the game trail. Probably would, in fact. And then he himself might have gotten a shot if he was quick enough.

No does, he told himself again. No doe season this year, and he wouldn't want to be caught with one—didn't want to bag a doe anyhow. No little spike bucks, either. There were plenty of those every year; but they weren't anything but meat, and Bet could buy meat at the meat counter. Let the little spike bucks grow up a few more years. Six points for him. Eight or ten if he was lucky, but he'd settle for six. A braggin' buck.

He grinned to himself, grinned to the little breeze and the silent wood.

That other hunter was coming nearer now, and he might very well be driving deer even if he didn't mean to. A deer heard better than a man, better even than most dogs. The lone hunter (Tom Hunter pictured a big man, middle-aged, moving quietly) was hunting upwind, which was the way to do it; deer had better noses than lots of dogs, too.

A terrified deer was on the game trail, small hoofs trap-drumming the hard, dry soil. Tom drew his bow, but it made the turn too fast for him to have shot even if he had wanted to, coming straight at his tree for a moment and flashing past—a small doe, scared out of her wits.

He got close to her, Tom thought. Got real close, probably kicked her up. Might have creased her with an arrow then. That would account for it.

He himself had put an arrow completely through a deer two years before, and watched it run away. It had run for more than a quarter mile, and it had taken him nearly two hours to find it, following the blood trail. If the lone hunter climbing the hill was following a similar trail, he would see him soon.

He listened for more, then for anything. This early in the morning, with the sun just rising, the birds ought to be making a fuss, but they were not. Had migration begun already? Even if it had, there should be plenty left.

It was the explosion, no doubt. It had scared—

Just then a jay started talking some distance down the hillside, the loud, hoarse danger-cries that warned all good birds of the presence of a cat or a man. Here he comes, Tom thought.

And then, that does it—that wraps up the morning. I'm not going to get a damn thing. Not even going to get a shot.

He had gotten up at three for this, left the house without breakfast. He returned the arrow to his quiver, put down his bow, and poured himself a cup of coffee, adding a few drops of rock-and-rye.

He sipped, then swallowed greedily, admitting to himself that it tasted great.

He would go home and eat, maybe take a nap. Bet would kid him, but it wouldn't matter because he'd kid himself worse. And before sundown he'd be back in the blind again, and maybe he'd at least get a shot. For a moment he regretted not shooting at the terrified little doe, but he pushed the thought aside. He could have, and he had chosen not to, so no more complaining about not getting a shot.

Maybe he should just go back to the van. He could sleep in the van for a couple of hours, then come back here. That way Rusty could make all the noise he wanted; this was Rusty's day off, too, after all.

He drank again, wiped his mouth on his right sleeve, and considered removing the wrist guard from his left. A wrist guard was there to keep the bowstring from slapping your wrist and to keep your sleeve from fouling the string. If he wasn't going to shoot his bow, why wear it? Although it was just possible that he'd get a shot at something he wanted on the way back to the van.

Or he could stay right here, hang in. The sandwiches he'd carried had been intended as his lunch. Was he going to tote them back to the van after carrying them out here? What would he think of himself—of the way he'd acted—when hunting season was over?

The stainless-steel cup that doubled as the thermos bottle's cap was nearly empty. As he swallowed the last drop, there was a sudden rattle as a deer broke just out of sight. Before he could grab his bow, it had flashed past, a little spike buck.

He picked up his bow and nocked the arrow again.

A minute passed, or an indeterminate time that seemed to him a minute or more; the playful wind carried the faintest possible odor of laundry day, a chemical smell from some factory miles away.

Then it sounded as if a riot were in progress just out of sight, the rocketing roar of a pheasant practically lost among clattering hooves and breaking twigs as an entire herd flushed from a thicket. He drew his bow as the lead doe rounded the turn and made for his tree, mouth open and tongue lolling, covering a good twelve feet with every jump, a big doe sleek and fat with autumn going full-out and still picking up speed. Behind her the ruck of the herd, bounding fawns and leaping does, perhaps eight in all, perhaps ten or twelve.

Last of all the buck covering their retreat, muscled like a wrestler and crowned more regally than any king, thick of neck and large of eye, frightened yet still in command of himself if not of his panicky harem. For an instant he halted at the bend, head high, to stare up at the tree-limb blind and the point of the arrow aimed at his heart. His tail twitched; he plunged ahead and was gone.

"God damn!" Tom said under his breath. "God damn, oh, God dammit!" It was inadequate, but what would be adequate? The bow had turned to concrete in his hand, its string sticking to his fingers as though they had been dipped in glue. Buck fever, he told himself. I got buck fever again.

After how many years? He tried to count back to his first hunt with Dad. Sixteen. No, eighteen.

Buck fever.

Yet it had not been. He'd seen buck fever, had experienced it himself. Your hands shook with eagerness, and as often as not you shot too soon. Or you gawked openmouthed instead of raising your gun, or knocked it over when you grabbed for it. His hands had been as steady as ever in his life; he had seen the buck and sighted, had known what to do. Something had stopped him.

Had Dad's ghost returned? Said spare this one, son, and for the rest of your life you'll know he's out there?

No. Tom pushed the thought aside. Only women saw ghosts. Ghosts! Women and nuts. Flakes, and he was no flake, was a rock-solid sober family man and a good bow-hunter. Something in his own mind had stopped him, and not for any silly, sentimental reason. What had it been?

When he rooted it out and held it up, he had to laugh. He had not shot because he might need the arrow—because something awful was coming. But the other hunter was merely a man like himself, and might easily be a man he knew, a man in a hunting cap and a camo shirt, walking along with his bow in his hand and his quiver on his back like anybody else.

Down beyond the bend there was a flash of brown, rich and reddish among the grays and blacks of trunks, the green of leaves. Not a camo shirt. Some kind of a brown shirt, maybe an Army surplus wool shirt, but it hadn't quite seemed like the Army color. A man—

There it was, just passing in back of a bush then gone in the shadows, red-brown with a gray streak and bigger than a pony, bigger than any man, as big as a bull almost but not a bull or a cow or anything like that.

A bear.

Not a black bear, and not even the kind of a black bear they called a cinnamon. A grizzly, a bear like people went a thousand miles to hunt. A grizzly bear for sure, even if there weren't any grizzlies in this part of the country and hadn't been since the people here wore three-cornered hats and fought Indians.

They said there weren't, anyhow.

There were coyotes now, and they said there weren't any of those either. Coyotes were supposed to be Western animals like grizzlies, animals you saw on the prairie in Texas, and out in the desert. But there was a dead coyote on the road a while back about a half mile from the house.

There it was again!

He pulled the arrow to his ear, then relaxed. Too risky, even if it wasn't too far. He'd only spook it, and this was the chance of a lifetime. Wait. Take your time. Even with a good shot, a big bear will need a lot of killing, and I mean to try and kill it, not just scare it away, and I sure wouldn't want to have it go off into the woods and take two or three months to die.

He put down his bow and wiped his sweating palms on his thighs. Where was it?

The woods were quiet. Even the jay had stopped talking. The jay had been a ways down the slope, probably it was still there, and the bear had gone far enough uphill that the jay wasn't worried, not that a bear would be much danger to a bird anyhow. The jay probably didn't know—it was a big animal, so it was scary. It would eat a bird if it could catch one, that was for sure.

The level sunshine streaked the woods with golden bars that seemed to him to obstruct his vision, illuminating a young sumac as though with a spotlight, leaving a clump of bayberries darker than they had been by night. If the bear was moving he couldn't hear it. It couldn't be snuffling; he would have heard that. No question about it.

There! Behind the fallen log.

Once more he drew his bow. The wind pushed aside a leafy branch, and a gleaming shaft from the sun struck the place on the other side of the log before his own shaft could. A few twigs and dead leaves lay there.

Nothing else.

The laundry smell had grown stronger. Air pollution! Even way out here, there was air pollution. He snorted, allowed the bowstring to straighten again, and wiped his nose on his sleeve.

And the bear rose on its hind legs at the sound, as bears will, and held up both paws.

No buck fever now. Back went the arrow to his ear. His release was clean and crisp, sending the long aluminum-shafted broadhead flying from his sixty-pound compound bow nearly as fast as a bullet.

Yet the bear tried to dodge. He saw it in slow motion, like movie blood flying off the teeth of a chain saw, the silver arrow streaking, the bear (almost as short-faced as a man, and not like a black bear very much) trying to writhe away before the arrow got it, the long orange hair on its chest crossed on a slant by a gray streak that was probably from an old scar, a crease from somebody's big-game rifle.

Quick as the bear was, it wasn't quick enough. The arrow hit it a little bit to one side of the breastbone, and buried the big steel head and half the shaft.

He had nocked another before the bear fell, and he let it fly, not so sure of his aim this time. Somewhere among the bushes and fallen branches the bear moaned, a deep, suffering noise that sounded practically human.

That first one got him good, and if you ask me the other one did, too.

A grizzly! His grizzly!

It seemed incredible. It *was* incredible. How many men in the whole damned country had taken a grizzly with bow and arrow? A hundred? Maybe. Maybe no more than a couple of dozen.

A couple dozen, and he was one of them. God had somehow, for some unknowable reason of His own, chosen to bless him beyond and above most other men, and he finally saw the level sunbeams for what they really were, God's fingers, and he thanked God for it, mentally at first, then muttering the words and half ashamed.

Was the bear still there? He peered and squinted, but could not be certain. A cloud passed before the sun and God's fingers were withdrawn, leaving the woods nearly as dark as they had been when he climbed into the blind. It was vitally important that he know; even a wounded buck could be dangerous.

Patiently he waited, twice thinking that he heard something big moving through the brush, each time assuring himself that it was just the wind, just his imagination. Either the bear was there (as it almost certainly was), or it wasn't.

If it was, everything was fine; he had his bear. If it wasn't, he'd have to track it and finish it off, if it still required finishing. He knew himself to be as good a tracker as anybody who hunted these woods, and knew too that he possessed a dogged persistence so great that his coworkers at the plant sometimes thought he was a little crazy, shimming and leveling, adjusting anew and trying again, working through break and then through lunch because doing it—getting it right—meant more to him than conversation or food. The bear would be found, if the bear was findable.

But the bear was probably dead already, lying no more than eight or ten feet from the point where he had shot it.

He took out another arrow just in case.

By degrees that seemed more than painfully slow, the sunlight returned, a little higher than it had been. He leaned from the blind, squinting. The bear probably wasn't—no, positively wasn't—where it had fallen. He could see the place now, see it as clearly as if he stood there, and there was no big animal there, so it had crawled away; with his arrow in it, it wouldn't crawl very far, not even if the second one missed.

And if it had, where was it? Could it have buried itself completely in the dirt? In dirt that was full of roots? That was possible, maybe, but it didn't seem likely, and he couldn't see either arrow.

The wounded bear might be anyplace—might even be waiting for him at the base of the tree.

He climbed down cautiously, stopping twice to look below him. If the bear was there, he couldn't see or hear it.

When he reached the ground, he got out his bow and nocked a third arrow. Bears could charge very fast. A well-placed arrow *might* stop a charging bear. But it might not, and a badly placed one certainly wouldn't. His first shot had been right on target though, and the bear had been losing blood for a good ten minutes. How dangerous could it be?

With his third arrow still nocked, he strode down the game trail, then through the underbrush until he reached the point at which the bear had risen on its hind legs.

There was blood, dark already, clotted and reeking. Here—he put down his bow and knelt to examine the ground—the bear had crawled off, still bleeding but not bleeding nearly as much as he'd have liked, pulling itself along with its front claws and leaving six deep gouges in the litter of twigs and leaves.

That way.

He hesitated. He was honor-bound to track down and dispatch a wounded animal, and doubly bound to dispatch one as dangerous as a grizzly. His honor did not demand that he start tracking right away, though, or even walk fast once he'd started.

There was a gleam—a dull, metallic wink—some ten or twelve yards away, probably brass from somebody's deer rifle. Cautiously he made his way over to it and picked it up. It was half an arrow, cleanly snapped in two: the blood-smeared head and a foot and a half of equally smeared hollow aluminum shaft. No bear, no animal of any kind, should have been able to pull that barbed broadhead out.

Looking around he found the other end tangled in a bush.

This was the second arrow, of course, not the first. It had made a shallow wound most likely, and had stopped with the head sticking out, having cut through a lot of fur, flesh, fat, and hide. Thrashing around, the bear had broken the shaft, and with the shaft broken both halves of the arrow had come out. That was what had to have happened.

He sat down on a fallen log. The bear was dying—that was absolutely sure. Very likely, the bear was dead already, and no more than a hundred steps away. However bad the second shot had been, the first one had been in the black. It had hit the bear's chest pretty near center, and gone in deep. As long as its sharp blades were in the wound, every movement, every breath, would do more damage. He'd have another cup of coffee, drinking it slowly and enjoying it, then track the bear, find its body, and skin it. No way in the world could he drag an animal that big back to the van to take over to Lakeside Sporting Goods, where they did taxidermy; but he could skin it and he would, and carry back the pelt and head. What had he done with the thermos? He stood up and looked around before remembering that it was still back in the blind, and returned the arrow to his quiver.

He had almost reached the tree again when he glanced up at his blind with the half-formed idea of checking its effectiveness from the ground (as he had so many times while building it) and saw the wide reddish face glaring down at him.

Sheer terror gripped him, and he ran. When he stopped at last, it was only because the stand of saplings through which he had tried to flee was too thick, almost, for him to move. He fell to his knees gasping, his own hoarse breath too loud for him to hear anything else. Insects looped and dove before his face, intent on entering his mouth, nostrils, and eyes.

As the minutes crept past, his self-possession returned. Wounded animals frequently turned on their attackers. It had never happened to him before, but he had read about such things in hunting and fishing magazines, and heard stories from other hunters. The wounded bear had supposed that he was still in the blind from which his arrows had come; and recovering a little from the initial shock of its wound, had climbed the tree in search of him. That was all.

He shuddered, every muscle shaking as if with cold.

He could have—should have—shot it there, standing solidly on the ground and putting two or three more arrows into it before it could get down. There had been two arrows left in his quiver—three, counting the one he had returned to it.

Thinking of his quiver, he groped for it. It was gone. Had he torn it away, dropped it in order to run faster? He could not remember, could remember only running, running and running, down the wooded slope and through a clearing. Maybe through more than one. Leaping over something that might have been a tree trunk or the trickling creek.

He got to his feet, his heart still pounding. Could bears hunt by scent? It seemed probable, and if they could it was possible that this bear was still on his trail, still after him. He tried to push aside the terrible memory of its eyes. It would have had to climb down from the blind first, and that had given him a lead.

A bear hunting by scent would move a great deal slower than a charging bear, too. He had seen coonhounds hunt by scent at a dead run, the coon-smell so strong and good they didn't even have to put their noses to the ground; but he had not seen it a lot, and though a bear might have a good nose, it probably wasn't as good as a coonhound's.

Closer every minute, though. It would be getting closer every minute, and not baying like a hound either, but hunting silently, maybe snuffling now and then, so he'd better move, get moving soon, get away from it and find a road or something, and he could hitch a ride back home and get his deer rifle, get a neighbor to run him back out to the van.

Struggling, half walking and half climbing, he freed himself from the saplings and looked around, took a few steps, stopped, and turned, realizing at length that he could not be sure of the direction from which he had entered it.

Walking or trotting—running, he felt sure, was no longer possible for him—at random might bring him nearer the bear. He found his bandanna and mopped his sweating face. It was fall according to the calendar, and the night had been crisp; but the sun was up now, and the day starting to get hot.

He stood still to listen and heard only birdsong. The bear had silenced the birds when it had driven the deer up the slope—silenced every bird around there except for the squawking jay. Birds were singing now, singing in every direction as well as he could judge, so the bear was probably nowhere near.

The best thing would be to circle around. Come up to the van from the other side. He reached into his pocket and found the keys. Once in the van he would be safe, and he could drive home for his deer rifle.

The woods should have been familiar. He had hunted these woods every season for almost twenty years, taken a dozen deer and scores of rabbits and squirrels out of them. He knew them, as he had often told Dean and Juan, like the palm of his hand; but this was a new place, or a place that he was looking at in a new way.

He had not brought a compass, and none was needed. It was early morning still, and at this time of year the sun rose almost due east; he found it without difficulty. North was left, south, right, west behind him; but where was the van?

Cautiously he set out. It was true, of course, still true, that he might be walking toward the bear. True, but not likely. Away from it or at right angles to it were the way to bet, so he would bet like that, and soon—very soon, he hoped—he was bound to see something he recognized, something that would give him his—mentally, he canceled the word *bearings*. Something that would tell him which way the van was.

His blind had been well up a hill, so he avoided them, threading blind, dry little valleys, and once discovering a stagnant pool shrunk almost to a mudflat by the heat of the summer that was only just over. He thought he remembered seeing it once (much fuller then, with a loon's nest at the edge) when he was out hunting with Dad; but he could not be sure, and he couldn't remember where it had been anyway.

Deer flies found him. He got out his repellent and sprayed, but it seemed to do little good.

The sun was too high to direct him now, and he blazed his trail, cutting six-inch strips of bark from likely trees with his hunting knife and letting them hang, and breaking the limbs of bushes to point the way he was going—not doing these things so much in the hope that anyone would follow the signs and find him, but to keep himself from circling. Knowing that lost men instinctively turned left, he turned right whenever a choice presented itself, and tried to walk toward distant hilltops or large trees when he could see them.

Toward noon the sun vanished and he heard the rumble of distant thunder. A cool front was on the way, clearly, with a storm for a roadie. He found shelter under a rocky outcrop, took off his boots and stockings, and waited out the rain.

How many times had he read that smart hunters were never without a compass? That it was always wise to carry emergency rations of some sort? Bet's little silver flask still held rock-and-rye. He sipped the sweet, potent liquor in the hope that it would assuage his hunger; but he was no drinker and soon recapped the flask, feeling slightly ill.

Thunder banged and rattled, rain pelted the dry woods, then slacked and faded to a shower as the thunder rolled away among the hills. Wearily he put on his stockings and boots again, rose, and set out, blazing his trail as before and soon encountering blazes that he himself had made only hours ago.

The sun was close to the western horizon when he came upon the road. It was not much of a road, only two streaks of muddy dirt, but among its rutted wanderings he imagined houses and farms, food and rest and telephones, and felt that he'd never beheld anything half so beautiful, not even Bet when chance had thrown them together at a high-school basketball game. Not even Bet, because she was there, too; and she was more beautiful now in the ruts of the dirt road, because she was his as he was hers, and she had given him Rusty.

Rusty ought to have a dog, a bird dog, maybe, that they could train together. A bird dog and a four-ten.

The road ran northwest and southeast, and there was no way to tell which direction might be better. Either one, he told himself, would be a great deal better than the way he had been going, better than wandering in search of landmarks that somehow weren't ever there.

Following his rule, he turned right. The shadows were long when he came upon the broken pine and stopped. He had seen it before, surely. Had noticed it several times that summer when he was going out to work on his blind. It had not marked the end of the road; the road went on for nearly a half mile more, past the firebreak the rangers had cut three years before. Yet it had been near the end.

His feet were blistered, and he was pretty sure that the blister on the side of the left one had broken, but he went on at a good clip just the same. Another half mile—more like a quarter mile now—and he'd reach the van. He could drive home, get something to eat and a good night's sleep. Come back Sunday morning to find his bear and skin it.

Two saplings up ahead . . . he stopped to look, then hurried forward. They had been bent and partially broken at several points, interlaced to form a knot that wasn't quite a braid. His first thought was that he had failed to notice them that morning, his second that it had been too dark to notice much of anything, his third that it had been done recently; the saplings' leaves were still green for the most part, and there was no sign that either had begun to grow into its tortured new shape.

His fourth was that it had taken enormous strength to do it. He had stopped to feel the bent and twisted trunks when something buzzed past him like an oversized hornet, and he felt that a red-hot poker had been rammed into his right arm. Whirling, he saw the bear, already nocking another arrow.

It missed as he dove into the undergrowth. Not long ago he had thought himself almost too tired to walk. Now he ran again, but not blindly as he had run before with abject terror grinding down his mind. There was a bend here, a pronounced one where the road skirted a hill. He cut across it and found the road again, sprinted down it—falling twice—and reached the van as the bear's third arrow scarred its steel side.

It's bigger than I am. (It was the first coherent thought since he had begun to run again.) And it's stronger, a lot stronger. But I'm faster and maybe I'm smarter.

His arm, limp and drenched with his blood, would not respond when he told it to get the keys from his pocket. He seized the edge of the pocket with his left hand and ripped it open with an effort he would in ordinary circumstances have found flatly impossible.

It was hard to open the door left-handed and maddeningly awkward to jam the key into the ignition switch and start the engine, but he did both, and with his almost-useless right arm managed to knock the shift lever from Park into Drive. He jammed his foot down on the accelerator as he spun the steering wheel one-handed.

Like an angry bull, the van smashed through the roadside brush to turn and charge the dark figure of the bear. There was a shuddering impact. Momentarily the van skewed sidewise. He fought the wheel and raced down the road, covering a mile or more before he dared to slow a little and pull out the headlight switch.

Only one headlight came on.

Suddenly (much too suddenly for him) there was gravel ahead, then asphalt and speeding cars. He should perhaps have slowed and waited for a break in traffic. He did not, charging the highway as he had the bear. Horns blared, and this time the crash was deafening and the world a kaleidoscope of tumbling objects that flashed past too quickly to be seen, though not too fast to strike blows that numbed instead of hurting.

When he crawled from the wreckage, the bear was upon him, a bear itself wrecked, its head and one arm dangling, drenched in its own nauseous blood. He ran, and knew not where he ran, heard the scream of brakes and the sickening impact behind him.

It was after midnight when he got home. Bet helped him out of Dean's car and into the house, ignoring his protests. "Oh my God," she said; and again, "Oh my God." And then, because he had been careful to limp, "Can you climb the stairs?"

And when he had insisted he would be fine on the couch, and eaten two pieces of cold chicken and drunk a glass of milk, and told her a careful mixture of truth and lies, he was able to get her to go up to bed, and opened the drapes.

He waited after that, sitting silent in the dark room, staring out the picture window at the dark street outside and thinking until he had heard the water turned off in the upstairs bathroom and the shutting of their bedroom door. A dozen bruises complained when he stood up, but his right arm, which had begun to throb, throbbed no worse.

"Daddy?"

Rusty was at the top of the stairs in his pajamas, his hair tousled.

"Was it really a bear, Daddy?"

For a second or two he debated, telling himself with perfect truth that Rusty was only a little kid. "Come on down, sport. We don't want to wake up Mom."

Rusty came down with alacrity.

"There really was a bear," his father told him. "But I'm not so sure it was a regular bear." Bending stiffly, he picked up the blue plastic bag the hospital had given him, feeling the paw stir inside.

"Mamma believed you about the car wreck."

He nodded, mostly to himself. "But not about the bear."

Rusty shook his head.

"I didn't tell her everything, either. Just a little bit. I tried to get her to believe it."

"Did you kill the bear, Dad?"

"No." He started for the family room, limping but trying not to. "There were a couple of times when I thought I had, but I didn't. You know my big arrows?"

"Sure."

"I shot it good with two of those, and I figured it was dead. It should've been." He handed Rusty the blue bag and fished his keys from his left pants pocket with his left hand. "It broke one of those arrows and threw the halves away. The kind of thing a man might do, mad because he'd got hurt."

"Was it big?"

He considered. "Yeah. Real big. Four or five hundred pounds, I guess. I took five arrows this morning, sport."

"Sure."

"There's no use carrying more than you need, and the bow license only lets you take one deer. If I missed a couple of shots, I'd still have three. So after it got my bow, I was thinking it only had three, and it shot three at me. One got my arm."

He pointed to the sling, and Rusty nodded, eyes wide. "But there's one more, the one I shot into it that it didn't break. I don't think it can use it now." He opened his gun cabinet. "The rifle would be better," he told Rusty, "but I can't on account of my arm."

The Redhawk was in its holster, and the holster on his gun belt, hanging from a hook. "You're going to have to help me get this thing on. Grab the other end."

Rusty did, and his father stepped into the belt, wrapping the buckle end around him, then turning until the tongue reached the buckle. "You know how these work. Think you can fasten it for me?"

Rusty thrust the tongue into the buckle and pulled back on it. "Tighter," his father said.

When it was fastened to his satisfaction, he drew the Redhawk and pushed the cylinder catch. "Six," he told Rusty. "Six forty-four magnums. I hope that'll do it."

"Sure, Dad."

"I hit it with the van." He snapped the cylinder back into the frame and reholstered the gun. "That was the second time I thought I'd got it. It dented in the right side of the van some and busted a headlight, but it wasn't hurt so bad that it couldn't grab on to something and ride along with me. I'm pretty sure that's what it must have done, because when that car hit me it was right there. It can move pretty fast, if you ask me, but not that fast."

"Is that when you got hurt, Daddy? When the car hit you?"

"Uh-huh. That and the arrow. The arrow first. But it got hurt, too. It went for me, and I was so scared I ran right out onto the highway without looking. You mustn't ever do that, Rusty."

"All right."

"I guess it didn't look, either. Anyway, a big truck hit it, an eighteen-wheeler. It messed it up pretty bad. Smashed the head flat. You ever see a cat or a squirrel that's been run over and flattened out like that?"

"Sure."

"That's what it looked like, and I thought it was dead. I'd wanted the head, but the head was a mess, and I hadn't killed it anyhow. What did you do with that bag I gave you?"

"On the chair." Rusty turned to get it. "It's gone."

"Yeah, I thought I heard it slide off a minute ago. You look in the living room, I'll look in the kitchen."

After half a minute Rusty joined him there, holding up the blue hospital bag in triumph. "Is it a snake? I can feel it moving around."

His father shook his head. "It's one paw. I don't even know which one." He paused, considering. "The left front. I know it was a front paw, anyhow. I cut it off. Somebody that had a car phone stopped and said he'd called for an ambulance. Think you can untie that?"

Rusty studied the knot in the top of the bag dubiously. "I'll try."

"It's pretty tight. I got a nurse to tie it for me, but then I held the end in my teeth and tightened it up as much as I could. Where was it when you found it?"

"Over in front of the door. I don't think it could get it open."

"After it tore through the bag, maybe. The man with the phone went over to see about the lady in the other car. She was hurt worse than I was, and while we were waiting for the ambulance I cut it off. I wanted something to show you and your mom."

Rusty's small fingers were picking at the knot. "You didn't, did you? Maybe she would've believed you."

"It had been wearing a sort of a belt over one shoulder. It was gray, and when I'd seen it before I thought it was a scar. I took it, but it was all messed up and I threw it away. Then I cut off that paw. It was real quiet till we got to the hospital. That was when I found out it was still alive and started to figure things out. They gave me that bag to put it in, and sewed up my arm and took care of some other stuff."

"I got it." Rusty looked into the bag. "It smells like Clorox."

"Dump it out on the floor," his father told him, and when Rusty hesitated, reached into the bag and took out the paw.

"Three toes." Rusty regarded the massively clawed digits with awe. "Don't bears got four like a dog?"

"Maybe it lost one in a trap." His father tossed the paw onto the floor between them. "Watch it."

For a minute or more it lay motionless.

"It was wiggling before," Rusty said.

"It's scared. You hit it or drop it or anything, and it keeps quiet awhile. I think it's hoping you'll figure it's dead."

"Can it hear us?" Rusty whispered.

"I don't think so."

As he spoke, one thick claw scrabbled the tiles and found a hold in the grout. The paw inched forward.

"It'll go a lot faster in a minute. It's waiting to see if we saw it move."

Rusty knelt beside the paw.

"Don't touch it."

The paw inched forward again, this time with all three claws scrabbling for purchase. "It's got my bow and that last arrow," his father said. "I figure it must have broken the first one, then it got the idea of using them."

As he spoke, the paw raised itself, running on the tips of its claws like a crippled spider.

They followed it to the living room, where he picked it up and returned it to the bag. "Tie this for me, will you, sport?"

"Sure. It's trying to get back to the bear, isn't it, Daddy? Only the bear's dead."

"I don't know. I thought it was dead when I shot it, and then when I ran over it." He sighed. "I was wrong both times, so this time I'm not going to count on anything. It can only fix itself so much, though. There's limits to everything."

Rusty nodded, his fingers busy with the bag.

"We can fix ourselves too. My arm'll heal, and I'll be able to go back to work. But if you cut me up enough like that, if you did it over and over, I'd die."

"You said the head was all mashed up."

"Yeah. That's going to take it a long time, this time, I think. That gave me time to get to the hospital and call Dean to come and get me there— all the things I did. It may not even start trying to put itself back together until the traffic on the highway lets up. That would be after one o'clock, I guess."

"Only the paw knows where it is?" Rusty put the blue bag down hurriedly. "It keeps trying to go there?"

His father nodded. "That's what I think, and it must know where the paw is, too. It'll come and try and get it back, and I think try and kill me like it did before. If it isn't till daylight, it won't get very far. Somebody'll see it and call the police. But if it does it at night, it might get all the way here. You go up to bed now."

Rusty gulped. "Daddy . . . ?"

"I wasn't going to tell you anything, and maybe I shouldn't have. But maybe something like this will happen again after I'm gone, and it'll be good if somebody knows. Don't you forget."

"Are you going to shoot it?" Rusty ventured.

His father nodded. "That'll stop it awhile, I figure. A forty-four magnum does a whole lot of damage, and I've got six, and twelve more in the belt loops. I'll cut it up then, and burn the pieces in the barbecue out back. If you hear shooting, don't let Mom come downstairs. Tell her I said."

Rusty nodded solemnly.

"Or call nine-one-one or anything. Now go to bed."

"Daddy—"

"Go to bed, Rusty." Rusty's father pointed sternly with his good arm. "Go up to your room and get in bed. Go to sleep. I've got to make coffee."

When the coffee was on, he turned out the lights and sat down on the couch again. It might be better to meet it outside, he told himself; but it might be worse, too. After a while he would get up and go out and walk around the house. It would keep him awake, anyway.

They'd want a kennel for Rusty's bird dog, and he could decide where to put it.

Thinking about bird dogs and kennels, and how kennels might be built, he stared out the picture window, waiting in his blind for a shambling figure that had not yet appeared.

Game in the Pope's Head

✦

"A sergeant was sent to the Pope's Head to investigate the case."
—FROM THE *LONDON TIMES*'S COVERAGE OF THE MURDER OF ANNE CHAPMAN,
SEPTEMBER 11, 1888.

Bev got up to water her plant. Edgar said, "You're overwatering that. Look how yellow the leaves are."

They were indeed. The plant had extended its long, limp limbs over the pictures and the sofa, and out through the broken window; but the weeping flukes of these astonishing terminations were sallow and jaundiced.

"It *needs* water." Bev dumped her glass into the flowerpot, got a fresh drink, and sat down again. "My play?" She turned up a card. "The next card is 'What motion picture used the greatest number of living actors, animal or human?'"

Edgar said, "I think I know. *Gandhi.* Half a million or so."

"Wrong. Debbie?"

"Hell, I don't know. *Close Encounters of the Third Kind.*"

"Wrong. Randy?"

It was a moment before he realized that she meant him. So that was his name: Randy. Yes, of course. He said, "Animal or human?"

"Right."

"Then it's animals, because they don't get paid." He tried to think of animal movies, Bert Lahr terrified of Toto, *Lassie Come Home.* "*The Birds?*"

"Close. It was *The Swarm,* and there were twenty-two million actors."

Edgar said, "Mostly bees."

"I suppose."

There was a bee, or perhaps a wasp, on the plant, nearly invisible against a yellow leaf. It did not appear to him to be exploring the surface in the usual beeish or waspish way, but rather to be listening, head raised, to their conversation. The room was bugged. He wanted to say, This room is bugged; but before he could, Bev announced, "Your move, I think, Ed."

Ed said, "Bishop's pawn to the bishop's four."

Debbie threw the dice and counted eight squares along the edge of the board. "Oh, good! Park Place, and I'll buy it." She handed him her money, and he gave her the deed.

Bev said, "Your turn."

He nodded, stuffed Debbie's money into his pocket, shuffled the cards, and read the top one.

> You are Randolph Carter.
> Three times you have dreamed
> of the marvelous city, Randoph Carter,
> and three times you have been snatched away
> from the high terrace above it.

Randolph Carter nodded again and put the card down. Debbie handed him a small pewter figure, a young man in old-fashioned clothes.

Bev asked, "Where did the fictional American philosopher Thomas Olney teach? Ed?"

"A *fictional* philosopher? Harvard, I suppose. Is it John Updike?"

"Wrong. Debbie?"

"Pass."

"Okay. Randy?"

"London."

Outside, a cloud covered the sun. The room grew darker as the light from the broken windows diminished.

Edgar said, "Good shot. Is he right, Bev?"

The bee, or wasp, rose from its leaf and buzzed around Edgar's bald head. He slapped at it, missing it by a fraction of an inch. "There's a fly in here!"

"Not now. I think it went out the window."

It had indeed been a fly, he saw, and not a bee or wasp at all—a bluebottle, no doubt gorged with carrion.

Bev said, "Kingsport, Massachusetts."

With an ivory hand, Edgar moved an ivory chessman. "Knight to the king's three."

Debbie tossed her dice onto the board. "Chance."

He picked up the card for her.

> You must descend the seven hundred steps
> to the Gate of Deeper Slumber. You
> may enter the Enchanted Wood or claim
> the sword Sacnoth. Which do you choose?

Debbie said, "I take the Enchanted Wood. That leaves you the sword, Randy."

Bev handed it to him. It was a falchion, he decided, curved and single-edged. After testing the edge with his finger, he laid it in his lap. It was not nearly as large as a real sword—less than sixteen inches long, he decided, including the hardwood handle.

"Your turn, Randy."

He discovered that he disliked Bev nearly as much as Debbie, hated her bleached blond hair, her scrawny neck. She and her dying plant were twins, one vegetable, one inhuman. He had not known that before.

She said, "It's the wheel of Fortune," as though he were stupid. He flicked the spinner.

"Unlawful evil."

Bev said, "Right," and picked up a card. "What do the following have in common: Pogo the Clown, H. H. Holmes, and Saucy Jacky?"

Edgar said, "That's an easy one. They're all pseudonyms of mass murderers."

"Right. For an extra point, name the murderers."

"Gacy, Mudgett, and . . . that's not fair. No one knows who the Ripper was."

But he did: just another guy, a guy like anybody else.

Debbie tossed her dice. "Whitechapel. I'll buy it. Give me the card, honey."

He picked up the deed and studied it. "Low rents."

Edgar chuckled. "And seldom paid."

"I know," Debbie told them, "but I want it, with lots of houses." He handed her the card, and she gave him the dice.

For a moment he rattled them in his hand, trying to imagine himself the little pewter man. It was no use; there was nothing of bright metal about him or his dark wool coat—only the edge of the knife. "Seven-come-eleven," he said, and threw.

"You got it," Debbie told him. "Seven. Shall I move it for you?"

"No," he said. He picked up the little pewter figure and walked past Holborn, the Temple (cavern-temple of Nasht and Kaman-Thah), and Lincolns Inn Fields, along Cornhill and Leadenhall Streets to Aldgate High Street, and so at last to Whitechapel.

Bev said, "You saw him coming, Deb," but her voice was very far away, far above the the leaden(hall) clouds, filthy with coal smoke, that hung over the city. Wagons and hansom cabs rattled by. There was a public house at the corner of Brick Lane. He turned and went in.

The barmaid handed him his large gin. The barmaid had Debbie's dark hair, Debbie's dark good looks. When he had paid her, she left the bar and took a seat at one of the tables. Two others sat there already, and there were cards and dice, money and drinks before them. "Sit down," she said, and he sat.

The blonde turned over a card, the jack of spades. "What are the spades in a deck of cards?" she asked.

"Swords," he said. "From the Spanish word for a sword, *espada*. The jack of spades is really the jack of swords."

"Correct."

The other man said, "Knight to the White Chapel."

The door opened, letting in the evening with a wisp of fog, and the black knight. She was tall and slender and dressed like a cavalryman, in high boots and riding breeches. A pewter miniature of a knight's shield was pinned to her dark shirt.

The barmaid rattled the dice and threw.

"You're still alive," the black knight said. She strode to their table. Sergeant's chevrons had been sewn to the sleeves of the shirt. "This neighborhood is being evacuated, folks."

"Not by us," the other man said.

"By you now, sir. On my orders. As an officer of the law, I must order you to leave. There's a tank car derailed, leaking some kind of gas."

"That's fog," Randolph Carter told her. "Fog and smoke."

"Not *just* fog. I'm sorry, sir, but I must ask all of you to go. How long have you been here?"

"Sixteen years," the blond woman said. "The neighborhood was a lot nicer when we came."

"It's some sort of chemical weapon, like LSD."

He asked, "Don't you want to sit down?" He stood, offering her his chair.

"My shot must be wearing off. The shot was supposed to protect me. I'm Sergeant . . . Sergeant . . ."

The other man said, "Very few of us are protected by shots, Sergeant Chapman. Shots usually kill people, particularly soldiers."

Randolph Carter looked at her shirt. The name CHAPMAN was engraved on a stiff plastic plate there, the plate held out like a little shelf by the thrust of her left breast.

"Sergeant Anne Chapman of the United States Army. We think it's the plants, sir. All the psychoactive drugs we know about come from plants— opium, cocaine, heroin."

"You're the heroine," he told her gently. "Coming here like this to get us out."

"All of them chemicals the plants have stumbled across to protect us from insects, really. And now they've found something to protect the insects from us." She paused, staring at him. "That isn't right, is it?"

Again he asked, "Don't you want to sit down?"

"Gases from the comet. The comet's tail has wrapped all Earth in poisonous gases."

The blonde murmured, "What is the meaning of this name given Satan: *Beelzebub*."

A tiny voice from the ceiling answered.

"You, sir," the black knight said, "won't you come with me? We've got to get out of here."

"You can't get out of here," the other man told them.

He nodded to the knight. "I'll come with you, if you'll love me." He rose, pushing the sword up his coat sleeve, point first.

"Then come on." She took him by the arm and pulled him through the door.

A hansom cab rattled past.

"What is this place?" She put both hands to her forehead. "I'm dreaming, aren't I? This is a nightmare." There was a fly on her shoulder, a blowfly gorged with carrion. She brushed it off; it settled again, unwilling to fly through the night and the yellow fog. "No, I'm hallucinating."

He said, "I'd better take you to your room." The bricks were wet and slippery underfoot. As they turned a corner, and another, he told her what she could do for him when they reached her room. A dead bitch lay in the gutter. Despite the night and the chill of autumn, the corpse was crawling with flies.

Sickly yellow gaslight escaped from under a door. She tore herself from him and pushed it open. He came after her, his arms outstretched. "Is this where you live?"

The three players still sat at their table. They had been joined by a fourth, a new Randolph Carter. As the door flew wide the fourth player turned to look, but he had no face.

She whispered, "This is Hell, isn't it? I'm in Hell, for what I did. Because of what we did. We're all in Hell. I always thought it was just something the Church made up, something to keep you in line, you know what I mean, sir?"

She was not talking to him, but he nodded sympathetically.

"Just a game in the pope's head. But it's real, it's here, and here we are."

"I'd better take you to your room," he said again.

She shuddered. "In Hell you can't pray, isn't that right? But I can—listen! I can pray! *Dear G*—"

He had wanted to wait, wanted to let her finish, but the sword, Sacnoth, would not wait. It entered her throat, more eager even than he, and emerged spent and swimming in scarlet blood.

The faceless Randolph Carter rose from the table. "Your seat, young man," he said through no mouth. "I'm merely the marker whom you have followed."

Empires of Foliage and Flower

✦

When the sun was still young and men fools who worshipped war, the wise ones of Urth took for themselves the names of humble plants to teach men wisdom. Sage there was, who gave his name to all the rest. And Acacia and Fennel; Basil, that was their anointed leader; Lichen and Eglantine, Orchis, and many more.

The greatest was Thyme.

Thyme's habit it was to walk westward over the world, ever westward and ever older, whitening his beard and waiting for no one; and if ever he turned east, the days and the years dropped from him. The rest are gone, but Thyme (thus it was said) will walk until the sun grows cold.

On a certain day, when dawn cast Thyme's shadow a league before him, he met a child in the road playing such a game as even Thyme, who had seen all games, had never seen before. For a moment Thyme halted. "Little girl," he said, "what is it you play?" For she gathered up seeds of the sallow-flowered garden pea, and ordered them in rows and circles, making them roll with her fingers; and scattered them to the winds, then gathered them again.

"Peace," she said.

Thyme bent over her, smiling. "I see you play at pease," he said. "Tell me what this game is."

"These are people," the child said. She held up her pease to show him, and Thyme nodded his agreement. "At first they're soldiers like ours," and she marshaled a column, with advance guard, rear guard, skirmishers, and outriders. "And then they fight, and then they can come home."

"And will they never go to war again? Or fight with their wives?" Thyme asked.

"No," the child said. "No, never."

"Come with me, little girl," Thyme told her, and took her by the hand.

All that day they tramped the dusty road together, mounting high hills and descending into bear-haunted vales where many say Thyme never comes. They crossed the wide valley of the Lagous, Thyme carrying the child on his shoulder at the ford of Didugua. Sometimes they sang, sometimes they talked, sometimes they went silently, walking hand in hand.

And as they walked on side by side, the child grew, so that she who had toddled in the beginning skipped and romped at the end. Thyme taught her to turn cartwheels, something he himself does very well.

That night they camped beside the road. He built a small fire to keep her warm, and told her tale after tale, for no one knows as many stories as Thyme. Green apples he picked for her, but they were red and ripe when they left his fingers.

"Who are you, sir?" the child asked, for now that Thyme had stopped, the ten watches of the night twittered and flitted like bats in the bushes about them, and she was a little frightened.

"You may call me Thyme," he told her, "and I am an eremite. That means I live with the Increate, and not with men. Do you have a mother, child?"

"Yes," she said. "And my mother will be worried about me, because I'm gone."

"No," Thyme said, and he shook his white head. "No, your mother will understand, because I left a prophecy with her when you were born. Do you know it? Think, because you must often have heard it."

The child thought; and when the cricket had sung, she said, " 'Thyme will take my child from me.' Yes, sir, Mama often used to say that."

"And did she not say anything more?"

The child nodded. "She said, 'And Thyme will surely bring her back.' "

"You see, she will not worry. Nor should you worry, child. The Increate is father to all. I take them from him—that is my function. And I return them again."

The child said, "I don't have a father, sir."

Again Thyme shook his head. "You have the Increate and you have me. You may call me Father Thyme. Now go to sleep."

The child slept, being still quite small. To make a small enchantment for her, Thyme moved his hands; gossamer covered her to keep her warm, and the flying seed of cottonwood and dandelion. She slept, but Thyme stayed awake all night to watch the stars.

In the morning the child sat up, rubbing the seeds from her eyes and looking around for Thyme. Thyme rose from the fields to greet her, sweet-smelling and wet with dew.

"I have to wash my face," the child told him. "I'd like something to eat too, and a drink of water."

Thyme nodded, for he understood that she indeed needed all those things. "There is a brook nearby," he said. "It lies to the east, but that cannot be helped."

He led her to it; and as they walked, his beard, which had been white as winter snow, grew frosty, and at last iron gray.

As for the child, because she walked with Thyme, she became younger and younger. When they reached the brook, she was hardly older than she had been when Thyme had seen her playing Peace in the dusty road. Nevertheless, she scrubbed her face and hands, then drank from her hands, scooping up handful after handful of clear, cold water from the brook while Thyme picked berries for them both.

"Why is the water so cold, Father Thyme?" she asked him. "Did it sleep out all night too, but with nobody to cover it?"

Thyme chuckled, for he was beginning to recall the ways of men, and even something of the ways of little girls. "No," he told her. "Trust me, my child, when I say that water you drink has been busy all night dashing down past rocks and roots. But it has run down from high mountain slopes where even Crocus has not yet set foot."

"Is that where the men fight?" she asked.

Thyme nodded. "For a thousand years your Easterlings have warred with the Men of the West, making the high meadows of the mountainsides their battlefields. Doubtless there is blood in that water you drink, though there is too little for us to see. Do you still wish to drink it?"

The child hesitated, but at last scooped up more. "Yes," she said, "because that's all there is to drink."

Thyme nodded again. "I drink pure rain, for the most part, mingled with a little dew, and there is no blood in either. You could not do that; you would become very thirsty, and die before the next rain. Drink as you must."

Hand in hand they walked west, eating wild raspberries from Thyme's old hat, the child hardly higher than Thyme's legs. But soon the top of her head had reached Thyme's waist; and when the last raspberry was eaten, she was nearly as tall as he, and they walked on arm in arm across the plain.

Thus they came to green Vert, that great city, the Boast of the East; and all who saw the two thought them a grandfather and his granddaughter, and smiled to hear Thyme ask if the road was not too weary for her, or the way too hard; for the child had grown lithe and long of limb, red-cheeked as an apple, with lips like two raspberries and eyes like the midnight sky.

Now it so happened that Patizithes, the Prince of the East, the Lord of All the Lands That Lie Beyond Lagous, the Margrave of the Magitae, and the Wildgrave of the Wood, the youngest son of the Emperor and heir to the Throne of Imperial Jade (for he mourned five brothers), saw them enter the city. Patizithes had been inspecting the Guard of the City Wall, a guard of boys and old men, and fretting at the duty, for he wished to ride to the war, feeling that he might win in a week what had not been won by his fierce father's war-tried warriors in a millennium. But when his gaze strayed from the boots and the buttons, the well-buffed broadswords of the boys and the burnished bucklers of the old men, he saw the child (grown a young woman) who walked with Thyme.

Quickly he dismissed that feeble formation, drew off three rich rings and dropped them into his pocket, and canting his cap at an elegant angle, dashed down to greet them at the gate while they were still being scrutinized by the sentries.

"Old man," said the senior sentry, "you must tell me who you are, and what it is you want in our city."

"I am but a poor eremite, my son," Thyme told him, "as you see. For myself, I want nothing from your proud city, and that is what I shall receive from it—a few broken bricks, perhaps, and a pretty fragment of malachite. But this child wishes to learn of peace, and of the war that took her father, and I have come with her, for she could not have reached this place without me."

Precisely at this point, Prince Patizithes appeared. "My friend," he said, smiling at the senior sentry (who was utterly astonished to be addressed so by the proud young paladin), "even you ought to be able to see that these travelers mean no harm. The old man's too feeble to overpower anyone, and while those eyes might vanquish whole armies, such conquests are no breach of the peace."

The senior sentry saluted. "It's my duty, sir, to question everyone who seeks to enter by this gate."

"And you have done so," Prince Patizithes pointed out. "I merely remind you that it's equally your duty to admit them when they've satisfied you as to their good intentions. I know them, and I vouch for them. Are you satisfied?"

The senior sentry saluted a second time. "Yes, sir! I am indeed, sir."

"Then come, dear friends." Prince Patizithes pointed to a little park, where a fragrant fountain played. "This quiet spot exists only to welcome you. Wouldn't you like to bathe your feet in its cool waters? You can sit on the coping while I bring you a little food and a bottle of wine from that inn."

While Thyme threw his long length on the soft green grass, the charming child permitted Prince Patizithes to hold her hand as she stepped across the cool stone coping and sat waving her weary feet in the fountain's chanting waters. "How could your city have known we were coming?" she asked. "So as to have this park ready for us?"

Prince Patizithes pursed his lips, feigning to ponder. "We knew that someone worthy of such a place must come at last," he whispered warmly. "And now we see that we were correct. How do you feel about duck? Our city's as famous for its teal as for its hospitality."

The child nodded and smiled, and when Patizithes had gone, stepped under the silver spray, washing the dust of many roads from her hair and face, and wetting the thin shift that reached now scarcely to her thighs. "Isn't he nice?" she asked Thyme.

"No," Thyme told her, sitting up. "No, my child, not he, though I may bring out some good in him before the end. He is brave because he has never been injured; generous, but he has not toiled for the food. You may trust me when I say that much more than that is required."

"But he likes me, and I'm a big girl now."

"Then ask yourself whether he would like you still, were you still a little one," Thyme told her. "That is the test."

"I still *am* a little girl inside," the child said. "It's only that going with you has changed my outside, Father Thyme."

"As he is still a little boy within," Thyme told her. "He has been changed as you have been changed, and in no other way. Do you see that woman with the basket of limes on her shoulder? She has borne many children; but the child in her is no larger than the child in you."

"Is there a child in everybody?" the child asked.

"Yes," Thyme told her. "But in some it is a dead child. And they are far worse than this young man."

Prince Patizithes appeared as he spoke. The proud prince bore a patinated brass platter—a servile service he had never performed before—but since he had seen the servants and slaves of his father's palace present comestibles in casseroles all his life, he lifted its lid with a fine flourish. "Roast teal," he announced, smiling. "Well stuffed with chestnuts and oysters, or so I am assured."

The charmed child served him an answering smile that pierced his poor heart.

"Wine too!" To cover his confusion, he brought a cobweb-cloaked bottle of Vert's best vintage from one pocket, popping the cork with a tug of his teeth and taking two tall tumblers from the other. "Wine for you, Father . . . ?"

"Thyme," Thyme told him.

"Father Thyme. And wine for this fair lady. Your niece, perhaps, sir?"

"My adopted daughter, my son." Thyme took the tumbler and tossed it down.

"Won't you join us?" the child asked as she sipped.

The proud prince shrugged sorrowfully. "Alas, that rat-infested inn had only those two tumblers. But if I might have swallow from yours . . . ?"

Shyly the child gave him her glass, and pointedly he pressed his lips to its rim, where her own ruby lips had lingered only a moment before.

Thyme cleared his throat. "We have come to your city so that this child might see of what stuff war is made. You seem to be a person of consequence here. Would it be possible for you to arrange an interview with one of your generals for her? I would be grateful, and so would she, I know."

The deceitful prince dipped into the dressing for a savory oyster. "I could try to set up an interview with our emperor's son for you two," he said slowly. "It wouldn't be easy, perhaps. But I could try."

The child asked eagerly, "Or with the emperor himself? I want to ask him to make peace with the Men of the West."

"Those yellowbellies?" The prince spat. "I don't think my—our beloved ruler would really go so far as to punish you for that. But to be honest, dear maiden, I don't believe it will be of the slightest use."

Thyme tipped the cobweb-wrapped bottle above his tumbler. "Nor do I," he said sorrowfully. "Except to her."

"If it will be of use to her, I'll arrange it," Patizithes promised. "But first she must be dressed for court. It won't do for her to be presented in that ragged shift, though you, as a peregrine holy man, may dress as you like."

Thyme tasted the wondrous wine in his tumbler thoughtfully. "Yes, I suppose you're right, my son. The child must have some new clothes."

"And I'll see to that too," the prince pledged. "I know the seamstress who makes gowns for the most fashionable court ladies. I suppose it might take her a month or so to run one up, though; you could stay with me till it's ready. Have you that much time?"

"All that we require, my son," Thyme told him. Thyme was taking charge of the teal, of which the lovely child had claimed no more than a leg, and Prince Patizithes was utterly astonished to see him bite the bare bones as easily as the child had eaten the meat.

"That's settled, then," the prince said with satisfaction; and as soon as the two had made their meal, he brought them both to the seamstress, who curtsied like a countess when she saw the royal patron at her drawing-room door.

"Madame Gobar." Patizithes pointed.

"What a wonderful figure!" The seamstress sighed, chucking the child beneath the chin. "You've hardly need of me, my dear, with that tiny waist and that face. Any little dressmaker could wrap you up in silk and slap on a few pearls and pack you off to court looking like a princess."

"Which she will never be, worse luck," the prince pointed out. "And I beg you not to be extravagant with those pearls."

"You're right, of course, Highness," the seamstress said. "Elegance and simplicity. And a silk that's like spring grass. I'll get it."

When the seamstress had slipped off to her storeroom, the child whispered, "Why does she call you *Highness*, kind sir?"

"It's merely a courtesy title." Prince Patizithes soothed her smoothly. "A bit of flattery our city's tradespeople lavish upon those whose station in life is somewhat more elevated than their own."

Thyme sighed. "I see."

The seamstress had brought a bolt of bright silk. She laid it on her table and put up a painted screen to close one corner of her chamber. "If you'll just step behind this, my dear," she chirped, "and slip out of that—that *thing* you're wearing, I'll take your measurements."

The beautiful child nodded dutifully, and slipped behind the screen, soon followed by the seamstress.

The prince looked grim. "This will take half the day, I'm afraid. We should have kept the wine."

"I did," Thyme told him, bringing the bottle from beneath his colorless old cloak. "No glasses, though, I fear. I have bad luck with them—they break so easily." He passed the black bottle to Prince Patizithes, who was somewhat surprised to find his wine gone sour.

"That should do it," said the seamstress, stepping from behind her screen. "I shall have her gown ready—"

Thyme's cold eye caught hers. There was the slightest of pauses.

"—by tomorrow. Tomorrow before nones, I should imagine."

"Fine," Thyme told her.

"And I've loaned her an old dress to wear until then," the seamstress proceeded breathlessly, "that is, she really doesn't have to return it."

"We thank you," Thyme told her; and as he spoke, the child stepped silently from behind the seamstress's screen, scarcely less lovely than a summer sunrise.

The prince gasped.

Thyme's mouth twitched, and he suppressed a smile. "This audience you promised to arrange for us, do you think you could make it for tomorrow afternoon?"

The child smiled too. "Yes, it would be marvelous. Could you?"

"I think so." Prince Patizithes nodded nervously. "Anyway, I'll try. I—my house is outside the walls. It's only a league or so. My carriage is at the gate. I'll bring it if you like."

"That might be best," Thyme told him. "This poor child and I have already walked some distance today."

"Of course, of course!" Prince Patizithes darted through the dressmaker's door.

Wearily, the child chose a chair. "He *is* nice," she told Thyme, "whether you think so or not."

"As nice as peace?" Thyme asked her seriously.

The seamstress simpered. "He's royal, my darling, and to be royal is ever so much better than to be nice."

"Perhaps." Thyme turned away and walked to the window. He had hardly reached it when a whip cracked outside. The prince's equipage came rattling over the cobbles, and four footmen leaped to open its doors and draw out a deep green carpet.

"Slippers!" The seamstress snapped her fingers. She flung herself into the search, but she had started too late. Lightly as any lady, the child smiled, gave her a little pat of parting, and put her hand into the prince's to help herself up the steep step. Frowning, Thyme followed, choosing a seat that faced the child.

Prince Patizithes raced around the high rear wheels to duck through the other door and sit beside her. "We've shoes aplenty," he assured her. "Guests are always leaving them. You know how it is. You may have whichever pairs you like."

The child thanked him with her eyes. "Are there any green ones to go with my new dress?"

Their coachman clucked his tongue to his team and cracked his black whip, the white horses leaped like lurchers after a leveret, and the prince's rich equipage jerked and jolted up the cobblestoned street.

Patizithes laughed. "Why, there's nothing *but* green ones, I'll take my oath. Because of the war, no lady of Vert has ever dared come to court in anything else."

The sentries snapped erect and saluted them smartly as the ghostly team galloped through the postern gate. Patizithes had lied about his lodge (for it was to such a hunting house in the forest royal that his carriage carried them) when he said it lay but a league away; their horses were heaving and lathered with sweat whiter than they before all the weary watches that brought them to that lonely lodge were done.

Yet it was lovely. The child stared at its tall chimneys and the thronging green trees of his father's forest with dazed delight. "Do you really live here?" she asked Patizithes in a bewitched whisper.

"It's just a shed," he said. "I've a little place in town as well, but I know you'll be more comfortable here, where each of you can have a private apartment."

At evening, while the whip-poor-will called from the tall cherry tree and the nightingale rained her sweet notes on the world, Prince Patizithes and the changed child watched lovely Lune's head lifted by the slow rotation of Urth, and strolled the strange walks of the grotesque little garden the prince's poor grandfather had graded and planted while weeping for his wandering wife.

Fragrant were the ramping pink roses and the fading forget-me-nots that night; but he found the child's musky tresses more fragrant far. And sweet though the birds' songs sounded, she found the prince's poor promises sweeter still.

The two thought themselves alone. But all the while, one watched with the night-wide eyes of love. While they paced the pebbled paths between the silent flowers' spiked arrays, sage Thyme spied upon each pale sigh, peeping between bloom and leaf. And while they sat side by side and hand in hand on the stained stone bench beneath the spreading wisteria, Thyme watched unwinking from the midnight face of the mute sundial.

And while they lay lazy on the soft grass, swearing the sweet oaths of love and longing, and whispering as they parted that though long lives might pass like a night and the New Sun sunder the centuries, yet never should they ever part, Thyme crept and cried, counting seconds that spilled with the sand from the hourglass, and scenting the soft breezes that cooled the child's burning cheek with his sad spice.

The cock crowed as Thyme tapped impatient toes at the lofty lodge's deserted door, but the lovers slept long. It was nearly nones before the coach came, bringing Prince Patizithes and a cheerless child. Together the three traveled over the rugged road that runs to the green gates of Vert; but they scarcely spoke one word, and though Thyme turned his anguished eyes from face to face, while watch waited upon watch, the cheated child never met his grim gaze. No more gave she her grave glance to the prince perched on the soft seat beside her, though her hand sought his, and sometimes failed to find it.

In a space scarcely short of miraculous, Madame Gobar, the seamstress, had sewn such a green gown as any virgin nymph would willingly have worn to Vert's stiff court. "No pearls, you see, Your Highness," she told Prince Patizithes in the honest tones of one who takes an open pride in having done her duty. "A few small emeralds, and a nice big aquamarine or two. And she loves it—don't you, my dear?"

She did. But before she could smooth her skirt and gaze a moment at the glass, off flew the coach, charging down the dirty streets of Vert and never pausing until it pulled up before the broad stair whose steps stretched to the portals of the palace.

Soon and swiftly they were sent before the emperor's own imperial throne; and there the poor child voiced her plea for peace through chattering teeth.

"I do not know how many men have died," she said. "Your Majesty will know that better than I; but I know my father was one of them, and that as we came here we saw unworked fields everyplace, houses falling to ruin, and women plowing—plowing badly—when the plowing should've been done weeks ago. We saw women sowing grain instead of shirts, cattle and sheep that had been killed by bears and wolves, and hungry children."

"Boys who can never grow into strong soldiers," Thyme added, addressing the emperor, "and girls who will never breed them."

Some shocked courtiers gasped at all this, grabbing their gowns and clutching their cloaks as though to keep them clear of contamination. But the stern, scarred old emperor never heeded them, nodding his head and neither smiling nor scowling.

"I have lost my father," the child continued. "I know that you have lost five fine sons. Only one is left to you. I love him, and so do all your other loyal subjects, I feel sure. Won't you make peace?"

"Peace has been made many times," the emperor said solemnly. "And each peace has only led to a new war. What is the good of treaties and truces where there is no trust? The fighting stops, and our enemy rearms."

With that, the elderly emperor's voice sank to silence, and a sullen silence hung heavy over all that gay green gathering. Some aged courtier coughed, and there was the faint scuffle of many shuffling feet. Prince Patizithes strode forward to stand beside the confounded child. Silently, he slipped his hand into hers and led her to an alcove. "I promised you an audience," he told the child coldly. "I didn't promise you that it would help things, and as you see, it hasn't."

Thyme told her, "You tried, and that's something not many have done."

Just then, they were joined by a general, an old officer whose bottle-green uniform bore many an enameled medal, besides the usual battle honors. His hair was gray, his visage grim, his eyes the green of Vert. "Your Highness," this green general growled, "may I interrupt? I think it will only take a moment."

"You already have, Generalissimo," the prince pointed out. "But yes. I think an interruption right now might be welcome."

"You are young," the green general said gravely. "And so you think wisdom is to be found in pink cheeks and bright eyes. We who bear the weight of past years know that white hair or a bald head is a better indication of it. Since you have brought this old, and I suppose holy, hermit to the court, I would like to make use of whatever hard-won wisdom he may possess while I can."

"Then speak, my son," Thyme urged graciously.

The hoary-headed old officer did not hesitate. "How can we win?"

"You may win," Thyme told him, "when your army is dressed in yellow."

For a moment the grim old general stood stunned. "You can counsel me to dress my soldiers like the enemy," he said slowly, "but I assure you that though I am master of all our armies, I cannot do such a thing. Nor would I do it if I could. I would rather lose the war than do as you suggest."

"Then you will not have to," Thyme told him. "Because I will do it for you."

The old officer turned upon his heel and left them without another word.

Thyme watched his retreating back, then said softly to the child, "Now I too must go, and you must come with me."

She shook her head. "I love Prince Patizithes," she said. Thinking that he still stood at her side, she looked around the alcove for him; but the prince of Vert had vanished.

"You will come with me." Thyme turned and walked away, his black boots tapping the tessellated pavements of the palace like the ticking of some slow clock.

"And he loves me!" the child whispered to herself; but there was no one but herself left to listen.

That night it rained, and Thyme sat drinking drop for drop with a broad banyan tree. As soon as the last drizzle stopped and the sun was seen, he rose and returned to the road. He had not walked much more than a watch when he heard the hurrying child calling. *"Thyme, Father Thyme, stop! Wait for me!"*

Without waiting, turning toward her, or even so little as looking behind him, he murmured, "Thyme waits for no one," and walked on.

It was early evening before she walked with him as she had when he had brought her to the city. "I want to tell you," she said.

"I know." He nodded. "And you are old enough now to tell Thyme, if you wish."

Slowly then she spoke of the old garden and the green lawn on which she had lain with her lover; then of the threats he had thrown in her frightened face, because she had wished to remain where he would reign, though she should be called his concubine.

"Did I do wrong?" she asked at last.

"No." For a second Thyme stopped, turning to take in the road that returned to Vert. "Very small, child, are the flying days of love, and men and women must catch them when they can, if they are to know love at all."

The child shook her head. "Wouldn't it be better not to know love at all, than to know a false love?"

"No," Thyme answered again, turning back to their way once more and taking her by the hand. "In the desert, travelers see pools of water where no water is; but those who see these pools know how real water must look, if ever real water is found."

So Thyme spoke, and soon no more was said, though arm in arm they walked together. Their road had reached the rugged hills, and now wound higher and higher, turning and twisting until at last it mounted mountains. There their road went with a wider, fairer way, where green grenadiers counted cadence for raw recruits, brave youths and young boys with pallid faces, who flaunted pikes.

With each cubit they climbed, the cherry-lipped child who had ventured to Vert vanished. Lines led from her eyes to her ears, and strands of silver streaked her once sleek hair. The food they found and the rough rations Thyme took from some of the soldiers seemed to thicken her hips and bulk her breasts; and at last, with their road long lost, when they went their way guided only by the green onrush of the emperor's army, she laid palsied palms on her broadened belly and knew the feeble flutter of new life.

Drawn the child looked before the dawn, in the hour when her own child came. Then Thyme himself knew terror; for it is not so (as some say) that Thyme heals all things, though healing he has. But Thyme himself tied the cord and comforted his tired child, pressing her babe to her breast.

"Now I must go," Thyme told her. "You must have food and good water, and rags with which to diaper your son. Keep him warm while I am away, and yourself as well." He set sticks by her hand, so that she might feed their fire, saying. "I will return as soon as the Increate wills it."

Then night closed over his old gray cloak; he was gone like some ghost. The chilled child lay alone save for her son, alone and lonely, shaking with the flickering, guttering flames in the white wind that whipped the wide green skirt Madame Gobar had made, shaking too with terror as she heard the wild howls of the wolves that batten on battles, the slayers of the slain.

More than these, she feared the fierce soldiers who surged about the wretched brush that sheltered her and her son. They who had been boys had been made beasts, bent if not broken by their battles, the henchmen of Hell and the disciples of Death—thus she thought. Then her babe embraced her breast, sucking his mama's sweet milk; and soon her heart soared. Such was the mutability of his mother. Such, indeed, are the shiftings in all human hearts.

Somewhere a stick snapped, and her bliss broke with it. She staggered to her feet, and would have fled if she could; but she could scarcely stand. Part of her wretched protection was rolled away. A short sword and a worn face caught the firelight. For a moment that seemed a month, her eyes met his. "By the book!" the startled soldier swore. "What in the name of awful Abaia are you two up to?"

"My son's having his breakfast, as you see," she said; "and I was resting, until you came."

The soldier lowered his sword and pushed through the brush. "Then sit down." He held out his hand; and when the child had clasped it, and sat as he had said, he sat himself, sitting so his broad back blocked the hole he had made in their screen of brush.

"Did you see our fire?" she asked. "I feared someone would, though Thyme piled as many dead bushes and branches as he could around this windfall before he built it."

"Thyme?"

"My father. Or at least that's what I call him, since he cares for me. You needn't be afraid. Thyme's an old man, you can kill him easily, I'm sure."

The soldier shook his head, his eyes on the baby boy. "I wouldn't do that. What's his name?"

The child had not yet chosen one, not knowing one would so soon be needed. Now she blurted, "Barrus!" Barrus had been her brother, in days that seemed a dream. Her bold brother, and her father's favorite.

"Ha!" the soldier said. "The handsome one, eh? Well, he's handsome enough, I'll admit, for somebody so new to this world. But may I ask what you're doing here, on a battlefield in a ball gown?"

"Seeing war," she said. "I think so that I'll know what it is when Thyme brings peace."

"You'd better go back home," the soldier told her. "Before you're killed—you and your child too. Before some fool shoots you, or you starve or freeze to death."

"We're going on, I think." Barrus had released her nipple; he was asleep. She slid the strap up so her silk bodice hid her breast. "Over the mountains to the Yellow Empire."

"In that green dress? That's suicide." A brass clasp held his soldier's sagum. He opened the clasp, pulled off the cloak, and handed it to her. "This was green when it was new, but it's gray now. It may not get you through alive, but it'll keep you warmer till you die."

Tearfully, she tried to thank him, though she only sobbed and stammered.

"Don't worry about me." The soldier shrugged. "There's plenty of dead men out there, and their cloaks don't keep the chill off any longer. I'll get another one—a newer one, with any luck." He rose to go.

Winking back her weeping, she blew him a brave kiss. He caught it, smiled suddenly (he seemed but a boy when he smiled), and was gone as the dark gave way to dawn. Hot tears streaked her tired cheeks; she closed his cloak about herself and Barrus, her baby boy.

So Thyme saw them when he pushed aside the brush—wrapped in warm wool, and peacefully asleep. When the child woke and Thyme chided her for crying, she would say only that those who have seen clean water in the desert's depths, without drinking, are entitled to tears.

Slowly they mounted the mountains' stony sides, old Thyme taking her hand and the child cradling her child. In time of peace, travelers would trudge the passes, as Thyme assured her. At present, divisions defended every defile, holding each high road against whole armies.

A bit before evensong, they were to witness such a struggle. Thyme stopped, pointing for the child with the pine staff he had chosen before they had left the last trees behind. "Do you see the green squares?" he asked sadly. "This is no skirmish, but some major matter."

It seemed a storm had struck the mountain-cut below. The arrows flashed like lightning, and they heard the thunder of the guns. A surging green square gained ground, then wavered and went out like the lambent flame of some snuffed taper; a second square crept up the slope, covering the corpses of the slain.

"See how resolutely they advance." Thyme tapped a stone with his staff as he spoke. "Determined to win or die! Would you care to say which you think it will be?"

She shook her head. She felt sure the soldier whose wool sagum she wore served in that square, though she told herself truly there was no way of knowing. Like the last, this square perished in the pass.

A yellow column came, sliding along like a snake from the wild wadis of the west. Green cavalry gave it check, then gave way. Scattered green soldiers followed, fleeing.

"The Westerners have the victory," she said to Thyme, "and soon they will take Vert. Then there will be peace."

Thyme took up his staff and stood, ready to resume their march. "That pass has changed hands many times," he told the child. "And the war is not yet won."

That night they camped near the enemy army. "Now wash your dress," Thyme told her. "I will keep my eyes off you." She did as he bid, scrubbing her soiled green gown in a sparkling stream. Sometimes soldiers stopped to talk with her. She was covered by her cloak, and she feigned a friendliness that was soon sincere. "Yellow will never yield," the newest recruits replied when she pleaded for peace. The older soldiers only shrugged, or spit, or spoke of something else. Although their accent was strange, she soon ceased to notice it, speaking just as they spoke. No one she had known had worn yellow, yet save for their yellow coats the young men could have been her cousins.

"Will there never be peace?" she asked Thyme when her dress was dry.

"You will see," he said, and would say no more.

When the next day dawned, her baby, Barrus, could walk with his mother. Thyme found him trousers and a shirt, she dared not ask where, and she shortened the little legs, and the sleeves of the shirt. From the peaks they could see the plains, and in the misty distance the spires of Zant, that unyielding yellow city, glorious with gold.

Barrus told tales of days she was sure he had only dreamed, chattering to the child of childish notions she had never known, then comforting her with kisses. "My mom forgets, doesn't she?" He giggled, grinning. "But you always remember, Father Thyme, don't you?"

Thyme sighed and shook his head. "It is my task to wipe away. As you will learn."

They found a road that roved from wood to wood. Stunted shrubs made way for white pine, alder, and pale aspen. Barrus had a knife now, and cut a clever whistle with which he piped their progress from peak to pass, and at last to the mountain meadows. He did as Thyme told him, but defiantly, not freely. At each step they took he grew taller, and more sulky and more sullen. "I can beat Thyme," he told his mother, tapping his toes to a tune he had taken from the thrush.

"Please don't!" She felt frightened; Thyme was their only friend.

The great sage grimaced. "They always think they can, at his age."

A day of drizzle brought them to the bright gates of Zant, weary and wet. Sentries stopped them, guards in gorgeous golden armor who addressed them in the babyish voices of boys or asked the quavering questions of senescence.

"We only want food and shelter," Thyme told them. "Food, and a fire, and a little peace. Those are our only reasons for coming to Zant."

Perhaps the guards pitied the palsied old man, for they opened the gilt gates for them.

"Are we going to go to an inn?" Barrus asked. He pointed to the painted boards grouped near the gate: the Golden Goblin, the Pilgrim's Pause, the Royal Roast, and many more, all pied with paint to picture the Goose Girl, the Pilgrim putting down his pack, the Singing Oriole, and so on, so that even those who could not read the names could take their ease at an inn in any case.

"No," Thyme told him. "Or at least I hope not. This is the country of gold, so nowhere does gold buy less than here."

He stopped at the step of a private dwelling, rapping its dark door with a ring hung for that purpose. "Madame," he said to the wary woman who came to his knock, "we are poor travelers, seeking a lodging for a night or two at a price we can afford. Can you tell us of some decent family who might take us in? We cannot pay much, but we will lay down ready money for whatever we get."

"No." The dour woman would have shut her door and shot its bar, but that Thyme's blunt black boot blocked its edge.

"If not yourself, perhaps some neighbor?"

"I don't dislike any of my neighbors that much," the dour woman told Thyme. "Now get your foot off my threshold, or I'll call the dog."

Thyme stepped back, bowing as her door banged shut.

A meager little man in a long yellow cloak stopped as it slammed, looking as wet as they were. "I heard what you said. I've got a room in a decent enough house, a couple of streets over. They might take you and your wife—"

"My daughter, my son."

"And your daughter, I meant to say. And your grandson, if you can pay."

Thyme thanked him, and they went with him, down one sodden street and up another, until at length they arrived at an old-fashioned high city house, ornamented with carvings now decayed, with a second story over-hanging the first, a third that overhung the second, and giddy garrets that overlooked the wall.

Cheapening with the landlady, Thyme got the child and Barrus a garret and rented a similar room for himself. When the meager man who had guided them to the house had gone, their new hostess asked how well they knew him.

"Less than you, I'm sure." Thyme knelt by the tiled hearth that was now his own, for this night if not forever. There was a little tinder and a log or two.

"You won't get *that* burning," said Barrus.

"In time," Thyme told him. His flint scratched his steel, sending a shower of flying sparks to the tinder.

"Because," the landlady continued confidentially, choosing to chat with the child, "we really know nothing about him here, except that he pays."

Thyme puffed his tinder. "He seems an honest enough man." A small swirl of smoke curled toward the chimney.

The child shivered; her cloak was soaked from hem to collar. "When he has that going," she said to her son, "you should borrow a stick to light ours."

Barrus snapped, "I'm not an idiot, Mother."

The landlady laughed. "Maybe not, but you could fool some people, boy. Now, none of your sass to me, understand? Or all of you will be out in the street.

"Our lodger, I was going to say, pays us by the month. But sometimes the only time we see him is when he pays."

"The very time," Thyme remarked tartly, "when so many are invisible."

The landlady laughed again. "And don't I know it! Still, you can't help wondering where he goes and what he does."

A feeble flame flickered beside Thyme's tinder, darkening the white wood before it dwindled and disappeared. "Does he share supper with your family?" He blew on the bright embers and fanned them with his hand.

She nodded knowingly. "Sometimes. Mutton tonight, like I told you."

Barrus said, "It's burning right now, I bet."

"It'll keep, boy. Besides, I want to see if you three need anything more before I go down to look at it. I don't climb the steps more than I have to." She was short and stout.

"More blankets," Barrus said bitterly. "And more firewood."

"There aren't any more blankets. You can spread your coat on your bed, the same as we do. And if you want any more wood, boy, you'll have to fetch it yourself—I'm not carrying another stick up here. Come along, and I'll show you where it is."

The child spread chilled fingers before Thyme's tiny blaze. "What do you think?"

"I think it will catch that smallest log now," Thyme told her. "Though it would be better if we had more tinder."

"About her lodger, Father Thyme. You know everything."

The old sage shook his head. "I *find out* everything," he said, "sooner or later. But I don't know everything. A fellow that rents a room and uses it only now and then? That's a rich man who wants someplace to go when he's not where he usually is. We'll learn more at supper."

And so they did. There were two sober tinkers who rented a room together, as well as themselves and the meager man who had helped them locate their lodging, and the landlord and landlady. The meager man asked clever questions of the tinkers until he learned that neither had left the city since he had last seen them. Then he turned to Thyme to ask about their travels.

"Over the mountains." Thyme took a pair of potatoes from the big blue bowl that the landlord handed him. "And it was the making of the boy, but the destruction of my daughter, or nearly."

"Bad weather there," their landlord allowed. His good wife gave him a long look, and he added, "Or so I've heard. I can't say I've ever been there."

The child peered into her chipped plate, which was still empty.

"It was worse here." Thyme tried to pass her the potatoes, but was waved away. Barrus took the big bowl. "Not as cold as it was in the mountains, but the rain makes you feel it more."

A worn old woman licked chapped lips in the child's plate, her wavering reflection as dim as her dead eyes.

"Of course, the war made everything ten times worse." An earthenware ladle drowned the dim woman in greasy mutton gravy.

"I'm sorry to hear that," the meager man muttered. He and Thyme talked for some time; he seemed eager to learn everything he could about both armies.

"Will there ever be peace?" the child asked them.

"When we win," their landlord said loudly. Hasty for his favor, the two tinkers banged the battered tabletop with their spoons.

Without speaking loudly, the meager lodger managed to make himself heard above the uproar. "Our emperor has pledged a rich reward for anyone who advises him on how peace may be achieved."

"Then your emperor is a wise man," Thyme told him. To the child, Thyme's tones seemed changed, as if an occult knowledge added weight now to words she did not wholly understand.

"And that is pleasant news for us," Thyme continued. "For we've come here expressly to see him."

Their landlady looked happy to hear it. "You may have to wait quite a while," she said, "if that's what you've come for. We don't often see him ourselves. We can give you your rooms for a week, for five times the daily rent."

"That's kind of you." Thyme tasted a piece of brown bread before laying it on his plate and larding it with a ladleful of the gray gravy. "I think you mentioned something of that sort while we were getting the fire started."

"About the rent?"

"About the emperor. You mentioned you didn't see him much."

"I don't remember that," she said.

"Then I was mistaken." Thyme turned from her to look at her lodger. "It was you she was speaking of, perhaps."

"Perhaps it was." The lodger pushed away his plate. "I don't want to take the time of the whole company, but if you could come to my room after dinner, I might be able to advise you about the best ways of getting a glimpse of our emperor, though he doesn't appear in public often."

"I've finished now." Thyme took the napkin from his lap and laid it beside his knife. "I see you're finished as well."

"Your poor daughter hasn't eaten much."

Thyme nodded. "True. But her appetite will be better tomorrow, I think."

The landlord laid a hand on his arm. "No bread pudding? My wife's bread pudding's quite famous."

The two tinkers looked ready to laugh with pure pleasure. "All the more for us," said the smaller. "I'll take the old man's," added the taller.

The child stood up, scraping back her chair. "May I come with my father?" she asked softly.

The meager man began, "Possibly—"

"She must." Thyme took her in tow. "Now what about you, Barrus? Which will it be, peace or pudding?"

"We don't have pease today," the landlady put in. "They're a bit tough, so far into the season."

"Then I'll take pudding," Barrus said sullenly.

"And we will see you later." Thyme led the child to the stair. "It will be on the floor below ours, I suppose."

The lodger nodded as he slipped past them. "I'll have to unlock the door."

"You are fortunate," Thyme told him when they were seated inside. "Our rooms have no locks. Of course, we've little to leave in them when we go."

The meager man smiled mischievously. "I'm afraid I enjoy frustrating our good hostess."

"She's the sort who snoops through drawers? I suppose so; she seems the kind of woman who would."

The meager man nodded. "Yet there are others who discover more secrets, without spying."

"True," Thyme told him. "And kind men who repent of their kindness when they find that others are clever."

"If you know my secret," the meager man said seriously, "you also know that I have means of silencing those who know secrets."

"Which need not be used in this case." Thyme rose and went to the window, where he stood staring out at the smoking chimney pots of Zant.

"I'm glad to hear that."

"My daughter and I will leave your city in the morning. In a day or two, we will have left its empire. I will not speak; nor will she, I assure you."

Bewildered, the child stared from Thyme to the meager man and back. "Please," she said. "What are you two talking about?"

Thyme turned. "The emperors of Vert trace their line from the first emperor for twenty generations," he said softly. "It is not so here in Zant. Here emperor has deposed emperor, till at last one who was well liked was murdered in a manner so foul that the people would not consent to his murderer's coronation. They chose another general in his place, a hero of humble birth who had risen through the ranks and was famous for his courage." Thyme glanced toward the meager man as he finished speaking, a charged gaze that told the child much more than his mere words.

"I understand—I think."

The meager man made a little motion of impatience. "Yes, I'm the Yellow Emperor. How did you know? Give me a simple, straightforward answer, please."

"I had your picture." From the purse at his belt, Thyme took a copper coin. "When we were going over the mountains, I stole some clothes for the boy."

"From my dead soldiers?"

"Yes. A few had a little money, which I thought might be useful in Zant. I confess I did not know how useful. When the Increate is with anyone, there rises a tide that bears into its harbor any ship that carries him."

"Millions of people have those coins."

"You asked me for a simple, straightforward answer," Thyme reminded the emperor.

"Give me your subtle and complex answer, then."

"Not terribly subtle, I fear. Nor terribly complex. It is true that millions have such coins, and yet do not know you when they pass you in the street; but that is only because they cannot conceive that they might encounter someone so exalted someday—someone who holds the power of life and death over every one of them. I know otherwise; there is someone who holds the power of being or unbeing over me, and I shall encounter that someone at the end of Thyme. Thus I understand that such meetings are not impossible."

The child smiled. "Isn't he wonderful?"

"Indeed he is," the emperor admitted. "It was nothing that I said?"

"Nothing specific," Thyme told him. "But our hostess had told us you seldom use the room you rent from her. My daughter asked me about it, and I indicated to her that you were perhaps a man of some wealth, and not what you seemed. You could have been a highwayman, but you lacked the blustering ways and the impressive physique those fellows use to overawe their victims. You had the manners of a gentleman, without the arrogance that is often conferred by birth—we had been with Prince Patizithes in Vert, and so my recollection of that sort of arrogance had been refreshed."

"I see."

"When you questioned me at our meal, my first thought was that you were a spy—an agent of the emperor's, or of whoever gathers facts for him; but such a spy would have been much more interested in the enemy's army than in his own. I asked myself who might have an equal interest in each. A general kept in the capital, perhaps, but such a general could not appear as a poor man in a place where rooms were let to lodgers. Then I recalled that the emperor had been a general, and that an emperor can do as he chooses. So I looked at the coin."

The child ventured a very small sound.

"Yes?" the Yellow Emperor inquired.

"Sir—sire—I thought emperors just sat on their thrones. In the palace."

"On occasions of state, I do," the emperor acknowledged. "But here in Zant, the occasions of state are as few as I can make them. Quite frankly, there are too many other things I have to do."

"But isn't it dangerous?"

"Just yesterday," the Yellow Emperor explained, "I learned of a plot to kill me as I slept. So you see it's less dangerous here than sleeping in my palace. More than a few of our august emperors have died in their beds, although not many were either old or ill. I find out everything that's going on in Zant this way, and that's a great deal less dangerous than not knowing."

He paused, his pale fingers fumbling the worn arms of his chair as he watched the child's face. "Now may I ask what your business was with Prince Patizithes?"

Spreading her hands helplessly, the child turned to Thyme, but he sat silent until she found her own anguished answer: "He let me talk to his father about peace. And he was my lover, at least for one night."

The emperor nodded. "Neither actually surprises me much. Your father said something about peace to the boy, and you're still a beautiful woman. This was some years ago, I take it?"

"No, only a few days—"

"Yes," Thyme told him.

"Perhaps fifteen years or so?"

"Yes," Thyme said a second time.

"I see." The emperor sighed. "They have a certain look about them, all that line. They're all a bit inbred, of course. I'm sorry, madame, but I can't permit you to take your son out of my domains. He's too valuable to me—too valuable even now, while Patizithes is still alive. If the prince dies, he'll be invaluable."

"If he will bring peace . . ."

"He *may* bring victory," the emperor explained. "Or at least assist it."

"And after the victory, will there be peace?"

"Of course. And I will be a generous conqueror, you may trust me for that. Why if—ah—"

"Barrus," she supplied.

"If Barrus proves a faithful vassal, he may well wind up upon the throne of Vert. The Easterners would be more docile with someone of their own royal family to rule them, no doubt."

The child felt that she was choking, but she said, "Then you may keep him. Please—will you remind him, sometimes, of his mother?"

"I will," the emperor answered. "I pledge my word to it."

"Father . . . ?"

"You have done well," Thyme told her. "Is that what you wished to ask me?"

His child shook her head. "No. In Vert you said that Vert might win when its men wore yellow clothes. Barrus will have a yellow uniform, I suppose. Is that what you meant?"

"Perhaps. Or part of it."

The emperor arose, strode across the room, and stared into Thyme's eyes. "You're a prophet! A sage! I should have known. And I take pride in my penetration—bah! What was it you meant? The whole of it."

Thyme told him; and late on the following morning, when the rain had at last relented, and long after the cock crowed, Thyme and the charmed child set forth from that tottering, high house, and the straight old street in which it stood, and the gilded gate of Zant itself.

While they walked, the child chirped, "I know this is very foolish, Father Thyme, but do you know I feel so happy! When I think back about it, I've felt sadder and sadder the whole time I've been with you. Now I'm happy again."

The old sage shrugged, and stroked his snowy whiskers, and whispered, "Such is life, child. Child, life is such."

So they proceeded, long league upon long league, the child chattering of the fields and flowers they passed, some pleasant pastures and their curious cattle. By the well-built bridges of the west they crossed its rushing rivers, the rivers that grind gold from their swirling sands. Soon they saw again the mighty mountains, standing like the walls of the world.

At first, the climbing child feared for her hoary father, feeling him too feeble to face their steep screes and perilous paths; but Thyme seemed to straighten with every step, and the snowy beard he had brought to Zant grew grayer and grayer from glance to glance. Once they were waylaid by a brutal bandit who threatened them, frightening the child with a fusil. Thyme took it from him and grappled him to the ground. Only one rose, and the two went on.

One morning, while they walked through a thicket of mountain laurels, the child lagged behind to look at them; for it seemed to her that some bore bright golden blossoms, and she had never seen laurels like them. Soon she found that the flowers belonged not to the trees, but to twining vines that choked them as they climbed. The child traced one down a trunk, ready to cut it at the root; but it grew from the eyes of a yellowing skull. She gasped and backed away.

"That is the trumpet vine," Thyme told her. "And that skull you saw once wore a green cap. Did you poke about the roots of the tree as well?"

In silent horror, she shook her head.

Thyme thrust aside the thick, tangled thorns with his stick, bent, and brought up a bone in a matted mass of mold. "Here is the rib of one who once wore yellow. You see, he has turned his coat, even though he has lost the back on which he used to wear it." Gay green moss had indeed wrapped the rib.

The child sighed, and sat herself upon a stone. "This is that place, isn't it? This is the pass where we saw the armies fight. I should have remembered it sooner, but then we were up there." Her eyes sought the spot along the snow line.

"Yes," old Thyme agreed. "This is the place."

"You said if each side tried to be more like the other, there might be peace. That's what you told the emperor."

The sage did not sit (for Thyme rarely rests). "What you say is so, child. During the long years in which I have ringed Urth, I have seen that the more nation differs from nation, the more difficult it is for one to trust another. Thus I advised each empire to make itself more like its foe. Alas, they were too much alike already. Each saw my advice not as a road to peace but as a ruse to win. The master of the green armies who rejected my counsel so rudely did so only that I might not guess what he planned; and the Yellow Emperor dressed legions in green only that they might not be fired upon as they advanced."

The child shivered. "And now the laurels war with the vines."

The old man nodded and struck a tree trunk (or perhaps the trumpet vine that twined it) with his staff. "I have changed their uniforms," he said. "But only they could halt their war."

Thus they came to green Vert, that great city, the Boast of the East; there they saw soldiers in argent armor standing guard at its gates, and a silver flag flying above the battlements of the bartizan. They did not stop. A gay girl the charmed child left the great green city, lissome and long-limbed, bright of eye and black of hair; but while she walked home with Thyme she dwindled, until such young men as they met on the way no longer stared but smiled. And ere old Urth turned her fair face from the sun, Thyme set her upon his shoulders.

Small and sweet and soiled she was when their long walk was ended at a place where pease had rolled hither and thither across the road.

"Good-bye for now," Thyme told her. "You may play with these pease, for the present."

"Good-bye for now, Father Thyme," she said. "I love pease."

"As do we all." Thyme took up his staff. "But it is so late in the season."

She was picking up her pease when her fond brother, Barrus, found her. "I *love* you," the child cried, and threw her chubby arms about him.

He fended her off as boys must, fighting to leave the love out of his voice. "You're a very bad girl," he mumbled, and he led her back to their mother's house.

Often afterward she talked of Thyme, until at last her dear mother declared she must have seen the ghost of her grandfather, who had died that day. But though Thyme walked with her always, as he walks over all the world, his adopted daughter did not see him again; and this is his story.

The Arimaspian Legacy

✦

*It is among the Issedonians themselves that the strange tales of
the distant north originate—tales of the one-eyed men and the griffins
that guard gold; and the Scythians have passed them on to the rest of us . . .*
—HERODOTUS, *THE HISTORIES*

Each year at about this time, I make the same resolution; but for you to
understand, I must first tell you of my old friend David. I intend to em-
ploy that first name since it was his—there are so many Davids that no ill-
intentioned person is apt to guess the David I mean. Certain members of
David's family are yet living however (an uncle, an aunt, and several
cousins, I believe), so I shall assign to him the surname of *Arimaspian*. Its
signification will become clear to you.

David and I were (as I have said) old friends. I might as truthfully have
called us boyhood friends, even though I lived on the southern edge of the
city and David on the eastern. We were of an age. We were alike in being
bookish but unstudious, and in being without sister or brother. We met at a
chess club for boys in the YMCA, and though we both soon abandoned
chess, we never quite abandoned each other.

The truth is that each of us found the other useful. It was the custom in
those days to require a boy to name his best friend. And then, cruelly, to investigate the matter with the boy named. Thus I specified David Arimaspian, and he me; and neither of us lost face.

In part in support of our own testimony, we met regularly once or twice
a month to talk, to trifle with chess or Monopoly or some other game, and
to read in each other's company. For the city was not so large in those days
that a determined boy could not ride his bicycle twice across it in a single

evening, and the distance between our homes was considerably less than the full diameter. Soon, indeed, I boasted a motor scooter in place of my bike; and in what now seems a short time, we both owned cars.

I said we met to talk, but I might better have said we met to boast. David began it, I believe. He was always exceedingly proud of whatever he possessed: his geese were every one a swan, as the saying goes. You will protest that if his boasting were objectionable to me, I might have mentioned the matter to him or even ceased to visit him; and you will be correct. The fact was that I did not find it objectionable, though possibly I should have. His latest possessions were often of interest—for he was something of a collector even then—and he took so much innocent pleasure in producing each and recounting to me the way in which it had come into his hands that I enjoyed his crowing nearly as much as he did himself. How well I recall the dubiously ivory chess set—the magnifying glass whose ebony handle bore *M.H.* in faded gilt, whose chipped and foggy lens David employed to burn his own *D.A.* into the birch grip of an old Finnish knife!

The years rolled by. With the triumphs and disappointments they brought to me, this brief tale has nothing to do; as for my boyhood friend, he became an astronomer—a discipline admirably suited to his largely nocturnal style of life—and an acquirer of old books.

I do not call him a *collector*, for it seemed to me that he followed no plan. Like many professional men, he was attracted to accounts of his own profession, and it sometimes seemed to me that he had a baseless predilection for gold edging. Scientific conferences of one sort or another took him to distant cities, where he rarely missed the opportunity of rummaging through such shops as they afforded. I have heard that he sometimes bought whole stacks of volumes as you or I might a single book, paying a trifle more to have them mailed home; the boxes in which his acquisitions arrived might be stacked in his foyer, unopened, for years. In our city, he haunted garage sales and would buy any number of decayed volumes and toss them into his rusty van. As far as I am aware, that van was emptied only when it became too full to hold more. He had inherited his parents' Victorian house, and it seemed to be his ambition to choke all its many rooms and hallways with old books, papers of his own, and the dusty instruments of science.

At the time of which I speak, he had nearly succeeded. On my increasingly rare visits, we had to clear a chair so that I might sit; and on the last, he grudgingly yielded his own to me and stood. That was three years past, and I never came again.

Thus I was astounded to find him at my apartment door so very early on the morning he died. His long sallow face seemed unchanged, as did his threadbare brown suit; but he carried a narrow carton embellished with golden foil—surely the kind that distillers of the best class provide at Christmas—and his eyes held such a light as I had not seen there since they had first met mine across a shabby chessboard.

His knock roused me from sleep; but I opened the door, and he handed me the carton, announcing that we must toast the dawn. "Hah. In glass, too! No plastic. Not for us—crystal! May I? Sofa's fine. Need a corkscrew? I could show you how to manage without one. No ice—it's melted, and the mammoth lives!"

I filled our glasses and said I was happy to see him, as quite suddenly I was.

"Course you are," he replied. "Hah! Lord! Have I ever lied to you?"

"Frequently," I confessed.

"Good, good! Then you won't flinch when I tell you I've fulfilled my life's ambition—that I'm—hah! Potentially the master of the world."

I admitted it could use one.

"Hah. Right." He gulped half his drink and grew serious. "Know what I've been after? Do you? All my life?"

I did not, yet I could see that he had found it.

"The book. Lord, the book. Hah! What a book! The one no one buys. Know what I mean?"

I shook my head.

"The one you almost buy but don't. The one you haven't got money enough on you for, that's too heavy to lug over to Seventh Street. The one you mean to come back for and don't, hah! The one that's gone, or some-where else, when you get back."

"Oh," I said weakly. "*That* book."

"Right! Didn't know I was looking till I found it. Eight hundred and sixty-five thousand miles across, but I've reduced it to a little thing, so big." (At this point he gestured with his glass. I think the size he indicated was roughly six inches by eight.) "Blue cover, I had the binder put on a gold griffin. Hah! Know about griffins?"

"Certainly," I told him. "Fabulous beasts with the head, wings, and legs of an eagle, and the hindquarters of a lion."

"Wrong! Not fabulous a bit. Spirits. Haven't you visited Sumer? Hah! Or Akkad? What about Ur?"

I shook my head. "No, David, and neither have you."

"All over the walls. Come midwinter, they fly from the sun with new strength for the Tree, get it? *There's* the gold that griffins guard—sun— civilization—nuclear fusion, too. Hah! Tells everything you've wanted to know all your life. Remember the one-eyed men? Tried to steal the gold, half blinded by the sun. Hah! *Spu's eye, Armia's one.* Arimaspians, race of one-eyed thieves. Know about sunspots? Disturb the solar spectrum, *in code.* Lasted eighteen months once—long chapter. Chaldean, not English. Somebody left it there to get us started. Hah! I ran it through a computer at Rice, put the English in my book."

God forgive me, I thought it was a joke, a game. I asked, "But this book tells you the secrets of life?"

He nodded solemnly. "Teaches you to read—thought I knew, hah! Didn't. Music in your head, after you read that. How to tie shoes, write a check. How old before you learned?"

"Seventeen, I suppose."

"Liar! Twenty-five at least. How to get the girl, easy as snapping fingers— all the ways. Make friends, influence people. Sports—quarterback— Olympics. Coordination and balance, that's all—anything your body *can* do. Hah! Meditation and exercises. Easy, really."

I think my look must have pierced his soul; he was proud, like all lonely men. Lonely men must be proud or die.

"Show you. Have to go anyhow. She's waiting." He stood, swaying a trifle.

"Dave . . ."

"Don't fret." He opened my window. I live on the seventh floor, and there is no ledge, no balcony or fire escape; yet he stepped over the sill as coolly as a man steps off a bus.

I rushed to look out. A red Jaguar idled at the curb. The lovely woman standing beside it appeared to be waving to me.

"Like it? Hah! Snap." David's voice was at my ear. He was standing beside my window, upon nothing.

"Got to go. Take care."

He descended on steps of air that only he could see; he had reached the third floor when dawn touched the sky and he fell.

His house went to a cousin, but he left his library to me, "my best friend." Was it merely a notebook, written by hand? Did he pay someone to set type, as he surely paid someone else to bind or rebind it? Or did he create his book himself by what is called desktop publishing? He seems to have owned equipment of that kind. His books are in storage now, for I lack the space for a tenth of them. Sometimes I go to the warehouse to open the crates and poke about—yes, still, especially at this time of year.

And in my dreams I see him falling, and griffins bent upon vengeance, bearing the treasures of the sun.

> *As when the gryphon through the wilderness*
> *With winged course, o'er hill or morry dale,*
> *Pursues the Arimaspian, who, by stealth,*
> *Had from his wakeful custody purloined*
> *The guarded gold; so eagerly the Fiend*
> *O'er bog or steep, through strait, rough, dense, or rare*
> *With head, hands, wings, or feet pursues his way,*
> *And swims or sinks, or wades, or creeps, or flies.*
>
> —MILTON, *PARADISE LOST*

The Seraph from Its Sepulcher

✦

The inscribed prayer was to be recited at each landing," Father Joseph explained. "The wrong turnings stand for miscalculations in life. They end in precipices, or become more and more steep until no one could climb them without falling, or else fade away altogether in screes of sliding stones."

"I took a couple of those," his visitor admitted. He felt rather lost, although he knew precisely where he was.

Father Joseph nodded. "Most people do."

"My name's Anthony Brook, by the way." Somewhat belatedly, Brook extended a sweating hand.

The priest accepted it. "Joe Krska." Together they stood looking down at the apparently unpatterned network of stairs that crossed and recrossed the steep defile.

"I ought to give you a card, I suppose," Brook added. He fished in a big shirt pocket for one and at last produced it, a stiff, tissue-thin flake printed in bold black capitals.

A slight smile tugged at Father Joseph's sun-browned face. "You have a great many letters after your name."

"You can put it in—"

"Oh, I can read. F.X.A.S. This last one. What does it mean?"

"Fellow of the Exsolar Archeological Society. That's why I'm here, actually."

Father Joseph sighed. "I hoped it had something to do with Francis Xavier. But you would like to sit down, Dr. Brook, and you won't want to climb more steps. Why don't we go in?"

The interior of the mission seemed cool, almost cold, and dark after the pounding sunlight of Mirzam. There were no pews for worshippers, Brook noticed, but two old wooden chairs stood just inside the heavy door, which Father Joseph wedged expertly with a small stone until it stood half open. When it had been fixed in place to his satisfaction, he motioned toward one and seated himself in the other.

"They built this under human supervision," Brook said, looking around.

Father Joseph shook his head. "They had seen our buildings and perhaps even studied them—if they needed to study anything so simple. But they built this themselves and presented it to the diocese. It was something of an embarrassment at the time, from what I've read. To some degree it still is."

Brook nodded, studying the airy columns and leaping arches of grainy, lion-colored stone. The arches traced a curve that appeared mathematical, though surely no parabola. The columns, he decided, were neither round nor ribbed; pierced by strangely shaped apertures like those in the cliffs outside, they seemed to breathe, sighing in the faint, hot breeze from the open door.

"As I am," concluded the priest. "How may I help you?"

"Just let me look around for a few days," Brook said. "I want to find out as much as possible about the Seraphs. I came here from the Motherworld to do that."

"It must have been extremely expensive."

"It was, but not for me—I've got a grant. I'll stay five or six years, visit every site I can, and dig when I have to."

"I see." The priest scratched his chin. In appearance at least, he was older than Brook; silver stubble gleamed beneath his fingers.

"When was this built, Father?"

"A hundred years ago."

Brook hesitated. "I've read that the last Seraph died in twenty-two ten."

"I saw a few as a boy." The sentence hung in the dry shade of the nave, at once an invitation and a challenge: *Credit this and I shall recount wonders that will be more to you than gold; credit this and you are twice a fool, a dupe and a fraud.*

"I don't know," Brook said slowly. "You must understand that I know them only from study." Footsore and legweary though he was, he rose and walked to the head of the tangled stairways. "They could fly. It's a point upon which all my sources agree, and some holostats show them winged. Why did they build this?"

Father Joseph joined him. "They were winged for at least one stage of their lives, but they flew only on certain well-defined occasions. There was a nuptial flight, for example."

"You've studied them, too, haven't you? And living here, you've had access to materials I've never seen." Brook paused. "Or did you learn that firsthand?"

"No, I read it in a book. In several, actually."

"You don't mind if I look around and shoot some holostats of my own?"

The priest did not answer, and after a moment Brook turned away. "If there's anything you don't want me to stat, just tell me. We'll discuss it, and if you won't agree I won't do it."

"It's all right," the priest said. "There's nothing here— Do you plan to leave today? Descend the stairs?"

Brook nodded. "I'll have to. My camping gear's down there on my roller. I saw your sign."

"Thank you. You'd have driven up them otherwise?"

"Of course. Oh, I realize that if enough people drove up and down, they'd destroy the stairs. But enough walkers, enough wear from enough boots, would do the same thing."

"You'll fall," the priest told him. "You're tired already. You'll be still more tired when you've examined and statted this church, and in places the steps are very steep. People have fallen before." He hesitated. "I'll sleep in my study tonight. I can lend you soap, a towel, and so forth."

"I couldn't take your bed."

"I'd much rather sleep in my study than have you sleep there."

"If you think I'd poke—"

The priest waved the objection aside. "Among my files? Of course not, and it wouldn't matter if you did. There's only one document—no, two— of any importance, and I'll show them to you when you come up to the rectory."

"All right," Brook said, "and thank you, Father. Thank you very much. I'd like to make a donation, if I may. Something in recognition of your hospitality."

"If you wish. I'll have need of it very soon, I'm afraid. You're not Catholic, Dr. Brook?"

Brook shook his head.

"Then you may not know what a sacristy is. Here, it's the small room to the left of the altar. You'll see my vestments hanging there. Go through the sacristy and out the door to your right; the steps lead up to my rectory. I'll have supper on the stove before you're through here, I'm sure."

Brook watched the priest's retreating back until it faded to near invisibility among the shadows. For the first time he realized that there were no lights in the mission except for a single candle, remote and golden as some faraway sun beside the altar. Holography would be unsatisfactory in an hour or less. He went to work quickly, creating images more permanent and in a certain sense more real than the stone.

"Stew," Father Joseph said. "I hope you don't mind. It's what I usually eat in the evening, and right now it's all I have ingredients for."

"Smells delicious." Without waiting to be asked, Brook dropped into a chair. "You're here all by yourself?"

The priest stirred and sniffed. "More onions—for my taste at least. I like to think that God and his holy angels are with me, Dr. Brook."

"I mean—"

"And the desert fathers, at least in spirit; Saint John of Damascus is a particular favorite of mine. But to answer your question as you intended it, yes. There's no one like yourself or myself here, except you and me. And save for a few visitors like yourself, there never is."

"How do you get your supplies?"

"I carry them on my back from Clear Springs. It's nearly all dehydrated stuff, of course. My little dewdripper cracks as much water as I require out of the atmosphere, though it has to work very hard here to do it."

Brook remained silent while the priest ladled stew into two bowls. When they were on the table, he said bluntly, "I'd think you'd go mad."

"Possibly I have." Father Joseph smiled. "Certainly my superiors thought I had when I asked them to send me here. I said I'd show you my only documents of any importance, didn't I? I will, after grace." He crossed himself and murmured a prayer Brook was too shy to join.

After the amen, the priest rose and stepped into the next room, returning with an outer and two of the flimsy sheets old-fashioned people still called *paper.*

The telltale flashed, and they were joined by an elderly man in black. "Dear Father Joseph Krska," this newcomer began, "I have good news for you. We want you to return here to Saint Ardalion's immediately. We require you for Senior Composition, Modern History, and Moral Theology. I feel sure it will be a great relief to you to leave such an isolated pastorate, and I congratulate you upon your new appointment." The elderly man's features tightened. "Don't wait for a replacement, Father. No one will be coming. Lock up, and leave at once. I am Monsignor Augustine A. Nealy, Dean. Today is Wednesday, the twenty-third of August, twenty-three seventy-three."

Monsignor Nealy flickered. "Dear Father Joseph Krska, for the time being please disregard my last. A certain Dr. Brook, a distinguished scholar from the Motherworld, desires to holostat your mission; please render him all possible assistance. Remain there at Saint Seraphiel's, please, for as long as you can be of help to him." Monsignor Nearly's eyes narrowed. "Father Graffe will have to take your classes temporarily. See to it, Father, that it's not for more than a few days. And don't write me any more of your letters! Simply come here as soon as you possibly can. I am Monsignor Augustine A. Nealy, Dean. This is Thursday, the twenty-fourth of August, twenty-three seventy-three." Monsignor Nealy vanished.

Father Joseph said, "You saved me, you see. Doubtless you thought that it was by your own will that you put out from the Motherworld so long ago—that you left to further archaeology, when in point of fact you left in answer to my prayers, though I was not yet born. I'm a thoroughgoing solipsist, you see."

Brook grinned. "I suppose we all are, Father, whether we admit it or not. You're going to do it, aren't you? Go back to the capital and teach moral theology and so forth?"

"I've sworn obedience."

"But you don't want to." Brook tested his stew, finding it (as he had anticipated from the steam) still too hot to eat. "I never liked teaching undergrads much either."

The priest brought glasses of cool water. "I'd like that better than teaching them little, but I'll have to teach them no more than they're willing to learn, I suppose."

"You've been studying on your own up here?"

"A bit. And writing a bit. There isn't much else to do. I say mass every morning, of course, read my breviary and other books, write when I think I've learned something worth writing, pray, and wait."

"For me?" At his first taste of water, Brook found that he was parched; he drained his glass and set it down.

"For them, Dr. Brook. This is a mission church, after all. They built it, but built it as a mission to themselves. They wished to become Christians, and some of them did." The priest fell silent, staring into his untouched bowl. "One's interred here. Did you find your way into the crypt?"

"A crypt? No. I want to see it. I must, before you go."

"Tomorrow, then," the priest said. "I'll show it to you."

"And you say there's a body there, the body of a Seraph? Remains are almost impossible to locate."

"I'll show it to you," the priest repeated.

Twilight never came to this high desert. Brook had sponged himself in the shallow basin and was reaching for a towel when the light from the windows deepened to amber. Before he found the antique touchswitch, a host of blue-white, crimson, and Sol-yellow stars hung above the tableland like innumerable torches suspended from so many balloons—close enough, or so it seemed to Brook, for anyone upon a hilltop to touch at will, close enough to sway in the chill, dry night wind that had sprung full-grown from nowhere.

In this desert, Brook reflected, this fellow Krska (how odd to think that he had been born when Brook's own voyage to Mirzam was nearly ended!) had lived year after year, hearing only the histrionic rant of the HL and the wordless moanings of the wind. Four rooms, and a church to which nobody ever came.

And the crypt. Where was it, and how could he have failed to find it, even without his sohner? He dressed again, testing his palmpilot before pulling on his boots.

Downstairs, the study door stood ajar, and Brook ventured to peer inside. Father Joseph lay on his back on the makeshift pallet he had contrived for himself, a hand on his chest, his eyes open.

"I thought I'd take another look around," Brook said. "I haven't quite been desensitized to the beauty of this corner of your world yet."

The priest did not reply.

"I might go back to my roller and carry a few things up."

Without looking at him, Father Joseph murmured, "You were afraid to sleep."

"I haven't tried, actually. I didn't feel like it."

"Do you understand why I painted the stone?"

"The sign at the bottom?" Brook hesitated. "We talked about that—so the rollers wouldn't spoil the steps."

"Rollers roll too fast," the priest murmured. And then, "Roll aside the stone." His eyes closed.

After a moment it occurred to Brook that Father Joseph had never, perhaps, been truly awake—that he, Brook, had spoken as a phantom in the priest's dream; for no reason he could justify he shuddered.

The narrow rear door by which he had left the church stood half open. He pointed a finger at it, letting golden light run down that finger like water to splash against the bare, cracked panels. The door was swinging a little in the wind; now that he saw it, he could distinguish the despairing creak of its hinges. He had neglected to shut it securely when he had left the church. Or perhaps the priest had visited the church afterward to recite some evening prayer before the altar. Or perhaps—

Brook pushed the thought from his mind as he went down the steps from the rectory. These, unlike the mazed stair that rose from the dry bed of the wadi, had been gouged out of the rock by the machines of men—for beings like himself, with legs shorter than a Seraph's. His knees ached again, just the same, by the time he had reached the bottom and entered the mission church.

His upraised, open hand flooded the sacristy with light. A half step down, and the gritting of wind-driven sand accused him afresh. He closed the door firmly behind him; its latch was of wood, hard brown twigs so oddly and cleverly shaped that he knew at once that it too had been the work of Seraphs.

A strangely shaped but quite unobstructed arch led from the sacristy to the chancel. There were no other doors save the one through which he had entered. A rough pole held the robes the priest had mentioned—green, scarlet, rose, purple, and white, all plain and rather cheap-looking. A cabinet held transparent vit chalices and corked bottles; it was not fastened down, and was not big enough to be the entrance to anything in any case.

The cloth-draped altar cast a dense black shadow, ungainly and (Brook felt) almost brutal, down the center of the nave. He pulled aside the altar cloth, and discovered that the altar was a rugged mass of native rock; its top, and presumably its bottom as well, had been cut flat. A twenty-centimeter square of some lighter-colored stone had been let into the top; this square was marked with the unbalanced cross he had noticed elsewhere.

A similar room on the opposite side of the chancel mirrored the sacristy; except for a mop, a pail, and a crude broom—this last clearly made by the priest from native brush—it was bare.

With little skill but great determination, Brook swept all four rooms. It took him a little over an hour, and when he was finished he had discovered no slightest crevice.

A reasonable man would return to the rectory now and go to bed, he told himself. On the other hand, a reasonable man would never have left every friend and relative he had to a death now past in order to cross interstellar space at near-light speed to Mirzam. He put away the broom, made sure that the rear door was latched, went out the front, and started down the Seraph-carved stair.

Descended, it lost most of its maze-like character; there was seldom more than one flight leading downward, and when there were two, either choice proved valid. He halted several times to rest, ruefully rubbing his aching knees and staring up at the stars, musing upon what the Seraphs might have become if only Mirzam had been granted a moon like Luna. Human beings—super-apes whose early evolution had certainly been arboreal—had been lured up and out by that yellow sphere, that great, ripe fruit hung in their sky for the plucking. Would the Seraphs (half insect and half pterosaur, wholly unique) have responded in like fashion?

Perhaps they would, Brook decided. The serpent, after all, was already well up in the tree when it urged Eve to taste the fatal apple. Or at least was always so depicted in art. Had it in cold fact been a mere snake in the grass? The priest would know, of course—ask him in the morning.

Brook rose and looked back at the mission he had left; it shone almost white in the starlight. After a long moment, he turned away to peer down into the dark cleft of the wadi. He was already more than halfway there, he decided; but climbing up again would be out of the question. He would have to drive the roller, sign or no sign; and if the priest was angry that would not matter, because he would have found the crypt by then without the priest's help.

In his dream the priest stood (as he had stood so often in life) before the open sarcophagus. The big kitchen knife was in his hand; but each time he raised it, his fingers grew weak. If he stabbed the Seraph it would, he knew, rise and seize him, a monster at once living and dead. He would awaken trembling, his nightclothes soaked with sweat. But he would awaken, the dream would end, and so he raised the knife.

His fingers were weak, numb. The heavy, broad-bladed knife nearly slipped from them.

"You must go," the Seraph said.

Its dry, shriveled mouth did not twitch, yet Father Joseph heard its voice. "That's what I've come to tell you," he said. And then, "I had hoped that if I slept in the study tonight you wouldn't bring me here—that you would take the man in my bed in my place." He sensed the Seraph's amusement. "I think he'll go tomorrow. I'm to show you to him, and he'll make pictures and go." Father Joseph hesitated. "I'd like—I should go with him. He can give me a ride as far as Treaty. That will save a day, possibly more."

"Yet you do not wish to go," the Seraph said. "Perhaps you are afraid that you will not be free of me? You will be free of me, or nearly."

"I feel it's my duty to stay; but it's my duty to go, as well. I wish my duties might be reconciled."

"I shall emerge very soon, Father."

The priest nodded, realized he was still holding the knife, and let his hands fall. "So you tell me night after night. I don't believe you."

Amused again the Seraph asked, "Then why are you eager to kill me?"

"I'm not eager to kill you. I want . . ."

"Yes?"

"To sleep. To sleep as other men do. To find peace, and rest, in sleep." The priest raised the knife again, but his fingers were weak, so weak it nearly slipped away.

"Is that all?"

"To pray. To say mass *here*. Not to— To wait here, at this mission, as I was intended to wait by your race and mine, for a living Seraph."

The Seraph's voice was a caress, and a blessing. "Not to betray us as your people betrayed us."

"*Yes!*"

"Come closer. You could not strike me from where you stand even if you wished to strike. Come closer."

Lowering the knife once more, the priest shook his head.

"Do you know why we became Christians, Father?"

The priest sighed. "By the grace of God."

"True, though you do not truly believe as yet. His grace makes use of means, of tools. Why?"

"Because you thought we'd spare you then." Father Joseph gazed at the knife in his hands; it seemed as inexplicable as any Seraph artifact. Was one to grasp both ends? "You thought we had decency enough for that, and you were wrong."

"Because we wanted to understand you, we became like you. You took lands that were never ours, and called them ours, and killed us lest we ask for them back. Now we are dead, but we shall rise again, in Christ."

The knife clattered to the stone floor.

"Like the flower from its seed, the moth from its cocoon. We become, come into being. If you were more like Christ, you would understand us better."

Fear struck Brook like a lash. With all his strength, he heaved back on the stick; the roller's big, soft wheels stopped . . . spun in reverse. For an instant it seemed he and it would surely go over. Instead they raced wildly backward, no longer following any stair, lost on the naked slope and out of control.

He pushed the stick forward to stop. The roller halted, canted at such an angle that he knew he would fall if he tried to dismount—fall and tumble, and at last drop.

Cold perspiration streamed from his forehead into his eyes. He wiped it away and eased the lever forward, edging the roller back in the direction of the stair. It was wrong, that stair, of course. The wrong one, though he had been so confident.

He stopped the roller again and dismounted. A hundred steps returned him to the precipice; golden light from his palm revealed a smashed roller far below—one certainly, and possibly two; he counted five wheels. Broken bones, bleached by Mirzam's young and pitiless sun, lay among the wreckage. A lonely wind sobbed between him and them, gritty with sand.

Some men would pray now, Brook thought. Some would spit. Why am I caught between them?

Slowly he made his way back to the roller and crept back to the landing. After lengthy deliberation he chose another of its diverging stairs and inched up it at a walking pace.

It took an hour to reach the top; once there, he parked the roller on a blanket-sized patch of nearly level ground and rooted through the cargo compartment for his sohner. With it, he circled the entire mission, scrambling wearily over insecure stones and hearing only the dull buzz of solid rock. The crypt was inside, clearly, under the baffling inlay of the floor; he had missed it, in spite of all his sweeping and careful peering.

Maybe they should've sent someone else, he thought; perhaps I'm not the right person after all. Aching with fatigue, he pulled open one of the massive doors, reflecting that it was he who had been sent in any case—the one who would have to do whatever was done, because there was no one else present to do anything.

Sohner in hand, he shuffled back and forth across the nave, hearing only stone, solid and dull, until he had almost reached the chancel. There (at last) there came the sharp *ping* of a cavity. Scarlet numerals rolled across the sohner's small screen: three hundred and forty-nine cubic meters. Brook nodded to himself, pulled off the earphone, and switched off the sohner. Here was the crypt, but where was its entrance? He puzzled over that for twenty minutes or more, poking here and prying there, and even considered waking the priest, before he realized that the priest had already told him.

"Roll aside the stone."

He had thought the priest dreaming, and doubtless had been correct. Yet that phrase surely contained the answer he sought; the priest, hearing his voice, had dreamt of exhibiting the crypt, as he planned to do in the morning.

The altar appeared far too heavy for one man to move, but he carried the translucent chalice and its small cloth into the sacristy, folded the clean white altar cloth carefully and laid it beside them, set his shoulder to the altar, and heaved with all his strength.

It trundled to one side so easily that he nearly fell into the opening beneath it, rolling onto one rough, rounded end to reveal a lightless opening through which even a large man (or a large coffin, Brook reflected) might easily pass.

For a moment he hung back, his left foot on the first step. Surely there had been some sound from below? Loudly, echoing, shocking, came the clang of metal on stone; it was followed by the murmur of the priest's voice.

As silently as he could manage, Brook moved the altar back into place, then spread the altar cloth once more and added the chalice with its pall. Wearily, he left the mission by the rear door and mounted the long, straight stair to the rectory. The priest slept as before upon the improvised pallet in the study, both arms stretched above his head now. Brook stared at him, snorted, and went up to bed.

It was indeed a different world.

"There were never more than two million or so," the priest said, "and they didn't need a great deal of food. Much of their lives was spent in dormancy. Much of ours is, too, although it doesn't seem to do us a great deal of good. Perhaps if we cared more for the worlds that we call ours, we'd discover that we too could get along on less food. And if we cared more for God. . . ." He shrugged, turning away from the brazen sarcophagus to study glyphs incised in the walls of the crypt.

"There would be fewer children to feed," Brook finished for him, "and better food and care for those we had. You're right, of course." He bent above the desiccated Seraph. "They changed like insects? Egg, larva, chrysalis, and adult?"

The priest shrugged. "No one really knows how many changes there were, or what the adult form actually was. In some cases, their transformations seem to have been self-directed."

"The flying, sexual stage would have been the last." Brook prodded the Seraph's open jaw; only by directing his palmpilot between the wasted lips could he make out the remains of what had once been a tongue (or something like one) inside the open mouth. "This individual isn't winged."

As though he had not been listening, the priest said, "I've wondered at times whether they hadn't visited the Motherworld."

Brook straightened up. "Because pictures of winged spirits go back to Sumer? They didn't call themselves Seraphs, did they?"

"Because of what you said a moment ago. And because others have said it so often—that word *larva*. It's Latin. Do you know what it means?"

Brook shook his head. "The Romans are supposed to be in my balliwick, but I've never learned the language, except for a few names. Try me on Ugaritic or Moabite. Let's see. The larva's what hatches from an egg, so I suppose it means a child—something like that."

"It means *ghost*," the priest said.

"I'm afraid I don't follow you." Brook tossed up a light; it touched the ceiling of the crypt and stuck there.

"I'm not sure I follow myself. Can't I help you with that? I'm perfectly willing to, if you'll tell me what you want me to do."

Brook shook his head. "I know what I need, and it'll only take a minute."

"Are you going to dissect?"

The archeologist glanced around sharply; there had been a change in tone. "No. I assume you don't want me to? Not now, and if you mean me, Tony Brook personally, not ever. This will be a job for a comparative anatomist, and a good one." He toyed with another light. "You don't really want that ride to Treaty, do you. You'd rather stay here."

The priest shrugged again. "What I want is scarcely the issue."

"Exactly. Do you recall what that superior of yours said? Monsignor whats-his-name? He said that you were to remain here as long as you could be of service to me. All right, I want you to stay right here and protect this body—this whole place, but our late friend particularly—until I talk one of your universities into sending someone out. It may take a while, I warn you."

The priest opened his mouth, and shut it again.

"I'm perfectly serious, and I'm going to put it in writing. Once you're gone, there won't be anything to keep any idiot who can borrow a roller from driving up here, taking this body, and burning it or tearing it to bits. I could tell you things that happened in Egypt— For a thousand years specialists will weep over this squandered opportunity to learn about a race that was in many ways, and maybe in every way, superior to our own. Stay here, Father—I mean it. He put you under my orders, didn't he? Very well, I'm ordering you to stay."

"It's extremely tempting," the priest said slowly.

"It's not a matter of temptation, Father. It's your duty."

"But, no. That isn't what Monsignor Nealy intended, and we both know it. No, I don't believe I can."

Brook made a final effort. "I'm going to spend the rest of the day on this, and a couple of things up there that I skimped yesterday; I'll leave in the morning. I want you to promise me, Father, that you'll think about what I said tonight—about your true God-given duty, as opposed to doing whatever you find least pleasant. I don't believe God's quite as cruel as you imagine."

The priest nodded and started up the steps to the chancel. "If you don't mind," he said mildly, "I always think best in the open air."

It was more difficult to drive the roller down the tangled stairs than it had been to go up them, something Brook had not anticipated; the priest's weight, and that of his luggage, added to Brook's two hundred kilos of clothing and equipment made it necessary to ride the brake constantly, even with the arrester on Full Regenerative.

"That way," the priest said. He pointed, one black-sleeved arm over Brook's broad shoulder. "This is one of the two places in which you can get lost—lost seriously—going down."

Brook nodded, steering to the right. "I didn't think there were any. Where's the other?"

"At the bottom." If the priest was joking, there was no hint of it in his voice.

Brook stopped there. "If you don't mind," he said, "I want to take one last shot, Father. I neglected to get this before I went up."

"Of course not. I'd like to remain here for a few minutes myself. I'll probably never come back."

The labyrinthine stone stairs gleamed like new-minted gold in Brook's holoscreen, flawlessly lit by the morning sunshine. At the top, the graceful Seraphic mission church seemed a pretty toy. Such a toy, Brook thought idly, as real angels might have built for the Christ child's crib set. Except—

He turned to the priest. "There's somebody up there. A man in black."

The priest nodded and smiled.

"But you were alone," Brook said, "that's what you told me."

"We didn't want to frighten you." The priest waved back to the tiny figure at the summit of the twining stairs. "Nor would you have believed us, and so that seemed best. But see how nicely things have worked out, Dr. Brook! Monsignor's instructions have been followed in both senses. I am coming in obedience to him; my brother remains to protect our mission, as you wished."

"Is he disfigured or something?"

"All of us are deformed in some degree by evil, Dr. Brook. That is its chief result. My brother is less hideous than most."

Brook took a deep breath. "Well, that explains a lot."

The priest did not reply.

His final holostat, taken as Brook repacked his equipment; and they started off in earnest. Fast though he drove, roaring up blind dunes constructed by the laboring winds, climbing mountains of sand not greatly inferior to the Jebel Seir while trailing a plume of sallow dust more lofty still, Mirzam's long day was three-quarters spent before the ocher and orange desert that dashed by their racing roller softened at last to green.

As they drew near Treaty, Brook spoke for the first time in hours. "I'm going to put up at Chesterton House, Father. It's reasonable and comfortable. I want you to let me pay for a room there for you, too. I stayed with you for two nights, after all."

"If you wish," the priest said. And then, "It's very kind of you."

A cheerful auburn-haired attendant supervised the robots that unloaded their baggage. "Been out in the desert long?"

"I haven't," Brook told her, "but Father Krska was there for more than ten years."

She smiled at the priest; and he nodded to her, affirming the truth of what Brook had said.

So this is unlawful desire, he thought, as his eyes traced the tender curve of her lips. This is the sensation they feel, the thing they fight against and rush to: this twitching in the shoulder blades.

I had not known.

Lord of the Land

✦

The Nebraskan smiled warmly, leaned forward, and made a sweeping gesture with his right hand, saying, "Yes indeed, that's exactly the sort of thing I'm most interested in. Tell me about it, Mr. Thacker, please."

All this was intended to keep old Hop Thacker's attention away from the Nebraskan's left hand, which had slipped into his left jacket pocket to turn on the miniature recorder there. Its microphone was pinned to the back of the Nebraskan's lapel, the fine brown wire almost invisible.

Perhaps old Hop would not have cared in any case; old Hop was hardly the shy type. "Waul," he began, "this was years an' years back, the way I hear'd it. Guess it'd have been in my great-granpaw's time, Mr. Cooper, or mebbe before."

The Nebraskan nodded encouragingly.

"There's these three boys, an' they had a old mule, wasn't good fer nothin' 'cept crowbait. One was Colonel Lightfoot—course didn't nobody call him colonel then. One was Creech an' t'other 'un . . ." The old man paused, fingering his scant beard. "Guess I don't rightly know. I *did* know. It'll come to me when don't nobody want to hear it. He's the one had the mule."

The Nebraskan nodded again. "Three young men, you say, Mr. Thacker?"

"That's right, an' Colonel Lightfoot, he had him a new gun. An' this other 'un—he was a friend of my granpaw's or somebody—he had him one everybody said was jest about the best shooter in the county. So this here

Laban Creech, he said *he* wasn't no bad shot hisself, an' he went an' fetched his'un. He was the 'un had that mule. I recollect now.

"So they led the ol' mule out into the medder, mebby fifty straddles from the brake. You know how you do. Creech, he shot it smack in the ear, an' it jest laid down an' died, it was old, an' sick, too, didn't kick or nothin'. So Colonel Lightfoot, he fetched out his knife an' cut it up the belly, an' they went on back to the brake fer to wait out the crows."

"I see," the Nebraskan said.

"One'd shoot, an' then another, an' they'd keep score. An' it got to be near to dark, you know, an' Colonel Lightfoot with his new gun an' this other ma' that had the good 'un, they was even up, an' this Laban Creech was only one behind 'em. Reckon there was near to a hundred crows back behind in the gully. You can't jest shoot a crow an' leave him, you know, an' 'spect the rest to come. They look an' see that dead 'un, an' they say, Waul, jest look what become of *him*. I don't calc'late to come anywheres near *there*."

The Nebraskan smiled. "Wise birds."

"Oh, there's all kinds of stories 'bout 'em," the old man said. "Thankee, Sarah."

His granddaughter had brought two tall glasses of lemonade; she paused in the doorway to dry her hands on her red-and-white checkered apron, glancing at the Nebraskan with shy alarm before retreating into the house.

"Didn't have a lick, back then." The old man poked an ice cube with one bony, somewhat soiled finger. "Didn't have none when I was a little 'un, neither, till the TVA come. Nowadays you talk 'bout the TVA an' they think you mean them programs, you know." He waved his glass. "I watch 'em sometimes."

"Television," the Nebraskan supplied.

"That's it. Like, you take when Bud Bloodhat went to his reward, Mr. Cooper. Hot? You never seen the like. The birds all had their mouths open, wouldn't fly fer anything. Lost two hogs, I recollect, that same day. My paw, he wanted to save the meat, but 'twasn't a bit of good. He says he thought them hogs was rotten 'fore ever they dropped, an' he was 'fraid to give it to the dogs, it was that hot. They was all a-sleepin' under the porch anyhow. Wouldn't come out fer nothin'."

The Nebraskan was tempted to reintroduce the subject of the crow shoot, but an instinct born of thousands of hours of such listening prompted him to nod and smile instead.

"Waul, they knowed they had to git him under quick, didn't they? So they got him fixed, cleaned up an' his best clothes on an' all like that, an' they was all in there listenin', but it was terrible hot in there an' you could smell him pretty strong, so by an' by I jest snuck out. Wasn't nobody payin' attention to *me*, do you see? The women's all bawlin' an' carryin' on, an' the men thinkin' it was time to put him under an' have another."

The old man's cane fell with a sudden, dry rattle. For a moment as he picked it up, the Nebraskan glimpsed Sarah's pale face on the other side of the doorway.

"So I snuck out on the stoop. I bet it was a hundred easy, but it felt good to me after bein' inside there. That was when I seen it comin' down the hill t'other side of the road. Stayed in the shadow much as it could, an' looked like a shadow itself, only you could see it move, an' it was always blacker than what they was. I knowed it was the soul-sucker an' was afeered it'd git my ma. I took to cryin', an' she come outside an' fetched me down the spring fer a drink, an' that's the last time anybody ever did see it, far's I know."

"Why do you call it the soul-sucker?" the Nebraskan asked.

"'Cause that's what it does, Mr. Cooper. Guess you know it ain't only folks that has ghosts. A man can see the ghost of another man, all right, but he can see the ghost of a dog or a mule or anythin' like that, too. Waul, you take a man's, 'cause that don't make so much argyment. It's his soul, ain't it? Why ain't it in Heaven or down in the bad place like it's s'pposed to be? What's it doin' in the haint house, or walkin' down the road, or wherever 'twas you seen it? I had a dog that seen a ghost one time, an' that'n was another dog's, do you see? *I* never did see it, but he did, an' I knowed he did by how he acted. What was it doin' there?"

The Nebraskan shook his head. "I've no idea, Mr. Thacker."

"Waul, I'll tell you. When a man passes on, or a horse or a dog or whatever, it's s'pposed to git out an' git over to the Judgment. The Lord Jesus Christ's our judge, Mr. Cooper. Only sometimes it won't do it. Mebbe it's afeared to be judged, or mebbe it has this or that to tend to down here yet, or anyhow reckons it does, like showin' somebody some money what it knowed about. Some does that pretty often, an' I might tell you 'bout some of them times. But if it don't have business an' is jest feared to go, it'll stay where 'tis—that's the kind that haints their graves. They b'long to the soul-sucker, do you see, if it can git 'em. Only if it's hungered it'll suck on a live person, an' he's bound to fight or die." The old man paused to wet his lips with lemonade, staring across his family's little burial plot and fields of dry cornstalks to purple hills where he would never hunt again. "Don't win, not particular often. Guess the first 'un was a Indian, mebbe. Somethin' like that. I tell you how Creech shot it?"

"No, you didn't, Mr. Thacker." The Nebraskan took a swallow of his own lemonade, which was refreshingly tart. "I'd like very much to hear it."

The old man rocked in silence for what seemed a long while. "Waul," he said at last, "they'd been shootin' all day. Reckon I said that. Fer a good long time anyhow. An' they was tied, Colonel Lightfoot an' this here Cooper was, an' Creech jest one behind 'em. 'Twas Creech's time next, an' he kept on sayin' to stay fer jest one more, then he'd go an' they'd all go, hit or miss. So they stayed, but wasn't no more crows 'cause they'd 'bout kilt every crow in many a mile. Started gittin' dark fer sure, an' this Cooper, he says, Come on, Lab, couldn't nobody hit nothin' now. You lost an' you got to face up.

"Creech, he says, Waul, 'twas my mule. An' jest 'bout then here comes somethin' bigger'n any crow, an' black, hoppin' 'long the ground like a crow will sometimes, do you see? Over towards that dead mule. So Creech ups with his gun. Colonel Lightfoot, he allowed afterwards he couldn't have seed his sights in that dark. Reckon he jest sighted 'longside the barrel. 'Tis the ol' mountain way, do you see, an' there's lots what swore by it.

"Waul, he let go an' it fell over. You won, says Colonel Lightfoot, an' he claps Creech on his back, an' let's go. Only this Cooper, he knowed it wasn't no crow, bein' too big, an' he goes over to see what 'twas. Waul, sir, 'twas like to a man, only crooked-legged an' wry-neck. 'Twasn't no man, but like to it, do you see? Who shot me? it says, an' the mouth was full of worms. Grave worms, do you see?

"Who shot me? An' Cooper, he said Creech, then he hollered fer Creech an' Colonel Lightfoot. Colonel Lightfoot says, Boys, we got to bury this. An' Creech goes back to his home place an' fetches a spade an' a ol' shovel, them bein' all he's got. He's shakin' so bad they jest rattled together, do you see? Colonel Lightfoot an' this Cooper, they seed he couldn't dig, so they goes hard at it. Pretty soon they looked around, an' Creech was gone, an' the soul-sucker, too."

The old man paused dramatically. "Next time anybody seed the soul-sucker, 'twas Creech. So he's the one I seed, or one of his kin anyhow. Don't never shoot anythin' without you're dead sure what 'tis, young feller."

Cued by his closing words, Sarah appeared in the doorway. "Supper's ready. I set a place for you, Mr. Cooper. Pa said. You sure you want to stay? Won't be fancy."

The Nebraskan stood up. "Why, that was very kind of you, Miss Thacker."

His granddaughter helped the old man rise. Propped by the cane in his right hand and guided and supported by her on his left, he shuffled slowly into the house. The Nebraskan followed and held his chair.

"Pa's washin' up," Sarah said. "He was changin' the oil in the tractor. He'll say grace. You don't have to get my chair for me, Mr. Cooper, I'll put on till he comes. Just sit down."

"Thank you." The Nebraskan sat across from the old man.

"We got ham and sweet corn, biscuits, and potatoes. It's not no company dinner."

With perfect honesty the Nebraskan said, "Everything smells wonderful, Miss Thacker."

Her father entered, scrubbed to the elbows but bringing a tang of crankcase oil to the mingled aromas from the stove. "You hear all you wanted to, Mr. Cooper?"

"I heard some marvelous stories, Mr. Thacker," the Nebraskan said.

Sarah gave the ham the place of honor before her father. "I think it's truly fine, what you're doin', writin' up all these old stories 'fore they're lost."

Her father nodded reluctantly. "Wouldn't have thought you could make a livin' at it, though."

"He don't, Pa. He teaches. He's a teacher." The ham was followed by a mountainous platter of biscuits. Sarah dropped into a chair. "I'll fetch our sweet corn and potatoes in just a shake. Corn's not quite done yet."

"O Lord, bless this food and them that eats it. Make us thankful for farm, family, and friends. Welcome the stranger 'neath our roof as we do, O Lord. Now let's eat." The younger Mr. Thacker rose and applied an enormous butcher knife to the ham, and the Nebraskan remembered at last to switch off his tape recorder.

Two hours later, more than filled, the Nebraskan had agreed to stay the night. "It's not real fancy," Sarah said as she showed him to their vacant bedroom, "but it's clean. I just put those sheets and the comfortable on while you were talkin' to Grandpa." The door creaked. She flipped the switch.

The Nebraskan nodded. "You anticipated that I'd accept your father's invitation."

"Well, he hoped you would." Careful not to meet his eye, Sarah added,

"I never seen Grandpa so happy in years. You're goin' to talk to him some more in the mornin'? You can put the stuff from your suitcase right here in this dresser. I cleared out these top drawers, and I already turned your bed down for you. Bathroom's on past Pa's room. You know. I guess we seem awful country to you, out here."

"I grew up on a farm near Fremont, Nebraska," the Nebraskan told her. There was no reply. When he looked around, Sarah was blowing a kiss from the doorway; instantly she was gone.

With a philosophical shrug, he laid his suitcase on the bed and opened it. In addition to his notebooks, he had brought his well-thumbed copy of *The Types of the Folktale* and Schmit's *Gods Before the Greeks,* which he had been planning to read. Soon the Thackers would assemble in their front room to watch television. Surely he might be excused for an hour or two? His unexpected arrival later in the evening might actually give them pleasure. He had a sudden premonition that Sarah, fair and willow-slender, would be sitting alone on the sagging sofa, and that there would be no unoccupied chair.

There was an unoccupied chair in the room, however; an old but sturdy-looking wooden one with a cane bottom. He carried it to the window and opened Schmit, determined to read as long as the light lasted. Dis, he knew, had come in his chariot for the souls of departed Greeks, and so had been called the Gatherer of Many by those too fearful to name him; but Hop Thacker's twisted and almost pitiable soul-sucker appeared to have nothing else in common with the dark and kingly Dis. Had there been some still earlier deity who clearly prefigured the soul-sucker? Like most folklorists, the Nebraskan firmly believed that its themes were, if not actually eternal, for the most part very ancient indeed. *Gods Before the Greeks* seemed well indexed.

Dead, their mummies visited by An-uat, 2.

The Nebraskan nodded to himself and turned to the front of the book.

An-uat, Anuat, "Lord of the Land (the Necropolis)," "Opener to the North." Though frequently confused with Anubis, to whom he lent his form, it is clear that An-uat the jackal-god maintained a separate identity into the New Kingdom period. Souls that had refused to board Ra's boat (and thus to appear before the throne of the resurrected Osiris) were dragged by An-uat, who visited their mummies for this purpose, to Tuat, the lightless, demonhaunted valley stretching between the death of the old sun and the rising of the new. An-uat and the less threatening Anubis can seldom be distinguished in art, but where such distinction is possible, An-uat is the more powerfully muscled figure. Van Allen reports that An-uat is still invoked by the modern (Moslem or Coptic) magicians of Egypt, under the name Ju'gu.

The Nebraskan rose, laid the book on his chair, and strode to the dresser and back. Here was a five-thousand-year-old myth that paralleled the soul-sucker in function. Nor was it certain by any means that the similarity was merely coincidental. That the folklore of the Appalachians could have been influenced by the occult beliefs of modern Egypt was wildly improbable, but by no means impossible. After the Civil War the United States Army had imported not only camels but camel drivers from Egypt, the Nebraskan reminded himself; and the escape artist Harry Houdini had once described in lurid detail his imprisonment in the Great Pyramid. His account was undoubtedly highly colored—but had he, perhaps, actually visited Egypt as an extension of some European tour? Thousands of American servicemen must have passed through Egypt during the Second World War, but the soul-sucker tale was clearly older than that, and probably older than Houdini.

There seemed to be a difference in appearance as well; but just how different were the soul-sucker and this Ju'gu, really? An-uat had been depicted as a muscular man with a jackal's head. The soul-sucker had been . . .

The Nebraskan extracted the tape recorder from his pocket, rewound the tape, and inserted the earpiece.

Had been "like to a man, only crooked-legged an' wry-neck." Yet it had not *been* a man, though the feature that separated it from humanity had not been specified. A dog-like head seemed a possibility, surely, and An-uat might have changed a good deal in five thousand years.

The Nebraskan returned to his chair and reopened his book, but the sun was already nearly at the horizon. After flipping pages aimlessly for a minute or two, he joined the Thackers in their living room.

Never had the inanities of television seemed less real or less significant.

Though his eyes followed the movements of the actors on the screen, he was in fact considerably more attentive to Sarah's warmth and rather too generously applied perfume, and still more to a scene that had never, perhaps, taken place: to the dead mule lying in the field long ago, and to the marksmen concealed where the woods began. Colonel Lightfoot had no doubt been a historical person, locally famous, who would be familiar to the majority of Mr. Thacker's hearers. Laban Creech might or might not have been an actual person as well. Mr. Thacker had—mysteriously, now that the Nebraskan came to consider it—given the Nebraskan's own last name, Cooper, to the third and somewhat inessential marksman.

Three marksmen had been introduced because numbers greater than unity were practically always three in folklore, of course; but the use of his own name seemed odd. No doubt it had been no more than a quirk of the old man's failing memory. Remembering *Cooper*, he had attributed the name incorrectly.

By imperceptible degrees, the Nebraskan grew conscious that the Thackers were giving no more attention to the screen than he himself was; they chuckled at no jokes, showed no irritation at even the most insistent commercials, and spoke about the dismal sitcom neither to him nor to one another.

Pretty Sarah sat primly beside him, her knees together, her long legs crossed at their slender ankles, and her dishwater-reddened hands folded on her apron. To his right, the old man rocked, the faint protests of his chair as regular, and as slow, as the ticking of the tall clock in the corner, his hands upon the crook of his cane, his expression a sightless frown.

To Sarah's left, the younger Mr. Thacker was almost hidden from the Nebraskan's view. He rose and went into the kitchen, cracking his knuckles as he walked, returned with neither food nor drink, and sat once more for less than half a minute before rising again.

Sarah ventured, "Maybe you'd like some cookies, or some more lemonade?"

The Nebraskan shook his head. "Thank you, Miss Thacker; but if I were to eat anything else, I wouldn't sleep."

Oddly, her hands clenched. "I could fetch you a piece of pie."

"No, thank you."

Mercifully, the sitcom was over, replaced by a many-colored sunrise on the plains of Africa. There sailed the boat of Ra, the Nebraskan reflected, issuing in splendor from the dark gorge called Tuat to give light to mankind. For a moment he pictured a far smaller and less radiant vessel, black-hulled and crowded with the recalcitrant dead, a vessel steered by a jackal-headed man: a minute fleck against the blazing disk of the African sun. What was that book of Von Daniken's? *Ships*—no, *Chariots of the Gods*. Spaceships nonetheless—and that was folklore, too, or at any rate was quickly passing into folklore; the Nebraskan had encountered it twice already.

An animal, a zebra, lay still upon the plain. The camera panned in on it; when it was very near, the head of a huge hyena appeared, its jaws dripping carrion. The old man turned away, his abrupt movement drawing the Nebraskan's attention.

Fear. That was it, of course. He cursed himself for not having identified the emotion pervading the living room sooner. Sarah was frightened, and so was the old man—horribly afraid. Even Sarah's father appeared fearful and restless, leaning back in his chair, then forward, shifting his feet, wiping his palms on the thighs of his faded khaki trousers.

The Nebraskan rose and stretched. "You'll have to excuse me. It's been a long day."

When neither of the men spoke, Sarah said, "I'm 'bout to turn in myself, Mr. Cooper. You want to take a bath?"

He hesitated, trying to divine the desired reply. "If it's not going to be too much trouble. That would be very nice."

Sarah rose with alacrity. "I'll fetch you some towels and stuff."

He returned to his room, stripped, and put on pajamas and a robe. Sarah was waiting for him at the bathroom door with a bar of Zest and half a dozen towels at least. As he took the towels the Nebraskan mumured, "Can you tell me what's wrong? Perhaps I can help."

"We could go to town, Mr. Cooper." Hesitantly she touched his arm. "I'm kind of pretty, don't you think so? You wouldn't have to marry me or nothin', just go off in the mornin'."

"You are," the Nebraskan told her. "In fact, you're very pretty; but I couldn't do that to your family."

"You get dressed again." Her voice was scarcely audible, her eyes on the top of the stairs. "You say your old trouble's startin' up, you got to see the doctor. I'll slide out the back and 'round. Stop for me at the big elm."

"I really couldn't, Miss Thacker," the Nebraskan said.

In the tub he told himself that he had been a fool. What was it that girl in his last class had called him? A hopeless romantic. He could have enjoyed an attractive young woman that night (and it had been months since he had slept with a woman) and saved her from . . . what? A beating by her father? There had been no bruises on her bare arms, and he had noticed no missing teeth. That delicate nose had never been broken, surely.

He could have enjoyed the night with a very pretty young woman—for whom he would have felt responsible afterward, for the remainder of his life. He pictured the reference in *The Journal of American Folklore:* "Collected by Dr. Samuel Cooper, U.Neb., from Hopkin Thacker, 73, whose granddaughter Dr. Cooper seduced and abandoned."

With a snort of disgust, he stood, jerked the chain of the white rubber plug that had retained his bathwater, and snatched up one of Sarah's towels, at which a scrap of paper fluttered to the yellow bathroom rug. He picked it up, his fingers dampening lined notebook filler.

Do not tell him anything Grandpa told you. A woman's hand, almost painfully legible.

Sarah had anticipated his refusal, clearly; anticipated it, and coppered her bets. *Him* meant her father, presumably, unless there was another male in the house or another was expected—her father almost certainly.

The Nebraskan tore the note into small pieces and flushed them down toilet, dried himself with two towels, brushed his teeth and resumed his pajamas and robe, then stepped quietly out into the hall and stood listening.

The television was still on, not very loudly, in the front room. There were no other voices, no sound of footsteps or of blows. What had the Thackers been afraid of? The soul-sucker? Egypt's moldering divinities?

The Nebraskan returned to his room and shut the door firmly behind him. Whatever it was, it was most certainly none of his business. In the morning he would eat breakfast, listen to a tale or two from the old man, and put the whole family out of his mind.

Something moved when he switched off the light. And for an instant he had glimpsed his own shadow on the window blind, with that of someone or something behind him, a man even taller than he, a broad-shouldered figure with horns or pointed ears.

Which was ridiculous on the face of it. The old-fashioned brass chandelier was suspended over the center of the room; the switch was by the door, as far as possible from the windows. In no conceivable fashion could his shadow—or any other—have been cast on that shade. He and whatever he thought he had glimpsed would have to have been standing on the other side of the room, between the light and the window.

It seemed that someone had moved the bed. He waited for his eyes to become accustomed to the darkness. What furniture? The bed, the chair in which he had read—that should be beside the window where he had left it—a dresser with a spotted mirror, and (he racked his brain) a nightstand, perhaps. That should be by the head of the bed, if it were there at all.

Whispers filled the room. That was the wind outside; the windows were open wide, the old house flanked by stately maples. Those windows were visible now, pale rectangles in the darkness. As carefully as he could he crossed to one and raised the blind. Moonlight filled the bedroom; there was his bed, here his chair, in front of the window to his left. No puff of air stirred the leaf-burdened limbs.

He took off his robe and hung it on the towering bedpost, pulled top sheet and comforter to the foot of the bed, and lay down. He had heard something—or nothing. Seen something—or nothing. He thought longingly of his apartment in Lincoln, of his sabbatical—almost a year ago now—in Greece. Of sunshine on the Saronic Gulf. . . .

Circular and yellow-white, the moon floated upon stagnant water. Beyond the moon lay the city of the dead, street after narrow street of silent tombs, a daedal labyrinth of death and stone. Far away, a jackal yipped. For whole ages of the world, nothing moved; painted likenesses with limpid eyes appeared to mock the empty, tumbled skulls beyond their crumbling doors.

Far down one of the winding avenues of the dead, a second jackal appeared. Head high and ears erect, it contemplated the emptiness and listened to the silence before turning to sink its teeth once more in the tattered thing it had already dragged so far. Eyeless and desiccated, smeared with bitumen and trailing rotting wrappings, the Nebraskan recognized his own corpse.

And at once was there, lying helpless in the night-shrouded street. For a moment the jackal's glowing eyes loomed over him; its jaws closed, and his collarbone snapped. . . .

The jackal and the moonlit city vanished. Bolt upright, shaking and shaken, he did not know where. Sweat streamed into his eyes.

There had been a sound.

To dispel the jackal and the accursed, sunless city, he rose and groped for the light switch. The bedroom was—or at least appeared to be—as he recalled it, save for the damp outline of his lanky body on the sheet. His suitcase stood beside the dresser; his shaving kit lay upon it; *Gods Before the Greeks* waited his return on the cane seat of the old chair.

"You must come to me."

He whirled. There was no one but himself in the room, no one (as far as he could see) in the branches of the maple or on the ground below. Yet the words had been distinct, the speaker—so it had seemed—almost at his ear. Feeling an utter fool, he looked under the bed. There was nobody there, and no one in the closet.

The doorknob would not turn in his hand. He was locked in. That, perhaps, had been the noise that woke him: the sharp click of the bolt. He squatted to squint through the old-fashioned keyhole. The dim hallway outside was empty, as far as he could see. He stood; a hard object gouged the sole of his right foot, and he bent to look.

It was the key. He picked it up. Somebody had locked his door, pushed the key under it, and (possibly) spoken through the keyhole.

Or perhaps it was only that some fragment of his dream had remained with him; that had been the jackal's voice, surely.

The key turned smoothly in the lock. Outside in the hall, he seemed to detect the fragrance of Sarah's perfume, though he could not be sure. If it had been Sarah, she had locked him in, providing the key so that he could free himself in the morning. Whom had she been locking out?

He returned to the bedroom, shut the door, and stood for a moment staring at it, the key in his hand. It seemed unlikely that the crude, outmoded lock would delay any intruder long, and of course it would obstruct him when he answered—

Answered whose summons?

And why should he?

Frightened again, frightened still, he searched for another light. There was none: no reading light on the bed, no lamp on the nightstand, no floorlamp, no fixture upon any of the walls. He turned the key in the lock, and after a few seconds' thought dropped it into the topmost drawer of the dresser and picked up his book.

Abaddon. The angel of destruction dispatched by God to turn the Nile and all its waters to blood, and to kill the firstborn male child in every Egyptian family. Abaddon's hand was averted from the Children of Israel, who for this purpose smeared their doorposts with the blood of the paschal lamb. This substitution has frequently been considered a foreshadowing of the sacrifice of Christ.

Am-mit, Ammit, "Devourer of the Dead." This Egyptian goddess guarded the throne of Osiris in the underworld and feasted upon the souls of those whom Osiris condemned. She had the head of a crocodile and the forelegs of a lion. The remainder of her form was that of a hippopotamus, Figure 1. Am-mit's great temple at Henen-su (Herakleopolis) was destroyed by Octavian, who had its priests impaled.

An-uat, Anuat, "Lord of the Land (the Necropolis)," "Opener to the North." Though frequently confused with Anubis—

The Nebraskan laid his book aside; the overhead light was not well adapted to reading in any case. He switched it off and lay down.

Staring up into the darkness, he pondered An-uat's strange title, Opener to the North. Devourer of the Dead and Lord of the Land seemed clear enough. Or rather Lord of the Land seemed clear once Schmit explained that it referred to the necropolis. (That explanation was the source of his dream, obviously.) Why then had Schmit not explained Opener to the North? Presumably because he didn't understand it either. Well, an opener was one who went before, the first to pass in a certain direction. He (or she) made it easier for others to follow, marking trails and so on. The Nile flowed north, so An-uat might have been thought of as the god who went before the Egyptians when they left their river to sail the Mediterranean. He himself had pictured An-uat in a boat earlier, for that matter, because there was supposed to be a celestial Nile. (Was it the Milky Way?) Because he had known that the Egyptians had believed there was a divine analogue to the Nile along which Ra's sun-boat journeyed. And of course the Milky Way actually was—really is in the most literal sense—the branching star-pool where the sun floats. . . .

The jackal released the corpse it had dragged, coughed, and vomited, spewing carrion alive with worms. The Nebraskan picked up a stone fallen from one of the crumbling tombs, and flung it, striking the jackal just below the ear.

It rose upon its hind legs, and though its face remained that of a beast, its eyes were those of a man. "This is for you," it said, and pointed toward the writhing mass. "Take it, and come to me."

The Nebraskan knelt and plucked one of the worms from the reeking spew. It was pale, streaked and splotched with scarlet, and woke in him a longing never felt before. In his mouth, it brought peace, health, love, and hunger for something he could not name.

Old Hop Thacker's voice floated across infinite distance: "Don't never shoot anythin' without you're dead sure what 'tis, young feller."

Another worm and another, and each as good as the last.

"We will teach you," the worms said, speaking from his own mouth. "Have we not come from the stars? Your own desire for them has wakened, Man of Earth."

Hop Thacker's voice: "Grave worms, do you see?"

"Come to me."

The Nebraskan took the key from the drawer. It was only necessary to open the nearest tomb. The jackal pointed to the lock.

"If it's hungered, it'll suck on a live person, an' he's bound to fight it or die."

The end of the key scraped across the door, seeking the keyhole.

"Come to me, Man of Earth. Come quickly."

Sarah's voice had joined the old man's, their words mingled and confused. She screamed, and the painted figures faded from the door of the tomb.

The key turned. Thacker stepped from the tomb. Behind him his father shouted, "Joe, boy! Joe!" And struck him with his cane. Blood streamed from Thacker's torn scalp, but he did not look around.

"Fight him, young feller! You got to fight him!"

Someone switched on the light. The Nebraskan backed toward the bed.

"Pa, DON'T!" Sarah had the huge butcher knife. She lifted it higher than her father's head and brought it down. He caught her wrist, revealing a long raking cut down his back as he spun about. The knife, and Sarah, fell to the floor.

The Nebraskan grabbed Thacker's arm. "What is this!"

"It is love," Thacker told him. "That is your word, Man of Earth. It is love." No tongue showed between his parted lips; worms writhed there instead, and among the worms gleamed stars.

With all his strength, the Nebraskan drove his right fist into those lips. Thacker's head was slammed back by the blow; pain shot along the Nebraskan's arm. He swung again, with his left this time, and his wrist was caught as Sarah's had been. He tried to back away; struggled to pull free. The high, old-fashioned bed blocked his legs at the knees.

Thacker bent above him, his torn lips parted and bleeding, his eyes filled with such pain as the Nebraskan had never seen. The jackal spoke: *"Open to me."*

"Yes," the Nebraskan told it. "Yes, I will." He had never known before that he possessed a soul, but he felt it rush into his throat.

Thacker's eyes rolled upward. His mouth gaped, disclosing for an instant the slime-sheathed, tentacled thing within. Half falling, half rolling, he slumped upon the bed.

For a second that felt much longer, Thacker's father stood over him with trembling hands. A step backward, and the older Mr. Thacker fell as well—fell horribly and awkwardly, his head striking the floor with a distinct crack.

"Grandpa!" Sarah knelt beside him.

The Nebraskan rose. The worn brown handle of the butcher knife protruded from Thacker's back. A little blood, less than the Nebraskan would have expected, trickled down the smooth old wood to form a crimson pool on the sheet.

"Help me with him, Mr. Cooper. He's got to go to bed."

The Nebraskan nodded and lifted the only living Mr. Thacker onto his feet. "How do you feel?"

"Shaky," the old man admitted. "Real shaky."

The Nebraskan put the old man's right arm about his own neck and picked him up. "I can carry him," he said. "You'll have to show me his bedroom."

"Most times Joe was just like always." The old man's voice was a whisper, as faint and far as it had been in the dream-city of the dead. "That's what you got to understand. Near all the time, an' when—when he did, they was dead, do you see? Dead or near to it. Didn't do a lot of harm."

The Nebraskan nodded.

Sarah, in a threadbare white nightgown that might have been her mother's once, was already in the hall, stumbling and racked with sobs.

"Then you come. An' Joe, he made us. Said I had to keep on talkin' an' she had to ask you fer supper."

"You told me that story to warn me," the Nebraskan said.

The old man nodded feebly as they entered his bedroom. "I thought I was bein' slick. It was true, though, 'cept 'twasn't Cooper, nor Creech neither."

"I understand," the Nebraskan said. He laid the old man on his bed and pulled up a blanket.

"I kilt him didn't I? I kilt my boy Joe."

"It wasn't you, Grandpa." Sarah had found a man's bandanna, no doubt in one of her grandfather's drawers; she blew her nose into it.

"That's what they'll say."

The Nebraskan turned on his heel. "We've got to find that thing and kill it. I should have done that first." Before he had completed the thought, he was hurrying back toward the room that had been his.

He rolled Thacker over as far as the knife handle permitted and lifted his legs onto the bed. Thacker's jaw hung slack; his tongue and palate were thinly coated with a clear, glutinous gel that carried a faint smell of ammonia; otherwise his mouth was perfectly normal.

"It's a spirit," Sarah told the Nebraskan from the doorway. "It'll go into Grandpa now, 'cause he killed it. That's what he always said."

The Nebraskan straightened up, turning to face her. "It's a living creature, something like a cuttlefish, and it came here from—" He waved the thought aside. "It doesn't really matter. It landed in North Africa, or at least I think it must have, and if I'm right, it was eaten by a jackal. They'll eat just about anything, from what I've read. It survived inside the jackal as a sort of intestinal parasite. Long ago, it transmitted itself to a man, somehow."

Sarah was looking down at her father, no longer listening. "He's restin' now, Mr. Cooper. He shot the old soul-sucker in the woods one day. That's what Grandpa tells, and he hasn't had no rest since, but he's peaceful now. I was only eight or 'bout that, and for a long time Grandpa was 'fraid he'd get me, only he never did." With both her thumbs, she drew down the lids of the dead man's eyes.

"Either it's crawled away—" the Nebraskan began.

Abruptly, Sarah dropped to her knees beside her dead parent and kissed him.

When at last the Nebraskan backed out of the room, the dead man and the living woman remained locked in that kiss, her face ecstatic, her fingers tangled in the dead man's hair. Two full days later, after the Nebraskan had crossed the Mississippi, he still saw that kiss in shadows beside the road.

Golden City Far

✦

This is what William Wachter wrote in his spiral notebook during study hall, the first day.

"Funny dream last night. I was standing on a beach. I looked out, shading my eyes, and I could not see a thing. It was like a big fog bank was over the ocean way far away so that everything sort of faded white. A gull flew over me and screeched, and I thought, *well, not that way.*

"So I turned north, and there was a long level stretch and big mountains. I should not have been able to see past them, but I could. It was not like the mountains could be looked through. It was like the thing I was seeing on the other side was higher than they were so that I saw it over the tops. It was really far away and looked small, but it was just beautiful, gold towers, all sizes and shapes with flags on them. Yellow flags, purple, blue, green, and white ones. I thought, *well, there it is.* I had to go there. I cannot explain it, but I knew I had to get to that city and once I did nothing else would matter because I would have done everything I was supposed to do, and everything would be OK forever.

"I started walking, and I was not thinking about how far it was at all, just that it was really nice that I had found out what I was supposed to do. Instead of thrashing around for years I had it. It did not matter how far it was, just that every step got me closer.

"Cool!"

He could not think of anything else to write, but only of the golden towers, and how the flags had stood out stiffly from them so that he had known there was a hard wind blowing where the towers were, and he would like that wind.

Someone passed him a note. He let it fall to the floor unread.

Mrs. Durkin took him by the shoulder, and he jerked.

"Billy?"

It was hard to remember where he was, but he said, "Yes, ma'am?"

"The bell rang, Billy. All the other kids have gone. Were you asleep?"

Thinking that she meant when he had seen the towers and the flags, he repeated, "Yes, ma'am."

"Daydreaming. Well, you're at the right age for it, but the period's over."

He stood up. "I should have done my homework in here. I guess I did, some of it. I want to get to bed early."

The sea was to his left, the ground beneath his feet great stones, or shale, or soft sand. The mountains, which had appeared distant the night before, were so remote as to be almost invisible, and often vanished behind dunes covered with sparse sea oats. There was a breeze from the sea, and though the scudding clouds looked threatening, it did not rain or snow. He was neither hungry nor thirsty, and was conscious of being neither hungry nor thirsty. It seemed to him that he had been walking a long while, not hours or days or years, but simply a long while, time as it had been before anyone had thought of such things as years or centuries.

He climbed dunes and rough, low hills, and beyond the last found an inlet blocking his progress; long before he reached the point near which she lay, he had seen the woman on the rock in the water. She was beautiful, and naked save for her hair; and her skin was as white as milk. In one hand she held a shining yellow apple.

He stopped and stood staring at her, and when a hundred breaths had come and gone, he sat down on a different rock and stared some more. Her eyes opened; each time he met her gaze, he felt lost in their depths.

"You may kiss me and eat one bite of my apple," she told him. "One bite, no more."

He was frightened, and shook his head.

"One bite will let you understand everything." Her voice was music. "Two bites would let you understand more than everything, and more than everything is too much."

He backed away.

The sun peeped from between clouds, bathing her with black gold. "What color is my hair?"

Perhaps its black was only shadow. Perhaps its gold was only sunlight. He said, "Nobody has hair like that."

"I do." She smiled, and her lips were as red as corals, and her teeth were sharp and gleaming white. "Men have found themselves in difficulties through biting my apple."

He nodded, certain it was true.

"But kiss me, and you may do anything you wish."

"I wouldn't be able to stop," he told her, and turned and ran.

He woke sweating, threw off the covers and got out of bed. The house was dark and quiet. The alarm clock meant to wake him for school said five minutes past four. He carried his books and notebooks to the dining-room table, turned on the light, and began to study.

In study hall that afternoon, he wrote this in his spiral notebook.

"One time Mr. Bates said how do you know this is real? Maybe what you dream is really real and this is a dream. How can you tell? People argued about it, but I did not because I knew the answer. It is because what you dream is different every night. Waking up you are wherever you went to sleep. Last night it was kind of the same as before, but different because the city was gone. Anyhow I could not see it. I met this girl who tried to get me to say what color her hair was, only I could not. She wanted to kiss me and I ran off."

He made a small round dot for the final period, and read over what he had written. It seemed inadequate, and he added: "I would like to go back."

He stopped upon the summit of a hill higher than most, and turned for a last look. She was standing on her rock now, sparsely robed in hair like fire that cast shadows upon her white flesh that were as black as paint. One hand held up her shining apple. When she saw he was watching her, she raised the other, kissed it, and blew the kiss to him.

For one brief instant he saw it fluttering toward him like a butterfly of cellophane. It touched his lips, soft and throbbing and redolent of the flowers that bloom under the sea. He shook, and could not stop.

A long time after that, when she and her inlet were many hills behind him and he had long since stopped trembling, he saw a black and white dog. It had a long and tangled coat, a long and feathery tail, and ears that would not stand up quite straight. He had never had a dog, but the people next door had a dog very much like that, a dog named Shep. He played with Shep now and then, and he whistled now.

The dog turned to look at him, pricking up the ears that would not quite stand up straight. It was some distance away but came trotting toward him, and he himself trotted to meet it, and stroked its head and rubbed its ears. After that the two of them went on together (the dog trotting at his heels) climbing and descending hills which gradually became less lofty and less rugged, sometimes catching glimpses of the sea to their left, where waves flashed in sunshine like mirrors, or stalked from darkling sea to darkling land like an army of ghosts.

The alarm clock was ringing tinnily. He got up and shut it off, stretched, and looked out the window. There were leaves, mostly brown, on the broken sidewalk in front of the house. He tried to remember whether they had been there the day before, and decided they had not.

Later, as he shuffled through the leaves, Shep joined him and accompanied him to the bus stop. He petted Shep and declared him to be a good dog, and found something strange in the way Shep looked at him, some quality that slipped away no matter how hard he tried to grasp it.

On the bus he told Carl Kilby, "He looked right at me. Usually they don't want to look you in the face. That was weird!" Carl, who had no idea what he was talking about, grunted.

In study hall . . .

"Last night I found this dog that looked exactly like Shep. Maybe it was him. He was a nice dog and we were way out in a pretty lonely spot. (I did not even see the ocean toward the end.) So I was glad to have the dog. Only what was he doing way out there? He was just walking along like me when I saw him.

"I have never had the same dream three nights. Not even two that I can remember."

"Billy?"

"Well, if it happens tonight too, I hope the dog is still there."

Mrs. Durkin touched his shoulder. "The period's over, Billy."

"Just a minute," he said. "I want to get this down."

"A kiss chased me and landed on my face."

It was inadequate, and he knew it; but with Mrs. Durkin standing beside him it was the best he could do. He shut his notebook and stood up. "I'm sorry, Mrs. Durkin."

She smiled. "The other kids rush out at the bell. It's kind of nice to have one who isn't eager to leave."

He nodded, which seemed safe, backed away, and went to his next class.

The dog was still there, lying down as if waiting for him. The weather was the same. The city he had seen had been on the other side of the mountains—he felt certain of that, and he could see the mountains far away, a low blue rampart.

He and the dog walked on together until the dog said, "Chief?"

"God bless you!" he told it, and leaned down a little to pat its head.

"Chief, would you maybe like a drink?"

It seemed entirely natural, but somehow deep underneath it did *not* seem natural. Not surprised but somehow (deep underneath) thrown a little off balance, he said, "Sure, if you would."

"There's a nice spring not far from here," the dog said. "Cold water, with a sort of drink-me-and-be-lucky flavor. I could show you."

He said, "Sure," but when they had gone some distance he added, "I guess you've been here before."

"Huh-uh," the dog said.

"Okay, then how do you know about this place?"

"I smell it." When they had climbed another hill and the spring was in sight, the dog added, "It might not work for me. Only for you."

The dog drank the water just the same, running ahead of him and lapping fast. There was a pool in the rocks, not too wide to jump over, from which a rill ran. He went to the other side and knelt. I've never drunk out of a dog's bowl, he thought, so this is a first.

It was good water, as the dog had promised it would be, cold and fresh. He had no idea what luck was supposed to taste like, so he tried to analyze the flavor, which was very faint. It was a taste of rocks and pines and chill winds, he decided, with just a little touch of sunshine on snow.

"Does he always follow you like that, Bill?"

Sue Sumner was blond and beautiful, and he knew he was apt to stammer like a retard; he also knew he had to answer. He said, "No, just yesterday and today. He's a nice dog, but I don't know why he comes to the stop with me."

She smiled. "You ought to take him on the bus."

"I'd like to," he said, and realized as he spoke that it was true. "I'd like to take him to school with me."

"Like Mary and her little lamb."

He grinned. "Sure. I've been laughed at before. It didn't hurt much, and it hasn't killed me yet."

It was Friday, which meant assembly instead of study hall. He would save his dream in memory, he decided, and write it down in study hall Monday, with his weekend dreams, if there were any. "Probably won't be," he told himself.

From his notebook . . . "The craziest thing happened yesterday. We got back from church and I went up to change back. I was putting on my jeans, and there was this bird singing outside. Singing lyrics. I thought this is crazy, birds don't sing words, and I tried to remember how they really did sing. I could remember the tune, but it seemed like I could not remember the words. I kept telling myself there were not any. I put on a CD, loud, and pretty soon the bird flew away. Now I cannot remember what the bird sang, and I would like to. Something about him and his wife (it rhymed with life, I remember that) building a house and don't come around because we will not let you in.

"OK, I went outside and right away the Pekars' dog started following me. I thought my gosh it is going to turn into The Dream—the hills, the rocks, the dwarf on the horse and all that, and I am crazy. So I walked about three blocks with the Pekars' dog along the whole time.

"We got to the park and I sat down on a bench and petted the dog some, and I said, listen, this is serious, so can you really talk? And he looked right at me the way he does and said yep. What is your name, I said, and he said Shep. I was going to ask if he remembered the naked lady with the hair, only he had not been with me when that happened. So I asked about the lucky water we drank, did he remember that? He said yep. He says he cannot talk to other people at all, only to me and other dogs. The dwarf said all that stuff about the writing on the scabbard and the writing on the blade, and I was not sure I remembered it. I still am not. So I asked him about that and he said he—"

"Billy, will you run an errand for me, please?"

He looked up and shut his notebook. "Sure, Mrs. Durkin."

"Thank you. Wait just a moment while I write this note." She wrote rapidly, not scribbling but small, neat, businesslike script. When she had finished, she folded the paper, put it in an envelope, sealed the envelope, and wrote "Mr. Hoff" on it. "Mr. Hoff is an assistant principal. You know that, I'm sure."

"Yes, ma'am."

"I'd like you take this to him, Billy, and I want you to wait for a reply, written or oral. If the bell rings before you get it, you are not to go to your next class. You are to wait for that reply. Leave your books here. I'll give you a note excusing you when you come back for them."

He explained about waiting to Mr. Hoff when he handed him the envelope; Mr. Hoff looked slightly baffled but told him to wait in the outer office.

Sue Sumner sat with him on the bus going home. Sue got off with him, too, although it was not her regular stop. Shep had been waiting at the stop, and she petted Shep until the other kids had gone. Then she said, "What's bothering you, Bill?"

"You could tell, huh?"

"I talked to you twice, and you didn't hear me. At first I thought you were ditching me—"

"I wouldn't do that!"

"The second time I saw that you were just so deep inside yourself . . ."

He nodded.

"Now you look like you're too big to cry. What is it?"

"First period." He cleared his throat. "I won't be there. I've got to go to the office. Are you going to tell everybody?"

Sue shook her head. She was wearing a guy's shirt, jeans, and very little makeup; and she was so lovely it hurt to look at her.

"I've got to talk to the psychologist. They think I'm crazy."

She put her hand on his shoulder. "You're not. You'll be fine."

He shrugged. "I think I'm crazy, too. I have crazy dreams."

"Everybody has crazy dreams."

"Not like this. Not the same thing, night after night."

"About me?" She smiled.

"Yeah. Kind of. How did you know?"

She smiled again, impishly. "Maybe I'll tell you, and maybe I won't."

They began to walk. He said, "Shep and I will walk you home."

"I kind of thought you would."

"Maybe I could leave the house a little early tomorrow and go over to your stop and wait there with you?"

Her hand found his. "I kind of thought you might do that, too. Tell me about your dreams."

"It's all kinds of stuff, only it's always about this place way far off. The gold towers. They're the color of your hair. Don't get mad."

"I'm not mad."

"Me and Shep are trying to get there. Shep can talk."

She squeezed his hand.

"I've got this sword. It's a beautiful sword, and there's writing on the scabbard and writing on the blade. The writing on the scabbard is important. Really, really important."

"Are you making this up?"

He shook his head. "If I was, it wouldn't be so scary. The writing on the blade is more important than the writing on the scabbard, but you have to read the scabbard, all of it, before you read the blade. It's all very hard to read because the writing's really old-fashioned. Shep can't read it at all, but I can a little. Last night I was able to make out the first three words."

"I bet you couldn't remember them this morning."

"Sure I can." He spoke the words.

There was an old woman in a rocking chair on the porch of a house they were passing. She called, "Hello, Sue. Hello, young man."

Sue stared, then smiled. "Hi, Aunt Dinah." (It seemed to him that there had been some slight obstruction in Sue's throat.)

"Would you and your young man like to come in for some iced tea?"

"Next time, Aunt Dinah. I've got to get home and do my homework."

A middle-aged man with glasses came out of the house and spoke to Aunt Dinah. She smiled at this man, and said, "I live here with you, sir." When she turned back to them, she said, "That's a fine young man you've got there, Sue. Hold on to him."

When they were a block past that house, he said, "We're going across these hills, Sue. Shep and me are. We found this girl, a beautiful girl with long black hair. Something had her foot, and it was pulling her into a hole, and—"

"I don't want to hear any more about your dreams," Sue said softly. "Not right now. Let's just walk for a while. Not talking."

He nodded. This was Spruce Street, and there was a house there where the people had actually planted spruce trees between the street and the sidewalk. He did not know the people; but he had always felt sure he would like them if he ever met them, because of that. Three houses down, a sleek Mercedes sedan was parked at the curb. He had seen it before, although he did not know the owner. He stared at it as they passed, because it looked different—different in a warm and friendly way, as though it knew him and liked him.

They had turned onto Twenty-third and walked another block before he figured it out. The Mercedes had always looked like something that would never be in his reach. Now it looked as if it was, as if it was a car he could own any time he decided he really wanted one.

Sue said, "I'm ready to talk now, Bill. Is that all right?"

He nodded. "I'm ready to listen."

"There were two things I had to say." She paused, small white teeth gnawing at her lower lip. "They are important, both of them, and I knew I ought to say them both. Only I couldn't figure out which one I ought to say first. I think I have, now. Have you ever been like that?"

He nodded again. "I usually get it wrong."

"I don't believe you." She smiled very suddenly, and it was as though the sun had burst from behind a cloud. "Here's the first one. Do you know why high school is so important?"

"I think you'd better tell me."

"It's not because it's where you learn history or home ec. It's not even because it's where you get ready for college. It's because it's where some people—the people who aren't going to be left behind—decide what they want to do with their lives."

He said, "My brother decided he was going into the Navy."

"Yes. Exactly. And I've decided. Have you?"

He shook his head.

"What I'm going to do is you, Bill." Her voice was low but intense. "I'm going to stick with you. I think you're going to stick with me, too. I'll see to it. But if you don't, I'm going to stick with you anyway. On the bus I thought maybe you were going to try to ditch me. Remember that?"

"I would never ditch you," he said, and meant it.

"Well, even if you do, I'll still be around. That's the first thing I wanted to say—the thing I decided ought to come first. Now I've said it, and I feel a lot better."

"So do I." He discovered that he was smiling. "You know, I've got this problem, and it felt really, really important. But it isn't. Not anymore."

She smiled. "That's right."

"I was thinking how to tell my parents. That was the part that really had me worried—how could I put part of it off onto them. I didn't think of it like that, but that's what it was. Well, I'm not going to. Why should they worry, when maybe they don't have to? If that school psychologist wants them to know, she can tell them herself. 'Oh, by the way, Mrs. Wachter, your son is crazy.' Let's see how she likes it."

"Here's the other thing I have to tell you," Sue Sumner said; her voice was so low that he could scarcely hear her. "That used to be Aunt Dinah's house, back there. But Aunt Dinah's dead."

The sky had not changed. The sun that was always to their left was to his left still. The racing clouds raced on, with more after them, and more after them, a marathon for clouds in which a hundred thousand were competing.

It must never change here, he thought. Then he realized that all his dreams had taken little time here, no more than a few hours.

The black-haired girl was still sitting on the ground, rubbing a slender white ankle that showed the livid mark of a clawed hand.

Soil wet with blood still clung to the blade of his sword. He wiped it with dry grass, wishing for rags and a can of oil. Reminding himself not to read the blade—not that he could have if he had wanted to.

The girl looked up at him, and her eyes were large and dark, forest pools seen by moonlight. "Not many men would have thought to do that," she said. Her voice was music, dark and low. "And no other man would have dared."

"I'm just glad it worked," he said. "What happened?"

For a moment she smiled. (When she smiled he felt he would have followed her to the end of the world.) "I didn't see the hole, that's all. The grass hid it."

He nodded and sat near her, though not too near. Shep lay down at his feet.

"I wasn't looking. I should have been looking, but I wasn't. It's my own fault. I might as well say that right now, because it's the truth and I'll never be at peace until I admit it. I hate stupid, careless people. But I was stupid and careless. Do you try to tell the truth?"

"Mostly, yes."

"I try constantly, but I lie and lie. It's my nature." She smiled again. "I have to keep fighting it, and though I fight it all time, I don't fight hard enough."

He recalled something his biology teacher had told him. "DNA is destiny."

"You're a wizard, aren't you." It was more accusation than question.

"No," he told her. "No, I'm not."

"Oh yes, you are." The smile teased her mouth; it was a small mouth, and its perfect lips were very red. "You've cast a spell on me, because I lie and lie but when I said you were a wizard that was the truth. How old are you? Really?"

He could not remember.

"You wizards can make yourselves young again. I know that, but I don't care. You're *my* wizard, and you saved me, and I love you. Now you look modest and say you love me too."

He tried.

She gave her ankle a final rub. "I *wish* this mark would go away. I know it won't, but I wish it would."

Rising, Shep licked it once, shook his head, and backed away.

"Your name is . . . ?"

"Bill."

She cocked her head. "Are you making fun of me, Bill?"

"No," he told her. "I wouldn't make fun of you. Not ever." He meant it.

"My name is Biltis." She rose effortlessly, and he stood up hurriedly. She took his hands in hers. "They'll want to know who my lover is, and I'll say Bill, and they'll laugh at me. Don't you feel sorry for me? Look! I've lost a slipper! Am I not richly deserving of your pity?"

"Maybe it's still down in there," he said, and knelt, and was about to thrust his hand into the hole.

"Don't!" She seized his shoulders, pulling him back. "I was only joking! Y-y-you . . ."

Surprised, he turned to look at her. Her crimson lips were trembling, the great, dark pools moist with tears.

"You mustn't! They're down there. You mustn't reach into holes, or go into caves or—or go down in wells or cisterns. Nothing like that, ever again. They never forget and they never forgive. Oh, Bill!"

She was in his arms. He clasped her trembling body, astonished to find it small and light. He kissed her cheek and neck, and their lips met.

"Come in and sit down, Billy." The woman behind the desk was dark, heavy, and middle-aged, with a warmth in her voice that made him want to like her.

"Are you really the psychologist?"

"Uh-huh. You were expectin' Dr. Gluck, I bet. She left at the end of the last term. I'm Dr. Grimes." Dr. Grimes smiled broadly. "Why don't you sit right there? I don't bite."

He did, on the edge of a chair more comfortable than most school chairs.

"Do you like bein' Billy? Would you rather be William?"

"Bill," he said. "I like people to call me Bill. Is that all right?"

"Sure, Bill. Bill, I'm goin' to start right off tellin' you somethin' I ought not to tell you at all. I like havin' you here. I been counselin' for close to twenty years now. That's what I do, I'm a counselor. And it's almost always drugs or liquor. Or stealin'. Here at this school, it's been drugs, up to now. Nothin' else. Let me tell you, Bill, a person gets awfully, awfully tired of drugs. And liquor. And stealin'. So I'm real glad to see you."

He waited.

"I got this notebook they took away from you." She opened the file folder on her desk and held it up. "I read it. Probably you mind, but I had to or else I wouldn't have known what was bein' talked about. You see?

I wouldn't have known what kind of things to say, either. Maybe you'd like it back?"

He nodded.

She put it down in front of him. "I'll tell you what I thought when I was readin' it. About that dog and the li'l bird singin' and all. I thought, why, this boy's got a real imagination! I told you about those drug people I got to talk to all the time. And the liquor people, too, and the stealin' people. All them. They haven't got— You know why people steal, Bill?"

He shrugged. "They want the stuff, I guess."

"You guess wrong. You ever see stuff you wanted? In a store or anythin'?"

"Sure."

"Uh-huh. You steal it?"

"No." He shook his head. "No, I didn't."

"They do. They take it. They take it 'cause they can't imagine anythin' will happen. They do that maybe a hundred times, and then they get caught. Only next time they can't imagine they're goin' to get caught *this* time. Why are you smilin'?"

"You reminded me of somebody. Not somebody real."

"On the TV?" She was watching him narrowly.

"No." He sensed that he had been cornered and would be cornered again. It would be best, surely, to tell the truth to this friendly woman and try to get her on his side. "In a dream I've been having. That's all."

"You like her. You wouldn't have smiled like that if you didn't. Is she pretty?"

He nodded.

" 'Bout how tall?"

"Up to my chin." He touched it.

"That's in real high heels, I bet."

"No, ma'am. Barefoot."

"Uh-huh. Hasn't got no clothes?"

It was going to be complicated. He said slowly, "She wasn't barefoot to start with. She had slippers, like. Really beautiful slippers with jewels on them. Only she lost one, so she took the other one off. She has on a—a dress with a long skirt. It comes down nearly to her feet. It's gold and red, and has jewels on it, all over."

He waved his hands, trying to indicate the patterns. "It's really, really pretty."

Dr. Grimes was nodding. "I bet she smells good, too."

He was glad to confirm it. "You're right, she smells wonderful."

"You smell things in this dream?"

He hesitated. "Well, I smelled her. And I smell the wind sometimes, the freshness of it. Or the ocean, when it was blowing off the ocean."

"You ever kiss this girl?"

"Biltis." He felt himself flushing. "Her name's Biltis. We laughed about it."

He waited for Dr. Grimes to speak, but she did not.

"I didn't really kiss her. She kissed me."

"Uh-huh. What happened after?"

"She whistled. I didn't think a girl could ever whistle that loud, but she did. She whistled, and this big bird came down. It looked like an eagle, kind of, but it was bigger and had a longer neck. It had a bridle and reins. You know? Those long leather things you steer with?"

Dr. Grimes nodded. "Uh-huh, I know what reins are."

"And she got on it and it flew away." He closed his eyes, remembering. "Only it talked to me a little first."

"This big bird did."

"Yeah. It said I better not hurt her. But I wouldn't. Then it flew away, and she waved. Waved to me."

"I see. That was real nice, wasn't it?"

He nodded. "I won't ever forget it."

"Maybe you'll see her again." Dr. Grimes was watching him closely.

"I don't know."

"Do you want to, Bill?"

"I don't know that either. She scared me, a little."

Dr. Grimes nodded. "Sure. You ever see her when you weren't sleepin'?"

"I don't think so."

"Only you're not sure?"

"No," he said. "No, I haven't."

"All right. I want to talk about awake now, Bill. Funny things happen to everybody, sometimes. I know funny things happen to *me*. Like just last Wednesday I saw a li'l boy that looked just like a certain li'l boy I had gone to school with—like he never had grown up, and here he was, just the same. Anythin' like that happen to you?"

He shook his head.

"Oh, I bet. You know there was somethin'. Tell me now."

He cleared his throat. "Well, I had walked over to somebody's house, and I was coming back. Shep and me."

"Shep."

He nodded.

"Can I ask why you walked over to this house, Bill?"

"Well, it seemed like I ought to. She got off at my stop. Off the bus."

"Uh-huh."

"So I had walked her over to her house. We talked. You know?"

Dr. Grimes chuckled. "She likes you, Bill. If she didn't like you, what's she gettin' off at your stop for? And you like her. If you didn't, what you walkin' her home for?"

"Yeah, I guess. Well, I was coming back home, and Sue's—this girl's aunt Dinah come out of her house and stopped me. She's an old lady, and she's not really this one girl's aunt. She was a friend of this girl's grandmother's."

"I got it. What she say, Bill?"

"She said she needed a big, big favor. She said she owed me already, but she needed another favor, a big one. Shep didn't like her."

Dr. Grimes leaned forward, her face serious. "Did she want you to do somethin' bad, Bill?"

"I don't think so. She just said that this girl's family probably has some pictures of her when she was young. Of Aunt Dinah. Now she'd like to have them, and would I see if I could get them for her. As many as I could. I said all right, but Shep says—I mean he doesn't like her. I don't think he likes me being mixed up with her."

"Shep's your dog?"

"No, ma'am."

"But he's a dog. Does he really talk, Bill?"

It was easier because he had just said it. "No, ma'am."

"You goin' to try to get the pictures?"

"Yes, ma'am. I asked this girl, and she said she'd look and bring them to school today, any she found. If she's got any, I'll take them over after school."

"That's not a bad thin' you're doin', tryin' to help out a old woman like that."

"No, ma'am," he said, "but I thought it was pretty weird. Why didn't she just phone Sue's mom?"

When they got off the bus that afternoon, he dropped his books at his house and put on Sue's backpack for the walk over to hers. The pictures, faded black-and-white snapshots, were in a white envelope in the pocket of his shirt, under his sweater.

There were more leaves on the sidewalk today; the maples had turned to scarlet and gold, and a bush in somebody's yard to a deep, rich crimson. "In my dream," he said, "where I've got that sword?"

Sue looked at him sidelong.

"It's beautiful. It's just so beautiful I can't hardly stand it sometimes. But it's just brown hills and purple mountains way, way off. And the blue sky, with the white clouds moving fast across it. What makes it so pretty is the way I feel about it. I see everything, and I see how great it is. The big bird with the girl riding him, and her hair and her scarf blowing out behind her. She waved, like this, and she had a gold bracelet on her wrist. The sun hit it, and it was the most beautiful thing I ever saw in my life."

"I don't think I like her," Sue said.

"Aunt Dinah?"

"This girl in your dream."

"Oh. I'm not sure I do either. But what I started out to say was that I'm getting to see things here the same way as there. That's really, really beautiful, like I said. But here it's beautiful, too. More beautiful than there, really. Biltis is beautiful. She really is, and her dress is really pretty, and her jewelry didn't just cost a lot, it's like looking at stars. But you're more beautiful than Biltis is."

Quickly, Sue turned again to look at him.

"If your dress was as pretty as hers and you had jewelry as nice as hers is, you'd be homecoming queen and she'd be a maid of honor. You know what I mean?"

Sue took his hand, and that was answer enough.

"So I've been thinking. Pretty soon I might be able to do that. Give you a dress that was so beautiful people would just stop and stare, and jewelry."

Shep said, "Good!" though Sue seemed not to hear him.

"I've been thinking about other stuff, too."

"Have you, Bill?"

"Yeah. Lots of things." He took the white envelope from his pocket. "Like I'd like to show her to you. Show you Biltis, if I could. If I was good in art, the way you are, maybe I could draw her. I'm not, but I can show you pretty close, just the same."

He took out a photograph.

"Like this. The sharp chin, and the little mouth. The big eyes, especially."

"That's Aunt Dinah," Sue told him. "Aunt Dinah, when she was about twenty."

"I know," he said.

"Anyway, she can't really be dead, can she?"

Shep growled softly, deep in his throat.

"I figured it out," Sue continued, "while I was looking for those pictures. See, my mother didn't want me going over there, so she told me Aunt Dinah was dead so I wouldn't. We went to some funeral, some old lady's, and when we got home she told me it was Aunt Dinah. I think I was in kindergarten then. Doesn't that make sense, Bill?"

"Sure," he said.

"I mean, you said she came out and stopped you on the street. Ghosts don't do that."

"I guess not."

"She didn't want to talk to me, because she knew my mother was mad. And she couldn't phone the house."

He said, "Right."

"But maybe you could get them for her. See? That's the only way everything fits."

He said, "We've still got to take her the pictures."

Sue nodded. "Yes, we do. That's why I brought them. I don't know what my mother was so mad about, and it was a long time ago anyway. You ought to forgive people after a while, unless it's something really bad. Dogs are good at that. We ought to learn from them."

She leaned down to pet Shep. "What about the big social studies test tomorrow? Have you been studying?"

"Yeah," he said, "only I missed class today. I had to talk to the shrink."

"It wasn't bad, we just reviewed Europe. Would you like me to fill you in a little, when we get to my house? I mean, I'll just tell my mother you weren't in class today, so I'm going to tell you what we talked about."

"Sure!" He smiled. "I've been hoping I could get you to do that. Boy! Am I lucky!"

"Okay. Suppose you got to go to Paris. Give me three or four things you'd like to see there."

He was silent for a moment, concentrating. "The big art museum."

"The Louvre. Ms. Fournier will give you a lot better grade if you use the French name. She teaches French, too."

"I know," he said.

They had reached the house. Still holding the snapshots Sue had brought to school, he climbed four steps to the porch and rang the bell.

"Maybe she won't be home," Sue said from the foot of the steps. "You could just leave them in the mailbox, Bill."

"I'm going out for football." He looked back at her, grinning. "Football players don't just leave them in the mailbox."

He rang again, hearing heavy male footsteps from inside the house.

Sue joined him on the porch. Her deliciously rounded chin was up, but she took his left arm and held it tightly.

A rumpled man opened the door and asked what they wanted.

"My mother had these . . ." Sue's voice faded away. "Tell him, Bill."

He nodded, and held them out. "There's an old lady living with you, I think her name's Dinah?"

The rumpled man shook his head. "There's no old lady living here, son. Forget it!" His face was hard and a trifle stupid, the face of a man whom life had defeated, who could not understand why he had been defeated so easily.

Bill said, "But you know who I mean. I promised her I'd bring her these pictures if I could, and—"

"Do you know her? You knew her name, so you've got to. You tell her to get out of my house and quit bothering me and my family."

Sue's grasp tightened. "Bill . . ."

"It's her house," he told the rumpled man, "or anyhow she thinks it is. She thought it was hers, probably, a long time before you were born, mister. I'll tell her what you said if I ever see her again, but I'm going to give you some advice right now. Take these pictures and don't tear them up or anything. Leave them someplace where they'll be easy for her to find. On the mantel or someplace like that. Let go of my arm for a minute, Sue."

He turned over the white envelope, took a pencil from his pocket, wrote "Dinah/Biltis" on the front, and handed the envelope to the rumpled man in the doorway. "That might help. I don't know, but it might. I'd do it if I were you."

After supper that evening, Ray Wachter asked his son why he was studying so hard, saying, "You've been at those books for a couple of hours now. Is it anything I can help you with?"

"Just social studies." He closed the book and looked up. "But I'm going out for football—"

"You are?"

"Yeah. It's sort of too late. Almost too late, but I just decided today. You've got to keep your grades up, or they won't let you play."

Ray Wachter tried to conceal the pride he felt; he was a simple man, but not an unintelligent one. "They might not let you play a lot anyway, Bill. You're not a junior, you know. Don't get your hopes too high."

"Well, this is the first big test in social studies, and I'm not too hot in that." Two words from the scabbard popped into his mind, and he pronounced them almost automatically.

"What the hell was that?" Ray Wachter took off his glasses, as if their lenses could somehow block hearing.

"What language, you mean?" Bill tilted his chair back, yawned, and stretched. "No language of this world, sir, nor do I know its proper name. I suppose it's nearer to Chaldean than anything else we have here."

"You're a funny kid, Bill."

He smiled. "Only too often, sir. I fall over my own feet, I know." When his father had gone, he murmured to himself, "I think it must mean, 'Let me be numbered among the learned.'"

He and the dog tramped over the plain, mile upon mile. There seemed to be no convenient way for him to wear the sword. He had tried thrusting its scabbard through his belt, but it slipped and tripped him, and proved to be much less convenient than carrying it, and the long blade it held, over his shoulder.

"Dark," Shep said.

"Pretty dark, yes. Do you mean that night is coming?"

"Yep."

"We ought to have a tent or something." He searched his pockets. "I don't even have anything we could use to start a fire, and there's nothing out here to burn except grass."

Shep said nothing.

"This is a little like a Jack London story. But I don't like that story and have no intention of repeating it. Are you getting tired?"

"Nope."

"Then we should keep walking, for a while at least. Why did she blow her kiss at me, Shep? Who was she, anyway?"

Shep said nothing.

"That's right, you never saw her. I don't mean Biltis, I mean the woman on the rock by the sea. She had an apple, a gold one. She wanted me to bite it, but you can't bite gold."

"Nope?"

"Nope. It's a soft metal, but not soft enough to bite, except for very thin gold leaf. They used to coat costly pills with that."

"Spring."

"This weather? Perhaps you're right, but it seems like fall to me. Very early spring, possibly."

"Water. I smell it. Smells strong."

He smiled. "Then it's probably not good to drink."

"Good water."

"If you say so. I'm learned now, or think I may be, but being learned isn't the same as being wise—I'm wise enough to know that, anyway. Wise enough to trust a dog's judgment of what he smells."

The wolf-wind that had driven the clouds before it like terrified sheep had come down to earth. It ruffled his hair and raced beneath his shirt. He shivered, conscious for the first time of both thirst and cold.

"Talking of water brings us back to the woman on the coast," he told Shep to distract himself from his discomfort. "Let's assume she's someone famous, or anyway someone known. A woman as lovely as she is and as mysterious as she is could hardly stay unknown for long. If we list what we know about her, we may find a clue to her identity."

Shep glanced up at him. "If you say so, Chief."

"Prima." He shivered again, and strove to walk a trifle faster. "She was on a rock in the sea. I'm tempted to say by the sea; but it was actually in the sea, although not very far out."

"Okay," Shep said.

"Secunda, she was nude. Both these seem to indicate that she had come up out of the sea. People on land wear clothing to keep off the sun and to keep warm." (At that moment he dearly wished his own would keep him warmer.) "People in the sea have no need to keep off the sun and cannot be warmed by ordinary clothing."

"Tertia, she was strikingly beautiful.

"And quarta, she held the golden apple I have already mentioned. That covers it, I think."

Shep made a small noise that might, or might not, have been of assent.

"You're quite right. There is more. Quinta, she had extraordinary hair. It seemed black and blond together. Not black in places and blond in others, but both at once. Sexta—a suggestive ordinal, Shep—wishing to give a blessing or something of the kind, she kissed."

"Did she, Chief?"

"Yes. Yes, indeed, she did. And if it was not her kiss that made me aware of the speech of animals, what did?"

They walked on in silence for a time. At length he said, "Do we know of any famous female who would appear to fit our description of her? It seems to me we do. We can call her Venus, or Aphrodite, or even Ishtar. She was born of the sea. Paris awarded her the golden prize called the Apple of Discord. She is the goddess of love, and we cannot understand any animal until we love it. Furthermore—"

"Over there!" Shep raced away.

The spring, when they found it, was wide and deep, and its water was clearer than any diamond. Shep drank, and he drank too, and marveled, by the sun's dying light, to see the cold, crystalline water welling from deep in the earth. It raced away as a noisy brook, narrow but by no stretch of the word feeble.

"Neither am I," he told Shep. "That water made me feel much stronger. I suppose I was becoming weak from thirst, and perhaps from hunger too."

He drank again, and the strength he knew was a strength he had never known before.

From his notebook . . . "Dr. Grimes has returned this to me. She wants me to record my dreams as I did earlier, and to show it to her at our next session. I will comply.

"Last night Shep steered me to a spring of strength. We drank from it. I felt much stronger and tested my strength by throwing stones, some so large I was astonished to find I could lift them. Shep ran as fast as my stones flew, which I think remarkable. (This morning he ran alongside our bus, following Sue and me to school. I believe he is out on the athletic field.)

"When I grew bored we sat beside the spring, I laboring to puzzle out the inscriptions on the scabbard by the dying light. The days must be longer there, or perhaps it is only that we move faster. I read each group of symbols again and again, if it can be called reading. Slowly, terribly slowly, the meanings of a few words creep into my mind. There are some I could pronounce if I dared, though I have no notion (or little) of what they may mean. There are others that I understand, or believe I may understand somewhat, although I have little or no idea of their pronunciation. It is a slow process, and one that may never bear fruit.

"And yet these spells are only a distraction, however hermetic they may be. What has happened to me? That is the question. Why do I find myself in that barren land each night? What land is it in which thaumaturgic springs rise from barren ground?"

"I want you to stay for a minute or two after the bell, Billy. Will you do that?"

His heart sank, but he nodded. "Yes, Ms. Fournier."

The bell rang even as he spoke. As the rest of the class trooped out, she smiled and motioned for him to join her at her desk.

"That essay of yours on the Louvre—I would have been amazed to see it from an undergraduate at Yale or Princeton, and delighted to receive it from a grad student. To get it here . . . Well, there simply are no words. I'm overjoyed. Flabbergasted. *Je suis noyé. Muet comme un poisson.* Was it really a lodge in the dark ages? A place where they hunted wolves?"

"*Oui, Madame,*" he said, "*c'était comme les jours du Roi Dagobert.*" Seeing her expression he reverted to English, and remained there.

"I shouldn't let you sign up this late," the coach told him. "I wouldn't, if we weren't short. What position do you play?"

"Whatever position or positions you want me to play, sir."

The coach grunted. "Damn right. Where do you think you might be good?"

"Nowhere, probably. But I'll try."

"Okay, we'll try you on the line. I want you to get down like this, see? One hand on the ground. That's good. When I count three, come straight at me as hard as you can. Don't use you hands but try to go through me. Try to knock me over. One—two—THREE!"

It was as though the coach were not in truth a man at all, but a sort of inflated figure, a man-shaped balloon to be shouldered aside.

Sue Sumner was sitting in the living room chatting with his mother when he came home. "I knew you'd be late because of football practice," she said, "but I didn't want to miss our walk. Is that all right?"

He nodded, speechless.

His mother said, "You're going to have supper at Sue's house, Billy. She phoned home, and then I talked with Mrs. Sumner myself. She'll be very glad to have you—she's looking forward to getting to know you. Pot roast. Are you hungry?"

He nodded again, suddenly aware that he was ravenous.

"Your father's so proud of you! What position will you play? I want to be able to tell him when he gets home."

"Linebacker."

"Well, try to catch a lot of passes."

Outside, they petted Shep. "Your mom has no idea what a linebacker does, Bill."

He grinned. "Yes, I know."

"Do you want me to tell her? You know, just girl-to-girl when I get a chance?"

He looked down at Shep, who said quite distinctly, "Yep."

"Yes, I do. She may actually be interested now that I'm playing."

"Do you think they'll really let you? Play? I know a lot of guys just scrimmage with the team for the first year,."

It was a good question, and he considered it for a block or more. "Yes," he said. "I'm going to have a tough time of it because I'm so new. Young men who have been on the team for what they consider a long while are not going to like my playing, and they'll like it even less if I start. But I believe I'll play, and even that I'll start."

"Don't count on starting," Sue said. "I wouldn't want you to be disappointed."

"Thank you. 'What if the rose-streak of morning pale and depart in a passion of tears? Once to have hoped is no matter for scorning. Love once, even love's disappointment endears. A minute's success pays the failure of years.'"

"Why, Bill! That's beautiful!"

He nodded. "It should be—it's Robert Browning. Can I tell you what I've been thinking?"

"I wish you would."

"I was thinking that football might just be a letdown. For me, for my parents, and for you. But it wouldn't matter, because you were here waiting for me when I got home from practice. What difference could football make after that? You were here, and it meant I had won. Practice and games are just bother. Busyness."

"Oh, Bill!" She took his hand.

"So after that, I thought what if you hadn't been here. And it hit me—it hit me very hard—that millions of other men will come home, and can't even hope that you might be there, waiting, the way you were for me. That even if you hadn't been there I would be privileged like nobody else on earth, because I could hope—really hope, not deluding myself—that you might be. That love's disappointments are better than success in other things."

He cleared his throat. "I realize I haven't expressed myself very well. But that's how my mind was running, and naturally I thought of Browning then, as anybody would."

"Can I tell you what I'm thinking now?"

He nodded. "Of course."

"I'm thinking what a jerk I was. I rode that bus for three solid weeks before I realized what was on it with me. That my whole future was sitting across the aisle, or three seats in back. What a jerk!"

He sighed, and could find no more words.

"Look sharp," Shep whined.

They were approaching the house at which he had left the snapshots, when a breathtaking brunette threw open its door. She was carrying a blue and silver jacket, and she held it up for their inspection before running across the porch and down the steps to meet them. "Remember me?"

He nodded. "Certainly."

Smiling, she held out her hand to Sue. "I'm Dinah—Dinah Biltis. I just want to give Bill this. It's cold, and he'll need it." She turned to him, holding the jacket open. "Here, take off that backpack and put your arm in."

He did.

"It's too big for him," Sue said, "and besides—"

"Bill's bigger than you know. Do you like it, Bill?"

"Yes," he said. "Very much." It was loose, but not excessively so. He lifted his arms to admire the sleeves: blue leather with silver slashes.

Without warning Dinah kissed him. At the next moment, she was fleeing back up the steps and into the house. He got out a handkerchief and wiped his mouth thoughtfully.

"Wow!" Shep barked. "Wow, Chief!"

Sue sighed. "I'm supposed to fly into a jealous rage, I think. Isn't that how it's supposed to go?"

He was snapping the jacket closed. "I have no idea."

"I think it is. Are you going to keep the jacket?"

"For the time being anyway."

"Suppose I asked you to give it back?"

He considered. "I'd want to know why. If you had a good reason, I'd do it."

"Suppose I didn't have any reason at all?"

Shouldering her backpack again, he began to walk. "I wouldn't do it. You told me what you had been thinking, a minute ago. Can I tell you what I'm thinking now?"

For an instant her eyes found his face, although she did not turn her head. She nodded without speaking.

"I've already got a mother. She's a good mother, and I love her. I need you, not another mother."

"If I say one more thing, will you get mad?"

"Nope," Shep told her.

"That's a letter jacket. You're not supposed to wear one unless you've lettered."

"There's no letter on it."

"Guys who've lettered are going to take it away just the same, Bill."

He grinned. "Then you'll have won. What's wrong with that?"

"Do you remember Grandma's friend Dinah?" Sue asked her mother over pot roast.

"Oh my goodness! Yes indeed—Auntie Dinah. I haven't thought about her in years and years."

Chick said, "Was she the one that collected shawls? You used to talk about her, Mom." Chick was Sue's brother.

Sue's mother nodded. "That's right. I don't believe you ever knew her, though."

"You will," Sue told her brother. "She's back."

Sue's mother picked up the green beans. "Won't you have some more, Bill?"

He thanked her and took a second helping.

Sue said, "You probably didn't notice how old-fashioned her clothes were, Bill. That dark dress and those black stockings. Jet beads. They didn't really shout it, but they were the kind of clothes people wore—I don't know. A long time ago."

He chewed and swallowed, and sipped milk. No one spoke, and at last he said, "They were in one of the pictures. She will have new ones next time, I think."

"Can she do that?"

He shrugged. "My jacket wasn't in those pictures."

"Take it off!" Seth Thompkins demanded, and Doug Douglas grabbed him from behind.

"Sure," he said. "If you want it, I'll let you have it."

Doug relaxed somewhat. He slipped out of the jacket, kicked Doug, and hit the back of Doug's neck when Doug doubled up.

Seth's right knocked him off balance, and Seth's left caught him under the cheekbone. He hit Seth in the pit of the stomach, knocking him sprawling.

Martha Novick had stopped to watch.

"People on television talk a lot when they fight." He picked up his letter jacket and dusted it with his hand. "I don't think it's ever really like that. You're too busy."

"I guess I ought to tell Mr. Hoff," Martha said, "only I'm not going to."

He thanked her.

"Did you hurt them bad, Bill?"

"I don't think so," he told her. "They'll get up when I'm gone."

Dr. Grimes closed the notebook and smiled at him. "This is interesting stuff, Bill. Did you really dream it?"

He nodded.

"Armor that looked like your school jacket?"

"Somewhat like it," he said. "Not exactly. Do you care?"

Dr. Grimes nodded.

"All right. My school jacket's blue and silver. You must have seen them."

She nodded again.

"This is a short black leather coat. It's not blue or silver at all—the leather isn't, I mean. But it has steel rings sewn on it, and steel plates across the chest. Some of the steel plates and rings have been blued. Heat blued, I suppose. Do you know how to blue steel?"

"I couldn't do it," Dr. Grimes said, "but I've seen it. Sure, Bill."

"The rest have been polished bright. They'll rust, I'm sure, unless I keep them shined and oiled. So will the blue ones. But I'm going to do the best I can to take care of them. I'll put a little can of oil and a rag in my jacket pockets tonight before I go to bed."

She cocked her head. "Will that work?"

"I don't know. I believe it may."

"Uh-huh. You tell me, if it does. You been fightin'?"

He smiled. "You get around, don't you?"

"You goin' to law school when you get out of here?"

"Why do you ask?"

" 'Cause you answer a question with a question when you don't want to talk. That's a lawyer trick, and lawyers make real good money if they're good. I don't get around a-tall, Bill. I just sit here in my office, talkin' and writin' down and answerin' the phone. But people come and tell me stuff. Got a li'l bruise on that sweet face, too. You really kick that one boy?"

He nodded. "Are you goin' to report me?"

"Huh-uh. Maybe somebody will. I don't know, Bill. But not me."

"I kicked him, and they would have kicked me if they'd gotten a chance. We weren't boxing, we were fighting. How can you play fair, when you're not playing?"

"You're on the football team now."

He nodded.

"Goin' to start against Pershing. That's what I heard."

"The coach hasn't said that to me. I can play halfback and linebacker—or at least he says I can—and I've been practicing those positions. I just hope I get in the game."

"Uh-huh." She smiled. "I was married to a football player, one time. Dee-troit Lions. I used to go to all the games back then, and I still watch a lot. On the TV, you know. You know what they tell me about you, Bill?"

He shook his head.

"They say you always catch a pass. Two men coverin' you. Three. It don't matter. You always catch it."

"I've been lucky."

"Uh-huh. Ms. Fournier, she says you're a genius. You been lucky there, too, I guess."

"I don't think so."

Dr. Grimes sat in silence for half a minute regarding him. At last she said, "If a boy's too smart, the other boys don't like that, do they? Maybe he was just lucky, but if he'd been luckier he would have missed a question. Maybe two. I ever tell you I like you?"

He nodded.

"I do, Bill. First time I talked to you, you seem like such a nice kid, and you got a good imagination. Now you seem like a nice man with a real good education and a kid's face. That first one was interestin'. This one here, this is real interestin'."

"You're wrong," he said.

"I get up in the mornin', and I want to come to work. That's because of you. How am I wrong, Bill? Tell me."

He rose, sensing that the period was nearly over. "You think I've grown up, somehow, inside. I haven't. I know a lot more than I did, because I've been trying to decipher the runes on the scabbard. But I'm still Bill Wachter, and I'm still young. Inside. 'When all the world is young, lad, and all the trees are green, and every goose a swan, lad, and every lass a queen. Then hey for boot and horse, lad, and round the world away. Young blood must have its course, lad, and every dog his day.'"

Dr. Grimes only watched him with thoughtful eyes; so when a second, and two, had ticked past, he turned and went out into the hall.

She said nothing to stop him, and he was ten paces from her door when the bell rang.

Sue and a tall, smiling man in a checked sportcoat were waiting for him when he left the locker room after the game. "This is Mr. Archer," Sue said. "He's going to take us to Perry's for a bite, if that's all right with you, Bill. Is it?"

He smiled. "Do you want to go?"

"Not if you don't."

"Then I do," he said, and her hand slipped into his.

Mr. Archer's car was a red Park Avenue Ultra with tinted windows. "You two sit in back," he told them. "It'll take twenty minutes or so, and I can't talk worth a damn when I'm driving."

Mr. Archer got in and tilted the rearview mirror up; and Bill opened the door for Sue, and got in himself on the other side. By the time that they had left Veterans Avenue behind, and with it the last traffic of the game, his hand had slid beneath her sweater and under the waistband of her skirt.

She was prim and ladylike when Archer opened the door of the car for her; but she left as soon as Perry's headwaiter had seated them, to repair her makeup in the restroom.

"Beautiful girl," Mr. Archer said appreciatively. "You know her long, Bill?"

"Yes and no." Although he had held the restaurant's door for them both like a gentleman, and had pulled out Sue's chair for her (beating the headwaiter to it by one tenth of one second), his mind was still whirling. "We rode the same bus last year, and she was in my homeroom and some of my classes. It was the forth week of the school year before we got to be close friends." He cleared his throat. "September twenty-second."

Archer smiled. "You remember the exact day."

"Certainly."

"You didn't play last year, did you? I don't think freshmen are eligible."

He shook his head, trying to recall his freshman year. Things had been so different then. So very, very different. So very much worse. "No," he said. "You're correct, they aren't, and I wouldn't have gone out anyway."

"She couldn't have known you'd be a star."

"She didn't even know I'd go out. That day—the day we really noticed each other—I hadn't decided to do it. Or even thought about it, really."

"Sue didn't tell you what I do." Mr. Archer took a card folder from a pocket of his sport coat, fished out a card, and laid it on the table between them. "I'm an assistant coach, just like that card says. I coach offense, and I go to high-school games whenever I get the chance, Bill, hoping to spot some real talent. Mostly I don't."

"In that case," he said slowly, "it was very nice of you to take us out like this."

A waiter came; Mr. Archer ordered a John Collins and two Diet Cokes.

"There are fifty players on each team this early in the season," Mr. Archer said, "so a hundred altogether. Why am I being nice to you?"

"I suppose because my parents weren't there. I ought to explain that. They wanted to come, but I begged them not to. I was afraid I wouldn't get to play at all, and that if I did I'd play badly."

Returning, Sue said, "You didn't, Bill. You made the Panthers look like monkeys out there."

Mr. Archer said, "The score was twenty-zip. Who scored all three touchdowns?"

"I was lucky, that's all."

"Five times I saw you catch passes that ought to have been incompletions. Three times I saw you catch passes that should have been interceptions."

A waitress brought their drinks.

"You know the three-times rule, Bill? Once, that's an accident. Twice, that's a coinkydink. Three times, that's enemy action. You were the—what school was that, Bill? Who were you playing?"

"Pershing." Sue had gripped his leg under the table and was squeezing hard, probably as hard as she could, but he had no idea why.

"You were Pershing's enemy," Mr. Archer said. "An enemy they couldn't handle. You weren't watching their coach, but I was—I used to coach high school myself. He was chewing nails and spitting them at his players."

"Bill," Sue whispered, "for just a minute I have to talk to you."

"So do I," Archer told her. "I need to tell him about some of the scholarships we've got. But all my talking will take quite a while, and maybe you won't. I'll go wash my hands."

Over his shoulder he added, "If you want nachos or anything just order. Steaks. Whatever. On me."

Sue leaned closer, her voice almost inaudible. "Our waitress. Did you look at her, Bill?"

He shook his head.

"It's Dinah."

Back in the Park Avenue Ultra, Mr. Archer asked where they wanted to go. Sue said, "Where Edison and Cottonwood cross. It's a white house, two stories, with a big porch. Okay, Bill?"

"We ought to take you home first."

"No way. You won't tell your folks a thing. Take us to Bill's house, Mr. Archer. Where I said. His mom and dad shouldn't find out he's a hero from the paper."

"Sue . . ."

Archer said, "You're afraid I'll go in and buttonhole your parents. You want some time to think it over yourself first. Am I right, Bill?"

He was not, but Bill said he was.

"I understand, and I won't do it. Listen, Bill, I want to tell you something and I want you to remember it. I was all-city quarterback once, back before you were born. Where you are now? I've been there, too. I know what it's like. You keep my card and I'll talk to you again in a few days."

"Your folks are nice," Sue said as he walked her home. "They let me tell them all that stuff before they told us they'd been listening on the radio. Did you notice?"

He nodded.

"College games get on TV. State's always do, around here, because there are so many grads. Mr. Archer didn't say that, so I'll say it now. Just something to think about, Bill."

"I am."

Sue glanced at him, then away. "Here's something else. My mom is a very good mother, but she works really hard. She has to be at work at seven, and when she gets home she has to clean and cook. I help as much as I can, and so does Chick. But she does most of it."

This time it was Shep who said, "Sure."

Sue did not seem to notice. "So she won't have listened to the game, Bill. I'm sorry, but she won't. I mean, I'll tell her tomorrow. But she won't have heard much about it on the radio."

He said, "That's good."

"In fact, she'll be in bed asleep by the time we get there. That's something else to think about, Bill."

Bill thought.

The hills were behind them, the plain ahead of them, flat and featureless, an empty expanse of dry brown grass across which a chill wind moaned. He had given the leather coat with its steel rings to Sue; its shoulders were too big for her and its sleeves too long, but that was good and the leather kept out the wind. "Where are we going?" she said.

He pointed. "See those mountains? There's a city, a golden city, on the other side. We're going there."

"What for?"

"Because it's the only place to go. You can go there, or you can die here. That's all the choices we have." He paused, considering. "I can't make you go there. I'd have to hit you or something, and tie you up when I slept, and I won't do that. Maybe there's something over that way, or over there. I don't know, and if you want to go look, I'll go with you. But—"

"I'm going where you're going, Bill." Sue's voice was firm. "I've already told you that. Only I've got a lot of questions."

"I haven't got any answers," he said.

There was a wild cry high overhead, as lonely and inhuman as the keening of a hawk. They looked up, and saw the great bird that had uttered it sailing through ragged cloud, and watched it circle and descend. "That's Biltis," he said. "Maybe she'll help us."

"She gave Sue a wand with which she can start fires," he wrote in his notebook the next day, "and said we would come to a river, and that there would be a cave in the bank which we were not to enter on any account.

"Sue clasped my arm and said, 'He belongs to me!' but Biltis only laughed and said I belonged to both of them, and that I had from the beginning."

"Come on in, Bill, and shut the door." Dr. Grimes waved toward a chair. "This here is Dr. Hayes. Dr. Hayes was my teacher a long time ago. Over there's Ms. Biltis from the school board. I told them I wanted to get Dr. Hayes to consult, and they said okay, but they had to have somebody here to see what was goin' on. So that's Ms. Biltis."

Dinah said, "Bill and I have met already. Hi, Bill."

He said hi in return.

Dr. Hayes asked, "Does he always bring the dog, Tacey?"

Dr. Grimes shook her head. "He talks about it, but I never did see it before. Is that Shep, Bill?"

He nodded.

Dinah said, "It's contrary to our regulations to have a dog in the building or on school property unless it's a guide dog for the blind. In this case, the board's willing to make an exception."

"That's good," Dr. Grimes said.

Dr. Hayes shaped a steeple from his fingers. "Why did you bring your dog today, Bill?"

"He's not really my dog," Bill said, "he's my lawyer."

Dr. Grimes looked surprised. Dinah laughed; she had a pretty laugh, and it made him feel better to hear it.

Dr. Hayes's expression did not change in the least. "I'm not sure I understand. Perhaps you'd better explain."

"I don't mean he's a real lawyer. He hasn't passed the bar. But I felt I needed someone to advise me, and I know Shep's smart and that he's on my side."

"I'm on your side too, Bill."

Dr. Grimes said, "So am I, Bill. I thought you knew that."

Dinah grinned; it was a attractive grin, and full of mischief. "We of the board are always on the side of the students."

"But you're over there." Bill gestured, "and Shep and I are over here."

"I can fix that." Dinah got up and moved her chair so that she sat on his left and Shep on his right.

Dr. Hayes nodded to her. "Is there a statement you wish to make on behalf of the school board before I begin?"

Dinah shook her head. "I'll reserve it."

"I would prefer that you not interrupt. Quite frankly, your presence poses a threat to the exploratory examination I wish to undertake. Interruptions may render it futile."

"What about the dog?" Dinah smiled.

Shep said, "Nope."

"If the dog proves to be an impediment, we'll dismiss it, although I doubt that will be necessary."

Bill said, "I'm missing social studies."

Dr. Hayes nodded again. "We're aware of it, and we've discussed it with your teacher. She says you have already earned an A, that you know much more of the subject than her course is designed to teach her students. What day of the week is this, Bill?"

"Monday."

"Correct. And the date?"

"October fifth."

"Also correct. We are in a building of some sort. Do you know what building it is?"

"Kennedy Consolidated."

"And why are you here, Bill?"

He stroked Shep's head, at which Shep said, "Dunno."

"Bill?" Dr. Hayes sounded polite but wary.

"I was thinking, sir. I could offer three or four explanations, but I don't have much confidence in any of them. The truth is that I don't know. Why am I?"

"In order that you can provide those explanations, for one thing. Will you?"

Dr. Grimes said, "You see, Bill, what you say to us is goin' to be a whole lot more help than anythin' we could say to you. You been sittin' in some class with a teacher, day after day, I know. This's kinda like that, only you're the teacher now, and me and Ms. Biltis and Doctor Hayes, we're the class you're teachin'."

Shep said, "Go ahead, Chief."

"All right." He paused to collect his thoughts. "I've been writing down my dreams in study hall. You told me to do that, but I was doing it before you told me, and Mrs. Durkin read my notebook over my shoulder and decided that I was psychotic. She likes me, but she still thinks I'm psychotic. She feels sorry for me."

Dr. Hayes said, "We all do, Bill."

"Not me," Dr. Grimes said. "Bill can take care of himself. I only wish he'd help me understand him more, 'cause I don't. I don't indeed."

Dinah grinned again. "Me neither. I feel sorry—"

The telephone rang. Dr. Grimes picked it up and said, "Counselin'. Oh, hello, Sue. You know I never have met you, but I've heard a sight about you from this nice Bill Wachter. He thinks you got angel wings, you know that?

"Why, no.

"Now don't you worry. I got my 'pointment book right here. Maybe two o'clock tomorrow?

"That's good. No, don't you worry none 'bout Shep. I got him right here. I been talkin' to him my own self." Dr. Grimes laughed. "Course he hasn't said much back, Sue. But maybe he will. What he say to you?

"That's good. That Shep's a good sensible dog, Sue. Don't you worry. You come see me tomorrow."

Dr. Grimes's smile faded as she hung up. "Shep's been talkin' to Sue too, Dr. Hayes. Sue's Bill's girlfriend."

Dinah said, "One of them."

"He didn't say nothin' bad, only wantin' to know where Bill was. So she told him and he went off. She'd like to see me, but the door was closed—just a minute ago, I guess—so she called from the phone in the cafeteria. Yes, Bill? You want to say somethin'?"

He nodded. "I've been pondering the speech of animals. It's not that the kiss that flew to me suddenly made animals talk. It's that the kiss let me understand what they were saying. Love is at the root of it. The more you love anyone or anything, the better you understand it. She kissed me, and I kissed Sue, and that may be the reason Sue understands Shep now."

"I got a cat I call Catcat," Dr. Grimes said. "I don't understand Catcat very good, but that Catcat understands *me* backward and forward too. She likes me more than I like her. That what you're sayin'?"

Shep said, "Yep."

Dinah said, "I'm going to interrupt here. Bill promised us several explanations and has delivered only one, that the Durkin woman thinks he's psychotic. I would like to hear the others. Also I want to say that I understand Shep perfectly—not that he's said much, but what he has said has been in plain Doggish, which is quite different from doggerel. If the student who called understands him too, she's no crazier than I am."

Dr. Hayes and Dr. Grimes stared at her.

"Bill's never kissed me. Is that supposed to make a difference? I've kissed him, though."

Dr. Hayes leaned toward Dr. Grimes. "I seem to be losing control of the situation, Tacey. My apologies."

"I guess you see now why I wanted you?"

Nodding, he turned to Dinah. "I take it you're a friend of Bill's family, Ms. Biltis?"

"Why, no. I don't know Bill's parents at all."

He cleared his throat. "She wants another explanation, and one just occurred to me. Would anyone like to hear it?"

Dinah said, "I would, Bill," and Dr. Grimes nodded.

"I don't credit this one either," Bill said. "I should make that clear. But I find it interesting." He held up his notebook. "Before I met Biltis I met a dwarf on horseback. Perhaps it would be more accurate to say that I was overtaken by him. It's all in here."

He paused, inviting them to read his notebook if they cared to. No one spoke.

"He gave me a sword. I want to call it an enchanted sword, and perhaps it is. Certainly the spells on the scabbard are magical, and doubtless those engraved on the blade are magical as well. I can read the spells on the scabbard somewhat. I read them badly and quite slowly, but eventually I can puzzle them out. Sue and Shep cannot read them at all."

Dr. Hayes said, "Do you feel that these enchantments explain your presence here, Bill? That the casting of a spell has compelled you to come, perhaps?"

He shook his head. "Not exactly. First of all, they are spells, not enchantments. That is to say, they're words of magical import. One merely speaks them, and no chanting is required, although I would think that many chants were required for the sword that was to bear so much magic."

Dinah giggled.

"Of course I have asked myself many times why such a sword should be given to me."

Dr. Grimes said, "It was your dream, Bill. You don't think that's reason aplenty?"

"That's like saying that all islands are inhabited because all the islands from which we've received reports are." He shrugged. "I've had many dreams in which I wasn't given an enchanted sword, or a sword of any kind. If—"

Dr. Hayes interrupted him. "Do you feel a connection between this sword and your penis, Bill?"

He laughed, and so did Dinah.

Dr. Grimes said, "What *do* you think that sword might be connected to, Bill, 'sides this dwarf? Comin' from a dwarf, I know why Doctor Hayes said what he did, and lots of people think like that. How do you think? What does this sword you got in your dream make you think about?"

"Biltis," he said. As he spoke, Dinah slipped her hand into his.

"Is that the girl in your dream that rides that bird? I told Dr. Hayes about her, and maybe he'd like to read about her too, by and by."

Dr. Hayes said, "Perhaps I would, Tacey. Perhaps I should."

"I think so. Why does this sword make you think 'bout her, Bill?"

He looked from Dr. Grimes to Dinah, and back again. "I think that Biltis must be a princess or a queen. Something of that kind, in any case—a woman with a lot of power. I told you about the fire wand."

Dr. Grimes nodded.

"The wand proves that she has magical possessions, and can afford to give them away almost casually. When Sue and Shep and I went into the cave—she had told us not to, but we went anyway, because Sue wanted to get out of the wind—we were attacked, and Sue's wand was at least as important as my sword and Shep's teeth in beating our attackers back and getting the three of us out alive."

Dr. Grimes nodded again, encouragingly. "It was a good thing you got it, Bill."

"It was a good thing Sue did, or we would probably have been killed. And Biltis gave it to her. Sue is jealous of Biltis, but I don't think Biltis is jealous of Sue."

Dinah said, "Neither do I."

"Sue wants to keep me," he continued, "but Biltis feels she already has me, and I think she may be right. When I made the thing that had her by the foot release her, she told me very seriously that I must beware of underground places. I didn't trust her warning then, not wholly. I should have."

Dr. Grimes leaned toward him. "You think that tells why you're here now, Bill?"

"Indirectly. Why did the dwarf give me the sword?"

Dr. Hayes said, "It's your dream, Bill, not ours. Why did he?"

"I don't know, of course. I can only guess. But my guess is that he did it because he had been ordered to—ordered by Biltis. When people talk of kings and queens, princes and princesses, these days, it's as stock figures in marchen—pictures in a nineteenth-century book that everyone is too busy to read. But I think that Biltis is a real queen, and real queens have subjects, hundreds of thousands of them, even in a small kingdom. Tens of millions in one the size of England. If a queen with real power had a sword written over with spells she couldn't read, she would look for someone who could, wouldn't she? And get him to read them for her?"

"Right, Chief," Shep said.

"It's your dream, Bill," Dr. Hayes repeated.

He nodded. "I'm not supposed to be explaining my dream, though, am I? I'm supposed to be explaining this—why you got me here. Very well. Suppose you got me here to tell you about the spells on the sword?"

Dinah said, "You've left something out. Perhaps you didn't think of it. Why didn't Biltis simply bring you the sword and ask you to read it?"

He shrugged. "You should know better than I. Possibly because I couldn't. I can read it only very slowly, and when I try, it's usually when we're going to camp, or rest for a while. To read it, I have to be able to see it, and we didn't have any way to make a fire until you gave Sue the wand. Now we'll have a fire and I may be able to puzzle out the writing by firelight."

He turned to speak to Dr. Hayes and Dr. Grimes. "Tell me something, please, and be just as honest as you can. It will mean nothing to you, but it's important to me. Haven't either of you noticed that Ms. Biltis here and the woman in my dream have the same name?"

"What are you talking about?" Dr. Hayes asked.

Dr. Grimes said gently, "They're not the same, Bill. This lady here's Ms. Biltis from the school board, and the one in your dreams is," she referred to her notes, "Biltis."

Bill turned back to Dinah. "So that's the way it is."

"Yes." She gave him her impish smile. "Don't worry. It won't hurt them."

"I wasn't worried," he said.

"Careful," Shep muttered.

"I have a sword," Dinah told Dr. Grimes. "It's out in my car. I'd like to bring it in and show it to Bill, if no one objects."

Dr. Grimes looked to Dr. Hayes, who said, "What do you think, Tacey? Is he apt to become violent?"

Dr. Grimes shook her head. "He's always been just as nice as pie, 'cept playin' that football, and he's generally just catchin' passes and runnin' then. You want to cut anybody, Bill?"

"No," he said. "Certainly not."

Dinah had already gone, seeming almost to have melted away.

"Somebody goin' to ask you to read that sword, you think, Bill?"

He nodded.

"Me, too. You goin' to do it?"

"I don't know yet."

Dr. Hayes said, "Do you really think that there may be writing on it, Tacey? An engraved blade? Something of that sort?"

"I guess we'll see. Bill thinks she's the same as the lady in his dream, and I see why. She does act sort of like it. You think she got that mark on her foot, Bill?"

He nodded.

"I been wantin' to ask you 'bout that. The first time you seen her, she had her foot down in that hole?"

"Correct."

"She do that on purpose?"

Shep said, "Yep."

"Bill?"

"I don't know. Shep thinks so. If it was intentional, it may have been to explain a preexisting mark on her ankle."

"A birthmark, like," Dr. Grimes told Dr. Hayes. "You can see it through her nylons if you look close."

He shook his head. "You're being drawn into the patients' delusional system, Tacey."

"Okay, maybe I wasn't seein' nothin'. Maybe it was just a shadow. What you think, Bill? You 'gree with Doctor Hayes?"

Shep said, "Nope."

Dr. Hayes murmured, "You must know, deep inside, that there is no such mark, Bill."

" 'I am Sir Oracle. When I ope my mouth, let no dog bark.' " He smiled. "Another possibility is that she wanted to warn me about the underground creatures—the cavern folk, or demons, or whatever we choose to call them. If she wanted to show me—not merely tell me—that they are real and dangerous, she chose a good way to do it."

"Only you went in that cave anyhow," Dr. Grimes said. "Can I see your book?"

He passed it to her, and she flipped it open.

Dr. Hayes said, "Some of the teachers here don't think your dreams are real dreams, Bill. They don't believe that they are dreams and not daydreams, in other words. Does that surprise you?"

"Yes," he said, "I didn't know they knew about them. Mrs. Durkin has been talking in the teachers' lounge, I suppose."

"Are they real dreams, Bill?"

"I don't believe so. I don't believe they're daydreams either."

Dinah returned, shutting the door behind her. "Here it is." She held up a package loosely wrapped in brown paper. "I got it from a company in Georgia." She unwrapped it, ripping the paper. "I had them send it UPS Overnight. It cost a little more, but it was worth it."

A glittering hilt protruded from a sheath of unadorned black leather.

"Here, Bill. I'll hold this part, and you can pull it out."

He looked to Dr. Grimes for permission. She nodded, and he drew the gleaming double-edged blade clear of the sheath.

Dr. Hayes said, "Is that the sword you've been telling us about, Bill?"

He rose, weighing the sword in his hand.

Dr. Grimes said, "That isn't a magic sword at all, is it, Bill?"

He moved the sword, not thrusting or slashing with it, only testing its weight and balance.

"There's writin' on the blade up close to that handle," Dr. Grimes continued. "I been tryin' to read it, only I can't. Not from here."

" 'Made in India,' " Bill said absently.

Dr. Grimes laughed. "It can't be no magic sword if it's made there, can it, Bill?"

Dinah sniffed. "It's my sword, and I think it's a very nice sword."

"It feels well in the hand," Bill said, "and I can't believe that anyone would waste so much good workmanship on poor steel." He seemed to be talking to himself.

Dr. Hayes said, "But not a magic sword. I hope you agree, Bill?"

"I do." He looked up. "It is becoming a magic sword, however."

Shep said, "Good!"

"Because I'm holding it. Magic is flowing from me into the sword. I didn't know that could happen, but it can."

Dr. Hayes looked at Dr. Grimes, who said, "Bill, I know you're just havin' fun, but you're makin' Dr. Hayes here think you got something really wrong with you. It's not nice to fool people that way, and you could get in a lot of trouble just doin' it."

"Because I said that?" He smiled. "Why is the Holy Grail holy, Dr. Hayes? Why does it perform miracles? It is the cup used by Christ at the Last Supper."

"Perhaps you can tell me, Bill."

"You don't know, Dr. Grimes?"

She shook her head.

"Because something—not magic, let's call it divinity—flowed from Him into the cup. We know that sort of thing happened, because once, when a sick woman touched Him, He said He had felt the power leave Him. *Dynamin* is the word employed in the Greek gospel—power, might. I might guess at the Aramaic word Christ actually employed, but I won't. Such things should not be guessed at. For me the word is *lygros*."

A glow like the light from blazing wood wrapped the blade of the sword as he pronounced *lygros*.

"The magical power of death, the power to kill," he whispered.

There was a knock at the door.

"You put that away, Bill," Dr. Grimes told him sharply.

He ignored her.

Dinah called, "Come in!"

The door opened, and Ms. Fournier looked in with a worried smile. "Sue Sumner isn't in here, is she, Dr. Grimes?"

Shep said, "Nope."

"One of the students told me she wanted to talk to you, and I thought—I hoped . . ."

Dr. Grimes said, "I haven't seen her, Ms. Fournier. She's in my book for tomorrow."

"The chem lab supplies are stored in the basement," Ms. Fournier continued, "I suppose you know that. Mr. Boggs sent her for some—oh!"

Shep had bounded past her, closely followed by Bill, sword in hand. With a murmured "Excuse me," Dinah followed him, kicking off her high heels to run before she was three steps down the corridor.

"Me, too, honey." Heavier as well as older, Dr. Grimes required most of the doorway.

"Pardon me," Dr. Hayes said. He was holding his pipe; although it contained no tobacco, he thrust it resolutely into his mouth and clamped it with his jaw before striding away.

"I looked!" Ms. Fournier called after him. "So did Mr. Boggs ! She's not there!"

They caught up with Bill and Shep in the furnace room, where Hector Fuente turned from his unsuccessful argument with Bill to demand, "What're you doing here, lady?"

"I'm Dinah Biltis from the school board," Dinah explained. "We're here to rescue Sue Sumner, if there's enough of her left to rescue."

"You got to have a pass."

"And I do. I'll show it to you in a moment. Have you looked in there, Bill? That iron door?"

He had not seen it. He lifted the steel bar and threw it aside.

It burst open, nearly knocking him down. The first hideous thing that rushed past him was not quite a corpse or a bear. The next had four legs and a multitude of arms, with an eye at the end of each. His first cut severed two, and they writhed on the floor like snakes. Others seized him; he broke their grip and drove his blade into the bulky, faintly human body. For perhaps five seconds, its death throes made it more dangerous than it had been in life.

Someone was shooting, the shots loud and fast in the enclosed space of the furnace room. He scrambled to his feet, reclaimed his sword, and saw Shep writhing and snapping in the jaws of a nightmare cat with foot-long fangs. With her back to the furnace, Dinah was firing a small automatic. Her last shot came as he took his first step, and the slide locked back. His blade bit the big cat's neck as though it had rushed into battle of itself, dragging him behind it. He felt it grate on vertebrae and cut free, severing the throat and the jugular veins, saw the great cat's jaws relax and the pitiful thing that dragged itself free of them and was so soon soaked by its own spurting blood.

Laying aside his sword, he embraced the dying dog. "Shep! Oh, my God, Shep!"

Dinah bent over them both, her empty gun still in her hand.

"Can't we heal him somehow, Biltis?"

She said, "You can, if you want to," and he repeated the words he had spoken once before, when he and Sue had walked past a certain house, whispering them into Shep's ear. The light of his blade shone through the clotting blood at that moment, purer than sunshine.

The three of them found Sue two miles underground and killed the things that had been guarding her. He wanted to carry her, but she insisted (her voice shaking and sharp with fear) that she could walk. Walk she did, though she leaned heavily on his arm.

Shep scouted ahead, sniffing the air and whining in his eagerness to be gone. After the first quarter mile, Dinah said, "This little flashlight's just about gone, Bill. See how yellow it is?"

"Yes. Out brief candle, and all that. Can we get back without it?"

"I think so. Remember the light from your sword? Do that again."

"I didn't think you saw that," he said.

"I see a lot. Do it again."

He muttered to himself, and when Sue released his arm, he fingered the blade; and a sapphire light crept up and down that deep central groove some call the blood gutter, and spread to the edges after a minute or two, and trailed, by the time they had gone another quarter mile, from the point. He relaxed a little then, and hugged Sue, and tried to make the hug say that they would make it—that she would see the sky again.

"Don't let them get me, Bill." It was a whisper from her mind, yet clear as speech. "Oh, please! Don't let them get me."

"I won't," he said, and prayed that he could keep the promise. "Are you on our side, Biltis? Really, really on our side?"

"Certainly," she said, and grinned.

Sue said, "You shot them. You wouldn't have, if you weren't on our side, would you?"

Dinah did not bother to reply.

"She wouldn't, would she, Bill?"

"Of course not," he said, "but I don't understand how she did it. Her gun was empty before we came in here."

"I had a spare magazine in my purse, that's all."

"One magazine?"

Dinah nodded. "Just one."

As they walked on (he with an arm about Sue's waist, she weeping and stumbling), he wondered whether Dinah had been telling the truth. She had sounded as though she might be lying, and it inclined him to trust her; she had been careful with her voice when she said she was from the school board.

The iron door was closed and latched. He lifted the latch, but the door would not open. He pounded on it with the hilt of his sword, which did no good at all, and the four of them threw their combined weight against it, which did no good either.

When the rest were exhausted he went back down the long tunnel, leaving Shep to protect the two women—or perhaps, Dinah and her little gun to protect Sue and Shep. By the fiery light of his blade he found something huge cowering in a crevice; he persuaded it to come out by telling it (entirely truthfully) that he would kill it if it did not.

When the two of them returned to the door, he called out to Dinah not to shoot, saying that the thing came as a friend. "If you will break this down for us," he told it, "we will leave the underground realm forever and trouble it no more. If you will not—or cannot—I will kill you. You've got my word on our departure, and on that too. Will you try? Or would you rather die here and now?"

The thing lifted the latch as he had, but the door would not open. It threw its weight against it, and it was bigger than any bull.

A crevice of light appeared. He put down his sword and got his fingers into it, and spread it as he might have opened the jaws of a crocodile, with veins bulging in his forehead and sweat dripping from his face, and the huge thing he had found throwing its terrible strength against the door again and again until the steel bar bent, and the boxes and barrels, the desks and chairs and tables that had been piled against it gave way.

They rushed out—Shep, Sue, Dinah, and he, climbing and stumbling over the fallen barricade. And the thing came after them, with Bill's sword in its hand; but Shep severed its wrist, Dinah put a bullet into its single eye, and he drove his reclaimed sword between its ribs until the quillons gouged its scales.

They found Drs. Grimes and Hayes dismembering the catlike monster that had seized Shep, and feeding the parts to a hulking old coal furnace, assisted by Hector Fuente and his machete. "They lef' this ol' furnace here for standby when they went to gas," Dr. Grimes explained. "They lef' coal, too. Hector here, he tol' us all 'bout it. This ol' coal furnace, it don't need 'lectricity, so when the 'lectric goes off, like in a ice storm, he can run it to keep the pipes from freezin'."

"It is a great loss to science," Dr. Hayes added, "but it is not *my* science. Besides, we would be accused of faking our evidence—the inevitable result of such discoveries."

Dinah said, "They shut the door on us, Bill, and barred it, and piled all that stuff in front of us. Shall we kill them?"

He shook his head.

The four of them went up the stairs and out onto the athletic field, past the volleyball court and the tennis court, and onto the field on which the football team would practice after school.

"It's so g-good to be o-outside." Sue was trembling. "Look! There's good old Juniper Street. It—it d-doesn't look the way it did, not to me. It looks like a toy under somebody's Christmas tree. B-but it's Juniper and I love it. I always will, after—after that. Don't you love it too, B-Bill?" Her eyes had filled with tears.

"I do," he said, though he was not looking at it. "See the hardware store? And Philips Fabrics?"

As Sue nodded, Dinah whistled shrilly; a huge black bird plummeted toward earth at the sound of that whistle, a minute dot that became a hurtling thunderbolt. They watched it land (barked at by Shep), watched Dinah mount, and waved good-bye.

"Who is she, Bill?"

He shrugged. "Who am I? Who are you?"

"Bill's girl," Sue replied.

Repeating those words to himself, he turned to look at her. Her eyes were of the blue light he had seen upon his sword, her disheveled hair the gold of the towers; the tilt of her nose and the curve of her smudged cheek filled him with a longing so intense that he dared not kiss her.

"Are you sure, Sue?" He had struggled to control his voice, and failed.

She nodded without speaking.

"Then I want you to look higher than the hardware store and the fabric store."

He watched her. "No, higher. Off into the distance. What do you see?"

"Mountains!" Her eyes were wide. "Bill, those are mountains! There aren't any mountains around here. There aren't any mountains like those for a thousand miles."

"That's right." He began to walk again.

"You're going?"

"Yes," he said. "I'm going,"

"Then I'm going with you."

Once they had left the town behind, the mountains were no longer impossibly distant. "One thing for sure," Sue said, "nothing will ever scare me after what happened today."

Shep wagged his tail in agreement. "Me too! Right, Chief?"

William Wachter shrugged. "I have a feeling that this was the easy part," he said.